SHIELD AND SACRIFICIAL HEIRS

ENERGY OF MAGIC
BOOK NINE

J.E. NEAL

*To my husband who absolutely deserves every single book dedicated to him.
Without him these books would not exist because he believed in me long
before I believed in myself.*

*So—to the magic of true love
and the power it holds in its hands*

CONTENTS

CHAPTER 1
ANSWERED PRAYERS
RAINER LAWSON

The mattress was bouncing. Rainer let one eye open. Immediately understanding that he was not going to be sleeping anymore, he opened the other eye.

"Hey there, baby." He rubbed his eyes and yawned as Emily continued to bounce beside him on the bed.

"Get up! We're getting married tomorrow!"

"Em." Rainer clasped his hands around her waist in an effort to hold her down. "It's six in the morning. Everyone won't be here for several hours to set up, okay?"

"How can you sleep? Aren't you excited?"

"I'm thrilled. I'm over the moon. I might just be a little more thrilled if the moon wasn't still out."

"Rainer!" she huffed.

With a defeated sigh, he sat up. "Okay, okay, I'm up." Excitement and nerves fought for dominance of his energy strains.

She brushed a kiss along his jawline. "Don't be nervous. We've done this a million times."

Rainer joined her laughter as he recalled the sheer number of times Emily had made him play wedding with her while they were growing up.

Somehow he was certain the ceremony the next day would be

1

nothing like their play weddings out in the back fields of her family's farm being conducted under duress by one of her older brothers.

But he wasn't terribly nervous about the ceremony or marrying Emily. That was all he'd wanted since he'd planted a kiss on the apple of her cheek when he was eight years old. His nerves were due to the surprise he'd been planning for the past several months that was supposed to be arriving in just a few hours. He fervently hoped it went off without a hitch.

"Let's go help Mom with breakfast, and then we can start working on everything." She tried to playfully scoot him out of the bed.

"Baby, we can go help your mom, but it has to be daylight before your brothers, or Dan and Fionna, or anyone is going to be out here to help us."

"I don't care. I'm too nervous. I have to do something."

Rainer slid out of the bed and pulled her to him. "I thought we weren't being nervous. No different from when we played out in the backyard, and Logan made you vow to eat slugs, and I gave you a grape ring pop. Like you said, we've done this millions of times."

She did giggle, but he hadn't succeeded in easing her anxiety. "Yeah, except there will be six hundred people here tomorrow. What if I trip? What if my hair does that frizzy floppy in the front thing? What if my dress falls off?"

It took a great deal of effort to keep from chuckling at her concerns. Rainer cupped his hand and drew from the ambient energy in the room. He converted it and pushed soothing energy into her.

"You will be stunningly beautiful. You always are. You will walk down the aisle on your dad's arm and back on mine, and you know neither of us would ever let you fall. If your dress falls off, then I say to hell with the ceremony, we're starting the honeymoon early."

She laughed and rolled her eyes, but she was still a bouncing bundle of nerves.

Two hours later, when Governor Haydenshire had been unable to fend her off any longer, he had Rainer, Logan, and Connor begin putting up the ornate archways and the tents for the reception.

Haydenshire men arrived at varying intervals and were given tasks to complete. The florists arrived next and began bedecking every surface with intricate floral arrangements under the direction of Emily's uncles, Tad and Nathan.

At ten, Dan and Fionna Vindico's Ferrari pulled through the massive wrought iron gates. This was the first time Rainer had seen Fionna since she'd been released from the hospital after suffering a gunshot wound that brought on her miscarriage. Emily had been over to visit her a few times, but Rainer had been at work. when Fionna had been released from the hospital after suffering a gunshot wound that brought on her miscarriage.

Rainer's shield shifted oddly and spun in an attempt to protect, even though the danger had long passed. At least, he hoped it had passed. He still couldn't stand to think about that horrific day and all that had happened when he'd helped Iodex, the Gifted police force he was a part of, take out the Interfeci Criminal Organization.

Keeping his boss's wife safe seemed like something he should have been able to do. Every Iodex officer felt the guilt, but there were too many guns, too many criminals, and too many unforeseen complications they just hadn't accounted for.

Emily wrapped her arms around his neck. "She's okay. Look at her. She looks so much better." She gestured her head toward the car. He had to agree. They did look happier than he could recall ever seeing them before.

The events that had taken place while Dan and Fionna had been in Hawaii raced through Rainer's mind. Two operatives Iodex had buried deep in the Interfeci had been murdered brutally, and hundreds of thousands of dollars were missing from the accounts Iodex had on lockdown.

While remembering the decree that Dan was not to know about any of that, as he had been ordered to step down as Chief of Iodex and deserved to move on, Rainer guided Emily toward the Vindicos.

They waved as Rainer mentally reminded himself that nothing had happened and no money had disappeared. It appeared Wretchkinsides had created some kind of contingency program if he were ever to be killed. As Dan had very effectively ended his life, his plans had been carried out. But Rainer didn't agree with the orders to keep Dan in the dark. Shielding a Shield never worked, and it often put people in danger. He thought of the years that his own father and the Haydenshires hadn't wanted him to know just how much danger Emily was constantly in due to Wretchkinsides.

Maybe now, it was done for, and everyone could move on. Maybe. Rainer couldn't quite buy that, but he was getting married, and he and Emily were spending the next two weeks deliciously alone in a hidden-away island villa deep in the Florida Keys.

No one would know where they were going. Not the relentless press that had hounded him since his father's death and certainly not anyone with any affiliation with Dominic Wretchkinsides. Rainer was certain he and most of his organization had been damned to hell, right where they deserved to be.

"Ni-on-na," Keaton, Emily's three-year-old brother, shrieked and raced toward Fionna as soon as he spied the new arrivals.

Dan caught him in his sprint and lifted him into the air to keep him from running headlong into Fionna. Keaton beamed and clapped excitedly. He wiggled in Dan's arms trying to get into Fionna's. He'd had quite a crush for the last several months, and Dan was doing a decent job of wrangling him.

Rainer was sure that though Fionna appeared to be the picture of health, she was still a little tender from her injuries. She probably wasn't quite ready to be assaulted by the ever-exuberant Haydenshire twins.

"That's just what Daniel does when she comes into the room," Governor Haydenshire teased as the entire family came to welcome Dan and Fionna.

"I hear congratulations are in order, Mr. and Mrs. Vindico," Will, Emily's oldest brother, chanted.

Fionna laughed as Dan beamed at her. "Thank you," they both offered as congratulations were echoed from everyone in attendance.

"You both look so happy and healthy." Mrs. Haydenshire hugged Dan and then Fionna. "And when Stephen told me you were getting married on Kauai where you'd grown up, that was just so perfect, and you didn't have to deal with the press, and you've just been through so much, and..." It seemed she was so elated for the newly minted Vindicos that she got lost in thought.

Dan chuckled. "It was perfect."

"Yeah, but his mom still won't speak to me." It seemed Fionna wanted a little advice from Mrs. Haydenshire. Rainer couldn't blame her. Mrs. Haydenshire was a vast well of practical wisdom, and there were very few problems she couldn't solve.

"Look, there's Chloe pulling up. Let's go get all of your gowns on and make sure Mom doesn't need to adjust anything." Mrs. Haydenshire grasped Fionna's hand and gestured back toward the farmhouse.

Rainer knew she would give Fionna advice about her new mother-in-law, but whatever she had in store for Fionna, it wasn't going to be something Dan would be allowed to hear.

Dan kissed Fionna's cheek as he released her hand and then went to help Will set up the altar area.

"Where's Garrett?" Emily quizzed as Chloe made her way toward them.

"Emily, come on. I want to see you in your gown once more before tomorrow," Mrs. Haydenshire commanded. She effectively saved Rainer's surprise.

Just before lunchtime, the men seated themselves at one of the dozens upon dozens of circular tables set up for the reception as the women moved in. They began putting flowers on every available surface and hanging the white garland roses and purple lavender over the seating area under the florist's directions.

It was going to be beautiful. Everyone could see that as Emily directed the florist's work to her vision. Fionna had to take breaks often. Dan watched over her obsessively, but she didn't seem to mind.

Finally, Rainer spied Garrett's Highlander making its way down the gravel path. A broad grin spread across his face.

"Hey, Em, could you come here a minute?"

Everyone tried to hide their excitement as Emily rearranged a few strands of pearls on one of the tables. With a distracted sigh, she turned to Rainer. "I'm a little busy." She gestured to the transformation of the farm at large.

Garrett threw the Highlander into park.

"Just for a second, please." Rainer took her hand and guided her toward the barn.

Suddenly her mouth hung open in shock and her eyes goggled as "Emily!" sang delightedly from the little girl Garrett lifted from the Highlander.

"Aida?" Emily gasped, looking from Aida to Rainer who was beaming at her.

Aida threw her arms around Emily as she lifted her up. "Oh my gosh! How did you…?" Tears flowed down her cheeks as she squeezed Aida tight.

"I kind of thought we needed a flower girl, and your mom and dad would like for Aida to stay on the farm through the summer if she'd like to."

Emily began to sob. She and Fionna had fallen in love with Aida when the Arlington Angels, the Summation team that they challenged for, had spent almost a month at an orphanage deep in Brazil.

"You are just too much. I don't deserve you." Emily set Aida down and threw her arms around Rainer again.

He kissed her cheek. "You've been worried about her since you got back. I wanted her to be in the wedding, and I'd like to see if we can't let her have an amazing summer even if we aren't quite ready to be parents. Your dad arranged the visit."

"Rainer said I could be in the wedding." Aida looked like she couldn't quite believe that was true.

"And I made you a fabulous dress." Fionna stepped toward them and beamed at Aida.

"Fionna!" Aida cried in absolute joy as she took off in a heated sprint toward Fionna.

Garrett caught her in her drive. "Whoa there." He lifted her off the ground and swung her in the air. "Take it easy with Fi, okay?"

Concern dampened Aida's earlier joy. She walked softly toward Fionna and clung to Garrett's hand.

"Am I allowed to hug you?"

The plea brought tears to Fionna's eyes as she nodded. "You better."

With tender care, Aida wrapped her arms around Fionna's waist, but worry still played in her eyes. "Are you okay?"

Before Fionna could formulate an explanation, Aida spied Chloe. She greeted her with similar tenacity and then moved back to Emily. She turned bashful as she clung to Emily's hand.

"Aida, this is Rainer." Emily made introductions. Rainer grinned down at her. She was adorable. He agreed with Emily's assessment as he knelt down and offered her his hand.

"It's so nice to meet you, Aida."

As her little teeth sank into her bottom lip in thoughtful consideration, she reminded Rainer very much of Emily.

"Emily really likes you," she whispered furtively. Emily covered her mouth to hide her giggle.

Rainer couldn't help but chuckle. "Do you think so?" Aida nodded vehemently. "Don't tell her this, but I really like her too." He winked at Aida and earned himself a sweet hug.

"What's wrong with Fionna, and who is that?" She pointed to Dan.

To Rainer's relief, Emily took over. "Fi is okay. She got hurt a few weeks ago, but she'll be all right. And that's Fionna's husband." She pointed to Dan. "His name is Mr. Vindico."

"He's very big." Aida's face fell in fear as she studied Dan's massive strength and somewhat foreboding demeanor. "Did he hurt her?"

"Oh no. He would never do that." Emily shook her head. "He saved her," she whispered.

Aida hesitantly moved to Fionna and grasped her hand. "My name is Aida," she offered Dan timidly.

He grinned at her. "Hi, Aida. It's so nice to meet you. Fi's told me all about you."

"She has?"

Dan chuckled at her. His kind smile seemed to assure Aida that he was a good guy.

After a few more introductions, Aida returned to Garrett. He spent a great deal of time at the orphanage where she lived, and they were very close. He coaxed her out of her shell by offering to let her help with the wedding preparations. She was thrilled with all of the flowers and decorations. She spun around the tables and played with

Keaton and Henry, but she often returned to Garrett and climbed in his lap when she needed a little reassurance.

"She's so good with them." Mrs. Haydenshire smiled.

Fionna nodded. "She helps take care of all of the toddlers in the orphanage. She loves them all."

When Dan and Will returned with eight buckets of fried chicken and all of the fixings for lunch, everyone was eager to take a break.

"Aida, come and eat," Emily called. Rainer noted the dark hollowness of Aida's timid brown eyes and that she was thin. He and Emily had started funding the orphanage as soon as Emily returned from her trip, but Rainer assumed it would take many months of Aida getting enough to eat on a regular basis for it to really make a difference.

Dan had fixed Fionna's plate and then sat down with a copy of *The Realm Times*. He flipped through the article on the takedown at The Tantra. So far, Iodex had effectively covered up the missing money and the murdered operatives.

But the *Times* claimed to have new information on the men who hadn't survived the takedown. Rainer wished Dan would put the paper away. He didn't want to think about it anymore.

"I know that man." Aida pointed to a color picture of Alexi Pravus, the man who'd shot Fionna and killed their unborn child. Everyone halted abruptly, and the endless expanse of fresh air normally afforded them by the farm seemed to be vacuumed from their lungs.

"You do?" Dan quizzed gently.

Nodding, she moved closer to him to study the paper. "Yes, he used to be my daddy's boss at the mine. He wasn't there when it collapsed, though," she stated softly. Her timid voice strangled in the fear of the life she'd been forced to live.

Rainer swallowed harshly as he recalled that the story of the mine collapse wasn't true. The nuns who ran the orphanage where Aida lived didn't want her to know her family had been murdered. Absolute terror marred Emily's beautiful face. Tears welled in her emerald eyes.

"I think he was a nice man. He used to bring me suckers whenever he came to get the money from Pai, but he made my tummy feel funny, so I'm not sure if he was a nice man." She sighed dejectedly as she read the newspaper with ease. "How did he die?"

"Aida." Emily moved to sit beside her. "Sweetheart, he wasn't a nice man. He's who hurt Fionna."

Aida looked confused as Fionna began to sob. "He told me as long as Pai kept paying him, he would make sure nothing bad would happen, but then he couldn't pay him one time, and that's when the mine collapsed. If Pai had kept paying him, I wouldn't have to live in the orphanage."

There wasn't a dry eye in the entire crowd. Dan wrapped Fionna up in his massive arms as she wept convulsively.

～

Dan Vindico

Dan's heart refused to accept the harrowing truth of Aida's horrifying tale. He tried to soothe Fionna. He couldn't stand for her to cry anymore. She'd been hurt so much, and it was all his fault.

Mrs. Haydenshire lifted Aida into her arms and gazed at her adoringly as she wiped tears from her eyes. "Aida, sweetheart, you can stay here on the farm with us for as long as you like. You don't have to live in the orphanage anymore." The Crown Governor wiped his eyes and nodded his adamant agreement.

"Fi?" Having no idea if he was ready to be a father to a seven-year-old or what might be in store for them down the road, Dan met Fionna's desperate gaze.

"Oh, please. Please, please!" Fionna begged.

He wiped away a few of her tears and turned to the Haydenshires. "Or she could stay with us."

He wondered momentarily if they should talk it over more or spend more time with Aida, but as he stared at the precious little girl that everything had been taken from, he knew she was the answer to prayers sobbed fervently from the hospital operating room, from the walls of their far too empty house, and from the island of Kauai.

"That's perfect," Mrs. Haydenshire gasped. She set Aida down and directed her toward Dan and Fionna.

Fionna moved to Aida and beamed through her cascading tears. "Aida, would you like for Dan and me to adopt you, so you could live here with us and never go back to the orphanage?"

Elation cast Aida's timid eyes. "And I could stay with you, and you would take care of me?" she asked hesitantly.

Fionna nodded. Her chin trembled as tears continued to roll down her cheeks. "Yes, you can stay in our house. You can even pick your own room, and be with us until you're all grown up."

"I promise I'll be good, and I won't make noise when I'm not supposed to, and I won't bother, and I'll help you do anything you need help with." Aida's promises unleashed more tears that Dan could no longer hold back. His heart ached physically as he gazed at his wife and his little girl.

"Does he want me to?" She clung to Fionna but eyed Dan speculatively. Grief shadowed her precious face once again.

Dan knelt down and took Aida's hands in his own. "More than you will ever know, sweetheart." Tears poured down his face now.

Garrett squeezed his eyes shut in what appeared to be utter relief. Everyone stared at the formation of a beautiful family.

A hesitant smile was just beginning on Aida's features. She was still nervous about the abrupt change in her life. "Do you know about little girls?"

She made Dan laugh through his tears. "I have lots of little sisters, and I've gotten pretty good with Fionna, but you can teach me the rest, deal?"

"Deal." Aida giggled.

In a move that melted through the remnants of terror and anger that still occasionally permeated his soul, the ones that Fionna was working on but that Dan hadn't yet been able to release, Aida reached and took his hand in her left and Fionna's in her right as a broad grin spread across her face.

CHAPTER 2
AIDA

Aida stood up on her tiptoes, and Dan noted the holes in her tennis shoes. He knew Rainer was sending a great deal of money to the orphanage, but maybe they needed more. He made a mental note to send them funding as well.

She tugged on Fionna's hand. She wanted to ask her something.

Fionna leaned her head down beside Aida's mouth. Aida cupped her hand and whispered in her ear. Whatever she'd asked had more tears flowing from Fionna's eyes.

"Yes," she assured Aida as she gazed up at Dan. "Dan gives the best hugs."

Aida seemed to have to will courage as she studied him, but then she extended her arms upward. After drawing a stuttered breath and blinking back more of his own tears, Dan hoisted her up into his arms and held her tight.

Aida's tiny frame melted into Dan's as she laid her head tenderly on his shoulder. She turned her face to his neck just the way Fionna did when she needed Dan to make her feel safe.

"Okay, you have to stop." Mrs. Haydenshire mopped tears from her eyes and face. Dan cradled Aida to his chest and felt his ragged soul begin to mend. She didn't seem to want to let go, and he wanted to hold on to her forever.

"Could we get a little help with this, Governor Haydenshire?" Desperation perforated his plea.

Governor Haydenshire chuckled as he nodded. "I don't know how often I cast and seal a marriage certificate and adoption papers in one month's time for the same couple, but for you two, this somehow seems appropriate." He slapped Dan on the back. "Let me go make a few phone calls."

"Thank you," Fionna called, but she was unable to take her eyes off Dan and Aida.

Garrett joined them. Dan tried not to mind when Aida exuberantly exchanged his arms for Garrett's. "Hey, this is pretty cool, right? If you go live with Dan and Fionna, I'll get to visit you all the time and we can play."

As he made his vow to Aida, he kept his eyes locked on Dan and Fionna. They both nodded their agreement. Dan was certain having Garrett around would help her adjust, and she clearly adored him.

"This is the best day ever!" Aida exclaimed. She hugged Garrett tighter.

"I think you're right, Aida Mae." Garrett lifted his eyes back to Dan. "Just remember that both of them are still my girls, but I guess I'll share them."

Dan could never thank Garrett enough for everything he'd done for both him and Fionna. As Garrett had just delivered them Aida, he knew he would always be deeply indebted. He didn't mind at all.

Rainer Lawson

The rest of the afternoon went by in a dizzying blur. As Rainer watched the aisle being constructed, his energy tensed. Another rise of excitement and nerves worked through his body.

He let his mind reel as he took a moment to recall images of Emily from the past. Memories formed in his mind of Mrs. Haydenshire picking him and Logan up from first grade when his father was out of town. Emily was seated in the back of the minivan with her hair pulled up in pigtails. She shared her jellybeans with Rainer but refused Logan any.

"Betcha won't kiss me." He could still hear her challenge. He could still feel his nerves. He could hear Logan and Connor's derisive groans and gags as he'd brushed his lips across her cheek.

He saw her long auburn hair whipped out behind her as she raced him on her bike. He always let her win.

"Will you push me on the tire swing?" He would have done anything if she'd just keep holding his hand. Rainer recalled the feeling.

He heard her terror-filled scream as she saw the copperhead, and his shield had emerged from his body though it was still largely undeveloped. His all-encompassing fervor to protect her, to put his body between her and the snake, washed through his mind.

Sitting down on the dock beside her, wishing there was something he could do to make her stop crying. *"Please, Em, don't be embarrassed. Isn't that what's supposed to happen?"* His confused plea echoed in his mind. He wasn't certain how to talk to her about starting her period. He just knew he didn't want her to cry and run away from him anymore.

Sitting in her loft trying to hide the effect she was having on his body. *"I know what you want to do."* He could still hear her sassy declaration.

"No, you don't." He could still feel the fevered burn in his face.

"You've been staring at them for two weeks straight." He'd wanted to melt into the floor right up to the point that she grabbed his hands and placed them on her breasts. After that, he'd only wanted to melt into her.

Walks on the beach and formals at the academy mixed with games of hide-and-seek as they flew through his mind. He landed on Emily dressed in a low-cut, hunter-green T-shirt, the exact color of her eyes, and a pair of tight blue jeans, sitting in his Mustang in a hidden-away cove at Great Falls Park.

His tongue in her mouth. His hands groping her breasts. Her grinding against him. Her jeans pulling away from her as he unbuttoned them.

Backing her up to the pier piling on Virginia Beach, the fragrance of her and of sex mixed with redwood in the humid salty air.

"Touch me, Rainer, please." He could still feel her whispered plea as it caressed his neck, the emerging wet heat on his fingers as he traced her, as his cock pulsed in her hands.

"Rainer, would you help them hang those lanterns in the cherry trees?" Emily's request jerked him back to the present. He gazed at her, completely overwhelmed by how much he loved her and the fact that the next day she was going to be his wife.

"Sure, baby." He helped her unpack the rectangular lanterns that she'd ordered to be hung throughout the blooming cherry trees on the farm.

Levi, Patrick, Dan, and Garrett hung the bubble lights inside the tents for the reception while Tad, Nathan, Logan, Connor, and Will listened to Emily explain how the dance floor should be situated.

Everyone paused when Fionna asked Aida if she'd like to try on her dress so that the hem could be pinned. They emerged from the house with Aida dressed in the deep-purple gown Fionna had created. It was fitted to her waist and then flared out into a long skirt. Fionna tied the large lavender sash into a bow at her back.

"It's the most beautiful dress ever, and purple is my favorite color!" Aida was exuberant. Dan beamed.

Rainer was certain there would be complications and issues as Aida grew used to the idea of living with Dan and Fionna, but at that moment, all three of them looked like they'd never been happier.

"I know," Fionna assured her as she leaned down to pin the hem. "That's why I made it for you, and my dress is purple too, so we'll match."

"You remembered that my favorite color is purple?" Aida couldn't quite seem to understand how much she was already loved.

"I remembered," Fionna promised.

Once the hem was pinned, Aida spun around making the skirt flare out. "Fionna says I get to keep it forever. I want to wear it every day. I feel like a princess!" She raced toward Dan.

~

"I think you look like a beautiful princess," he assured her. She beamed up at him, and it was apparent to everyone watching them that he made her feel safe. She was aware of the power of his shield, and she wanted to be near him.

"And here's your crown, my little princess." Fionna handed Dan the circle of purple and light pink flowers that Fionna had made to match the bridesmaids' bouquets.

Dan leaned down and placed it tenderly on Aida's hair.

"Do you know what that's called?" Fionna adjusted it slightly.

Aida shook her head and reached to grasp Dan's hand.

"It's called a haku, and we wear them for very special things and special dances in Hawaii," Fionna explained.

Dan carefully lifted Aida back into his arms, making certain that the pins didn't scratch her calves. "Fionna wore a beautiful haku when we got married."

Aida's eyes lit as she beamed at Fionna. "And then she was the most beautiful princess ever!"

"She definitely was." Dan's vow strangled in his throat.

Holding Aida seemed almost as natural as holding Fionna. He could feel the light traces of her burgeoning energy soothe when she was near him.

"When do I get to go home with you?" Aida asked timidly. She sounded afraid she would get in trouble for being curious. Fionna gazed at Aida in Dan's arms. The smiles she kept giving him made him feel like maybe her world had finally settled into perfect accord.

"We thought we would take you home in just a little while, and I can finish sewing your dress, and then you can pick out your room. But then we're going to come back here because tonight Emily is having a slumber party with you, and me, and Chloe, and Adeline at the farmhouse. No boys allowed!" Fionna tempted her.

Aida's eyes lit in delight, but Dan was concerned. "But if you'd rather stay in your new room tonight, you and Fionna could stay at home." He wanted Aida to know she didn't have to stay overnight if she didn't want to.

Garrett, Logan, and Rainer all chuckled. Suddenly aware that they were being watched, Dan assumed they knew he didn't want to sleep without Fionna. He wanted to take his girls home and start working on becoming a family.

Aida looked concerned as she studied Dan and Fionna. "Won't you miss Dan?"

Fionna nodded. "I will miss Dan, but we'll see him in the morning while we get ready for Emily to marry Rainer. Tonight, he's going to a party with the boys."

Aida drew her mouth to the side. "Slumber parties are a lot of fun. I think maybe even more fun than boy parties."

He was certain she was the cutest child that had ever existed in the history of the world. "I have no doubt," he assured her. "But I need you to do something for me tonight, okay?"

"Anything," Aida vowed.

"I need you to take care of Fionna for me and to remember that she still has a hurt tummy, okay?"

"I promise I will."

Her little head hit Fionna's abdomen in the approximate place where she'd been shot, and Dan was well aware that with each exuberant hug, Fionna twinged in pain.

"Dan, Fionna," Governor Haydenshire called from the back deck. He was holding up a stack of paperwork. "Why don't you let Aida play with the boys?"

Dan hoped against hope that nothing had gone wrong with Aida's paperwork.

Emily moved in. "Actually, why don't I help you take off your dress so the pins don't stick you, and then you can help me with a very important job for the wedding."

Dan set Aida back on the ground. "But you'll be right back?" Her voice shook and she clung to Fionna's hand.

"We'll be right back."

"Okay." She nodded at Emily. "Sister Tabitha says I'm a very good helper."

Emily smiled. "You're an excellent helper!"

Fionna clung to Dan's arm, drawing from his ample energy

reserves. He supplied her with strength and soothed her as they made their way into the farmhouse.

They followed Governor and Mrs. Haydenshire into the office. "All right, you two have a seat." The governor's grin put Dan at ease. He certainly didn't appear to have bad news.

Dan and Fionna seated themselves and waited with bated breath.

"Here are the papers establishing you as Aida's guardians and stating that someone from the Auxiliary Office of the Senate will check on her occasionally to make certain that you're caring for her properly. As I have no doubt that she will be both adored and thoroughly spoiled rotten, I wouldn't worry about it, so just sign them." Governor Haydenshire set a stack of paperwork down in front of them.

"Says the man who allowed a six-year-old Emily eleven gumballs out of the machine at the grocery store because, and I quote, she wanted a pink one. The same man who has already purchased Abigail a tricycle," Mrs. Haydenshire chastised.

Dan and Fionna laughed heartily as the governor gave her a goading smirk.

"Now," he went on. "The Brazilian government doesn't believe she has any known living relatives left, so when these papers are signed, she becomes a Vindico. She gives up the last name of Santos and her family crest the very same way Fionna did when she married you, Dan."

"But Stephen and I just wanted to suggest, if you don't mind," Mrs. Haydenshire stepped in. Dan and Fionna nodded adamantly. "You might not want to bring up the change of her name for a few weeks still. Let her get used to being taken care of and relying on you for what she needs."

The governor grimaced. "It's not something she's accustomed to. I'm certain you've noticed her ragged clothing and the fact that she probably hasn't been eating enough food. You're going to have to work slowly and methodically to make sure that she eats foods that she needs. You'll need a pediatric medio's guidance. Going from not quite enough food to an abundance of it can be difficult for little bodies."

The pain of it being stated out loud made Dan's heart ache.

"It was only three years ago that Pravus killed her parents and her older brothers." Disgust leaked into the governor's tone. "She was only four when it happened. According to the nuns at the orphanage, she remembers snippets of her family but not the events surrounding their death."

Mrs. Haydenshire gave Fionna a sorrowful gaze. "She might not ever really feel comfortable calling you Mom and Dad."

The governor nodded. "Rainer never did. Of course he was much older when Joseph was killed."

"That's completely fine," Fionna vowed. "I don't want her to forget her parents. I want them to stay with her in her heart forever. They'll always be a part of her."

Dan squeezed Fionna's hand. No one else in the room was aware of the depth of knowledge from which she spoke. She'd buried her mother when she was barely thirteen.

"All right, get these signed." The governor handed over the next stack of papers before he continued. "There are a few allowances the Realm gives with international adoptions. Because there are really only seven weeks of the school year left, Aida won't be expected to begin attending elementary school until next fall."

When Dan had awoken that morning with Fionna tucked up on his chest, he had no idea that by that afternoon he would have become a father. He tried to locate panic about that fact within his body or his mind but found none. He hadn't allowed himself to think through the radical changes this was going to bring about though. It was truly going to be a trial by fire, but he was more than ready.

Thoughts of outstanding school systems, vegetables, and Internet safety suddenly became extremely important. He tried to envision Aida leaving them every day to go to school. His shield tensed.

"She seems exceptionally bright. She read that paper in English quickly and adeptly for seven. And she remembered Pravus from a very young age," the governor reminded them. "But you might want to do a few educational things with her that her classmates will probably have already done that she might not have. Take her to the zoo, to see a movie, to a park, on a picnic, to the beach, things like that."

"I want to take her to Kauai." Fionna turned the full power of her pleading gaze on Dan.

He'd been thinking the very same thing. "Why don't we call your grandparents when we get home? We could spend the summer there if you want, baby doll."

She threw her arms around him and squeezed him tightly. The governor cleared his throat when the hug extended for several minutes.

"Sorry." Fionna reseated herself. A rosy heat colored her olive cheeks.

Governor Haydenshire chuckled and shook his head at them. "She'll have to be immunized," he continued down his list. "And, she does seem to have accepted the mine collapse story. She's reconciled that in her mind. I would leave it at that. I wouldn't try to explain to her what actually happened unless she asks when she's much older. Rainer still has no clue as to the gruesome details of his parents' deaths, and he never will." The governor looked visibly pained as he recalled their murders.

Fionna and Dan shared his grief as they signed the last few papers.

"She doesn't have a middle name," Fionna noted as she signed her name under Dan's.

"No, and that isn't uncommon in the village where she was born, but you could give her one if you'd like."

"We'll let her choose," Fionna stated firmly as Dan smiled and winked at his beautiful wife.

"Or, we could make Santos one of her middle names, but I think she should have two. She could choose the second, just like you did."

Fionna swallowed down another round of emotion as she nodded her agreement.

CHAPTER 3
COOKIES AND MILK

"What do they taste like?" Aida was quizzing Logan when Dan and Fionna returned to the deck. He'd offered her one of Mrs. Haydenshire's famous chocolate chip cookies. "They're amazing!" Logan scrubbed Aida's scraggly hair. Dan noted that she seemed to bring peace to him as well. He'd phoned Logan when they'd returned from Kauai and invited him and Adeline over. They'd discussed Pravus and what Logan had done and how it affected him.

It had been cathartic for both of them, but Aida seemed to bring Logan peace, a reminder that life went on in the wake of all of the evil atrocities Pravus had committed.

Dan watched as Aida took a hesitant bite. Her eyes goggled. "It's so yummy!"

"She's probably never had a cookie," Fionna whispered.

"Ever?" Dan was unable to believe the depth of poverty that Aida had lived.

"Her family was really poor, and when I was there the orphanage fed them stew every day because it fills them up. I'm sure it's better now, but it wasn't that long ago that we were there."

"I'll give you the recipe," Mrs. Haydenshire assured Fionna.

"Thank you! And Mrs. Haydenshire," she pled, "if I get confused or I'm not sure how to handle something with her…?"

She embraced Fionna. "Then Stephen and I are just a phone call away."

After thanking the Haydenshires profusely for all of their help, Fionna gazed at Aida who'd been supplied with milk and another cookie via Logan and Adeline.

"We need to get her home, so I can sew the hem on her dress and then get back for the parties." Fionna laid her head on Dan's shoulder. He brushed a kiss in her hair and pulled his car keys from his pocket.

A sudden realization had him reeling momentarily. "Uh, baby, I don't have a way to get you both home." His two-seater Ferrari was definitely not a family car.

"Here." Rainer tossed Dan the keys to Emily's Hummer. "Give Sam a call, but we won't be needing it for a few weeks."

"Thank you." Dan still couldn't quite wrap his head around everything that had changed in one day's time.

"Okay, but I don't want a minivan." Fionna's plea made everyone laugh.

Dan helped Aida up into the Hummer and showed her how to buckle in. He added a booster car seat to the list of supplies they needed to acquire immediately. Fionna took a quick inventory of the suitcase Aida had brought from the orphanage.

"I got to fly in an airplane, and it was so high. And then I got to ride in Garrett's car, and he has a phone that has movies on it!" Aida declared in shock.

Dan and Fionna shared a grin.

"We need to take her by a few stores. The things in her suitcase are falling apart, but we need to be careful. She'll be embarrassed," Fionna whispered as Dan cranked the Hummer.

He recalled Adeline's face and her horror when Lucas had taken them shopping in Sydney. His willingness to buy her anything at all had done nothing more than make Adeline uncomfortable and further the wedge between them.

He kept the warning planted firmly in his mind as he drove them to a local Target. He and Fionna tried not to overwhelm Aida as they encouraged her to try on tennis shoes that fit.

"I've never had new shoes before," she admitted shamefully.

"Well, we'll just get one pair for now, and that way your feet won't hurt, so you can run really fast."

Aida nodded, but she was still uncomfortable. She finally picked out a white pair with light-purple laced butterfly designs and purple laces. She carried the box in her arms like Dan and Fionna had given her precious metals. They moved on to clothes.

"You need a new nightgown for the slumber party." Fionna pointed to a rack of little girls' pajamas.

"My nightgown is in my suitcase. Sister Mary Francis packed it for me."

"It's so small and full of holes," Fionna whispered to Dan.

Not certain what else to do, Dan reached and pulled a purple pair of pajamas off the rack that appeared to be Aida's size. They had hot pink hearts all over them. "I really like these."

Aida's eyes lit, but she said nothing.

"And, I think you would be so pretty in them."

"You do?" Aida quizzed. Dan and Fionna nodded adamantly.

"But I already have a nightgown, and you aren't allowed to have more than one because someone else might need it." Aida explained the rules of the orphanage.

Dan thought momentarily that his recently mended heart was going to break all over again. Fionna drew from him as she took a deep breath. He felt the energy she pulled leave his body. Somehow, her draws never depleted him. The always seemed to give him strength.

"Well, now that you're going to live with Dan and me, it's okay to have more than one, and if you'd like we could give your other nightgown to a little girl that's a little bit smaller than you. You've grown so much since I saw you in Brazil. I think it's time for you to get clothes that are a little bit bigger." She kept her tone soothing, but Dan knew she was fighting tears.

"Are you sure?" Aida's brow knitted tightly. She didn't want to break a rule.

"I'm sure." Fionna nodded.

"Do you have more than one nightgown?"

"Uh," Fionna stammered. Truthfully she only had one nightshirt other than her vast collection of negligees and nighties because she normally slept naked. It was a preference that drove Dan wild and that he sincerely hoped she would continue even though they'd suddenly become parents.

"I sometimes sleep in one of Dan's T-shirts," Fionna supplied in a partial truth.

Aida nodded her understanding. "It's so nice if you get clothes that are too big because then they don't pinch like all your others."

Fionna and Dan shared a heartbroken gaze as Fionna nodded.

"Is it okay if I have those?" Aida whispered suddenly in a terror-filled plea as she pointed to the pajamas in Dan's hands.

"Of course, sweetheart. Do you see any others you might like?"

After several long minutes and a great deal of convincing, Aida admitted to liking a pink nightgown with Moana and Maui on it and another pair of short pajamas with crowned frogs all over them. She said the frogs were very funny, and Dan considered purchasing two pairs.

Fionna picked her up a new toothbrush and children's toothpaste. Aida hadn't fussed too much over this as Fionna mentioned that she was buying her and Dan new toothbrushes as well.

Time was running short, so Fionna simply picked up three pairs of blue jeans, a few small shirts, panties, and two cotton dresses that she thought Aida would like. She added them to the buggy without discussion.

While Fionna had been grabbing clothes, Dan had done a quick Internet search on the safest booster car seats. He put that in the cart on top of the clothes.

After the purchases had been made, Dan installed the new car seat and drove his family home in Emily's Hummer. He liked the way it handled and wondered if Fionna might like one. They certainly needed a larger car.

Aida clung to Fionna's hand and gnawed on her lip as they entered the house. "Your house is very nice."

Dan wondered if it would take Aida as long to call it *her* house as it had taken Fionna.

"Would you like to look around?" Fionna eased softly, but Aida shook her head. It had been too much in one day. She was visibly overwhelmed and exhausted.

Fionna gave Dan a pleading stare. Drawing a deep breath, he leaned and hoisted Aida into his arms. She immediately turned and hid her face in his neck once again.

Fionna's eyes closed in defeat. "We should've had Garrett come with us for this. He's her favorite," she mouthed.

Dan debated calling Garrett as he moved to the couch, sank down, and cradled her in his arms.

"Aida, would you like for us to stay home with Dan and not go to the slumber party?" Fionna was struggling under the weight of Aida's emotions. She read her with ease, and Aida's fears and confusion must've been all-consuming. Her own rhythms were vibrating.

"I would like to go to Emily's slumber party, please."

"Okay." Fionna smiled in relief. "Well, if we're going to stay with Emily tonight, then you don't have to pick your room out today."

Aida's energy eased. They understood that she didn't want to make any more decisions. She continued to glance around the house until her beautiful brown eyes landed on the quilt on the back of the couch.

"Hey, you know Fi made those quilts." Dan gestured to the others hung over the armrests of the couch and love seat.

"You did?"

Fionna smiled and nodded. "Maybe in a few weeks we could make one for you."

"A purple one?" Aida asked. Her energy soothed and then began to spin happily.

"Sure!"

Aida turned back to Dan. "Did you know that Fionna has this stuff that she can put on your skin and make it not itchy anymore?"

"Fionna is amazing." He studied her arms as he made his vow. Her olive skin looked patchy and dry.

"They don't make them wear suntan lotion at the orphanage, but they play outside most of the day in Brazil. She has eczema. Garrett always heals the patches when he's there, but he couldn't heal what was causing it. I put Tutu's kukui oil all over her while I was there and her skin cleared up, but then we left. We'll need Tutu to help us figure out what's causing it."

She forced a sweet smile as she took Aida's hand. "You know, when I was a little girl, my mom used to put that same stuff on my skin every night after my bath so that my skin wasn't itchy. I still put it on every day, so maybe we could put it on together."

This idea seemed to thoroughly delight Aida. "Is that how you got to be so pretty?"

Dan beamed at both of his girls.

Fionna swooned. "Oh, thank you. How about if we all go in the kitchen and have a snack? Then I'll go finish your dress, and we can pack for Emily's."

Elaborating on what they were going to do seemed to bring Aida peace. Everyone understood that she was fine as long as Dan and Fionna didn't force too much on her at once.

Dan watched Aida dutifully eat the apples and cheese that Fionna had cut up for her, but she was thoroughly delighted with the Dr Pepper Dan provided her.

Fionna's new sewing machine was flying upstairs, and he felt a sense of peace and wholeness flood through him. It was an odd sensation, not one he was accustomed to feeling unless he was in physical contact with Fionna.

After getting everything packed, Dan drove back to the farm. Aida had requested she be able to bring her new frog pajamas. She was certain Emily would think they were funny as well.

The Haydenshires seemed pleased to be throwing one last slumber party in Emily's honor. They shared nostalgic gazes when they thought no one was paying attention.

"Okay, I ordered the pizzas," Governor Haydenshire informed his wife as she was preparing bowls of chips and dip.

"Pizza is delicious!" Aida explained to Dan. "Garrett brought it to us when Fionna and Emily made us the slumber party at the orphanage."

"Yeah, I did." Garrett hoisted Aida up onto his shoulders, making her giggle with delight. "And why did I bring you pizza?" he chanted.

"Because you're the man!" Aida supplied in a clearly well-rehearsed routine.

Dan and Fionna laughed at the two of them.

"I guess Dan can be the man too," Garrett pledged.

She nodded her agreement, completing the perfection of Dan's day.

"Would one of the *men* like to make the child something to drink?" Mrs. Haydenshire rolled her eyes at the macho spectacle playing out in her kitchen.

Garrett lifted Aida off of his shoulders.

"What would you like to drink, sweetheart?" Dan winked at her. She gifted him with another one of those heart-melting grins.

She turned to Mrs. Haydenshire timidly. "Do you have the stuff that Dan gave me at Fionna's house?"

Mrs. Haydenshire raised her eyebrows to Dan in question. He chuckled and scrubbed Aida's head, making her laugh. "Dr Pepper, but maybe just one more today."

"I do have that." Mrs. Haydenshire supplied Aida with a prepared glass.

"They have it here too," Aida whispered in shock, making Fionna, Dan, and Garrett beam at her.

"We need to get going," Logan urged all of his brothers, Rainer, and Dan. Aida's face promptly fell.

She clung to Dan's hand. "You and Garrett are going to come back, right?"

Dan leaned down so he was gazing into Aida's frightened eyes. "I promise, baby. I'll be back to get you and Fionna bright and early tomorrow morning."

"What if you forget to remember us?" She sounded terrified.

Dan hugged her close. "I would never ever forget you and Fionna, okay? You two are the most important people in the entire world to me," he explained as all of the Haydenshires offered him sympathetic gazes.

She nodded but then pulled away and held her hands up to Garrett. He tucked her head on his shoulder. "Listen to me for just a minute, okay?" She nodded. "Remember, every single time I promised I'd come back to the orphanage to see you, I did, right?" Another nod. "I also promise that Dan and I and Fionna will never forget to remember you, okay?"

"Okay," she whispered. He squeezed her tight and set her back down.

She grasped Fionna's hand. "I will take care of Fionna for you. I remembered."

"Thank you. I know you'll take good care of her. If you decide you want to come home, you tell Fi, and I'll come and get you both, even if it's late tonight."

The governor smiled. "Good dad." He gave a slight nod of approval, bolstering Dan's waning confidence. He still didn't know what he was doing.

CHAPTER 4
THE MAN YOU HAVE BECOME

Kisses were shared by most of the Haydenshire men and their wives, fiancées, and girlfriends who were staying for the party. Dan pulled Fionna in for a long drawn kiss. As sweet, happy giggles reached their ears, they knew their little girl had spotted them.

"She'll have to get used to that, because we're still doing that all the time." Fionna laughed.

Dan gave her a rather lascivious smirk that said when their little girl was asleep they'd be doing a whole lot more.

Aida promised again to take good care of Fionna for Dan before he left to join all of the Haydenshire men at Lesco's Pub. They took the back room that Logan had booked for Rainer's bachelor party after Rainer adamantly insisted that the party would not be held in a strip club or even a bar.

"Okay." Garrett poured himself a beer from the numerous pitchers Les was setting on the long table. "I know that we're here to harass and chastise Rainer, but could we all just take a minute and raise a glass to the guy who not only scored one but two of my favorite women in the world in like one month's time?" He raised his mug to Dan.

Laughing, Dan nodded his acceptance of the toast.

"Yeah, let's just talk about you having a little girl," Will chimed in as everyone took a seat. "First of all, you will be broke very, very soon, like as soon as Fionna and Aida decide that she needs new clothes. And I'm pretty sure this has already happened, but she will wrap you so tightly around her little finger it will be painful, but you will be woefully unable to extricate yourself from her grip."

"That has definitely already happened," Dan assured everyone. He turned to Rainer with a goading grin and chuckled. "You know, I will say, all of that stuff Governor Haydenshire used to complain about constantly with you and Emily suddenly makes perfect sense to me."

Rainer rolled his eyes and braced for the incoming harassment he was certain to receive over the next few hours. "I am marrying her tomorrow," he reminded everyone.

Les carried in platters of wings, hot dogs, burgers, and onion rings. He grinned at Rainer. "All right now, Mr. Lawson, you better take care of my favorite little redhead."

Rainer laughed. "She's my favorite redhead too. No worries."

"If anything gets too confusing tomorrow night, you just give me a call and I'll talk you through it," Les harassed.

Everyone laughed heartily as Rainer shook his head. "I think I got it, but thanks."

"Yeah, but go ahead and write your number down for him, Les." Patrick brought on another round of laughter.

"So, do we get to find out where you'll be stiffing our little sister tomorrow night?" Will chanted.

"Not a chance in hell. I grew up with you all. You'd show up there."

"We could talk him through it," Garrett guffawed.

"Em, where am I supposed to stick this?" Connor chimed in immediately.

Dan felt genuinely sorry for Rainer as they continued. He was thrust back in time as a memory seared through his mind. The clinks of mugs on the tables and the bellowing laughter coupled with derision faded away for just a moment. *"Taking Governor Haydenshire's baby girl to the beach for vacation? I knew you had guts, Lawson."*

"I suppose."

"Relax, you'll be fine. Just take everything nice and slow, really slow."

Dan had used every ounce of ample muscle in his body to keep from laughing at Rainer's wide-eyed terror over what he was about to do.

With another glance down the table, he let the memories flip through his mind. Trying to make the governors understand that Rainer had to know the truth so he could keep Emily safe. Training him to shoot, to cast, trying to teach him a little bit about life. Trying to take that wide-eyed kid and turn him into a man. Dan would not take credit, but the confident guy seated across the table from him prepared to marry the love of his life the next day had come so very far so very fast. Dan couldn't have been more pleased to call Rainer Lawson his friend and a hell of a good guy. Rainer's father, Governor Haydenshire, Sam, everyone who had a hand in raising him should be proud. Dan certainly was.

"She's been asking to touch it since she was four, so...." Levi laughed as the story of Emily's childhood curiosity was retold much to Rainer's chagrin.

"No, Rainer. You don't pull that hair!" Garrett upped the ante to groans from the table.

"You know," Connor goaded, "all this time you've been buying her ring pops, you should've been getting her Blow Pops."

Will chuckled. "Trust me, you don't walk around grinning like he does unless you're getting blow pops."

Garrett chuckled. "Hey, he's Elite Iodex. He knows how to search it out, cover it up, bury it deep, and get the job done."

Pitchers of beer and platters of food were consumed. Logan and Dan refrained from harassing Rainer, but he took it in heavy doses from everyone else.

By midnight, only Logan, Garrett, Dan, and Rainer remained. None of them were looking forward to returning home to a cold, empty bed. The press had been swarming around the farm earlier and had located the bachelor party but had been refused entry into the pub by Les.

They seemed to have given up and gone home. Everyone was well aware they would be out in force the next day.

"We could go by Mom and Dad's and check on the girls," Logan suggested.

Dan's face pulled into a hopeful smile. "Yeah, that'd be good. Fionna was hurting some earlier, and Aida's so convinced I'm going to forget her."

"That orphanage is rough, man. Give her some time. Not a lot of people have kept their promises to her." Garrett looked pained.

"You sure your parents won't mind?" Dan felt the sudden need to move. He had to make certain Fionna and Aida knew he would always be there and how much he loved them.

"Nah," Logan scoffed.

"Let's go," Dan commanded.

"Yeah, but Em was big on the whole *me not seeing her before the wedding* thing." Rainer hesitated.

Logan rolled his eyes. "As your best man, I volunteer to go in and make certain that she doesn't mind you feeling her up before she goes to sleep."

They drove back to the farmhouse, and Dan followed Logan and Garrett silently through the kitchen door. Rainer waited on the porch until Logan returned and gestured him inside.

Emily blinked heavily, but then smiled as Rainer eased out of his shoes and slid in behind her on her pallet.

"Hey there," he whispered.

"Hey." She took his hand and pulled it over her and snuggled into his chest.

Dan tiptoed over to Fionna and Aida. Fionna's arm was around Aida's waist tenderly. They were sound asleep on their sides. Leaning down, he brushed a kiss across Fionna's cheek and then one across Aida's.

Her eyes blinked open hesitantly.

"Dan?"

"I'm sorry. I didn't mean to wake you, sweetheart."

A broad smile stretched across her face. "Is it time to put my dress on?" She yawned deeply.

Smiling, Dan shook his head. "Not yet. I just wanted to come check on you and Fi."

"I took care of her," she whispered.

Panic set in his gut as he studied Fionna's abdomen looking for any sign of distress.

"You did?"

"Yes, I held her hand while she fell asleep because she said she missed you."

Dan's heart tumbled over the next beat. "Thank you." He brushed another kiss on Aida's sweet face.

"Can you stay here with us?"

"Uh," Dan turned to Logan who was already tucked in next to Adeline and Garrett who was kissing Chloe's cheek.

"Sure, they won't care," Logan scoffed.

"Okay." Dan smiled at Aida as he kicked off his boots and moved behind Fionna. She sighed contentedly in her sleep and wiggled her body into Dan's embrace.

"Thank you." Aida lay back down, still holding Fionna's hand in both of her own.

Just as everyone was beginning to doze off came one of the sweetest things Dan had ever heard.

"Hey, Dan?" Aida whispered.

He leaned up. "Are you okay, baby?"

Nodding, she smiled. "I just wanted to say I love you."

Emotion cinched his throat. The last two months assaulted his mind. Wretchkinsides, the baby, the gunshot, the miscarriage. Blinking back tears, Dan nodded. "I love you too, sweetheart, so much."

Garrett raised his head off of Chloe's pillow. He gave Dan a knowing grin. "Just makes everything seem like it might've been worth it, doesn't it?"

"Yeah, it definitely does."

CHAPTER 5

THE END OF AN ERA

RAINER LAWSON

"Oh, good grief," Rainer heard Governor Haydenshire huff as he took in all of the late-night additions to Emily's slumber party.

Everyone who'd been sleeping in the governor's vast living room sat up and yawned while rubbing their eyes.

Nerves twisted uncomfortably in his stomach. Rainer wondered if he was the only one who noticed Emily's absence from their pallet.

Mrs. Haydenshire followed in behind her husband. Rolling her eyes, she began navigating her way through the pallets carrying a crying baby Abigail.

"And now I suppose you would all like breakfast." She chuckled as she handed the baby and her bottle to the governor. She seemed very pleased they'd all ended up there in the middle of the night.

Aida promptly stood and straightened her new frog pajamas as Dan and Fionna participated in what Rainer assumed was their customary morning routine of cuddling, kissing, and whispering to one another. They seemed momentarily unaware that anyone else was in the room at all.

Aida carefully stepped over Chloe to get to Governor Haydenshire. He was settling into one of the recliners, gazing at Abigail.

"I'm sorry," Aida apologized.

"What are you sorry for, sweetheart?" Concern furrowed his brow.

"I don't want you to be upset with Dan because I asked him to stay. It's my fault he's here."

"Oh, sweetie, no," Governor Haydenshire insisted kindly. "I'm not upset at all. I can't think of any other place that Dan should be other than with you and Fionna, but,"—he winked at her—"these other boys are nothing but trouble."

She giggled and seemed pleased that the Haydenshires weren't upset with Dan. She returned to Fionna's pallet and was immediately tucked between Dan and Fionna in what Rainer was certain was going to be a very happy family.

Everyone headed into the kitchen to help with breakfast.

"Are you going or you want me to?" Garrett asked Rainer.

He smiled and waved Garrett off. "I've got her."

"You always have." Garrett slapped him on the back in a gesture of confidence and belief that Rainer would always take care of his baby sister.

The heavy spring dew gathered on the legs of his jeans as his body propelled him toward Emily. He tried to will away his nerves so he could calm her. Whatever had driven her to her childhood loft early in the morning, he wanted her to know he understood.

He eased the door to the barn open and drew a deep breath. A lifetime of memories wafted in the air. So much had happened in the last twenty years up in her loft. Their playroom as kids, a hideaway in their youth, a refuge when life was too much to deal with, and a secluded haven of explorative sensuality as young adults.

Rainer checked the watch that had been his father's. In six hours, she'd be walking down the aisle. His heart sped as he climbed the rungs of the ladder.

"Hey there," he soothed softly as he crawled into her loft.

She smiled, but she'd been crying. His heart ached for her. He knew how hard this all must be. He seated himself beside her but was careful not to touch her. He wasn't certain she wanted him up there.

"Are you okay, baby?"

She nodded but still hadn't spoken. She was holding a doll in her hands, tying a ribbon on the outfit the doll was wearing.

"I just wanted to come up here one more time, you know?" she confessed in a strangled whisper.

Rainer's heart pricked. "I'm sure your dad will let you come up here whenever you want."

She nodded but continued staring down at the doll. "I know."

Rainer brushed her hair behind her shoulder as he studied her. "Are you gonna give her to Aida?"

"Yeah, she doesn't have any toys." Emily picked up a package of Abigail's baby wipes. She carefully scrubbed the doll's plastic face and hands.

"Give Dan and Fi a little time. I'm sure they'll take care of that."

"Remember when I used to carry her around everywhere and make you say that you were her daddy?" Emily laughed at the memory.

"Yeah, and I remember you throwing her at me when I wouldn't hold her."

She laughed harder causing more tears to escape, giving haunting imagery to all she was gaining and all she was losing on their wedding day.

"I don't remember what you named her," Rainer confessed.

"Phoebe." She tried to draw steadying breaths.

"Right, from *Magic School Bus*."

Emily seemed pleased he'd remembered. "I hid her up here because Connor and Cal kept taking her and doing horrible things to her."

Rainer laced his fingers through hers. "Yeah, I remember that too."

"I just miss him so much. I really wish he was here for today." The fissure in her heart, unable to be healed, gave way to sobs she'd tried futilely to dam back. Her rhythms shook with the effort.

Rainer ached for all of the people who weren't going to be there with them today. "Me too, baby. I just kind of keep thinking that maybe Cal and my parents will have the best seat in the house."

They sat in silence for several long minutes. "Hey, Em, do you want me to go? I didn't mean to interrupt."

"No." Emily shook her head frantically.

"Good. I don't want to go." Rainer wrapped his arm around her.

"It's just,"—she stared down at Phoebe—"whenever I think about hundreds and hundreds of people sitting out there watching me, or of all of the press, or of not living here anymore, I just want to stay up here. I know that's stupid." She blinked back another round of tears.

"If you want, I'll get the minister to come up here, but I do really want to marry you today." He brushed a kiss on her cheek in the approximate location of the kiss she'd dared him to give her when she was seven years old.

Emily drew a deep steadying breath and took one last look around. She clung to Rainer's hand and drew deeply from his energy reserves. He let his eyes close and supplied her with calm in heavy doses. Everything he had was always for her. She was all that would ever matter. As their energy combined, he was overcome with the love that flowed between them.

"Okay," she whispered. "Let's go get married."

He nodded and helped her down the ladder.

They headed back into the kitchen with Emily carrying Phoebe behind her back.

Governor Haydenshire gazed at Emily. He blinked back the tears that threatened his eyes and then gave Rainer a wistful smile.

Everyone was gathered in the kitchen with Mrs. Haydenshire preparing pancakes by the dozen and Fionna frying bacon and eggs. They were having an involved conversation. Fionna was listening intently to whatever Mrs. Haydenshire was sharing—advice about being a mother, Rainer assumed.

When the last batch came off the griddle, everyone took a seat and dug in. Emily moved to Aida who'd seated herself on the window bench between Garrett and Dan. "I wanted to give you a present since you're being so nice to be our flower girl."

Surprise lit Aida's face as she offered Emily a sweet smile. "You don't have to get me a present. I already got a dress, and a flower princess crown, and purple pajamas."

Dan's eyes closed momentarily as Fionna laced her fingers through his.

"Well, I really want you to have this, but you have to promise to take good care of her."

Aida bit her lip and nodded.

Emily pulled Phoebe from behind her back, and Aida's mouth hung open in shock. Her eyes danced in elation.

"She was my favorite." Emily gently laid Phoebe in Aida's arms. "But I think she needs you to take care of her now."

Aida gazed at the doll like she'd never seen anything more perfect. "Thank you! She's so beautiful! What's her name?"

"Her name is Phoebe." Emily wrapped Aida and Phoebe up in a hug.

Aida began to rock the doll and run her fingers tenderly over her hair.

"I bet Fionna could make her some more dresses," Emily offered.

Fionna nodded. "Sure! We could make her some dresses and outfits and maybe even a blanket or two."

"You know…" Mrs. Haydenshire stood from her seat at the kitchen island. "Wait just a second."

She returned several minutes later with a doll bottle and Phoebe's blanket.

"Oh wow!" Aida gasped as Mrs. Haydenshire handed her the accessories. She immediately wrapped her new baby tenderly in the blanket and began feeding her the bottle.

"Hey, remember that time Cal and Connor…" Logan began.

"Logan!" shouted from Rainer, Emily, Garrett, and both of his parents.

"Geez! I'm sorry. Never mind."

Dan and Fionna urged Aida to finish her pancakes. She agreed as long as Dan would hold Phoebe and give her the bottle.

Rainer, Logan, and Garrett laughed hysterically as they watched all six-feet-five, two hundred fifty pounds of solid muscle that was Dan Vindico, former Chief of Elite Iodex, feed a baby doll a fake bottle.

He leveled a glare at all of them. "I may not be your boss anymore, but I can still kick your ass," he huffed, making certain that Aida couldn't hear him.

The threat coupled with him cradling the doll only served to make them laugh harder as Emily and Fionna cried from their own laughter.

After the breakfast dishes were done, all of the men were shooed away to the guesthouse so everyone could get ready.

Rainer's nerves set in again as he noted the press vans lining up outside of the Haydenshires' gates.

"Are you okay?" Logan elbowed him as they entered the kitchen.

"Yeah, I just kind of can't believe it's here."

"Hey, you've been getting ready for this since you were, like, five. If I were ordained, you and Em would've been married dozens of times by now."

Rainer laughed and tried to ignore the plaguing twists in his stomach and the gnawing ache in his heart. He just wanted to talk to his dad.

"Aww, sweet!" Garrett chanted as everyone entered.

Emily had arranged a large stack of dozens of Dr Peppers to look like two four-tiered cakes that she'd chill casted. A huge platter of Adeline's nachos were on the table set to stay warm. There were bottles of beer lined up on the table along with bowls of nuts and platters of Big Mickey's subs.

Though they'd just consumed masses of pancakes, Garrett grabbed chips and dug into Adeline's dip. Rainer grabbed a Dr Pepper. He hoped the beverage would settle his stomach.

Logan joined Garrett at the nachos. He studied Rainer sipping the Dr Pepper. "Are you really nervous?" He sounded shocked.

"Yeah, a little. I guess." Not really appreciating being called out, Rainer shrugged. "I'm not sure why though."

Garrett laughed. "Well, my baby sister can be quite frightening, especially if you piss her off."

Over the next hour, Will, Levi, Patrick, and Connor joined the assembly. Will sank down on the sofa beside Rainer. He studied him knowingly. "You know, as soon as you see her, you won't be nervous anymore." Rainer was certain he was right. "And girls take ages to get ready for their wedding. She probably has six of them over there working on her hair, and it will really only take you like five minutes to shower and two minutes to put on the tux, so there's really no reason why we can't let the footballs fly for a little while."

Will had thrown him a lifeline, just as he'd always done and just as he always would do. Will was the big brother everyone wished they had.

Rainer nodded his adamant agreement. He was desperate for a distraction. He just needed to be able to forget momentarily that neither of his parents would be there to watch him marry the love of his life, or to reconsider for the thousandth time moving Emily off of the farm, or to worry that he wasn't good enough for her and didn't deserve her.

"Let's go," Will called to everyone as he tossed a football in the air.

"Hey, Rainer." Logan rushed to catch up to him as they made their way to the back fields. "You remember how freaked I was, don't you? I was a disaster before Ad and I got married, but I have to tell you *everything* is so much better after you're married. I'm talking everything."

Rainer's brow furrowed. How could sex with Emily possibly be any better, assuming that's what Logan was referring to?

"And this is you and Em, and then we'll really be brothers." He punched Rainer in the shoulder.

"I thought that happened that afternoon when we crashed our bikes."

Logan laughed and nodded his agreement. "I get to be on Rainer's team," he chanted loudly just like he would've when they were eight. Everyone laughed as he and Rainer performed the secret handshake they'd established the day they'd become blood brothers.

Minutes later, a rough and rugged game of shirts versus skins was beginning. They played for two hours straight with the press lurking on the outskirts of the farm trying desperately to get shots of the pre-wedding game.

Rainer noted the arrival of the rental company delivering hundreds of wooden, white folding chairs, but he tried to focus on nothing but the game.

Connor snapped the ball, and Rainer stepped back. Garrett moved in to sack him, but he leapt and hurled the ball down the field hard.

Dan raced forward and caught the long pass just as he slid into the end zone. Everyone became aware that they had an audience as Fionna whistled and she and Aida applauded Dan's efforts. He looked thrilled that his spectacular catch had witnesses.

After tossing the ball back to Will, Dan headed toward his two favorite women.

CHAPTER 6

FOOTBALLS, LIP GLOSS, AND BOWS

DAN VINDICO

"Nice catch, Mr. Vindico."

Impressing his wife would always make him feel like a king. Dan gave her a cocky smirk. "Not quite as good as the night I caught you."

"Maybe you should go pro."

Noting that she was still dressed in her Angel sweats and hadn't yet showered, he pulled her into his sweaty, bare-chested embrace. She pretended to gag.

"There are other sports I'd rather go pro in," he explained wryly.

She wiggled away from him, still laughing. "I don't think that's a sport, but you're definitely the MVP if it is."

Aida was holding Fionna's hand, swinging their arms wildly.

"Emily needs a little bit of help with an errand. We're going to go into town for a few things. Aida wanted to come see what you were doing and if she could hang out with the guys for a little while."

Dan nodded his understanding that whatever Emily and her bridesmaids were doing, it wasn't something Aida needed to know about just yet.

"Sure." Dan grinned at Aida, reveling in the way she made him feel like he had a purpose, like maybe all of the hell they'd been through had a real resolution.

Aida's eyes lit as she grinned up at Dan. "And Fionna says that once I have my dress on, I can wear blush and lip gloss."

"Did she?" Dan immediately hated the idea and was surprised Fionna had allowed it.

Garrett, Will, Logan, and Rainer were walking back to the guesthouse in time to hear the exchange. They were all chuckling as they paused on the sidelines, downing bottles of water.

Aida raced to Garrett, so Fionna gave Dan a goading grin. "You've been a dad for twenty-four hours. Are you already overprotective?"

"I'm a Shield, and I know how guys think, and I love you both more than life itself, so yeah. But I can ramp it up for you if you'd like."

She laughed and shook her head at his challenge. Leaning in to brush a kiss along his jaw, she whispered, "It's just strawberry-flavored Chapstick." Dan nodded his hesitant defeat as she turned and called out to Aida. "Okay, you and Dan have fun, and I'm going to go help Emily. When I come back, it will be time to put your dress on."

Aida exchanged Garrett's hand for Dan's. He was pleased she seemed excited to hang out with him even if Fionna wouldn't be there.

"And then I can put on my lip gloss?"

Fionna kissed her cheek. "And then you can put on your lip gloss."

Dan's head fell in mock defeat as all of the men laughed at him outright.

Fionna blew Dan and Aida kisses, climbed back in the Ferrari, and headed back to the farmhouse.

Dan led Aida inside the guesthouse followed by the rest of the Haydenshire men.

"It seems like somebody gave me some advice about something like this recently," Logan drawled as Aida continued to discuss wearing lip gloss for the wedding.

"Yeah." Rainer laughed. "Something about fighting a losing battle." He batted Logan's pitch out of the park.

They both cracked up as Dan rolled his eyes. "This is obviously entirely different."

Aida took in the superfluous amounts of food as everyone who'd been playing football dug in.

Dan popped open a Dr Pepper. "Would you like one, sweetheart?"

"Yes, please."

Dan handed her the can he'd opened and grabbed another for himself. He fell onto the sofa, and his heart warmed as Aida promptly climbed in his lap. He'd been preparing for the sting of her sitting with Garrett instead.

She sloshed the Dr Pepper on the leg of his basketball shorts he'd run home that morning to get. "I'm so sorry." She panicked. Tears formed in her eyes.

"It's okay, baby. Watch." Dan summoned a very faint heat cast and dried the spot in a matter of seconds. "See, no big deal."

She looked somewhat mollified as she tucked her head under Dan's chin and drew a long sip of her drink.

Dan felt her little finger begin to trace the tattoo of the cobra on his bare chest. He swallowed uncomfortably. He didn't know what to do or say. He'd certainly never considered how to explain that particular tattoo to a child.

She sat up, studied him momentarily, and then smiled. "This is so good. I never had anything but water before I came here."

Dan's heart ached, and his stomach turned uncomfortably. It was a feeling he was growing accustomed to experiencing every time he heard another story about Aida's life before she'd been adopted. He wasn't certain that Dr Pepper was something she should have had before, but he knew she should probably have at least had milk.

She sat up suddenly as she took in Rainer falling onto the love seat with a huge sub and a beer. "Emily looks so beautiful! You're going to want to kiss her as soon as you see her!"

"He always wants to do that," Garrett teased her. She beamed at him.

"I can't wait to see her." Rainer winked at Aida.

"Her hair is very fancy, just like this." She handed her Dr Pepper to Dan and piled her straggly brown hair up on top of her head. It stuck out in every direction. Everyone chuckled at her affectionately.

"And Fionna made her do her mouth like this." She poked her lips out in a heavy pucker. "And then Adeline put lipstick on her, and then she did like this." Pulling in her pucker, she rubbed her lips together dramatically.

"Emily and Fionna are wearing very beautiful red lipstick, but Fionna says my lip gloss is prettier on me."

"I think Fionna is definitely right about that," Dan assured her.

She turned her head back momentarily and nuzzled her head on his neck. Then she wrinkled her nose. "You smell not as nice as you did yesterday."

Dan laughed. "I promise I'll take a shower in just a second."

Everyone was perfectly content to let Aida regale them with her morning events as they settled in to listen to her.

She blushed slightly and reached for Garrett's hand as she realized everyone was staring at her and listening intently.

"What other fun things did you do this morning?" Dan urged her on.

"Emily let me see her dress, which is a secret, and I'm not allowed to tell you about it." She put both of her hands over her mouth for a few seconds indicating that she wasn't going to tell the secret. "And all of the bridesmaids are wearing very fancy, purple, very high heels, and I am wearing purple shoes too, but mine are only this high." She sighed as she held her thumb and index finger minutely apart. "But they *do* have bows on the back just like Fionna's." She pointed to the back of her right foot. The bow seemed to make up for the lack of heel.

Dan was quite certain he'd never seen anything cuter. "I'm sure they'll be very pretty."

Governor Haydenshire entered through the garage door. "Your sister told me I had to leave." He sounded highly offended.

Everyone laughed at him which did nothing to ease the pain of his dejection.

Aida turned back to Rainer. "And Emily gets to wear very beautiful, very lacy panties that tie with bows on the sides, and if you want to take them off you can just untie the bows!" she announced as she pointed to her own hipbones.

Rainer's eyes goggled as he choked and spluttered on the beer he'd just taken a long sip of.

Garrett, Logan, Patrick, Levi, and Connor all guffawed. Will and Dan shared a horrified grimace.

Dan didn't know what to do. He needed Aida to stop discussing Emily's undergarments, but he was terrified to scold her when spilling a drop of Dr Pepper made her cry.

She turned to Dan, her eyes still lit in utter joy. "And I want to wear panties just like that when I get married!"

He head dropped as he grasped his chest. It was too many emotions to sort through, but trying to envision his baby girl on her wedding night, letting some unnamed boy that Dan instantly hated untie her panties, made him want to strangle someone, preferably any boy who wanted date Aida in the future.

Governor Haydenshire chuckled as he recognized the horror Dan was currently experiencing. "Uh-huh, talk to me when she's twenty and putting on a wedding gown."

Rainer still hadn't raised his head from his hands. What they could see of him was glowing crimson. Garrett began asking him if he needed to practice tying and untying his shoes.

Aida seemed shocked by Rainer's reaction. She studied him and then turned back to Dan. "Does he not like bow panties?"

Rainer whimpered as the Haydenshire brothers cracked up again.

"Oh, trust me, Aida Mae. He'll like them," Garrett assured her.

Governor Haydenshire stepped in after making certain that Dan was watching. "Aida, sweetie, we probably shouldn't talk about that. Emily might not want us to."

Aida nodded her understanding. "I'm sorry. Will Emily be mad at me?"

"Of course not. You didn't know and now you do," he explained kindly.

Aida looked distressed for a moment, but her smile returned as she nuzzled down under Dan's chin once again.

The governor chuckled at Dan's relief. "Just takes a little practice. You'll get the hang of it."

"Would the groom like the first shower?" Will gallantly tossed

Rainer another lifeline. Dan was certain Rainer was thankful to be making an exit as he headed into his and Emily's room.

The men cycled through the showers, and an hour later, Fionna returned for Aida. Dan was only slightly aware of the chuckles that echoed around the room as his mouth hung open and his eyes goggled as he took in his wife.

She was stunning. Her hair was pulled up in a loose twist with several tendrils cascading down by her face. The dress was a deep-purple satin gathered at the bust, displaying her luscious cleavage. The skirt portion was short, hitting her midthigh and doing an outstanding job of showing off her long legs. The heels were indeed very high with satin strappings across her toes that formed an x across her foot with a bow tied behind her heel.

She was wearing more makeup than Dan was accustomed to, and the deep-burgundy lipstick she'd applied had her luscious lips displayed in a perfect pout.

The diamond rings shimmering brilliantly on her left hand that told the world that she was his completed what Dan was certain was the picture of the most stunningly beautiful woman on the planet.

"Wow," he growled and let a low whistle slide through his teeth, making her beam.

"You look very beautiful!" Aida gasped.

"Thank you." Fionna looked extremely pleased with Dan's reaction. "Are you ready to go put on your dress?" She leaned down to take Aida's hand.

Patrick, Rainer, Levi, and Governor Haydenshire all turned their heads. It was a gesture Dan immensely appreciated. When Fionna leaned forward, you could see straight down the dress. Saliva flooded his mouth as he stifled a low groan.

Aida nodded excitedly. "Bye, Dan!" She threw her little arms around his legs in a hug. "I'm going to go put on my dress and my lip gloss."

"All right." He lifted her up into his arms and planted a kiss on her cheek. "But not too much."

Fionna chuckled as she leaned up on her tiptoes and kissed his jawline. Dan's heart thundered out his approval.

Just as Fionna led Aida out of the house, Garrett walked into the kitchen tying his bow tie. Laughing, he shook his head at Dan. "Man, what is it with you and lipstick?"

Dan headed to the bathroom to shower and wipe off the imprint of Fionna's lips from his jaw.

CHAPTER 7

HERE COMES THE BRIDE

RAINER LAWSON

While trying not to let his mind reel over all of the things that could possibly go wrong, Rainer wondered if Emily had received the roses he'd ordered for her.

His brain offered him nothing but all of the potential points of disaster. Grandpa Haydenshire was going to be there, and that was always potentially catastrophic. Governor and Mrs. Vindico would be coming, and they'd yet to be informed of Dan and Fionna's very recent adoption. The press was out in alarming force. They were desperate for pictures of the wedding, reception, and of Abigail. Garrett had helped the Stylers unload the cakes and had been wearing a disturbingly mischievous grin ever since he'd returned.

Son, if you can't change it, and you can't control it, then figure out what you can learn from it, and then just hang on and try to enjoy the ride because you never know when it might end. Rainer heard his father's voice echo in his mind.

It had been an odd statement from his father. Joseph Lawson had done the impossible. With his closest friends by his side, he'd set out to overturn a corrupt Senteon and governing board. He'd ratified a new constitution that kept the Gifted from using their powers to abuse the Non-Gifted and those less fortunate. He'd set up a balancing division of power. He'd solved the problems and controlled the Realm.

But that day at Disney World when Rainer had been a little concerned about riding his first full-fledged roller coaster, *hang on and enjoy the ride* had been his father's advice.

Rainer stared in the mirror as he began attempting to tie the bow tie for the third time, just the way his father had taught him. *Cross, loop under, double over, then back.*

A knock sounded on the door. Jerking the tie back out, he opened the door.

Governor Haydenshire met him with his kind, knowing smile. "Need some help?" He gestured to the tie.

"Oh, it's okay. I think I've got it," Rainer assured him. What was wrong with him? He'd done this hundreds of times.

Governor Haydenshire gazed at Rainer for a long minute. "Could I come in, son?"

Rainer nodded. He felt badly he hadn't made the offer sooner. He couldn't seem to think straight. He stepped back to the mirror.

"He would be so proud of you," the governor choked out.

Rainer feebly fought tears. He didn't have to ask whom the governor was referring to. "I hope so." *Cross, loop under, double over, then back.*

"I know he would be because I know how proud I am of you."

Cross, loop under, double over, then back. His hands shook. The knot slipped through again.

"Dammit!" Rainer jerked the tie from his neck and threw it on the dresser. He stabbed his fingers through his hair, ordering himself to calm down and tie the damn tie.

Governor Haydenshire chuckled, stepped behind him, and lifted the collar of Rainer's shirt. He retrieved the tie, and with steady hands he completed the bow and then lowered the collar.

Rainer lifted his head and met the governor's wise gaze in the mirror. "I'll take care of her always. I swear, sir."

Governor Haydenshire blinked back tears of his own. "I have no doubt. You always have. When you were just a little guy, barely out of diapers, you used to get so angry at her big brothers if they did anything to upset Emily. You came out swinging. It didn't matter how much bigger they were than you. And a few years later, I stood on the side porch and watched you and Logan teach her to ride a bike without training wheels. You wouldn't let her go until you knew she could do it no matter how exhausted you were or how fast you had to run. You never let her crash. You were only thirteen years old when you put yourself between her and a copperhead. And a few years after that, you took her out in your Mustang, and she offered you the whole world and you turned her down. Honestly, son, I cannot think of a finer man to be marrying my baby girl."

"Thank you, sir." Rainer ordered his tears away. This was the happiest day of his life. Why was he crying?

Governor Haydenshire offered Rainer his hand, but Rainer shook his head and wrapped his arms around the man who had made him who he was.

"Thank you for everything you've done for me for my whole life!" Overwhelmed by the magnitude of all the Haydenshires had given him, he shook his head in disbelief.

With tears now streaming down his face, Governor Haydenshire nodded. "The pleasure was all mine, son. Believe me."

With a final adjustment of the tie, Governor Haydenshire stepped back. "I guess I better go. My baby girl's getting ready to marry the only man in the world I ever would have approved of for her, and I'm supposed to walk her down the aisle."

Rainer chuckled. "Yeah, I think they're expecting me at the end of that aisle soon."

"You better not make her wait. I'll still throttle you if you make her cry."

"Don't worry. I'll be there. I've been waiting for this my whole life," Rainer vowed as he watched the governor exit the room.

"You ready?" Logan gave Rainer his version of the signature Haydenshire smirk.

"Yeah." Rainer willed the sub sandwich he'd had after playing football to stay in his stomach.

"Good, cause it's about that time." Garrett gestured his hand to the back door.

Adeline and Fionna were on the deck pinning on all of the milky white rose boutonnieres.

Dan chuckled as he took in Rainer who was certain that his pallor reflected his nerves. "Just wait 'til the moment when you finally see her. That's when I could breathe again." He offered Rainer a pride-filled gaze.

Rainer nodded and prayed that Dan and Will were both right, as he assumed that he would need to be able to breathe to say his vows.

"You have the ring, right?" He panicked and all but shook Logan.

"Right here." Logan patted his jacket pocket. "And I have this." He pulled out a piece of pink notebook paper folded in the intricate fold that Emily used to do when she gave him notes in elementary school.

Rainer took it and pulled it open. It was a page from Emily's school binder. Doodled all over it in Emily's adolescent handwriting was RL and EH inside of hearts. *Emily Haydenshire Lawson* was written along the sides, and Rainer and Emily Lawson was drawn elaborately in the center of the paper. In one corner that had formerly been blank was an added note in Emily's much more polished, adult handwriting.

Today I get to make all of my lifelong dreams finally come true. Even at four years old I could see what an amazing man you are. Thank you for loving me when I least deserved it, for always protecting me even from myself, for putting up with me when I'm being impossible. Most of all, thank you for being the man of my dreams. Love, the future Mrs. Lawson.

"She gave it to me last night. I guess she thought it might help." Logan slapped him on the back.

Rainer refolded the note and placed it in the pocket of his own tux jacket very near his heart. "Thanks." He met Logan's eyes.

A million memories, a thousand sworn secrets, skinned knees, welts from paintballs, hundreds of football games, and cheeseburgers shared in his 'Stang, more crude jokes than he could ever count, his entire life, his best friend since birth, stood before him. He'd never faltered, and he never would. "You've got this, man. I'll be right beside you. Just like always."

~

Several minutes later, Rainer stood off to the side of the seated guests and the platform altar. Music swelled from the orchestra, and Logan smiled. "You ready?"

"I think." Rainer's mouth had taken on a Sahara-like dryness.

"Good, because that's our cue." He gave Rainer a slight push and then followed him as they moved to stand at the front of the enormous crowd.

Cameras clicked feverishly both from the hired photographers and the press with long-range lenses from outside the gates.

The music faded and then bled into another song. Rainer forced air into his lungs. He was determined to remember everything about the day. He studied the people staring back at him and the space around them.

Emily had outdone herself. The backdrop and altar area were bedecked with beautiful flowers in every shade of purple and pink and cream. The long, pearl aisle runner was in place with the Lawson and Haydenshire crests embroidered in gold.

Purple, lavender, and cream-colored flower petals were scattered along either side of the runner. The light pink cherry trees in perfect April bloom stood reticent alongside the guest chairs. Lanterns, waiting to be lit for the reception, hung from their limbs.

Swallowing hard, Rainer watched as Garrett and Chloe appeared and then smoothly glided down the aisle. Garrett walked her to her assigned location and then offered Rainer his hand.

He slapped Rainer on the shoulder as they shook hands.

Aida beamed at Rainer as she moved slowly down the aisle just like Emily had instructed her. She dropped pink and purple rose petals as she made her way down.

Dan and Fionna followed behind her, gazing at her adoringly. Dan offered Rainer another slap on the back as he took his place beside him.

Adeline appeared alone and walked down the aisle with her eyes fixed on Logan's. "It's so worth it, man," Logan whispered as he took in his own bride gazing at him sweetly as she took her place.

Keaton made a dashing appearance in a tiny tuxedo, grinning and giggling as he carried a small chalkboard that read, "Hey Rainer." He raced down the aisle and then turned to show off the sign to the crowd before taking a seat near Aida.

Henry followed him, looking more nervous than Keaton but carrying another chalkboard that read, "Here comes your girl."

Everyone chuckled as Rainer beamed. Mrs. Haydenshire was patting tears from her eyes as was Nana Anderson.

And then suddenly, the trumpets blared. The six hundred guests stood, and "Here Comes the Bride" swelled as the most beautiful woman in the world appeared, blinking back tears and gazing into Rainer's eyes.

While trying not to tremble, Rainer drew a deep breath as Emily was escorted in on her father's arm.

Tears sprang to his eyes. My God, she was ravishing. The dress was made entirely of antique lace with a satin underpinning. Small, gathered lace straps came across her shoulders, and the neck formed a deep V, showing off her cleavage.

The lace skirt billowed at her waist and trailed out behind her elegantly in a long train. The straps hooked just above her shoulder blades and the skirt attached just below her waist leaving her entire back exposed. Rainer had never seen anything so breathtaking.

Her hair was fixed in loose curls, most of them caught up in pins at the nape of her neck with a few loosened tendrils curling down the sides of her face. A milky white rose, matching the one on Rainer's coat, was tucked loosely in the auburn tresses just behind her ear.

She looked angelic, absolutely stunning, and Rainer couldn't halt the tears that escaped his eyes. She was trembling on her father's arm, and Governor Haydenshire was rapidly losing a war against tears of his own.

Every step she took made Rainer love her more. He longed to touch her, to feel her hands in his. At that moment, it seemed impossible that she was even real, and that he was lucky enough to be standing where he was, waiting on her.

She was some magical dream he never wanted to awaken from, a drug he'd gladly take every single day of his life.

Finally making her way there, Emily gazed into Rainer's eyes as he looked at hers. They both willed away their tears.

"Who gives this woman to be married?" The minister smiled kindly at the Crown Governor. He choked and looked like he'd never uttered anything more difficult in his entire life, as he barely managed, "Her mother and I."

Emily beamed at her daddy with tears leaking down her cheeks. She swallowed hard as he kissed her cheek and put her hands in Rainer's.

Rainer let her hands go for just a moment. He reached and wiped away her tears as he whispered, "You are the most beautiful thing I've ever seen." This only served to make her cry harder.

After taking her hands again, they turned to the minister. They repeated the vows spoken by couples over and over throughout the centuries. Rainer promised to love her and to take care of her forever. She cried quietly as she made the same vows.

At the appropriate time, Rainer forced himself to take his eyes off her long enough to turn and take the ring from Logan, who was blinking back tears of his own as he stared at his little sister. Rainer smiled at her earnestly and spoke, "With this ring I thee wed." Rainer raised the ring to show the engraving he'd had her Uncle Tad add to the wedding band.

Her chin quivered. She shuddered out sobbing tears as she read the words, "My everything."

A moment later, Emily turned to Adeline, who handed her Rainer's wedding band. She repeated the vow and then turned the ring between her thumb and index finger, showing Rainer the words, "My hero."

Closing his eyes, Rainer was overwhelmed. When he'd regained his slipping control on his emotions, he opened them again and gazed at her in utter adoration.

A few moments later, the minister murmured, "Well, Mr. Lawson, you may kiss your bride."

Rainer cradled her face in his hands, gazing at her before he leaned in, and she whispered, "Betcha won't kiss me!"

Laughing, he dipped her back and devoured her mouth. She threw her arms around his neck as he laved her lips with his own.

The crowd hooted and wolf whistles echoed all around them from all of his groomsmen.

After several long minutes, he released her. A brilliant smile lit her entire face as she wrapped her arm through his and they turned to face the crowd.

Governor Haydenshire stood, cupped his hand, and amplified his voice.

"Ladies and gentlemen, it is my distinct honor as the Crown Governor of the American Gifted Realm to introduce Mr. and Mrs. Rainer Emory Lawson." The crowd cheered. "And he better take good care of my baby girl," he added as Rainer led Emily back down the aisle.

CHAPTER 8

OFFERS AND INTRODUCTIONS

The wedding bled seamlessly into the reception. The guests took their places at the candlelit tables and enjoyed the catered meal.

But Rainer suddenly found himself quite finished with the festivities. After an endless number of photographs had been taken, he backed Emily up to the side of the farmhouse, desperate for just a moment alone.

"So, Mrs. Lawson, can I get another kiss?" His heated breath caressed her neck, and the hungry fire burning in his eyes seemed to drive her wild.

Her eyes danced deliciously as he caged her between his body and the white plank board siding. With his hands on either side of her head, he consumed her. They broke apart after several long minutes, both gasping for breath.

"Can't we just go on our honeymoon now?" Emily whimpered.

Rainer kissed his way up her cheek and then nipped her earlobe. "I think we're supposed to make an appearance at this shindig your parents are throwing today, baby, but don't worry. I'll make it worth your wait."

They made their way back into the tented reception area to cheers from the crowd. While being slapped on the back and having his hand shaken constantly, Rainer followed Emily's lead and tried to speak to each of their guests.

Suddenly Emily gasped. Rainer spun, effectively ending a conversation with Chancellor Wilshire. "What's wrong?"

"Look at what they did!" She pointed to the cake table. Rainer bit his lips together and tried not to laugh.

On top of the elegant five-tiered cake complete with fondant icing made to appear that it had been draped over each layer and then bedecked with tiny purple flowers and pearls, that Emily had designed and Mr. Styler had created, sat a cake topper.

Rainer knew Emily hadn't wanted a cake topper at all, but she certainly hadn't picked out a topper that displayed the groom with his tux pants down around his ankles holding the bride with her legs open wide and wrapped around his waist, with her gown pushed all the way up to make it appear that they were having sex against a wall.

All of Emily's brothers were howling with laughter as Emily turned the color of her hair. The groom's cake, which was supposed to be an exact model of Rainer's Porsche, had been altered as well. On the windshield, someone—Levi, Rainer assumed as he was certainly creative enough to have pulled it off—had cut an outline out of black paper of a woman lying back against what would be the passenger side door and window with her legs spread and her dress flared out. The groom was holding her legs apart and appeared to be in the process of leaning his head down to fit between her thighs.

Rainer headed toward the cakes to remove the additions, but the crowds booed. With a shrug, he pulled Emily in for a kiss as the crowd cheered once again.

After everyone ate the elaborate meal, Rainer guided Emily to the dance floor for the first dance. "Hey there, baby," he whispered as he wrapped her up in his arms.

She beamed as she laid her head on his shoulder and tucked her face next to his neck. Cameras clicked feverishly as he swayed her and whispered how much he loved and adored her in her ear.

She lifted her head, and suddenly they were barely moving as they kissed passionately for the crowd.

Just as the song was ending, Governor Haydenshire pretended to shove Rainer away as he cut in. The crowd laughed and applauded raucously.

"Can't Help Falling in Love," by Elvis spun from the DJ booth, the first song Mr. and Mrs. Haydenshire had danced to at their wedding and the governor's request for his dance with Emily.

～

Dan Vindico

"They need you there. You should never have left Iodex, but after everything I've seen, I think you're the man for the job. Wilshire's going to offer it to you. Take it."

"Sir, I'm honored that you thought of me." Dan was taken aback by Mentor Sullivan's insistence that he replace him as the head of Ioses Order at Venton Academy. What the hell was going on at Venton? Why was Sullivan suddenly willing to retire? He was certainly of age, but he'd never expressed any interest in giving up his position.

Just as Sullivan had promised, Chancellor Wilshire headed Dan's way. He took the seat beside him, and they chatted for several minutes. Dan noted that Wilshire didn't seem as thrilled about Dan accepting an offer to teach as Sullivan had been.

"Let's cut to the chase. Sullivan insists you're the man for this job. We'd be happy to match your previous salary at Iodex as a start." The Chancellor sighed.

Dan wasn't certain how to proceed. He'd never worked anywhere but Iodex, where your pay was set by your rank and years of service. This was happening quickly, and the level of urgency was odd. "Thank you for the offer...sir. I need to discuss this with my wife and think it over. I'll let you know soon," Dan assured him.

The chancellor all but rolled his eyes. "I'm offering to make you the Mentor over Ioses Order, Daniel. That's a very prestigious position."

"I'm not telling you *no*, but I'm also not accepting any position until I talk with my wife. I've also promised her that we'll spend the summer on her family's farm in Kauai, so I wouldn't be able to start until just before the school year resumes."

Chancellor Wilshire suddenly looked slightly more enthusiastic about his offer. "I understand. Talk it over with Fionna. I would like to hear from you before this year's graduation."

"I'll let you know," Dan agreed as Aida raced toward him on the verge of tears.

"What's wrong, sweetheart?" Dan panicked as Aida crawled up in his lap and laid her head on his shoulder.

"That little boy over there pinched my arm very hard." She rubbed an angry red mark on her forearm. Her voice trembled.

Fury lit through Dan like he'd never felt before. His shield flared around her. "Which little boy?" He stood while keeping Aida caught up in the safety of his arms.

"Dan." Fionna raced to them. "Calm down. Wes is taking care of it."

Dan scanned the crowd. His blood boiled. His eyes landed on Wes Willow and his father, Governor Willow, scolding the little boy in question. The demon spawn looked remarkably like Wes had when he was eight.

Dan started to march over, but Fionna caught his bicep. "Dan, she's all right, and they're going to make Kendrick apologize."

"Kendrick?" Dan huffed. The kid deserved to be beaten up for his name alone.

"Dan!" Fionna tried to physically halt his advance toward Wes Willow. "That is Wes's wife's maiden name. Please calm down."

Suddenly, Kendrick was upon them followed by a very sheepish-looking Wes Willow. "What do you tell her?" Wes demanded.

"I'm sorry I pinched your arm." Kendrick rolled his eyes. Dan glared at him hatefully.

"Dan." Fionna elbowed him and voiced his name through her teeth.

Aida turned and stared down at Kendrick. "It's okay, but it isn't nice to pinch people because it hurts them and it makes them sad."

"Oh my gosh, Dan, she's adorable," Wes tried.

"Obviously!" Dan glared at the spawn's father.

"Dan!" Fionna shot him a look that said for him to tone it down.

"Uh, come on, Kendrick. Let's go get some more punch." Wes grasped his son's shoulders and steered him away.

Fionna shook her head. "Later we will discuss appropriate responses when people who we've been friends with since elementary school tell you that your child is adorable, but right now we really need to introduce our daughter to your parents."

Dan sat Aida down but kept a close eye on Kendrick Willow as he guided her toward his parents who were talking with several members of the Senteon. "Come here, sweetheart." He stopped her and summoned. He touched her arm and drew the heat away from the sting and soothed where the little brat had hurt his baby girl.

"Thank you very much." She gave him a sweet grin. Timing their arrival well, Dan, Fionna, and Aida arrived just as his parents' conversation wound down.

"Daniel, Fionna, nice to finally see you," Governor Vindico sniped. Mrs. Vindico's face bore her preferred mask of martyrdom as she glared at Fionna.

Dan sighed. "Mom, Dad, there's someone I'd like you to meet. This is Aida." He fought the desperate urge to put his body and his shield between his daughter and his mother. "Fi and I adopted her yesterday."

The governor's mouth hung open as Mrs. Vindico began fanning herself and gasping for breath.

"Son, do you have some kind of terminal illness you haven't told us about?" his father demanded.

"Uh, no, Dad. I'm fine."

"Aida, why don't you go play, and you can have another juice box if you want," Fionna urged sweetly.

"Yes, ma'am. Thank you." Aida turned toward the children's table that Rainer and Emily had thoughtfully provided for their many younger guests.

"You come and get me or you get Garrett if that Kendrick kid comes anywhere near you again," Dan commanded. Fionna rubbed her temples.

"Yes, sir. I will."

The Crown Governor and Mrs. Haydenshire raced toward them.

"Isn't it wonderful!" Mrs. Haydenshire insisted as she instinctively edged Fionna away from Mrs. Vindico. "I mean, it certainly takes very, very special people to adopt especially after all Dan and Fionna have been through."

"Is this some kind of horrible joke, Daniel? Oh yes, Mom, we're getting married in Hawaii and then adopting a little girl just to spite you." Mrs. Vindico demanded in a heated whisper, terrified that someone might overhear her. "Do you just not care about us at all? Does our family's pride and reputation mean nothing to you?" Her voice shook in her fury.

Dan narrowed his eyes and worked his jaw. Fionna grasped his hand, but he unhinged it anyway. "No, Mother, my wife and my little girl are not a joke, and I'm so sorry that we didn't do things just the way you wanted them done, but this is our life and not yours!"

Kara and Meredith raced to Dan's rescue. "Isn't it great?" Meredith urged forcefully. "You've been wanting Dan to settle down, and get married, and start a family."

"And Aida is just adorable, Mom. She's been playing so sweetly with Olivia and Oliver." Kara pointed to Dan's niece and nephew. Aida was teaching them how to blow the puffy leaves off the dandelions, delighting both Olivia and Oliver.

Aida followed Olivia over to Meredith and Tim.

"Watch what Aida can do!" Olivia was in awe.

Aida blushed deeply from having the attention of the crowd of adults. She demonstrated blowing the flower.

"Did you make a wish?" Kara asked her sweetly.

Aida shook her head as she reached and took Dan's hand. "No, ma'am, but I told Olivia and Oliver that they were supposed to make a wish before they blow them. I don't need any more wishes because I get to go home and stay with Dan and Fionna, and live near Garrett, and live near Emily and that's the best wishes ever. I didn't want to use up any more wishes because someone else might need them."

Tears pricked Fionna's eyes as she knelt down and pulled Aida into her embrace. "Dan and I wished for you too, sweetheart," she vowed.

"You did?" Aida sounded astonished.

Dan joined his wife in a low squat and nodded. "We did."

Aida glanced around at the adults whose eyes were fixed on her. "I've never been wished for before. Thank you for wishing for me. I'll try to be a good wish," she pledged to Dan.

After lifting Aida up into his arms, he swallowed back another round of emotion. "You are the very best wish I have ever wished for, baby. The very best." Dan fixed his glare back on his parents. "Have anything else to say, Mother?"

"No." Governor Vindico gazed at Aida caught up in Dan's arms. "She doesn't."

Olivia tugged on Meredith's hand. "I want Aida to come to my house and play. She has a baby doll named Phoebe."

"Well, you and Aida are cousins now, so she's welcome to come to our house anytime she likes." Meredith kept her pleading gaze fixed on Dan's eyes. "We would really love that."

Dan nodded as Aida turned back to the crowd but kept her arms draped around his neck. "Yeah, we need to do that." He had quite a few bridges to mend, and Aida deserved a family beyond him and Fionna.

"You understand it was just all a little sudden," Governor Vindico tried to explain their trepidation.

"For some people," Dan allowed. "But for us it was perfect."

"I'm a cousin?" Aida asked thoughtfully after the exchange. "I've never been a cousin before." She looked concerned that she might not be up to the task.

"Well, Fi and I have never had a little girl before, so how about if we learn to do all of this new stuff together?"

"Okay." Aida leaned and whispered in Dan's ear.

He nodded and set her on the ground. "Aida wants to give you a hug," he explained to his parents and sisters.

Kara blinked back tears as she embraced Aida immediately. "And if you come and play with me and Zach, we'll watch movies, and eat ice cream, and I'll paint your fingernails."

"Wow!" Aida was delighted as she turned back to Fionna. "Is that okay?"

"Only if I get to come too," Fionna teased.

Aida giggled. "Only if Fionna comes too!"

"Of course."

Aida moved on to Meredith. She hugged Olivia and kissed Oliver's cheek tenderly, which he promptly wiped off. She slid to the governor. He knelt down and studied her precious face. "You know, Olivia and Oliver call me Gramps. Does that sound okay to you, sweetheart?"

Aida nodded and hugged him timidly. She moved to Mrs. Vindico while biting her lip as she studied her.

Drawing a deep breath, Dan's mother knelt forward and patted Aida's back as she hugged her waist. "It's so nice to meet you, Aida," Mrs. Vindico forced.

"It's very nice to meet you too, ma'am."

"Perhaps you and Olivia could both bring your dolls for dinner at our house sometime soon. And you may call me Grandma just like Olivia, if you'd like," she managed through her clenched teeth.

Aida smiled but immediately turned back to Dan and Fionna, not certain what to say.

"I would at least like to see photographs from your wedding, Daniel." She let everyone know that she still wasn't pleased.

"We'd be happy to show them to you, but there aren't many," Fionna explained hesitantly.

"Well, we still want to see them, and Marion and I are thrilled that both you and Aida have joined our family," Governor Vindico vowed.

"Thank you." Fionna looked truly touched as Aida crossed Fionna's arms over her. "How about if we invite Gramps and Grandma, and Olivia, and everyone over to our house tomorrow night and me, you, and Dan can throw a luau just like Dan and I had after our wedding?" Fionna prompted Aida.

"Would you like to come over to Dan and Fionna's house, and we'll have that thing that Fionna said?"

Everyone chuckled and smiled at her. "We'd love to," Meredith assured her.

"We'll be there, sweetheart." The governor cradled Aida's face in his hand, making her grin. "Hey, we finally have another Mrs. Vindico," he announced as he placed his arm around his wife. Dan bit back his hysterical laughter as he took in the momentary look of horror Fionna tried to hide.

"How's the happy family?" Rainer quizzed as they worked their way through the guests.

Kara smiled at the newly minted Lawsons. "Thank you so much for inviting us. The wedding was gorgeous!"

"Thank you." Emily smiled. "We're so glad you came and that you're getting to meet Aida." She winked at Aida who'd moved to hold Emily's hand.

"She really was just the perfect little flower girl. I can't wait to tell everyone that she was in your wedding," Mrs. Vindico declared proudly.

Dan rolled his eyes. He should have opened with "your new granddaughter was the flower girl in the Lawson-Haydenshire wedding. Think of how jealous the bridge club will be."

"Of course I know how very much it must've meant to your parents that you had a proper wedding, and Aida just made it perfect." Mrs. Vindico was unwilling to let it go.

Dan laced his fingers through Fionna's. He leaned and whispered, "I much preferred ours actually."

"She was perfect." Emily tried not to laugh outright at Mrs. Vindico's sudden pride over her granddaughter and her quip about Dan and Fionna's wedding.

"I guess I'll let you go live with Fi and Dan, but you have to come visit Rainer and me a lot, okay?" Emily knelt and hugged Aida fiercely.

"I will. I promise, and thank you for letting me be in the wedding." She startled Rainer with an exuberant hug.

"I think it was definitely meant to be," Rainer assured her.

Sam sauntered over just then, smiling at the assembled group. Emily threw her arms around Sam and kissed his cheek.

"Girl, I told you to run for the hills. Now, Rain Man's gotten you down the aisle, and you're in it thick."

"I think I've been in it thick since I was about four, Sam." She mocked concern.

He hugged Emily fiercely and then turned to Fionna and smiled. "And if I heard correctly, I believe Big Man Vindico turned you from

Miss Amazing Girlfriend into Mrs. Amazing Wife." Sam winked at Fionna as she nodded and showed off her rings.

Sam let a low whistle slide between his teeth. "See, this is what happens. He gets you all distracted with shiny stuff, and then you don't see what a sorry sack-a-goods he really is."

"Aww, I think he's perfect." She kissed Dan's cheek.

"Good Lord, he's gotten you good." Sam winked at her. "Well, Mrs. Vindico, I'd say if you keep right on thinking he's perfect even when he isn't, and if he keeps right on looking at you like he been drooling over you all afternoon, then I'd say the Vindicos are gonna do just fine."

Dan and Fionna shared an excited glance over the proclamation. Dan put his hand on Aida's shoulder. "Sam, this is our little girl, Aida."

The immense respect he held for Sam welled in his soul when he grinned down at Aida. There was no quizzical gaze, confusion, or look of disbelief. Sam gave Aida a sweet grin. His eyes twinkled as he took her in.

"Well, hello there, Miss Aida. I'm Sam." He held his hand out to Aida.

She giggled. "Hi Sam!"

"And Fi and I were just realizing that we need a new car." Dan gestured his head to Aida without her seeing.

Sam chuckled as he pulled himself back to full height. "Funny how we go from cool boss man, throwing his leg over a custom Brutale built for one, to I'm gonna wedge my cool self into her convertible built for one and a quarter because it's complicated, to that day when all those pieces finally seem to fit together. Suddenly we have ourselves a minivan, and the cool boss man on the bike would never have believed the big ole smile on your face right now."

He was absolutely correct. "Yeah, I should have listened sooner."

"Don't you know they all tell me that, and then they go do something else stupid, and I wonder when the world is ever gonna listen to me, don't I, Rain Man?" Sam urged Rainer.

"Every single time," Rainer pledged.

"All right, well, Mrs. Amazing Wife, what are we gonna drive all them precious little Vindicos around in?"

Dan could feel the pride and elation fill her soul. "Not a minivan, please."

Sam chuckled. "All right, well, if I tell you to come see me, are you gonna have to pack my sweet little Aida up in a box and mail her, or do you have something you can at least get her to the shop in?"

"Rainer and Emily very kindly loaned us the Hummer while they're gone," Dan explained.

Sam slapped Rainer on the back. He couldn't quite hide the extreme pride in his eyes.

"You bring Mrs. Amazing Wife and Miss Amazing Aida"—Sam tugged on Aida's left ear making her giggle—"out to see Sam, and we'll see if we can't make all of big man Vindico's girls happy."

"That's all that matters," Dan vowed.

The DJ's voice echoed throughout the tent. "If the bride and groom will move to the center of the tent, it's time to throw the bouquet and for Rainer to remove Mrs. Lawson's garter."

Emily giggled over her new name as they made their way to the designated location.

"Do you have any idea how happy I am not to be trying to catch that bouquet?" Fionna laid her head on Dan's shoulder.

He turned to kiss the top of her head as Aida led them toward Rainer and Emily. "Do you have any idea how happy I am?" Dan gazed at her with all of the love and adoration that swelled inside of his chest. He wasn't certain he could contain it all as she swooned.

Emily tossed the bouquet to the gaggle of single women gathered behind her. They all looked prepared to fight.

Garrett marched over to Dan and Fionna. "What the hell is wrong with Wes's kid? He pinched her. I'll kick his little punk ass."

"Precisely," Dan agreed.

Fionna gave them both a bewildered glare. "Oh my word, she has two of you. The punk in question is only eight, and woe be unto her boyfriends."

"She's never dating," Dan and Garrett announced simultaneously.

Fionna shook her head at both of them and turned back to Rainer and Emily.

"Come on, Lawson. Do it right!" Dan chanted, making everyone laugh.

Emily sank down on Logan's knee. Her cheeks were the approximate color of her long auburn hair.

"Legs," by ZZ Top swelled from the speakers. With a pompous swagger and a mischievous grin, Rainer turned to the assembled crowd, waggling his eyebrows.

Dan's whistle was joined in by several catcalls and applause.

"Behave, Mr. Lawson," Governor Haydenshire ordered though he was laughing.

Upping the ante, Rainer pointed to his own wedding band and shook his head at the governor. This brought on more raucous laughter.

Rainer fell to his knees. He delicately lifted her foot high as her eyes goggled. Logan pretended to gag for the audience.

Suddenly, Rainer threw the long skirt of the dress up over his head. Emily squealed. Several long moments later, he emerged, pulled the garter from his teeth, and dangled it between his fingers. He waggled his eyebrows again.

The crowd whistled and applauded as Rainer turned and shot the garter right at Garrett.

"Oh, fuck no!" Garrett reflexively leapt out of the way, and the garter landed in Levi's hands. His mouth hung open in shock.

Rainer Lawson

As Rainer pulled Emily off of Logan's knee, she shook her head at him.

Right on time, the chop of helicopter blades drowned out the noise around them.

"What is that?" Emily panicked.

Rainer pointed to the chopper descending into one of the unoccupied back fields. "That's our ride, baby." He very rarely showed off his vast fortunes, but today, of all days, he wanted to spoil her.

Her mouth dropped in shock, as he guided her toward the chopper.

"But, where is it taking us?"

Rainer wrapped her up in his arms and whispered in her ear where they would be spending the next two weeks in complete, opulent privacy.

"You rented a whole island?" Her shocked whisper delighted him.

"Yes, and I wanted to get there quickly. Pete's a Gifted helicopter pilot as well. He'll have us there in just a few hours. That is one of the largest and fastest helicopters in the Realm." He pointed to the helicopter that was cooling down in the Haydenshires' pasture.

Their guests offered them congratulations and well-wishes as their luggage was loaded.

Aida hugged Emily. "What do you do on a honeymoon?"

Emily and Fionna giggled as Rainer and Dan tried not to laugh.

"Emily and Rainer are just going to relax and spend some time together," Fionna explained.

Aida looked concerned. "Maybe you should take a book and one of those phones like Garrett's that has movies in case you get bored."

Dan laughed outright. "If she gets bored, Lawson, we need to chat."

Rainer smirked. "Don't worry. I'll keep her entertained."

After giving the Haydenshires hugs and thanks for the tremendous day, Rainer and Emily raced through a shower of flower petals as he helped her up into the helicopter.

"Are the Lawsons ready?" Pete Namphis chuckled. Rainer assumed his eagerness was evident on his features.

"We're ready," Emily squealed. The crew of six pilots and coolant officers had the chopper off the ground in seconds.

Just a few hours later, they landed on a custom helipad on Hatchpointe Island, an all-inclusive, private island deep in the Florida Keys. There was only one villa. The staff stayed on the other side of the island and only came when they were called, leaving Rainer and Emily completely alone in the lap of luxury.

"You two have fun." Pete helped Rainer unload their luggage.

"Thanks, Captain Namphis. We will." Rainer shook Pete's hand.

"My pleasure, son. You take good care of her, and I'll pick both of you back up right here in two weeks."

The sun had set a few hours before, but the beach was bathed in moonlight and the glowing lights of the estate. It was a decent climb up the island landscape to the abode they would be sharing, the place where he was going to make her his wife. His heart was already flying, and he hadn't even begun the climb.

"This is amazing! Do I even want to know what this cost you or what that helicopter ride cost you?" Emily seemed overwhelmed.

"Based on your tone, I'm gonna go with no."

She laughed and took in the lush landscape set off in sparkling blues and greens. The moonlight danced on the lapping waters.

"No one knows we're here?" Her voice lowered as she began to really understand.

"No one, sweetheart. Just you and me."

Relief flooded through her energy. She'd been chased relentlessly for weeks. The wedding, the takedown of the Interfeci, Dan and Fionna, little Abigail, everything the press felt they deserved to know about they'd dogged her every step to discover.

"There is a serving staff on the island, but they stay on the other side and only come if they're called. So, for all intents and purposes, except for when you want them to bring meals, we're all *alone*."

His breaths came quicker as Emily took his hand and began leading him up the long wooden planked staircase that led from the beachfront to the villa.

Unable to stop himself, Rainer watched the way her hips swayed as she climbed. He skipped a step to touch her bare back surrounded by the lace of the dress.

He willed patience by reminding himself that he should at least let her see where they'd be staying and maybe even unpack before he claimed her.

They stepped up onto one of the wooden decks of the house. She turned and gazed out at the moonlit ocean. It seemed to take her breath away. "This is so perfect."

The long sultry glances she cast Rainer did nothing to quell his overwhelming desire. He grasped her waist and pulled her into him.

He pressed himself against her. "I know you feel that, baby. If you don't stop looking at me like that, I'm gonna lay you down and take you on this deck. So, before I get too carried away, are you casted?" Making a baby on their wedding night was definitely not in his plans, but when he got her out of that dress he was likely to lose the ability to think at all.

She smirked. "Yeah, I kind of thought I might need to be today."

He chuckled just before he leaned in and pillaged her mouth. A soft moan escaped her when he finally released her. He reminded himself again to be patient and led her into the villa.

Her emerald-green eyes were dark and craving. "But you could take me on the deck, right? Because no one can see us." Her question was low and breathy.

A low, needy groan worked from his lungs as he nodded. "No one."

He forced his mind off of her body as best as he was able. "They'll do our laundry if I decide to let you wear clothes at all over the next two weeks, which isn't likely. And they'll get you anything you want." Giving her a lust-filled, longing gaze, he took her hand and led her to the largest deck off the front of the house. "But anything you need, baby, I'll take care of." His voice turned the consistency of gravel, rough and reverent in his desire. A delicious shiver rocked through her as she nodded her understanding.

The villa was open on all sides. Being the only two people on this side of the island made doors and windows unnecessary for privacy. There was a magnificent ocean view from three sides of the villa.

Rainer guided her up a few steps into a living room. It consisted of a high counter in the corner with two bar stools and a huge, wicker, heavily cushioned, double lounge that faced the beach. Heat casted candles were placed strategically throughout the room on all of the side tables. The roof was constructed of driftwood and thatch.

"Wow," she whispered as she took it all in. They traversed the few steps that led to a kitchen only large enough to make a cup of coffee or a simple meal.

Emily's mouth pulled into a sexy, sultry grin as she spied another deck. He followed her eyes as they took in the biggest Jacuzzi tub either of them had ever seen. It was constructed out of cream-colored tiles and was easily big enough for ten people.

This side of the house, though open to the views, was blocked by enormous palm trees. Candles, bubble baths, and massage oils were placed on the corners of the large tub. The room also held a low-slung wicker bench topped with thick white pillows, plenty big enough for two people to lie on. *Especially if I'm on top of her* Rainer thought savagely.

Huge, plush white towels were rolled and strategically placed on wicker side tables situated throughout the room. Two large bamboo-framed mirrors filled both of the only walls the room offered.

The next deck was by far the most magnificent. A dining table set for two sat on the smooth wooden floor. A chilled bottle of champagne and two flutes awaited them. The deck was curved around a large infinity pool, shaped to look like it would spill off the sides of the deck and right into the ocean, which was the majority of the fantastic view from this side of the house.

Candles were lit every few feet surrounding the pool, and as the moon lit Emily's alabaster skin, the effect was stunning.

"This is amazing." She stared out at the lapping ocean as she laid her head on his shoulder. Another large wicker bench with a matching white mattress-sized pillow was on the deck—this one larger than the one beside the tub.

With a wry grin, he gazed at her longingly. He didn't think the ocean view had anything on her.

"It's nice." He lifted her chin tenderly between his thumb and index finger until she was staring into his eyes. "But I'm looking at the most stunning thing I've ever seen in my entire life."

Her eyes closed and a small moan escaped her as he traced his hands around her face, then glided his thumb over her lips just before guiding them to his own.

He whispered kisses on her mouth until her lips parted. He settled for another deep exploration, but he was desperate for so much more.

The kisses built in intensity until she pulled his tongue in her mouth and sucked. She mimicked the moves she used when she took him in her mouth. It drove him wild from sheer anticipation.

He let his hands slide from her bare back to her chest, tenderly drawing his index finger over the swells of her breasts. He slipped one hand under the lace bodice of the dress as she threw her head back in a panted moan. Her nipples pebbled tightly under the lace of her bra.

He reclaimed her mouth, sucking her bottom lip and then sliding his teeth over it, nipping her, *owning* her.

She pulled away slightly, and he forced himself to wait. He wanted the anticipation to build. He wanted to make love to her all night long, and he was determined to take his time worshipping her gorgeous body.

He stared at her, eager in his greed. She was his, and he planned on making certain she knew that, and felt that, and that she was glad of it.

"Would you like some champagne, Mrs. Lawson?" He made another path with his index finger along the scalloped V neckline of her dress. Her breath caught deliciously.

With a sultry grin, she nodded. Her eyes grew darker still. They were heavy-lidded, and her lips were kiss-swollen from his teeth. "I really, really like it when you call me that."

He moved to the bottle casted to stay chilled on the silk-draped table. He loosely wrapped the provided cloth over the neck and popped the cork. He set the bottle down, waiting as the foam bubbled before pouring two glasses of the amber liquid.

Handing one to her, he grinned. "I really, really like that it's your name."

She moved to the edge of the pool and hiked her dress upward. A quick grunt of approval sounded from him as his heartbeat sped. She kicked off the heels she was wearing and sank her feet and calves in the cool water. The dress splayed out around her.

She beckoned him as he stared unabashedly from the dip between her shoulder blades all the way down the perfect curvature of her back that led to her gorgeous ass still covered in lace. *Not for much longer.* Fire burned from his groin. It seared through him, incinerating any patience he tried to cling to, as he walked to her and toed off his shoes.

He'd changed in the helicopter, but she'd wanted to remain in her dress.

"I want you to take it off of me," she'd drawled in his ear heatedly when he'd returned from pulling on a Polo shirt and shorts.

He let his legs dangle in the water beside hers. The rippling water moved her feet as she sipped the champagne. He was woefully unable to take his eyes off her.

"Eager for something, Mr. Lawson?"

Chuckling, he shook his head at her teasing. "You have no idea."

She gave him a half grin. Her eyes danced as fire burned from his. She turned and looked back out at the ocean. She was going to make him work for it, and he was more than up for the challenge.

She seemed to decide to tease him a little more. She set her champagne on the tile edge of the deck and then leaned and outlined the strain protruding at his zipper line with her fingers.

A low groan echoed from him.

"You seem a little turned on." Her eyes were longing as she continued to taunt him, never actually making contact with him.

He grasped her hand and pressed it to his cloth-covered, throbbing cock. "I've been aching for you since you walked down that aisle, baby. You're gonna take it all for me."

Rushed breaths made her chest rise and fall rapidly.

With a wry chuckle, he shook his head. "No, wait, that's not true." He smiled as he took another sip of the champagne.

She furrowed her brow. Quickly deciding that if she could tease, he could too, he winked at her. "I've been aching for you since Aida told me what kind of panties you're wearing." He watched her mouth fall open as she squeezed her eyes shut.

"She didn't!"

"She did," he confirmed as she covered her face with her hand.

"I can't believe she said that. I didn't think she even noticed." Blood filled her cheeks only adding to Rainer's overwhelming desire.

Still chuckling, he let his hand glide over her backside. An ocean breeze reached them. It ruffled her hair, and he caught the scent of her perfume and her own sexy musk. He clenched his jaw in effort not to lay her out immediately.

He slipped his right hand over the folds of lace gathered in her lap until he reached her exposed knee. The feeling of her silky skin set him on fire. He slid his hand under the bulk of lace that covered her thigh. Her eyes begged him with each delicious inch his hand gained as he slowly worked his way to where she was wettest.

He stopped just before he reached the very heart of her. "So, can I see them, Mrs. Lawson?" His question rang with mock nonchalance. His voice was consumed with rough desire.

He watched the storm swirling in her eyes as she cocked her jaw to the side and shrugged. "Maybe."

His eyes flashed with ardent desire. His blood ran thick with aching need. He leaned in and kissed just below her earlobe, letting his hot breath caress over her exposed neckline. He spun his tongue an inch above her collarbone, then sucked the thin skin before he demanded in a heated whisper, "I want to see them, Mrs. Lawson. Right now. I'm losing my patience. Don't make me wait."

She trembled. Her eyes flashed as her breath came in frantic pants, hot from his demands. A hungry moan escaped her.

Attempting to regain her slipping control, she let her eyes close as he began to rub her inner thighs, thick and fevered with wet heat. She squirmed in anticipation.

"You're already wet for me, aren't you, baby?"

She panted and visibly willed his hand higher. Her mouth hung open momentarily as she gave him a heavy nod. "Someone will have to help me out of this dress." Her hot breath teased his lips in challenge.

He closed his eyes and forced himself to be patient as he fought tearing the dress off and exposing all of her to him.

With a determined clench of his jaw, he stood and reached for her hand. She scooted back out of the water and stood.

He kissed her again, devouring her mouth, running his hands over her in scorching caresses.

"I'll take care of the dress," he assured her as passion coursed through him, making him pulse and ache, a sensation he pulled her close enough to feel through the tight lace covering her body. She moaned in sweet anticipation. Their energy spun in craving pulses desperate to be joined. "Then I'll take care of you."

She nodded heavily as he led her to the center of the villa. "I can't have my baby hot, wet, aching, and needing me to make everything feel better."

A frantic groan echoed from her. Her entire body trembled against his.

A gargantuan bed was situated in the very center of all of the rooms. No walls blocked it from any other part of the house, so they could hear the ocean's steady, lapping waves and feel the breeze it provided.

The bed was a high, substantial, four-poster with net hangings surrounding it, and curtains that could be drawn to block it from view. Rainer had no desire to draw them, and had no intention of doing anything that would take time away from getting his hands on her bare skin.

Still hungry, she ran her tongue over his lips. With a covetous groan, he ravaged her mouth.

She lifted his shirt over his head. Her hands grazed over his chest, grasped his pecs, and then she spun her thumbs up over his nipples. She dropped her head and swirled her tongue over the sensitive skin and made him pant.

He forced himself to concentrate, to make this night all she deserved for it to be. He traced his fingers over her kiss-swollen lips then slid his hands down her delicate neck. The contraction of her swallow tensed in his groin as she lifted her head in invitation. With gentle presses, he tempted her to give him full control. Using gentle persuasion, he spun his tongue in the hollow of her throat.

He slipped his right hand back and pulled several pins from her hair, releasing the long, thick, auburn waves as he sucked and licked the succulent skin of her neck.

Her hair cascaded down over her chest, and his eyes lit with greed.

"You are so fucking beautiful." His eyes traveled from her lips, red and swollen, down her neck stained with evidence of his hungry kisses, to the dress that covered too damn much.

She stared at him in expectation.

He brushed the hair he'd just released from her neck and kissed the skin he'd revealed.

Rainer worked his way behind her. She leaned her head down, and he gathered her hair in his hands, swept it to the side, and revealed the tender skin at the nape of her neck.

Kissing, licking, and occasionally letting his teeth tempt her resolve, she trembled as he worked his way down to the dip between her shoulder blades. Tracing his hands down the trail his lips had just forged, he tediously unfastened the pearl buttons on the top of the dress.

His mouth trailed over every tiny space of her spine that he revealed as he made it through the top three buttons. The bodice fell away from her as his lips mapped their way down the curvature of her spine.

She arched her back deeply. Her body tensed. She began to roll under his touch.

He edged his way down her back slowly. He dropped to his knees as he reached the low waistline of the dress where five pearl buttons stood between her and him, the only things blocking his way.

With a thundered groan, he worked the buttons loose, revealing the top of her backside.

He slipped his hands in the opened dress, massaging what he'd just revealed. He cupped her ass, grabbing what he wanted, as he spun her back around still massaging her greedily.

Finally freeing her, he glided his fingertips up her arms until he reached her shoulders. He slid the gathered straps of the gown down and let it fall in a lacy pile at her feet.

A voracious growl thundered from his chest as he grabbed her and pressed her body to his. He melded them together, fevered flesh on flesh.

He lavished her mouth with his lips, as he popped the clasp of the bra. After freeing them from their white lace trappings, he lifted and massaged her ample breasts. They swelled in his hands. Her nipples drew into tight, puckered mounds that strained for his affection.

She threw her head back with a loud moan and hoisted them in his face as he panted.

"Tell me what you want, baby. Tell me every single thing you've ever wanted me to do. Every fantasy. It's just you and me. No one else will ever know, but I want every part of you to belong to me. I want to make them all come true," he demanded in a husky whisper as he licked and kissed his way over her collarbone. An excited moan covered the slight hesitation swirling rapidly in her hungry eyes.

Timid, fearful, hope flooded her energy. Finally giving in to the persuasion of his urgent pleading kisses, she threw her head back again, letting her eyes close as she whispered, "Suck me hard. Bite me. Please, I want it."

With another thundered growl, he worked slowly. He kissed tedious circular patterns around her breasts, lifting their heft, kneading them as he pulled her right breast in his mouth, sucking and tugging, bathing her with the heat of his lips as she cried out for him.

"Oh god, harder, please," she begged.

He almost lost control as he took more of her in his mouth. He grasped the other in his hand, kneading it with fervor. Her breaths stuttered deliciously. He spun his tongue over her swollen nipple, feeling her energy pour into his mouth.

She gasped his name. Her energy spiked in hard, jagged arcs. She was close. He could tell, and this would be a hell of a way to start the evening. He kept up the motion, pulling and tugged her forcefully. He matched his sucks and licks to the rhythm he kept when he took her. She cried out in a long desperate moan.

"Oh god, please, please don't stop." She lost all sense of restraint. It drove him wild.

She pitched forward as he caught her nipple in his mouth between his teeth and pinched the other in his hand. He forced her surrender. The slight climax stole her breath. Her eyes flashed unrestrainedly as she clung to him. Her body shuddered as it rocked through her.

She buried her face in his neck, and he held her tenderly. Her breath came in harsh pants. Her energy unfurled all around them. He'd certainly never brought her like that before, and she seemed embarrassed that she'd begged for it.

"Shh." He caressed his hands lightly over her body. "I've got you, sweetheart. I'm right here, and when you beg me for it, nothing turns me on like that. Please, baby, please tell me what you want. You're my wife, and I want to show you how much I love you."

Her body seemed lost between desperate desire and fearful hesitation. He kissed her sweetly and then kissed down her neck and over her breasts again. He edged her closer toward desire, which was his only goal.

His mouth traveled down her stomach. He traced his hands over his Phoenix crest inked on her hipbone. As he grabbed and massaged her backside, he dropped to his knees.

Her hands hung loosely by her side. She seemed to surrender her body to his will. Rainer took her right hand in both of his. She stared down at him. Her gaze was greedy and eager as he let his breath caress over her inner wrist and then he brushed kisses across it. Her pulse raced under the thin skin.

Inhaling the scent of her mixed with the perfume she'd applied there, he moaned with desire. He released her wrist and kissed her outer thigh and worked up her hip until he reached the bow on the panties that Aida had informed him of. With a slight chuckle, he whispered, "You know, Aida told me if I wanted to take them off I just had to untie the bows."

She gave him a sultry smirk. "Do you want to take them off?"

"Oh, hell yeah, baby." He caught the ribbon in his mouth, tugged, and watched one side of the panties fall away from her. "I want to taste that sweet cum you just gave up for me."

Her body trembled deliciously. He huffed hot breath over what he'd just revealed. She was waxed bare again. His cock throbbed in desperate anticipation as he moved to the other side.

She trembled from the hot breath caressing her. He began brushing kisses up her right hip. Desperation to fully see her bare lips surged through his shield. He tugged the ribbon again with his mouth. She spread her legs and let the panties fall to the floor.

"So beautiful, baby." He gently tempted her mound with teasing strokes of his index finger. She was swollen and soaking wet. The tender skin was fevered with a dark pink heat from her desire. She let her head fall back again as he caught her backside in his hands and tilted her pussy toward his hungry mouth.

His tongue danced along her slit, never entering her but still able to taste the wet heat and energy emanating from her. She gave him a yearning moan. He repeated the motion this time, moving from front to back as she quaked and begged.

"You taste so sweet, baby. So good."

"Please, please." Her voice was deep and husky from need.

"Tell me," he instructed, "tell me what you want me to do."

A pleading groan filled the air around him, saturated with the heady scent of her arousal.

"Lick me." She leaned back against the bed and spread her legs, offering him an undeniable invitation.

He delved between her bare lips with not one trace of a tender red curl to block his mouth from her swollen skin. He used two fingers to coax her clit to his tongue. It swelled, eager for his tongue. He slowly devastated the tender bundle of nerves.

He added to the intensity and the pressure. She began to beg in earnest. Her body shuddered against him.

He steadied her and then used his thumbs to open her wide. She laced her fingers in his hair and pushed him deeper. He drowned her clit with his mouth, stroking her constantly with his tongue as he sucked. She screamed out for him as he sent her spiraling over the edge again.

Her nails dug into his scalp as her orgasm seared through her. He forced her to relent only to him. Her energy flooded his mouth as he sucked the heavenly liquid pouring from her body.

Her legs trembled, and her body quaked. He stood and held her again. She couldn't quite get her footing, weak from all he'd done.

In one quick movement, he scooped her up and cradled her in his arms. He scooted the soft silky sheets and blankets down the bed until he could lay her gently on one of the pillows.

Begrudgingly, he covered her and then made quick work of dispensing with everything he was wearing before he slid into the bed beside her.

"Want to take a break, baby?" He guided her to his chest and wrapped his arms around her tightly.

"No." Her face displayed a replete smile. Her blinks were heavy, as she let him cuddle her closer. "I feel so safe in your arms."

The statement was intoxicating, a delicious drug he craved. The truthfulness that seemed to have seeped from her soul and out of her lips made his heart beat disjointedly.

His eyes closed as he reveled in her proclamation. With one phrase, she tapped into the core of his very being. He was a fierce Ioses Shield. His desperation to protect her was all-consuming.

Suddenly, she worked down his body. With a sultry, luscious grin, she kissed his chest and lapped at his nipples with her tongue. She followed the trail of chest hair down his abs until she reached his cut lines. His breaths came in ragged pants. His eyes rolled back in the ecstasy of what she was doing.

"But now I want to know what you want." She brushed open-mouthed wet kisses on either side of his cock and traced her index finger down the line between his right hip and leg. A shuddering groan overtook him.

She followed the same path with her tongue, sweeping it back and forth down him. She was going to make him beg as well it seemed. He supposed that was only fair. He watched her work.

Her hot breath teased his cock. She licked a pearl of desperate need that leaked from him and spilled on his abs. She moaned her approval.

With a ragged groan, his hips rose of their own accord in a mimicked thrust. "You like that, don't you, baby? I'm about to fill you full of it."

Upping the ante, she dropped her head between his legs, spun her tongue over his sac, and then sucked him. It was exquisite. Unable to take much more, he began to writhe.

"Oh god, please," he growled.

"What?" She feathered her tongue from his hilt to his ridge as he groaned.

He leaned up to watch her tongue glide over him, as he demanded, "Suck me, baby. Put my cock in your hungry little mouth and suck me hard."

He pulsed hot and heavy in her face. His body contorted as his muscles seized.

With an eager moan, she wrapped her fist around his shaft. She drew him into the heat of her mouth and sucked with ferocity. She swirled her tongue over his head.

A moan thundered from deep in his chest. She was exquisite. Her hair was splayed across him. She released him, traced back up him with her tongue, and then pulled him in deeper than before. The bed, the room, the entire world spun away from his understanding.

The only thing he was capable of feeling was her mouth surrounding him, her nipples grazing his inner thighs, and her hair brushing across him softly.

He clenched his jaw. He didn't want her to stop, but he wasn't letting her do this, not tonight of all nights.

She drew the erotic energy flooding his body straight from its source. He had to stop her. A shuddering growl escaped him. Their energies combined in her mouth.

She released him and began kissing back up his abdomen and stomach, dragging her fingers over him as he willed away the imminent explosion.

Rainer grabbed Emily's waist and jerked her underneath him. "Baby, I need you. Right now. I need to be inside you. I need to make you mine." He traced his fingers tenderly along her slit, making her buck.

He slipped them inside the slick, wet heat and felt her shudder from the heady sensation. He knew right where to go. The tightly ridged nerve endings coiled and begged for his touch. He watched her body pitch and toss as she ground against his hand.

He groaned in heated passion as he watched the liquid form of her energy flow around his fingers and seep into his soul.

Rainer rushed his lips back to hers. He devoured her mouth and kept his strokes deep and driving.

She gasped his name as she bucked underneath him. Her breath began to stutter again as she flushed pink for him. Her body slowly began to give him what he was after.

"That feels good, doesn't it, baby? Right there. I know. You need to come for me, don't you?"

Emily's breath washed from her body, and her energy arced high. She was swollen and throbbing. Her energy twisted in desperate arcs until her breath caught, and her body contorted. She screamed out for him.

Releasing everything, taking it all for himself, his body tensed as he watched her come. Her hair was splayed across the white pillows. Her gorgeous body curved and arched as she gasped for breath. The waves seared though her as she convulsed.

She quieted after several minutes. He held her to him, wrapping her up in his arms until her breath steadied, and she clung to him.

He knew she was tender. He caressed her back and backside, hoping to give her a few minutes.

As he traced her cheek with his hand and brushed whispered kisses in her hair, she pled, "Rainer, please."

Perfectly willing to give her anything in the world, he soothed, "What, baby?"

"I've waited my whole life for this night. Please don't make me wait anymore. Please."

Unable to help himself, his hands traveled back to her breasts with magnetizing force. He massaged as she continued.

"Please make me yours, really yours, really your wife."

Insatiable yearning desire flooded through him as he growled, "You are really mine." He braced his body against hers, feeling her spread her legs under his. He pinned her hands over her head.

"Oh god, yes!" She quivered as his body tightened against hers.

He paused for one moment more. Gazing deeply into her eyes and watching their fiery depths fill with his love and adoration, he pushed inside her, claiming all of her as she bucked under his deep thrust.

He halted momentarily. It was different. He could feel it. It was so much more than it had ever been. He kept his gaze locked on her eyes. She felt it too.

It was indescribable. He lost himself in her as he began to thrust to the rhythm of her pulse. The past melted away. The future was tied solely up in her. The energy their bodies possessed was nothing compared to what they were creating together this night.

He'd never felt anything so astounding. As many times as he'd been with her like this before, it couldn't have prepared him for what it was like to know she was his forever.

This. This he knew was what heaven must be like. He was unable to imagine anything more astounding.

His body released all of the horrors of his past. They seemed to fall from his grasp like sand through his open hands. It all drowned in the ecstasy of being deep inside her.

The air around them vibrated and pulsed with their united energy flowing with utter dedication and a love so deep it was unfathomable to him as he made her his.

The glint of his ring caught his eye as he held her captive under his body. He kept her pinned to the bed. A deep yearning coursed through his blood, running thick and hot with utter devotion.

He pushed her harder. His thrusts were unrelenting as she closed her eyes in the ecstasy of what he was doing to her body. Her breath caught. Her skin seemed to pulsate under his grasp. She writhed and lifted her body as he pounded into her, listening to her call out his name, begging and pleading for release.

He forced her body to form around him until she'd taken him to his hilt, and she cried out. She swelled around him. She drowned him, and he moaned as she bound him tighter in the hot wet space that he permeated fully.

"I'm...coming," stuttered from her in broken syllables. She was unable to catch her breath as the climax began to claim her.

Her warning had him hot-wired. Every nerve ending in his body was set to detonate. Unable to fight it any longer, he buried himself deep inside her as she cried out, and he filled her with all of him.

Their releases mixed inside her, and he could feel them combine around him as he gasped for breath. He was unable to withdraw as she continued to writhe.

When her body collapsed under his, he pulled away, still trying to catch his breath. He kept her tucked tight against him. He didn't speak. He didn't know what to say. It was overwhelming, so he just held her. She refused to allow any space between them as their intoxicating energy joined together and spiraled and wound its way around them.

"You are amazing," he finally managed.

"Did it feel different to you?" Her body gave a slight shiver.

"Yeah," Rainer assured her. "It was the most incredible thing I've ever felt."

She burrowed down in his embrace and made him smile. She was relieved he'd felt it as well. He could feel her every emotion.

"Please don't let me go," she pled suddenly.

He made certain every part of her touched some part of him. Rainer gently mated their mouths again before assuring, "Never, baby. I'll never let you go." He whispered kisses across her forehead, willing calm into her. "I'm right here. Right beside you. That's all that matters. I'm never going anywhere. I never want to be anywhere unless you're there with me."

With a deep breath, she kissed his chest before she relaxed completely in his embrace. "I love you," she whispered.

"I love you too. Go to sleep, baby. I've got you." He ran his fingers through her hair and surrounded the two of them in his shield until she was sound asleep.

He gave a prayer of fervent thankfulness for all that he held in his arms and all that he'd been given. It was so much more than had ever been taken away.

CHAPTER 9

INTRUSIONS

DAN VINDICO

Fionna was pretending to still be asleep curled up on her stomach with her hands buried under her pillow. Dan gazed at her, still unable to fathom what he would always consider to be utterly unbelievable—she was his. She and she alone had pulled him from the terrifying and drowning depths of hell, and even after all he'd put her through, she'd somehow made his life everything he'd been too afraid to dream it ever could be.

Carefully, he surrounded her. He kept his weight on the mattress as he wrapped his arms over hers and kissed her cheek. Her back melded with his hardened chest.

"Good morning, Mrs. Vindico." He watched a broad smile spread across her face as he traced his hand down her back and grabbed a handful of her exposed ass. He squeezed tight and braced his morning wood between her cheeks. She gave him a luscious moan.

"Would my gorgeous wife like some coffee before our little girl gets up and I watch in awe as you accomplish everything you've decided we're going to get done today?"

Fionna wiggled until he moved enough that she could roll over.

"We can do it. I just need a little help." Her words drowned in a heavy yawn.

Dan kissed the top of her head. "I'm all yours, baby doll, but if I need to build an imu pit in our backyard for a pig roasting, I might need to get started on that now."

She laughed, a sound that Dan was quite certain could bring about world peace. "I think we'll just have chicken for this particular luau."

"We don't have to do all of this. We could just go out," Dan pointed out yet again. He didn't want her going to all of the trouble of cooking traditional luau foods for his entire family.

"No." Fionna's right hand glided up his chest and caressed Dan's face. His heart beat disjointedly. "This will be fun, and maybe your parents won't feel like they completely missed out on our wedding, and Aida and Olivia can play. Of course, she needs some toys besides Phoebe if they're going to play, and we need to get the stuff for her room."

"Why don't you do the food, and I'll take her toy shopping?" Dan was rather excited by the thought of spending the day bonding with Aida.

Fionna giggled. "Because, if I let you take her toy shopping, she would either come home with every single toy in the entire store or she would come back with only Matchbox police cars, army men, and tanks."

"Are you saying I have no restraint?"

"I kind of like that you have no restraint when it comes to me."

His left eyebrow arched. His hands grasped her tits. "That's because you, Mrs. Vindico, are entirely irresistible."

"Plus, I want to spend the whole day with both of you." Her breaths came up short as he rolled her nipples under this thumbs.

Dan brushed kisses along Fionna's jawline until he was laving her mouth with his own.

"That sounds perfect."

She braided her fingers in his hair and pulled his mouth back to hers until they were consuming each other, and Dan wondered just how long they had before Aida was awake.

Rainer Lawson

Rainer's eyes peeked open and then squeezed shut tight again. He realized immediately what the hangings on the bed were for. He eased from the covers and pulled the hangings shut. He reheated the sheets and blankets with his hand before he slid back into bed with his wife.

Emily slipped back to his chest immediately. He took several long minutes to let his hands tenderly explore her naked body pressed against his. Their wedding night replayed in his mind.

He was thankful the early sunrise hadn't disturbed her slumber. His head fell back on the pillow in the now darkened bed. His soul filled with replete satisfaction. She was his. All his, and no one else's, not ever. He would never take that for granted.

He glanced down at his left hand and smiled at the sight of his ring against her bare shoulder. Love and devotion overwhelmed him. He tucked her closer to him and fell back into a peaceful sleep.

Several hours later, he awoke when Emily returned to the bed. She slipped quickly through the curtains with a deep yawn as she crawled back under the covers.

He slid his hand down her back and scooted her closer to him. "Hey there, Mrs. Lawson."

A broad grin spread across her face as she planted a kiss on his cheek. "I didn't know how late it was. When did you close the hangings?"

"When the sun was right in my eyes at about five thirty this morning, and I didn't want it to wake you. You were up kinda late last night. Seemed a little worn out."

"I know. Someone just wouldn't let me sleep."

Laughing, he kissed her forehead. "Yeah, well, don't plan on getting too much sleep for the next two weeks, baby, 'cause I'm just getting started."

The intrigued grin that formed on her beautiful pink lips made him throb. His cock was awake and more than ready for more honeymooning.

"It's almost noon," she informed him.

"Seriously?" He'd had no idea how exhausted they really were. He'd been teasing her, but the past few months had worn them out thoroughly.

He stood and opened the hangings to reveal the brightly lit shoreline. "Are you hungry?"

She gave him a hesitant nod.

"Baby, why didn't you wake me up?" *Nice job taking care of her, Lawson.*

"I just woke up, remember?"

Rainer headed to the kitchenette while attempting to pull on his boxers as he went. He almost fell flat on his face from trying to do the two things at the same time. She laughed at him.

He quickly started a pot of coffee, once he'd determined how the maker functioned. He headed back to the bed and handed Emily the menu.

"So, the people just bring whatever we want to eat three times a day?" She studied the many varied options.

Another yawn contorted his jaw, but he managed a nod. "Yeah, or we can order everything for a day or two and then reheat it, keep it cool, or whatever needs to happen."

"Let's do that. I want to be all alone with you." She gave him his favorite mischievous grin and wriggled beside him. "You know, so if I want to walk around naked all day and make you drool, I can."

Rainer gave her the voracious growl she was after as he pulled her body down the mattress, dispensed with the menu, hopped over her, and pinned her underneath him.

"What is it you wanted to do all day if we're naked and alone, baby?"

That fire he loved sparked in her eyes. She slipped her hand down and then wound it into his boxers.

"Oh, you know, I thought maybe we could have wild, crazy sex on every available surface of this fantastic villa that you've rented for us, and I've always wanted to do it on the beach." Her fingers traced the ridges and straining veins that carried raw need to his head.

He lost all sense of what they'd been discussing and of the fact that he was supposed to be acquiring food for his wife. His eyes rolled back in his head.

"That's it, baby. Grab me."

Emily seemed to have forgotten eating as well. She moaned as he throbbed in her hand.

"You're so damn beautiful. Feel how hard you make me," he commanded. Rainer leaned and kissed her heatedly. A shuddering moan echoed from her mouth into his. It drove him wild. "God, I need you again. I need to fill you full."

Suddenly, there was a knock on the door. Only…there really weren't any doors. Panic surged through Rainer.

Emily gasped as Rainer threw the covers over them quickly. "Excuse me! What the hell do you think you're doing?" He slid from the bed as Emily buried her naked body under the covers up to her neck.

Rainer pulled on a pair of shorts while he glared at a tall, lanky man and a short woman dressed in uniforms from the company that owned the island.

Rainer cast his shield and positioned his body between Emily and the intruders.

"We're so sorry to interrupt, Mr. Lawson," the man drawled in a thick Eastern European accent. "I'm Aldus. We wanted to bring you a sampling of the food available to you while you stay on the island, and we wanted to say welcome to Hatchpointe and congratulations to you and Mrs. Lawson."

They stepped into the villa carrying two large trays containing numerous dishes of food.

"Rainer!" Emily panicked, but he was already on it.

He halted them before they took another step. "We didn't call for any food. And let me be perfectly clear, do not return unless we call, or I will arrest you for wrongful intrusion, invasion of privacy, and breach of contract. I'm certain the Crown Governor would see things my way. Leave! Now!"

The woman spoke in quick irritated Spanish to Aldus. Most of the staff of Hatchpointe was Non-Gifted, but the owner, Mr. Langfield, was Gifted, and Rainer knew the staff was aware of the Realm. They knew who the Crown Governor was and what kind of power Emily's father wielded.

"Certainly, sir." The man leaned and managed to set the trays of food on the kitchen counter. "We'll await your call, Mr. Lawson. We didn't mean any intrusion. Your father was an acquaintance of Mr. Langfield's, and he wanted you to know that if there is anything we can do during your stay, to make your honeymoon everything you desire for it to be, just simply say the word."

The fact that his father knew the man that owned the island location distracted Rainer for a moment, but he reminded himself that Emily was buck naked in their bed and there was a man standing not ten feet away from her.

"We'll be in touch, but right now I'd like a little privacy with my wife!"

"Certainly, sir. Just phone with your desires. Remember that it takes us a little time to reach you from the other side of the island," Aldus drawled as he and the woman paced back down the stairs.

Uncertain what to do next, Rainer eased back toward Emily.

"Are they just gonna show up whenever they want?" She sounded terrified.

"Not unless they want me to bankrupt their company with several lawsuits and own this entire island." Vengeful fury burned through his veins.

"Maybe we should call Daddy."

Without meaning to display his defeat, Emily saw it set in his eyes and certainly felt it in his rhythms. He'd wanted desperately to bring her here, to tuck her away in safety and solitude, and to get her to completely rely on him instead of her father, not that he didn't appreciate everything Governor Haydenshire always did to protect all of his children.

Rainer wanted so badly to prove to her that he would take care of her and be to her what her father had always been to her mother.

Emily forced an uneasy smile. "I'm sure they won't be back. I mean it is noon. We slept really late. I know you'll take care of me," she reassured.

"I swear, if they come back without us calling, I'll take care of it. I don't share, baby. You know that. I would never let anyone see anything that's meant only for me and for you. That's a private show, and I guard everything you give me with my life."

She gave him a sweet smile as she nodded. "I know." Glancing around as if the view might offer her a change of subject, she smiled. "Let's eat!" She pulled on a tiny white spaghetti string top and a pair of denim cutoffs so short they made Rainer's mouth water, then she poured cups of the coffee he'd made earlier.

CHAPTER 10

PREPARATIONS

Soon, they were sitting on the bed devouring the provided food and talking. Rainer's shoulders eased. It had been several weeks since they'd really talked about anything other than the wedding or the Wretchkinsides takedown. He allowed himself to wonder if any progress had been made in his absence on the missing money or the murdered operatives, but then he forcibly channeled his thoughts back to his beautiful bride. That was the past, and he wanted to stand with her and gaze into their future.

"I'm going to need lots of sunscreen if we're gonna go play on the beach," Emily drawled flirtatiously.

He was extremely pleased that she seemed to be letting their morning interruption go. Rainer gave her a cocky grin. "I'd be happy to help you with that."

"You're sure if I want to lie out topless or to make you take me in the waves, no one's going to see?"

"Not unless they don't ever want to see anything ever again," Rainer vowed. "Does this mean that my baby would like to go play in the waves?"

"We are on this beautiful island where the water is nice and warm, and I'm with this really hunky guy that I made marry me." Her delighted giggle made him laugh.

"The pleasure was all mine, trust me."

Emily crawled out of the bed and began going through one of her suitcases. She glanced around at the villa as she extracted a black bikini and matching cover-up. "It's just so hard to decide where to do you first. We could have sex in the bath tub, or the pool, or the ocean, or on the many various bed-like structures here." She gestured around the villa. "You'd think they made it just for that purpose."

"Yeah, I really couldn't get my brain anywhere above my belt when I was making the reservations for our honeymoon," he confessed somewhat sheepishly. "Is that okay? I'll take you somewhere else if you want? Anywhere. You name the place."

She shook her head at him and rolled her eyes. "I was kidding. This place is amazing, and I plan on making use of every available surface for its intended purpose."

He tried to shake off his nerves. Something about Aldus bugged him. His shield was taking over his brain. He needed to take care of her. "I could give you a bath."

"Let's wait for tonight. It'll be more romantic once it's dark."

He slowly drew her into his body and whispered a gentle kiss along her cheek. "Okay, then why don't you go put on that bikini, and I'll take you down to the shoreline, and we'll see just how quick I can get you back out of it."

Emily trembled in his arms. The effect drove him wild.

"Then after that, we can hang out, relax, order some dinner, and then I'm gonna lay you out in that tub, baby. I'm gonna rub my hands all over you until you're begging me to get you wet and dirty all over again."

She moaned in furtive need as her eyes flashed and darkened. "You won't let anyone see us."

"Never, baby. That's all for me and no one else, not ever. You're all mine. Forget this morning. Just go get ready."

She gave him a heavy nod. The sweet sultry scent of her mixed with need and sex hung in the humid air around them. Rainer tried to draw deep breaths. He watched her turn and walk to the bathroom in the villa, the only room with four solid walls and a door.

When Emily emerged, Rainer's mouth gaped as he fished around in his head for a full minute trying to remember how to close his jaw.

She was wearing a black bikini he'd never seen before. The top consisted of two thin black straps of material covering an inch or two over her nipple line, leaving the majority of her ample cleavage exposed. It joined in the center by three small strands of black material that hooked together with a gold medallion. Finally recalling how to make his lower jaw join with his upper, Rainer swallowed hard as his eyes traveled down her torso over her tattoo to the skimpy bottom of the bikini. A very insubstantial diamond cut of black fabric barely covered the parts of her only he had seen. The back was nothing more than a thong.

"Oh my god." Rainer gasped for breath.

Glee lit Emily's face as she giggled at him. "Close your mouth, baby. You're drooling."

A quaking moan thundered from his lungs. "That should be illegal."

"If you don't like it, you could take it off of me."

Ardent desire seared through Rainer's veins. "Come here to me." She let her hips sway as she moved to him. "You are just so damn gorgeous." He wrapped his hands around her waist. He was desperate. Everywhere on her body he touched seem to ignite like they'd been doused in gasoline.

She pulled away with a naughty grin as she slipped on her flip-flops. She slung the beach bag over her shoulder, grabbed a book she'd packed, and blew Rainer a kiss. With a look that said she wanted to be chased, she paced down the wooden steps that led to the shoreline.

Dan Vindico

"Best husband ever!" Fionna kissed Dan's jawline as she accepted the Starbucks cup he'd just surprised her with. Aida was almost as thrilled with her proclamation as Dan was. They continued to move through the grocery store they were currently in.

Aida was reading Fionna's list to them and helping them locate the items. She was astonished by the sheer amount of food in an American grocery store and the fact that she was getting to help shop and cook.

Every few minutes, she would tend to Phoebe whom she'd placed in the seat of the cart. Dan and Fionna found this particularly adorable and grinned at one another every time she explained something to Phoebe or offered her the bottle she'd brought along.

"Okay, your mom's bringing an appetizer, and Kara's bringing dessert." Fionna glanced at the list in Aida's hands. "Remember after we get all of the groceries, we get to go get a few toys and books and things for your room."

Aida nodded but was still concerned about Dan and Fionna buying things for her. An idea struck Dan as they moved to the checkout. "So I'm a guy, and I don't know these things, but don't baby dolls need stuff so you can take care of them?"

Fionna mouthed the word "brilliant" as she nodded. "Oh yeah, I mean Phoebe needs a cradle, and some clothes, maybe a stroller."

Dan melted as Aida tried very hard not to look as excited as she clearly was by the idea that she was allowed to have toys all her own.

"And Aida needs some books to read to Phoebe," Dan added nonchalantly.

Shivering in delight, Aida drew a deep breath. "When I lived in the orphanage, sometimes people would let us have books that they didn't want anymore, and they put them in the book room. I read them all, and I would hope every day that other little girls would give us their books they were finished with because even though they were already read they were still really good. But if they didn't give them to us, I would read *The Paper Bag Princess* because it's my most favorite story in the whole world, and it makes me laugh. I miss it a little bit." Her excitement dampened as she realized the book was no longer with her.

Quickly deciding that if he had to drive to Brazil to get Aida the book, he would, Dan kissed the top of her head. "I bet they have that book at the bookstore here so you could have your very own copy and several others. If they don't have it, we'll order one when we get home."

"Really?" Aida's beautiful eyes twinkled.

"Absolutely!"

"Oh wow!"

Fionna blinked back tears as Dan prayed that they could locate the book in question that day.

Pride and love filled his entire being as Dan drove his girls home several hours later. Under a fair amount of persuasion, Aida had relented and picked out a white, wooden, rocking cradle for Phoebe. It matched the white wood headboard of the bed that used to sit in one of Fionna's guest rooms. Dan had moved it to what used to be his office. To his shock, that empty room, once a shrine to the vengeance that consumed him, was the one Aida had chosen.

She wanted her room to be close to Dan and Fionna's, and when he'd offered to paint the walls lavender, she was overjoyed.

With a quick glance in the rearview mirror, he saw Aida holding Phoebe in her lap, but she was lovingly running her hand over the purple and white quilt that Fionna had picked out for her bed.

It had small pictures of fairy princesses sewn delicately into the squares. There were unicorn throw pillows that Fionna had been thrilled to show their little girl. When Aida declared that she wasn't special enough to get to sleep with a fairy princess quilt and unicorn pillows, Satan himself couldn't have stopped Dan from buying it and every available accessory that went with it.

Given that Dan despised his mother's lifelong obsession with drapes, Fionna had laughed hysterically when he'd added the curtain set to the cart.

They'd also purchased a small, white, wooden bookshelf to hold the books Aida picked out and a desk complete with a cork board that ran along the back. By the time Fionna finished loading up every single thing she wanted Aida to have, the sales associate was visibly delighted.

Fionna located *The Paper Bag Princess,* and tears leaked down Aida's tiny precious face when she opened it and saw that it was the very same book only in English instead of Portuguese. She'd been thanking them for a solid hour.

Fionna had added several books she remembered reading to Aida or that Aida had read to her while she'd worked at the orphanage and then several of her own favorites growing up.

When Aida wasn't caressing her new bedding, she turned back to the book she'd decided to start on, calling out the letters to the very few words she stumbled over for Dan and Fionna to help her.

"Fionna!" she gasped.

"What, baby?"

"Matthew and Marilla adopted Anne just like you and Dan adopted me only I rode an airplane and not a train." She held up the junior edition of *Anne of Green Gables.*

Fionna grinned. "That's right. They did, and those were my very favorite books when I was a little girl."

"Oh wow!" Aida breathed as she turned another page.

Fionna's phone rang.

With a wry grin, she answered, "Hey, Daddy."

To Dan's shock, the Stylers had been overjoyed that Dan and Fionna had married and adopted Aida.

He hadn't expected their exuberance when they'd refused to fly to Kauai for the wedding. The excuse had been that they couldn't afford to unexpectedly close the bakery, but Fionna had explained that her father didn't like coming back to Kauai. It was too painful. There were too many memories of her mother.

Dan understood that only too well, but he was still shocked that the Stylers weren't upset with Fionna's rapid life changes. Her father wanted her to be happy, and he was extremely pleased they were marrying and that she was considering quitting the Angels.

To Mr. Styler, Aida was the linchpin that would have Fionna resigning from her professional sports career, so he approved of the adoption completely.

"Yes, she's fine. She's reading." Fionna rolled her eyes as her father talked. "I do have to go to the arena tomorrow for a little while."

Per her contract, Fionna had to be in the stadium for several hours the next day and at least one practice day a week until her contract was up at the end of April. She couldn't challenge or participate in practice though.

Adeline had explained that the physical energy drain would be much harder to recover from for the next several weeks. Since they'd been very actively trying to conceive again, this all worked well. Once Fionna was pregnant again, she couldn't be under the field aegis. It would be dangerous for her health and the health of their child.

In one five-minute conversation, they'd both agreed that they wanted Aida to have younger siblings. The sooner the better. They'd already been trying anyway. They were certainly enjoying the process, but Dan knew she was very ready to conceive again.

"Okay, love you too." Fionna hung up the phone. "Daddy wants you to bring Aida by the bakery tomorrow while I'm at practice. He basically wants to load her up with cookies and show her off to all the customers."

"That sounds perfectly logical to me."

"It would." Fionna laughed.

"You're going away tomorrow?" Aida's tiny, frightened voice pierced through Dan. They shared a heartbroken expression.

"Just for a little while and then I'll be home," Fionna assured her.

"Can't Dan and I come with you?"

The press would be out in force with everything that had happened to Fionna in the past several weeks. This was her first return to Angels Arena. Neither Dan nor Fionna wanted Aida bombarded by the press, and Fionna was adamant that she not know about the miscarriage.

"I was thinking maybe Garrett could come over and play tomorrow while I'm gone," Fionna explained. "And then when I get home, we'll all go do something special together. I think Garrett misses you."

Aida seemed excited Garrett might be coming over, but she was visibly distressed as they pulled into the driveway and began unloading all of their purchases.

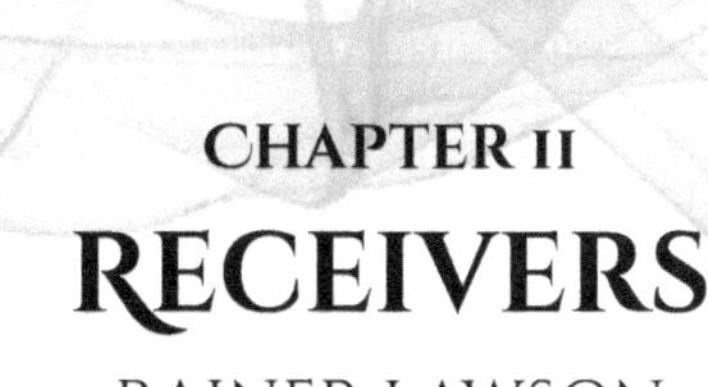

CHAPTER 11
RECEIVERS
RAINER LAWSON

Simply unable to touch enough of Emily's body to ever satisfy himself, Rainer continued to massage sunscreen into her skin. Finally forcing his hands off her luscious ass that was completely exposed, he fell to the towel beside her.

"Take that top off for me, baby. I need to put on a little more."

She gave him a sexy half grin and popped the clasp on the bikini top.

A low, hungry growl echoed from him as he lathered his hands and began massaging her breasts. He groped and pulled until she was arching her back and her energy spun in waves of tantric need.

She shuddered and gasped deliciously as he spun his thumbs over her nipples, watching them as they rose in stiff peaks that made him weak from desire.

"I want you." Her body rolled with her plea.

"Is here okay?" He grimaced at the sand on their feet and calves. "I don't want anything to…." The word *chafe* was decidedly unsexy. He bit his lip to keep it from escaping.

She stood, grabbed his hand, and led him toward the water. An entire beach all to themselves. The reward without any of the risk filled him with reckless abandon.

Edging a few steps in to the warm, breaking waters, she spun. Her exposed breasts danced all for him. His hungry cock tented his boardshorts. Freeing himself of them, he tossed them out of the water's reach and seated himself in the shallow surf.

Emily straddled over him, hoisting her exposed breasts in his face. Grasping her waist, he brought them to his mouth and licked the sweet, salty flavors of her from between them.

With the taste of her filling all of his senses and flooding his brain, he jerked the insubstantial bikini bottom to the side and revealed her swollen lips. She reared up on her knees and shook her ass for him as his fingers made certain she was ready.

"Ride me." He grasped her waist and lowered her over him. Her eyes flashed from his gruff command, and as the surf broke over him again, she slid down his cock.

The water washed over them as she pulled away and lowered herself back repeatedly. He'd never felt anything so utterly amazing. He watched her work.

Still sucking and licking her breasts, he held her to him via her lush ass cheeks as she rode him hard. Her body slid over him slowly, inch by delicious inch. She pulled him deeper with each pass. She threw her head back, giving him a hell of a show.

Her hands slipped down her own breasts, and he went wild. A low, desperate growl echoed from him as he grabbed her waist, spun her, and laid her out in the incoming surf that trailed under her body.

He formed her around his length. Everything in him drew tight. His muscles seized as her body swelled and encased him in a tight heavenly grip. His vision clouded, and his shield pulsed in craving hunger.

With a loud whimpering moan, she broke as the waves washed over her and a set all her own crashed through her.

Her body taunted and nursed the climax he'd been fighting. "Oh, fuck," he moaned, "I'm gonna fill you up, baby. You feel so damn good."

"I want it. Give it to me," she commanded.

With that, he collapsed on top of her as he flooded her body with his release. The water surrounded them, and he made her his own.

Worried his weight was too much for her against the sand, he rolled off of her and pulled her up onto his wet, sandy chest. "Are you okay?"

Laughing, she sat up. "Well, I'm a little sandy, but that was amazing."

"I probably can't do that again for a while, but my ability to give showers is still top notch." He grimaced when she turned. "And I think I might have a few things I need to heal up. He gently touched the sandy scratches on her shins, knees, back, and her inner thighs. "I'm thinking ocean sex only works in the movies."

Emily grinned. "Totally worth it, and my husband always knows how to make me feel better."

He winked at her and pulled his shorts back on. When she wobbled slightly, he took the towel she'd been folding and threw it in the bag. Pointing to his back, he offered, "How about another ride?"

With his help, she threw her arms around his shoulders and wrapped her legs around his waist, letting him give her a piggyback ride back to the villa. As they approached the deck, he bounded rapidly up the stairs. She squealed and tightened her grip. Rainer was quite certain this was the perfect honeymoon.

Dan Vindico

Aida seemed to have decided not to think about Fionna being gone for a few hours the next day. She flitted back and forth from her new room where she watched Dan drill holes above her windows to hang her curtains to the kitchen to see if Fionna needed help with the food for the luau.

Eventually Fionna joined Dan in Aida's room. Aida watched with glee as Dan lifted the mattress off her bed, and Fionna pinned the bedskirt to the box springs.

She helped Fionna put her new fairy princess sheets, fresh from the wash, on the bed. Dan spread the quilt wide in the air and let it fall over her as he laid it on the bed. She laughed delightedly as she crawled her way out.

They watched her carefully arrange all of her new books on her shelf. She cradled each one in her hands like she was holding fragile glass. She put her favorites from the orphanage between the unicorn bookends Fionna had found.

As she ran her fingers over the titles and authors' names, she informed Phoebe the order in which she planned to read them to her.

Fionna helped her put the pram stroller she'd spent thirty minutes picking out in the corner to hold Phoebe's bottle and blanket and the pretend baby food she'd chosen.

Dan snapped together the wooden cradle, and Aida tenderly laid Phoebe in it and covered her with her blanket. She began rocking it slowly and sang a lullaby in Portuguese.

Suddenly, she raced to Dan and Fionna and threw her arms out wide to embrace both of them. "Thank you so much for everything you got for me! And for letting me live here and be a family! I feel like the whole sunshine is inside my tummy!"

Fionna hugged her tight and blinked back tears.

"Yeah, I know just how she feels." Dan gazed deeply into Fionna's eyes.

~

Rainer Lawson

"Finally!" Rainer pointed to Aldus pulling up on a vehicle equipped to drive through sand and low-level water.

They carried trays containing Rainer and Emily's dinner and enough food for the next day that they'd requested two and a half hours ago. Rainer helped them with the load.

"We certainly hope you enjoyed your day here at Hatchpointe, Mr. Lawson." Aldus's smile seemed sinister. The woman who'd been with him earlier in the day was back as well. Rainer noted her name tag this time—Bryna.

"Very much. Thank you." Rainer kept his tone cool. He was still pissed about the interruption at lunchtime and the wait after they'd ordered food.

Emily, fully clothed this time, offered them a half smile as she studied Bryna. She moved to Rainer and laced their fingers together.

Panic rocketed through his shield. His heart thundered in his chest. She felt something in the woman's energy she hadn't liked. He positioned his body between Emily and Bryna.

"That will be it for a while. We'll call in a day or so when we need more food."

Aldus offered a slight chuckle. "We will leave the honeymoon couple to their villa. Enjoy your evening. There is to be a meteor shower tonight if you'd care to watch it. The sky is clear, so it should be quite a show."

"Thank you." Rainer adjusted his stance. When Bryna moved closer, he narrowed his eyes.

"Do let us know if there is anything else we can bring you," Aldus drawled.

Bryna offered Emily and Rainer a rather cool, "Have a nice night," before she followed Aldus back to the truck.

"What did you feel?" Rainer wrapped Emily up in his arms. He set his shield around her.

She let him restore her for a moment before she pulled away. "Fi's been trying to help me with this. Well, she was helping me with it before everything happened. And she's a much, much stronger Receiver than I am."

Fionna was a much stronger Receiver, but Rainer believed that with the help of the extra energy in her engagement band, by the time Emily was thirty she might be nearly as strong.

"What was she teaching you?"

"You know I've always been able to pick up on dark energy, black energy, anything like that. All Receivers can do that. And you know I'm able to sense if you're upset or Logan or any of my family or anyone I've spent time with without touching them. I can do it without being anywhere near them. You or Logan can be upset at work, and I sense it when I'm all the way at the arena." She flushed, embarrassed by her own abilities.

Rainer caressed her cheek. Her smile soothed his soul.

"Anyway, Fionna said that you can kind of channel that energy read and read anyone who's near you. Fi has always been able to do it without even thinking about it, but she's incredible. I've been trying to do what she taught me, and I've gotten better with it."

Rainer's heart sank. "Em, why didn't you tell me all of this?" She used to tell him everything.

Emily offered him a sorrowful gaze. "When she first started trying to get me to feel it, I never thought I could actually do it. I just thought Fionna wanted me to because sometimes all of her power freaks her out. But then you were telling me about what happened at The Tantra with Wretchkinsides. And when you said that he'd had people at Dad's inaugural ball, I remembered that I'd felt something weird from a few people. It wasn't dark and it certainly wasn't black, but I'd felt the other energies that Fionna had been talking about. And then when Bridgette stayed at Mom and Dad's. I know that I didn't like her because I was still being awful about her job, but I think I also got a really bad feeling from her. I didn't want to bring it up after the takedown, because I wanted to be there for you. You weren't yourself for a little while after that," she explained hesitantly.

Rainer sank down on the reclined lounge in the seating area of their villa and seated Emily beside him. He certainly hadn't been himself. That was an understatement. He just hadn't realized she'd needed him as much as he'd needed her the days following the takedown.

"What other energies?" He wanted to know everything. He could listen and process it now, and truthfully, he couldn't then.

Emily kissed his cheek before going on. "Fi can feel Non-Gifted people's emotions all of the time." She sounded thoroughly impressed. "And I can only do that if their energy is running in one solid emotion. For most people, that's never the case, but since the takedown, I've been sort of practicing whenever I'm around other people."

"What did you feel from that woman?"

"Well." Emily sighed thoughtfully. "I felt her deceptive energy. It was kind of strong. It may not have anything to do with us at all, but she isn't a nice person."

Rainer racked his brain as to how to handle this turn of events.

"What about the guy, Aldus? Did you feel anything from him?"

She shook her head. "I didn't pick up on anything, but she was closer to me. It was so strong. I'm sorry. I know you wanted this to be perfect, and it is perfect. I feel terrible now."

"Hey." Rainer cradled her closer. "Listen to me. I had Dan check and re-check this place when I made the reservations. He even had Fitzroy double check it on the international records, but my only concern is that you are safe and happy, okay?"

"I doubt it had anything to do with us. She could hate Aldus, or hate working here, or be irritated that we're on vacation and she isn't. There are a million things she could have been thinking that would've read as hateful."

"That's true, but I need to make certain nothing's going on that shouldn't be." After brushing a quick kiss on her forehead, Rainer picked up his cell phone.

"Man, I explained all of this to you when you were fourteen. You cannot already be confused," was Garrett's snide greeting.

Rainer rolled his eyes. "Unless you want me to tell you all about what I've been doing to your sister since I got her here, could you can it for a minute?"

Garrett chuckled. "All right. Well played. So, why exactly are you calling me from your honeymoon?"

"Could you do me a favor?"

"Oh, this should be good."

Quickly growing weary of Garrett's mocking, Rainer sighed. "I need you to run a couple of names for me."

"Why?" Garrett's tone changed immediately.

Rainer briefly described what had happened and gave Garrett Aldus's first name and Bryna's full name. He'd carefully noted it from her nametag.

"That's not cool. If Fi's been teaching Em, she's probably right. You need to keep a close eye on everything going on. I'll run the names and call you back."

"I will. I swear."

"You got some way to get my baby sister off that island if something goes down?"

Defeat settled on him harshly. "No, not really. It would take several hours to get a helicopter back out here."

"Fuck. All right. Just chill. Let me see what I can find out about your overly helpful help. I'll call you back."

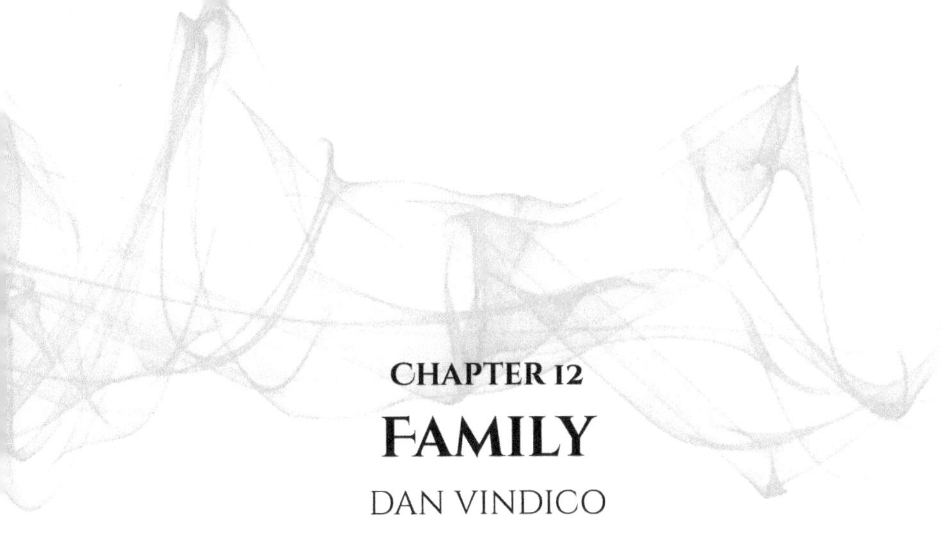

CHAPTER 12

FAMILY

DAN VINDICO

"Hey, could you do me a favor?" Dan asked Garrett hopefully.

Garrett chuckled. "Sure. It seems I'm in the favor business tonight."

Dan had no idea what that meant. "I was just wondering if you'd want to come hang out with me and Aida tomorrow while Fi's at the arena. She's been asking for you."

He couldn't stand the thought of Fionna entering the arena alone while the press chanted and screamed about whether or not she was going to sign her contract, or about Aida, and the miscarriage, but he didn't know how to be two places at once.

"Actually, I'm not too crazy about Fi being at the arena alone tomorrow. The press has gone crazy. They're outside of my apartment still asking if I know if she's gonna sign for another season and if I'm sure the baby wasn't mine. How about if I pick up Miss Aida Mae and take her out to breakfast or bring her out to the farm? Mom and Dad would love that, and she could play with me and the twins while you take Fi to the arena."

Accepting that he owed his entire life to Garrett Haydenshire, Dan sighed. That sounded perfect. "Thank you. She'll love that."

"I'll get her by eight. Tell them both I love them. I gotta go do something for Rainer."

"I will, and thanks, Garrett, really," Dan offered humbly before ending the call.

He grinned at Aida tucked up in the corner of the sofa with *Anne of Green Gables,* reading intently. Phoebe was beside her, and occasionally Aida would explain the story to her.

He headed into the kitchen. Fionna was hunched over the sink, scrubbing Okinawa sweet potatoes. Dan breathed hot kisses down her neck.

"Need some help, baby?" He let his hands slide up her waist and over her breasts. She spun. Her hands were in gloves and she was holding a potato, but the flirty smirk she gave him made him hungry for far more carnal things.

"And what would you like to help with, Mr. Vindico?"

"Well...I was thinking...after I kick my family out of here...that maybe we should recreate...some of our trip to Kauai." He paused between every few words to spin his tongue up Fionna's neck and let his teeth graze over the thin skin.

"I haven't given you a bath in several days, and that stuff Tutu makes is pretty incredible. I wouldn't mind rubbing it all the right places just before I take you to all the best places," he assured her with a great deal of arrogance.

Her breath caught and her body tensed beside his. Dan gave her a cocky grin. "That sound good, baby doll?"

"Oh yeah," she vowed in a passion-filled plea. Suddenly she spun back, pulled off the gloves, and laid the potato in the colander with all the others.

She wound her arms around Dan's neck. "But now I'm all wet," she murmured in his ear while letting her hot breath set him on fire.

Dan's body tensed and shuddered as he wrapped his hands over her stunningly sexy ass. He let his mind reel over all of the things he planned to do to her once Aida was asleep.

"I could take you upstairs and take care of you really quick," he offered. "Or you could just keep thinking about how hard you make me, baby doll. Such a good girl for me. You hang me so hard I ache.

You take it so good for me. Think about how good that's gonna feel when I finally give it to you. You think about how hard I'm gonna take you once I get you swollen hot and dripping for me, or about how wet your sweet little pussy is gonna be when I finally explode deep inside of you and watch it drip back out. Let it build for me until we're all alone tonight and I tear you up." He kept his tone low and commanding as he whispered his requests.

"Oh god." Fionna ground her body against Dan's now straining erection evident through his jeans. He lifted her up onto the counter as he devoured her mouth. He laced one hand in her hair and let the other slide down the side of her breast and then to her back.

"Feel it, baby. Feel what you do to me. So fucking perfect."

The doorbell ringing had them breaking apart and gasping for breath. Aida entered the kitchen carrying the doll and her book. Fear cast her sweet face. She moved to Dan and grasped his hand timidly.

Ordering the erotic pleasures he planned on indulging in much later from his brain, he realized she was nervous about his family coming over and that she felt safe when she was near him. He leaned and hoisted her up into his arms.

"Let's go see who's here first."

She laid her head on his shoulder. Fionna relieved her of her book, but she wouldn't relent Phoebe.

Rainer Lawson

Rainer answered his phone on the first ring as he paced in the villa. "What'd you find out?"

"Aldus's last name is Kamen. I found him on the website you gave me, but that's about it. He's worked for the company for a couple of years. No record here in the States. You'd have to get Portwood to check the International records to see if he has anything going on in Europe anywhere. But the woman, Bryna,"—Garrett hesitated and Rainer's stomach clenched—"she's worked for other all-inclusives, and she's been fired three times."

"For what?"

"Things apparently went missing from a few patrons' villas, and she was blamed. She was indicted twice but let off for lack of evidence. I'm betting if she's up to anything, she's after Em's ring. Just tell her to keep it on and you should be fine. Unless you've got other stuff down there that's priceless."

"No." Relief washed through Rainer. His imagination had run away with him in the time that he'd waited on Garrett to call back. "Well, Emily is absolutely priceless, but nothing else."

He could almost hear Garrett's smile from a thousand miles away.

"I think she's just a petty crook. She might know the legend about how the ring was made, but I'm thinking she saw those big, huge diamond bands and her fingers started itching. As long as Em's wearing it, then it shouldn't be a problem. You've seen the casts she can throw with it." Rainer's entire body eased. "You two relax and do all those wild, kinky, crazy things people do on their honeymoon. Just keep an eye on your phones, wallets, and jewelry. I think you're fine."

"We will," Rainer assured him. "Thanks, man. I really appreciate it."

"No problem. That's what brothers do. You know that."

~

Dan Vindico

As it turned out, Aida was wiggling out of Dan's arms almost immediately. Meredith and Tim arrived with Olivia and Oliver. Meredith and Olivia were loaded down with dolls and every available accessory to play with them.

"Oh wow." Aida gasped as she took in all of the toys.

"Olivia came prepared." Meredith sighed.

Dan tried very hard not to scowl at his brother-in-law who was carrying nothing while his sister was barely visible over the load of doll clothes, blankets, and a toy high chair.

Olivia was beaming as she showed Aida her baby whose name was Christina.

"May I touch her?" Aida asked timidly while the adults looked on.

"Yes, and you can play with her, but Oliver is not allowed to touch her or play with her because he puts hair bows in his mouth," Olivia informed Aida with an air of disdain for her little brother.

Aida beamed. "Do you want to see my new fairy princess bed?"

The girls took off for Aida's room as Dan relieved his sister of her burdens. After he'd made the toy delivery, he led everyone into the kitchen.

"That smells delicious." Meredith gave Fionna a hug.

"I hope everyone likes it." Fionna had lost a little of her confidence in light of his mother coming over. That always made Dan regret having to expose her to his family at all.

Oliver followed his parents into the kitchen with his lip poked out as he gazed up the stairs after Aida and Olivia.

As soon as Fionna cooked the potatoes in her hands and heat casted them on the counter, she scooped Oliver up. "You got left behind, didn't you?" She kissed his cheek. "Can he have an animal cracker?"

Meredith nodded, and Fionna supplied Oliver with a few crackers they'd picked up at the store. He promptly shoved an elephant in his mouth.

Kara and Zach arrived next. Zach was carrying the cake plate, a motion Dan appreciated immensely.

"This is probably super lame, but I made a coconut cake. I couldn't think of anything else. I have horrible pregnancy brain." Kara uncovered the cake after Zach set it on the counter. "And I shouldn't have said that either. I'm so sorry. I'm going to stop talking." Kara covered her face with her hands.

Fionna hugged her. "Coconut cake will be delicious. It's very tropical. And I'm okay."

But a moment later, Fionna's chin trembled. Dan pulled her close and wrapped her up in the sanctuary of his massive arms. She buried her face in his chest.

She certainly didn't begrudge Kara any pregnancy-related issue, but she wanted so badly to be pregnant again. And what she most wanted was to have never lost their first child. "I love you so much," Dan whispered in her ear while Zach and Meredith tried to loudly discuss foods they thought were Hawaiian. Everyone pretended not to see Fionna's tears.

She drew a deep steadying breath. Dan set his fierce shield around her. His siblings were visibly devastated that she was so upset.

He supplied her strength and calm while keeping her cradled closely to him.

"We'll get there. I promise."

"I think maybe a bath tonight would be good," she whispered so quietly Dan barely heard.

Quickly kissing the top of her head, he smiled. "I know, and I'll take care of you. Otherwise, Tutu might fly out here and come after me." He earned a slight giggle.

The doorbell rang again just as Fionna seemed to be perking back up.

"Oh, good. Mom and Dad are here," Dan sneered to chuckles from his siblings.

He pulled open the door to welcome in his parents. His mother hoisted a leaded glass tray into his tightly clenched stomach.

"Thanks, Mom." He rolled his eyes as she forced her way inside. Dan tried to hide his chuckle. The governor, in effort to show his support, had worn a bright red Aloha shirt that had white hibiscus flowers all over it.

Dan studied the tray. In juxtaposition to his father, his mother had to show her disdain. She'd halved olives, placed them on top of precut cheese cubes, and had speared the horrendous creation with pretzel sticks.

"Gee, Mom, you shouldn't have gone to so much trouble." Dan lifted the tray slightly before he placed it on the island in the middle of everyone.

Ignoring him thoroughly, Mrs. Vindico turned on Fionna. "Now, dear, I'm not certain what you might be making for this luau event, but I've just gone on a very special diet."

"Of course you have," Dan huffed under his breath. Marion Vindico dieted with regularity—whenever a diet would inconvenience someone she was irritated with, or gain her attention, or help her regain control of a situation that had shifted away from her.

Fionna was the consummate hostess. "Oh, well, I didn't know you were on a special diet since yesterday, but if there's anything you can't have I'd be happy to prepare something special just for you." There was a heavy note of irritation in her tone. Dan started to panic.

"I wouldn't want to put you out. I'll just have water." She lifted a large bottle of some kind of electrolyte-infused water.

"Mother, that water is for Gifted people who work out constantly," Dan spat.

"Well, this diet was featured in *Women of the Realm* this month," his mother announced proudly. "Didn't you see it, Fionna?"

"No, I'm sorry, Mrs. Vindico, I must've missed that issue." She feigned sorrow. "You know with being in the hospital and all," she huffed under her breath.

Dan cracked up at her remark, earning him his smile from Fionna.

Mrs. Vindico forged onward. She always did. "It's a kind of rotation diet where you only eat one protein each week along with raw greens, and you drink eight bottles of this special water each day. It's to help with stress and weight gain in your midsection. Maybe you should consider it, dear."

Fionna's mouth hung open, and Dan was prepared to murder. He suspected there was a very good reason that his beautiful wife had thickened just a little in her midsection, but he sure as hell didn't need his mother pointing it out.

He jerked the water bottle from his mother's hands and checked the manufacturing information. "Uh-huh, it's made by Jaredon, and that is also the publishing company of *Women of the Realm*. It's a racket!"

"Unfortunately, I've decided to go with poultry this week." Mrs. Vindico feigned the half apology.

Dan couldn't quite hide his smirk.

"Well, that's perfect." Fionna stifled a giggle. "I've been working on this Huli Huli chicken all afternoon." She lifted the aluminum foil off of the chicken pieces that she'd marinated and grilled with pineapple. It smelled heavenly.

Mrs. Vindico's face fell as Dan moved in. "Fi's amazing, Mom. I'm so glad that you'll be able to eat with us. It's delicious."

His mother, the queen of the cliché, had clearly been under the impression that for the luau Fionna would be serving pork.

"My best friend, Malani, made it for our picnic after the wedding." Thoughts of Malani and the wedding seemed to ease Fionna. "And I made some cabbage with papaya and strawberry, and some spinach salad with maca dressing so you could have the greens in that as well." She continued to infuriate Mrs. Vindico. It was a sight Dan was thoroughly enjoying.

"You had a wedding picnic?" Mrs. Vindico snipped.

Dan narrowed his eyes. "Why don't we go into the living room and have these appetizer-like things. Grab a beer or I can pour up some wine. There are POGs, which are really great fruit drinks we brought back from Kauai, in there as well." He gestured to the cooler where he'd chilled the beer, wine coolers, and Hawaiian Sun POG.

Pulling beers out of a cooler was something Mrs. Vindico considered to be barbaric which was the main reason Dan had set the drinks up this way.

Everyone fixed themselves a drink and settled in the living room. Oliver began pulling the pretzel sticks out of the appetizers, dispensing with the olive, and eating the pretzels and cheese which he seemed to enjoy.

"Can we see the pictures of the wedding?" Kara pled.

"Oh, sure." Fionna handed her a small four by six album that contained the printed snapshots Kai had taken with his phone of the wedding and reception.

"We didn't have a photographer or anything. It's more about being in the experience with the island," Fionna tried to explain without giving too much of herself away.

Dan rubbed her back. "It was perfect." He dared anyone to argue.

"Fionna, you look so beautiful!" Kara flipped to the photo of Fionna walking down the sand aisle.

"Thank you!" Fionna beamed over the assessment.

"You don't have on shoes." Mrs. Vindico gasped as she noted

Fionna's feet. She was taking a step when the photo had been snapped.

"Nope, just the dress." Fionna gave Dan a mischievous grin.

He winked at her. He could never love anything more.

"Mom, it was on the beach. See, Dan and Garrett don't have shoes on either," Meredith pointed out as they landed on the shot of Fionna's Papa placing her hand in Dan's.

"And of course Garrett was there. You've been best friends for as long as I remember." Kara beamed. "I'm glad he's such good friends with Dan too. I'm not sure he would've agreed to be your maid of honor." She giggled.

Mrs. Vindico looked set to maim. She glared at the photograph of Garrett as if that might in some way let him know she was furious he'd been at the wedding.

Fionna beamed. "He would've if I asked him too, but having him there was perfect."

Kara nodded. "Now, what is the floral crown called?" She was genuinely interested in learning all about Fionna and where she'd come from.

"It's a haku." Fionna was still grinning as she explained the pictures. Dan felt her energy soothe and begin to roll in replete happiness.

I feel like the sunshine is in my tummy he recalled Aida's earlier description of how Fionna made their entire family feel. He couldn't think of a better way to describe her all-encompassing loving powers. He gazed at her adoringly.

"Did you make yours?" was Kara's next question.

Mrs. Vindico scoffed. "Of course not, Kara. Certainly she had a florist." She slapped her hand on a photo of the Hawaiian blooms that formed a circle around Dan and Fionna in the photos.

Fionna shook her head. "We didn't have a florist, but my Tutu made my crown, and Malani made my lei." She pointed out the photo of Dan placing the white ginger lei around her neck. "And I made Dan's lei."

"That is just so cool and so perfect for you two. After everything..." Meredith blinked back tears.

"It was perfect." Fionna laced her fingers in Dan's hand.

Mrs. Vindico huffed audibly as she rolled her eyes. Dan knew his mother felt she'd been sorely wronged. He tried to remind himself of that before he began shouting and ruining the family gathering.

She'd planned his and Amelia's wedding down to picking out Amelia's gown. After she'd been killed, it hadn't taken Mrs. Vindico long to restrategize. Once Crown Governor Lawson had gotten Dan cleaned up and named him Chief of Iodex, her plans had vastly expanded. He was to have a huge wedding, a full Senate affair so she could show off the Vindico money and the status she felt she was owed, being married to a governor and with her son having a high ranking title in the Senate.

She'd given up hope for several long years when Dan did nothing more than talk with a woman just long enough to get her into bed and then moved on. When Fionna had come into the picture, she'd been elated, and the plan had expanded yet again.

Her son, Chief of Elite Iodex, was now going to marry the Senior Receiver of the Arlington Angels, one of the most famous Angels to ever challenge. It would have been an extremely high-profile wedding. She couldn't quite compete with Joseph Lawson's son marrying the current Crown's daughter, but she would have given it a shot had she been allowed.

Dan shuddered to think of the exhaustive fights that would have ensued.

"What is a tutu?" Mrs. Vindico brought Dan back to the present.

"Oh." Fionna chuckled. "Well, Tutu is grandmother in Hawaiian, but everyone on the whole island calls my grandmother Tutu. Her first name is Tua, and she sort of takes care of everyone."

Lost again, Dan let his mind reel back to Kauai to her grandparents' large farm. Fionna's grandparents could be millionaires. The lubricating ointment Tutu created would make her famous for the overwhelming sensations it added to lovemaking. But fame and fortune weren't what Tutu wanted.

She wanted to take care of the people in her corner of the world. She wanted to grow and care for each plant or flower that she used in her creations. Her hands, her energy, her spirit went into every brown bottle she created. Every screw-top jar she filled was a labor of love, a passion that filled her soul.

Dan was overwhelmed that he got to be a small part of such an incredible family that had created the woman he'd fallen completely, inexorably, and irrevocably in love with.

Kara turned to the last few pages of the album. There was a shot of Dan leaning Fionna back and kissing her heatedly. Laughing, Kara and Meredith looked delighted with his exuberance.

"Very nice," Zach complimented.

"Hey, she'd just made me the happiest guy on the planet."

There was a shot of Dan slipping the hibiscus bloom over Fionna's ear, giving her a lust-filled, hungry grin.

"You put it over your left ear because that means you're taken," Fionna explained.

Pride and contentment swirled through her energy as she shared a reminiscent glance with him.

"You look quite pleased to be taken," Kara teased her.

"Dan doesn't look like he minds being the one doing the taking." Zach slapped Dan on the shoulder. Governor Vindico gave Dan a pride-filled smile.

Kara turned the page. The pictures of the reception picnic on the beach had Mrs. Vindico's lips pursed in fury.

Kara smiled. "Oh, that looks so much more relaxed than our wedding." She pointed to a shot of Fionna reclined on the beach with her head in Dan's lap, and to the one of Dan stealing another kiss as the sun set. There was a picture of Garrett embracing her tenderly. And Kai had snapped a shot of Dan cradling Fionna's face in one hand and slipping his other under the slit of her dress.

On the last page was an image of the Styrofoam coolers that contained numerous beer bottles and of the very few guests eating off recycled cardboard plates at their reception.

Fionna's Papa had taken a shot of the mountaintop chalet overlooking the ocean where Dan and Fionna had spent their wedding night. It was the last photo in the album.

"Is that your grandparents' home?" Mrs. Vindico demanded.

"No, ma'am. That's where Dan took me for our wedding night."

The rustic chalet didn't meet Mrs. Vindico's standards. That was evident by the scowl on her face.

Fionna bristled. She'd taken Mrs. Vindico's lack of approval as a direct assault on Dan's ability to plan their wedding night. "It was so romantic. There was a huge bathtub and hammocks on the porch where we lay and watched the sunset. The bed was in this sweet little nook. It was perfect. I hope we get to stay there again." She glared at her mother-in-law.

Dan put his arm around Fionna, trying to soothe her and prevent her from lunging at his mother, not that anyone would blame her.

Noting the heated standoff ensuing between the two women, the governor stepped in. "Why don't we eat?"

"Yes! What can we do to help?" Kara leapt. Fionna drew a deep breath and allowed Dan to push calm into her rhythms in heavy doses.

"Why don't you get the girls?" She finally sighed. "I'll put the food on the table."

THE DEMON INSIDE

Dan convinced the girls to put the dolls down for naps while they ate. Soon everyone was seated in the dining room devouring grilled Huli Huli chicken, Hawaiian sweet potatoes, cabbage, long rice, poi, and a delectable macaroni salad. There was a massive bowl of the spinach salad with maca dressing that Tutu recommended for women trying to get pregnant.

Aida was thrilled with the POG and the sweet potatoes. "I've never had anything to drink that was pink and potatoes that are purple!"

Dan and Fionna shared an amused grin as they watched her inhale the strawberry and papaya in her salad and avoid the cabbage.

"This chicken is amazing, Fionna." Zach helped himself to another two pieces.

"Zachary, I never took you for a big eater," Mrs. Vindico huffed. There was a reason no one ever ate with any exuberance at the Vindicos'. His mother was a horrible cook.

Coughing to hide his chuckle, Dan awaited Zach's response. "Oh, just hungry tonight, I guess."

Dan's mother picked at her chicken and ate a little cabbage from the salad.

"Now," she drawled when there was a lull in the conversation. "Daniel, your father and I really feel that though you've gone ahead and married without us, we would very much like to host a reception for the two of you here so that we can celebrate with you.

"We would like to allow our friends to be a part of your celebration. I'm not certain what you were thinking with all of that." She gestured to the photo album in the living room. "But your father holds an extremely important role in the Realm Senate. I don't mind telling you that your decision to elope in Hawaii isn't the image our family is trying to uphold.

"I've taken the liberty of booking the Fairmount Garden Room in a few weeks' time. This will be a formal affair, black tie, so if you're going to insist that Aida attend, she'll need to understand that her best manners will be expected. Perhaps I'll just take her shopping so I know she'll be dressed appropriately for the evening." She shot an expression of disdain at Aida's outfit. "Fionna, you will need a gown and *shoes* for this event."

Fury pulsed from every cell in Dan's body.

"Dan," he heard Fionna's warning tone, but she sounded distant as anger rang in his ears.

"If I insist that my daughter attend my wedding reception! The reception I never agreed to having!" he roared. "And not that I give a damn what image you're trying to uphold, *Mother*, but just for your information we did not elope in Hawaii! We had a wedding ceremony where we were married!" He narrowed his eyes in fury. "You know what, you go right ahead and have yourself the reception you've always dreamed of. Book the Fairmount. Invite your friends. Serve whatever the hell you've decided we're having, and by all means have it all on fine china, but you can do it without Fionna and me because we won't be there!" He seethed.

"Dan," Fionna tried again, but he was too far gone.

"What you seemed to have missed out on entirely is that my marriage, my family—that's what matters to me. In fact, they are all that matter to me! Our wedding was perfect because it was for us. It was what we needed after all of the hell we went through at the hands of Wretchkinsides. After all of the hell I put her through." He threw his hands toward his wife.

"She'd done nothing at all but somehow manage to love me, and that's what we needed to heal. That's what we needed to move on after all of the loss. The commitment I made to her standing on the shores of Kauai isn't something I take lightly. It's forever, for the rest of our lives no matter what life may bring. My marriage is so much more important than some fucking reception so that you can show off your money and your power to all of your friends. And you know what else, Mother? Our wedding was perfect because you didn't have one fucking thing to do with it!"

Unable to see anything at all except violent red throbbing energy spilling out of his pores, Dan tossed his napkin down, grabbed his riding jacket, and raced to the garage. His Brutale roared to life. He let the soothing rattle of the motor ease his incensed rhythms as he flew away.

An hour later, after riding endless road after endless road, not certain how he'd even gotten there, Dan shut down the bike and slung his leg off it.

Governor Haydenshire must've heard the gates open and the bike pull into the barn. He met Dan in the grassy lane between the barn and the farmhouse.

"Want a beer?" He handed him the bottle he'd carried out with him.

Neither certain nor caring where he was being taken, Dan followed the Crown Governor to the backyard and toward the small lake on the property.

Dan listened to the gravel on the shoreline crunch under his boots as they walked.

"Your lovely wife phoned me. She seemed to think you'd end up out here."

Harrowing guilt flooded through Dan. "Oh my God, I left them with my mother!" He turned to sprint back to the bike to go back home.

"Dan." The governor halted his escape. "Your dad took your mom home. Fionna and Kara are playing with Aida. You scared her, son."

Dan's head dropped in abject defeat. He was a horrible husband and a horrible father. He jerked his bicep out of the governor's hand. "I have to go apologize and swear I'll never do that again."

"Don't do that," Governor Haydenshire soothed. "Aida will be all right. Kids are shockingly resilient. You are human, and forgive me for stating the obvious, but you have always had a temper. I will say that it's dramatically improved since you and Fionna decided to cram three or four years' worth of life into three or four months."

"I have to go back and tell them both how sorry I am," Dan continued to argue.

"They already know that, but I'm not going to force you to stay here. It probably wouldn't be great for my health if I tried, but since you did fly in here on your escape vehicle, how about a little advice before you head home?"

Assuming he could use all the advice he could get on being a better husband and father, Dan hoped Governor Haydenshire would talk quickly.

"I heard the tale from Fionna's point of view, and I'll tell you what I think might've set you off. You tell me if I'm wrong. Your mother has always been your mother." He chuckled and shook his head. "And you've never really accepted her for who she is any more than she can bear to accept you for you.

"Don't feel bad for losing your temper with her. She drove Lillian over the edge at the hospital, and my wife has the patience of a saint. But let's talk about why her planning a party for you and Fionna pissed you off so much."

Dan rolled his eyes. The disgust of his mother's words began to permeate his mind again.

"If I were to take a guess, I'd say that you aren't the same guy you were even six months ago. Is that a safe bet?" he asked wryly.

"Yes." Dan was still eager to try and repair the damage he'd done.

After giving him a quick grin that said for him to simmer down, the governor continued, "But there's a little more to it than that. Over the last ten years, you turned yourself into something almost unrecognizable to those of us who raised you and loved you. You got yourself into a fair amount of trouble. Joseph pulled you out of the wells of death you continued to throw yourself headfirst into, and he gave you a goal. But then the goal became the drug.

"Fast forward ten years, and you walked out of a bar with a gift from heaven. You walked into a real life. She is the only thing that made you forget all of those wells you so often considered going back to drink from.

"Forgive me for not giving this the gravity it deserves, but I understand you'd like to go back home and soothe the pain you created so I'm going to try to get to the point as quickly as I can. You accomplished the goal. You walked through hell again. Only this time, life was waiting on you on the shores of Kauai, and you knew she was your saving grace. So, you held on with both hands, and here we stand on my lake. Nothing has ever pissed you off more than something that scares you because so few things ever really have. You're terrified of losing her, and you're scared of what you did to save her. And that infuriates you."

Dan knew the governor was right, so he listened more intently.

"You want so badly for everyone around you to see and to understand that you aren't the guy you pretended to be for the last decade. You want people to understand what Fionna did for you. You want her to get all of the credit she deserves for being the tremendous woman she is. You want to know that people believe you've changed, that you're better. You want to rid yourself of what you took on when you killed him, and your mother wants to throw a party for her friends." The governor shook his head again, and Dan fought the urge to throw his arms around the man who'd always understood him better than he'd understood himself.

"There's nothing wrong with a party, but you understand the difference in the wedding and the marriage. You know which one really matters, and you still feel so guilty for what happened with the baby, for Fionna's injuries, and for her having been so afraid to tell you she was pregnant. So, when your mother made her feel unimportant, when she attacked all of the healing that Kauai offered both of you, you came out swinging because that's who you are. You're her Shield. And you couldn't stand to allow her to be hurt again, certainly not at the hands of your own mother.

"You also can't stand that Marion refuses to see all that Fionna's done for you. But Dan, she can't see it because first she'd have to admit that you weren't okay. She refuses to admit that."

He shook his head. "Here's the thing about life—you can't change what you did. You can't make people open their eyes and see. People will always only see what they want to see and hear what they want to hear. If that weren't the case, about half of the news stations in the Realm would be out of business tomorrow. On the other hand, you do know what she did for you, and you know how much you love and adore that woman and that little girl that God just literally handed to you."

Dan nodded and attempted to dam back tears with his fingers. God, he'd never deserve either of them.

The governor gave him another wry grin. "Maybe put all of the guilt-driven energy you used to chew out your mother into making certain that Fionna and Aida know and never doubt how much you love them. You'll find that the more you feel like you've done right by them, the less your mother's—or anyone else's—opinions will matter to you. It will also convince you over time that no matter how much of Nic Wretchkinsides's energy you took on, it won't change the man you are. And maybe let your mom throw her ridiculous party."

Dan tried desperately to believe Governor Haydenshire's words. He was just so afraid that he'd done nothing more than trap the demon inside of himself.

"You know, Joseph used to say you didn't have to hold all the aces, you just have to play the hand you're dealt well," Governor Haydenshire reminded Dan. "You've had a hell of a game to only be thirty-two years old. No one would've blamed you for throwing the hand in and walking away, but you didn't. Now, you're not only getting to play with a whole new deck, you've turned up the queen of hearts. Play this hand with a little more thought, a little more consideration than you played the last few with, okay? It's just a party. It would make her happy, and it might be a nice opportunity to show off the new Daniel Vindico and his beautiful family.

"You already know life doesn't have to be perfect according to someone else's definition. It just has to be right for the people living it. So, let your mother throw her party because to her that's perfect. You pull your lovely bride into your arms, hold her close, and dance at the party that's for the two of you. Laugh and whisper about how neither of you wanted it at all, and in that moment, realize that you can't change the past. You took him on, and you won. If you're scared he's the reason you ran away tonight, then learn to control your temper and you'll have beaten him again. Let it go, and let Fionna and Aida finish healing you."

Summoning and making the Agusta fly, Dan arrived home in less than fifteen minutes.

"I'm so sorry," he pled as soon as he vaulted through the door. Fionna gave him his smile.

She was drinking tea on the couch. "I'm glad you're home."

"Fi, I'm so, so sorry!"

She reached for him, and he raced to hold her close. "It's okay. It actually means a lot to me that it pissed you off so much, but maybe dropping f-bombs in front of our little girl wasn't the best idea."

Dan squeezed his eyes shut. He wished he could somehow take it all away.

"Is she okay? Where is she?" Dan scanned the room in search of Aida.

"I let her take a bubble bath, and we talked about why you'd gotten so upset. She knows it had nothing to do with her, but you might need to go over that again. I promised her you were coming back after you calmed down. She fell asleep while Kara read to her. She's okay, but we do have to deal with your mom a little differently."

"I cannot tell you how sorry I am." *Learn to control your temper and you'll have beaten him again.* He'd taken down Wretchkinsides, but he wasn't certain he could fight his own base nature.

"This has been a lot lately. It'll be okay. We'll figure it out. As long as I have you, we'll make this work, okay?" Fionna vowed.

She set her mug on the table beside her, and her warm, soothing love began to flow through his hands as she held them.

"Always. I swear to you, I will always be here. I don't know what I was thinking leaving like that. It wasn't to get away from here or you or Aida. I was just so furious."

"I know," Fionna continued to soothe him, to accept him even though he didn't deserve her offered reprieve. "Please stop beating yourself up for this. You have no idea how much it means to me that you think our wedding was perfect. I was a little worried it was only perfect for me and not you."

Shock worked through Dan's sorrow. "No, baby, believe me, I loved every moment of that day and every moment of every day that I get to spend with you. Being your husband, being Aida's dad, everything that's happened, I just freaked out."

Fionna nodded. "If anyone deserved an epic freak-out, it was you. You're still way behind me on the freak-out scale since we started dating, fell in love, moved in together, fell even more in love, ended an evil crime organization, lost a baby, got married, and adopted a little girl in five months' time."

Before Dan could respond, Aida appeared, barely awake and carrying Phoebe. "You came back." Her voice was just a whisper, and she stayed out of Dan's reach. It killed him that he'd frightened her.

Not certain he could take her pulling back, Dan didn't reach for her. "I'm so sorry. I shouldn't have lost my temper like that. Please, baby, believe me, I was never upset with you or with Fionna. And even if I had been, I still shouldn't have yelled like that. And I certainly shouldn't have left. I will do anything to make it up to both of you." He had an overwhelming desire to throw himself at her feet and plead for mercy.

She smiled at him and then brought tears to his eyes as she crawled up in his lap and formed herself into a tight ball.

Fionna's hand flew to her mouth as Dan cradled her closely just the way he cradled Fionna when she formed herself in the same shape.

"It's okay, but when you get mad you're supposed to breathe in roses." She drew a deep, audible breath. "And blow out the candles." Aida blew the breath back out of her mouth.

Shocked by his own smile, Dan chuckled. "Roses and candles. I promise I'll do that next time."

"I don't like it when you leave," she confessed in a heartbroken plea as she clung to him.

"Aida,"—Dan watched as she raised her tear-filled eyes to his—"I promise I won't ever get mad and leave like that ever again, but sometimes Fi and I are going to have to leave and go to work, or the store, or some other place, but we will always come back and get you, sweetheart."

"Like tomorrow." Fionna rubbed Aida's back. "Dan and I are going to go to the arena for a little while because I have to work, but you get to go have breakfast with Garrett and play on the farm. When we're finished, we'll be back to pick you up."

Aida's entire body convulsed as she started to sob. Panic shot through Dan like a bullet. "What's wrong, baby?"

"My mamãe and pai and all of my big brothers went away and then they didn't come back. They didn't ever, ever come back!"

Dan's heart shattered and fell into the pieces that Fionna had so recently put back together. Huge tears flowed down Fionna's beautiful face as Dan attempted to hold both of them.

Suddenly, Fionna drew a deep breath and determination set on her features. "Aida, when I was a little girl, just a little bit older than you, my mommy went away and didn't come back."

Aida's breath caught. She trembled in Dan's arms. She sat up as he tried desperately to soothe both of them.

"She did?"

"Yes, but sweetheart, she didn't want to go away, and your mamãe and pai and all of your brothers didn't want to go away either. They wanted very much to come back to you."

Aida looked unsure.

"If you'd like to tell Dan and me about your mamãe and pai and your brothers, we would love to hear about your family."

Stunned disbelief etched Aida's precious face. "You would?" she whispered to Dan.

He nodded through his own tears. "Very much, baby."

"Sister Mary Francis said I shouldn't talk about them because it made me sad."

Fionna wiped away her tears and kissed Aida's cheek. "She just didn't want you to be sad, but sometimes talking about them helps us not be sad anymore. It helps us keep them safe in our heart."

Dan and Fionna shared a heartbroken gaze. Their precious baby girl hadn't dealt with her crippling losses, and she hadn't even been allowed to discuss them.

"Will you tell me about your mommy?" Aida whispered.

"Sure," Fionna agreed.

Two hours and two mugs of tea created by Tutu out of passion flowers and chamomile later, Dan carried his little girl to her bed. She was sound asleep. She'd told Dan and Fionna what she remembered about her parents and her brothers.

Fionna shared a few stories of things she and her mother used to do when she was Aida's age. Dan had listened intently to every story, soaking them up like life's breath to a drowning man.

He settled Aida's fairy princess quilt over her and brushed a kiss across her cheek.

He smiled as he heard the bathwater running. Several minutes and numerous drops of Tutu's oils later, Dan and Fionna soaked away their arduous night.

"You're an incredible mom."

"It helps to know what she's going through."

"I imagine it helps to be an incredible woman."

She sighed out her disagreement.

He rubbed his hands slowly up and down her back, rubbing the oils into her soft skin. "Governor Haydenshire thinks we should let Mom have her thing." He was still furious about the entire concept.

"I kind of thought that too. It hurts my feelings that to her we're not really married because we didn't do it her way, but on the other hand, I would be hurt if my son got married without me."

Dan didn't comment on the thirty-year relationship between him and his mother that had led to her being cut out of their wedding.

"Honestly, baby, that's why I got so mad. I saw that she was hurting your feelings, and I snapped."

Fionna smiled against him. "I know and that was really, really sweet. Kara told me that you'd never blown up at her like that."

A defeated sigh echoed from Dan's chest. That point did nothing to convince him that his temper wasn't getting worse. Thoughts of why that might be threatened to unravel him.

"I don't know. We've had our share of arguments, but I've never stormed out like that. I saw how hurt you were, and when she said that about Aida, I came unglued. I'm scared about why I did that," he finally confessed to her.

She unleashed the full power of her soothing Receiver's cast. It worked through him, restoring him. "I love you, and I love how much you love us. Even after everything we had to go through to get here. I just..." she choked out, "I can't tell you how happy you make me or how much I love you, all of you, even the parts that scare you. I'll help you work through them. I'll help you do anything." Her tears splashed into the bathwater.

Dan was overwhelmed, but he knew he shouldn't be. She always managed to see the good in him when he saw nothing but bad. She always seemed to understand why he did the things he did even when he didn't understand them himself.

She loved and accepted his every flaw. With every hideous scar, she was somehow able to make him whole in spite of himself. She wound her way inside of the darkest, most battered parts of his soul and soothed the places he'd thought were malignant and dead that no one else had ever been able to access.

"Take me to bed," she whispered. With the implicit offer of her all-consuming healing powers driving him, he helped her out of the tub, gently dried her off, and then set to tend to her thoroughly.

Several hours later, he awoke to a small hand touching his bare shoulder.

"Dan?" Aida sounded terrified.

While trying to get his bearings, Dan sat up and then remembered that neither he nor Fionna were wearing anything at all. He quickly slid back down in the bed. "What's wrong, baby?"

"I had a nightmare," she confessed in a heartbroken whisper.

"Okay." He debated how to proceed. "Go get back in your bed, and I'll be in there in just a minute."

Her lip trembled as she nodded and headed back out the door.

Certain it was his fault for shouting at his mother and then bolting that had given Aida nightmares, Dan pulled on sweatpants and a T-shirt and moved into Aida's room after covering Fionna carefully and heat casting the sheets.

"Phoebe wanted to know if you would lie down with us because we feel safe if you're here."

"Sure, baby." Dan reclined in Aida's bed beside her. She crawled up on his chest, and he cradled her to him. His shield spilled from his pores, filled with his love and fierce protection for his precious baby girl. He held her tightly. He'd never let anything hurt her again. He would keep her safe.

His eyes blinked open hesitantly two hours later when Fionna's lips caressed his cheek. "She's in my spot," she whispered sweetly. He laid Aida beside him in the bed as he sat up and tried to stretch the crick out of his neck and to work the kinks out of his compacted spine. His size didn't lend itself to lying in a double bed with his seven-year-old for any length of time.

"Nightmare," he whispered.

Fionna covered Aida back up. She gazed down at her sweet face as she slept soundly.

They headed to the living room to have coffee before they got Aida up to go to breakfast with Garrett.

"When did she wake up?"

"About four. I'm sure my blowup freaked her out."

"Or talking about her family, or coming to live with us, or having her very own room. She's used to sleeping with a dozen other little girls."

Dan supposed all of that might've been the cause, but he doubled his determination to learn to quell his temper.

When Garrett arrived an hour later, Aida was nervous, but she flew into his arms. He seemed to always bring her peace.

"Dan and I will pick you up at the farm in just a little while. I promise," Fionna vowed.

She gave them a frightened nod but allowed Garrett to move her to his back for a piggyback ride to the Highlander.

They'd phoned Mrs. Haydenshire before Aida awoke to ask if she thought Dan should stay home with her. She'd urged Dan to go with

Fionna, stating that the only way Aida would learn that they would always be there to pick her up would be to prove it to her.

There certainly wasn't a better source of advice anywhere in the Realm, so Dan and Fionna followed her suggestion.

"When we pick her up this afternoon, she'll be better." Fionna begged Dan to reassure her that they'd made the right decision.

"That's the only way." Dan sincerely hoped he was right.

CHAPTER 14

STORMS

GARRETT HAYDENSHIRE

"Aida, sweetie, would you like me to make you something else to eat?" Mrs. Haydenshire asked Aida. She'd had two bites of her egg and picked at the muffin on her plate.

"No, ma'am. This is very good. Thank you for my breakfast."

"Come on, Aida Mae, you always eat for me." She clung to Garrett and refused to get out of his lap. He loved that, but also hated that she wasn't eating and was so thrown by Dan and Fi not being there.

"Dan and Fionna will be here in just a little while, and once you eat, maybe Garrett will take you out and let you feed the guppies in the pond," Mrs. Haydenshire offered.

Aida was intrigued but unsure. An idea sprung to Garrett's mind. "How about you eat your blueberry muffin and then we'll take your picture feeding the fish and send it to Dan's phone, then he can send you a message back."

Her eyes lit. "Really?"

"Really," he promised.

She began eating rapidly as Mrs. Haydenshire and Garrett shared a smile as she went to retrieve Abigail.

The governor looked relieved as well. He winked at Aida as he continued sipping his coffee.

Logan stalked sullenly through the kitchen door. "Sweet!

Blueberry muffins!" His mood improved rapidly. He fixed himself a plate and took his seat.

Garrett knew he was bored out of his mind with Rainer away in the Keys and Adeline working long shifts at the hospital as she fully began her own practice.

Something caught Garrett's eye as Logan scrubbed Aida's head.

"What's that?" He lifted the sleeve of Logan's T-shirt.

"Nothing." Logan jerked his arm away, but he still wasn't nearly as strong as Garrett.

"When'd you get inked?" Garrett studied the decent-sized, banded tattoo that was now circling Logan's bicep.

The governor rolled his eyes. "Why do you all feel the need to do that?"

"It's just something I wanted to do. Ad likes it." The wrath in Logan's reply was unnecessary.

"Tone it down." Garrett gestured his head to Aida but then gave his brother an approving nod. "It looks good. I like it." He didn't comment on the fact that he knew the tattoo was of great significance to Logan. A representation of what he'd been through, what he'd done, and a reminder for him to make each day count in light of all he'd lost and all he'd gained as he'd pulled the trigger on his pistol that fateful day.

"Yeah, I went to that shop that did all of yours." Logan grasped for the camaraderie, and Garrett realized that his brother needed him more now than he ever had before. Garrett vowed to himself to be there for Logan always, just like he'd promised Cal he would be.

They were the only two Haydenshire brothers who'd ever ended someone's life in retribution for something they'd done.

~

Dan Vindico

"Fionna! Fionna! Fionna!" Her name was chanted constantly as they moved toward the arena.

"Are you planning on signing your contract for the next season now that you're married?"

"Did you and Chief Vindico decide to adopt because of the miscarriage?"

"How are you feeling?"

"Are you able to practice"

"Will you be ready to challenge in August?"

"Looks like you've put on a little weight there, Fionna. Are you pregnant again?"

"Are you going to walk away from your career to pursue motherhood?"

"What kind of message does that send to your fans?"

"Do you still consider yourself a role model for young girls after everything you've done?" The questions became more relentless and more rude as the reporters realized she wasn't going to comment.

"Back the hell off! Get out of her face!" Dan demanded of the reporter lecturing her about her public image and being a role model.

⁓

Garrett Haydenshire

"Dan and Fionna have those." Aida studied Logan's arm.

"Have what, sweetheart?" Mrs. Haydenshire reseated herself with Abigail and her bottle.

"Those pictures on their skin that don't come off when you take your bath."

Garrett was pleased Aida sounded like her old self.

He winked at her. "Yep, they do." He didn't want his parents to give her their opinion on tattoos.

"They have two that match."

Garrett nodded as he added more eggs and bacon to his plate. His heart swelled when Aida suddenly kissed his chin. She dropped her fork and squeezed her arms around him.

He followed suit and wrapped her up in his arms. "I love you, Aida Mae."

"I love you too!" she urged with a great deal of exuberance. "Do you know about Dan and Fionna's skin pictures that match?"

"I know some about them."

"Fionna has it on this ankle." She settled back in his lap and pointed to her left ankle. "And Dan has it on his back right here." She stretched to try and reach her own shoulder blade.

Chuckling, Garrett continued to nod. "They got those done together."

"And Dan has another one on his back that's a cross, and he has a yucky snake one right here." She pointed to her chest. "I don't like that one," she admitted hesitantly to Garrett.

"Well." He wondered how to handle that particular bit of information. "The tattoos that Dan and Fionna have mean something important to them."

"And he has one where Logan's is." She pointed back to Logan's bicep.

"What?" Mrs. Haydenshire turned on Logan immediately.

"Mom!" Garrett tried to get her to calm down at least in front of Aida.

"And Fionna has water, and flowers, and a funny shape on her other ankle, and a word I don't know. And she has a tattoo here on her back." She pointed to her own tailbone. "And she also has flowers here, but I only saw the top of it when she took me swimming at the orphanage. I think the rest of the flowers are under where your bathing suit goes, and that's private."

Garrett watched his parents and little brother become extremely uncomfortable. "That's right. It's always private." He'd arrested enough child molesters to know never to let the opportunity pass by to remind her of that.

"Have you seen her flower tattoo?" Aida pierced him with those huge brown eyes. He promptly choked on his bacon.

Swallowing down a large swig of coffee, Garrett shook his head. "I've only seen the top when I went swimming with her. Just like you."

She took another bite of eggs as she considered. "Do you think Dan's seen her flower tattoo?"

After drawing a deep breath and glancing at his parents, who were clearly going to let him fend for himself on this particular matter, he nodded. "Dan and Fionna are married, so I think Dan has seen her tattoos."

He sincerely wished she'd pick a new topic.

"I think so too because they took a bath together last night."

The entire table cringed over her realizations.

"Emily has a tattoo here." Aida pointed to her hip bone. The bath didn't seem to have bothered her. Garrett let himself relax slightly.

"She said it was something of Rainer's. I don't remember what. Have you seen hers?"

"I have seen Em's tattoo."

"Maybe when I'm older, I'll get flowers like Fionna."

Garrett's parents both shuddered.

"Maybe when you're much older." He wondered what Dan would say to that.

Much to Garrett's relief, Aida was quiet as she finished her muffin.

"May I please feed the fish now?" she asked him sweetly.

Mrs. Haydenshire expertly kept Abigail tucked on her shoulder and handed Aida a bag of stale bread from the breadbox. "Just hold Garrett's hand when you're by the lake, okay?"

Aida agreed as she raced out the back door.

Rainer Lawson

"But it's a good idea," Emily insisted for the third time.

"I'm not going to let you cook on our honeymoon. We're supposed to be relaxing and spending time together not cooking and cleaning."

"Those people give me the creeps, and I swear I felt like someone was watching us in the pool this morning."

"Then they got a hell of a show." Rainer shot her a cocky grin.

She giggled. "True, but not the point."

She wrapped her arms around his neck as he rested his hands on her backside.

"They keep asking us if there's anything else we want, so if you just get them to get us groceries, we can cook and eat things off of each other."

"I'll think about it." A grin formed on Emily's face. She thought she'd just gotten her way, but he'd meant what he said. He would consider it.

"What would my beautiful bride like to do this afternoon?"

Her hand moved to his zipper line, and his heartbeat quickened as she began to massage him. "In the very brief time that you've actually left my clothes on, I have been reading a very good book."

Rainer throbbed in her hands. He shuddered from the exquisite sensation. "Oh, so you want to read, baby?" he rasped in her ear as he began kissing from her earlobe to her neck slowly. Taking firm hold of her backside, he thrust against her.

"I could read unless there's something else you want to do." She grasped him tighter with a needy moan.

A low rumbling growl echoed from Rainer's chest. "There are so many things I want to do." His hands wound their way under the T-shirt she'd thrown on after their tryst in the pool that morning.

"Like what?"

"Like this." He jerked the shirt off of her. "And this." He released her luscious breasts from the white satin bra. Her eyes closed as he traced delicate patterns over her breasts, watching her nipples darken and beg for his attention.

"I want to suck you, baby, until you beg me for more. I want you to ache for me to fill you full."

Her body pitched. Her breaths stuttered as she moaned.

He laved her right nipple with his tongue. He flicked it back and forth over the sensitive skin drawn into a taut cherry confection all for him.

Thunder echoed in the distance as the sky began to darken.

"Rainer," she panted as he began to trace his fingers over her mound through her shorts. He wanted to build her desire so high he was her only craving when he finally gave in to his own heady desires and plunged her depths.

"What, baby?"

She continued to pant and writhe in his arms. "It's going to storm."

"I'm right here. I'll keep you safe," Rainer assured her with his customary response for her fear of storms.

"I know." She seemed to force herself to go on. He dipped his hand down the waistband of her shorts, pulled the scrap of lace covering her lips aside, and lightly teased her slit.

She gasped for breath. "Yes," breathed from her as the sweet liquid heat she made for him began to ease around his fingers.

"Tell me, baby. Tell me to touch you."

She trembled in his arms. Her breaths were shallow and quick. "Oh god, I want you to touch me, but don't we need to do something so everything doesn't get wet?"

He forced the head above his beltline to reengage as he pulled his hand away. Thinking about anything but laying Emily out and pounding into her was next to impossible while she was standing topless beside him.

He kissed her forehead as an idea formed in his mind.

"Go get in bed for me. I'll close everything up, and then I'm going to give you some better memories of storms."

As he pushed away the harrowing guilt Emily's terror always brought him, Rainer lowered and attached the huge plastic sheeting that covered every open space of the villa.

Clouds rolled in, darkening the shoreline. Lightning fractured the sky. Emily squeezed her eyes shut and clenched her jaw in an effort not to whimper.

She'd hated storms ever since she was a little girl. All Receivers hated them. He wondered momentarily if Fionna's fear equaled Emily's, but he suspected it didn't.

"You have to stay in my room with me and hold my hand because you're my boyfriend," she'd informed him one day after school when she was five and a spring thunderstorm had darkened the fields over the Haydenshire farm.

"I'm your boyfriend?" Rainer had been shocked. He recalled the excitement he'd felt.

"Yes." Her eye roll made him feel stupid for asking.

"How do you know?" he'd asked innocently.

"Because I said so and because you're my best friend."

He'd followed her to her room, seated himself on the hardwood floor beside her bed, and held her hand.

"I think I have to be Logan's best friend because we're blood brothers, but I'll be your boyfriend." He'd hoped against hope she would agree.

"Okay." She accepted the terms of the deal and that had been it. Their fates sealed inside of her room in front of a checkerboard and against the echoing thunder of the impending storm.

Ten years later, he'd stupidly driven to Norfolk to check on his uncle even though she'd been a disaster all day. She knew something bad was happening. She could feel it.

That day would be the very last day of his life he would ever doubt her abilities. The call had come. Cal had been killed. Emily had raced out of the kitchen into the furious storm. She'd called and called. He'd left his phone in the Mustang. The press had gotten word of Cal. They were all eager to profit off of the pain. Unable to get to any of the other Haydenshires, they'd chased her, and she'd wrecked.

"Rainer, man, you gotta come back. Cal's been killed in Berlin and Em's in the hospital." Garrett had barely managed to get the words out through his harrowing tears.

Throughout her recovery, the day of the funeral, and the day Rainer had left her to keep her safe, she'd projected all of the horrifying feelings, the energy that her body could barely contain, into the unbalanced, violent, electromagnetic energy of the storms.

While sliding the last of the plastic sheeting into place, he kept his eyes locked on hers as he moved back to her. He wondered why he'd never thought to try and replace her harrowing memories of storms with something much more pleasant.

Removing his cutoff shorts and boxers, he climbed into bed beside her. She clung to him fiercely.

"I'm right here, baby." He slid his hands down her torso and removed the shorts and G-string she was wearing. "Just be right here with me. I'll never let anything hurt you. I'll always keep you safe."

CHAPTER 15

SAM AND AIDA

DAN VINDICO

"Good morning, Mrs. Vindico." Dan kissed his way down Fionna's temple to her exposed shoulder.

"Mmm, I love Saturdays that start out like this."

Dan loved them as well. He was thrilled she didn't have to go back to the stadium until the next Monday, that Aida had slept through the night, and that Fionna was naked and curled up next to him, after he'd rocked her luscious body with his own the night before.

"Would you like coffee in bed before our sweet little girl gets up?"

"You know you're spoiling me rotten."

He continued his kisses. "I thought that was my job."

A few minutes later, Dan returned to their bed carrying large mugs of coffee. Fionna gave him that dazzling smile that lit his entire world as he handed her the mug. He wrapped his arm over her as they sipped the warm soothing liquid.

Heaven couldn't possibly be any better than this. He reveled in the contentment he felt holding her safely beside him as Aida slept soundly in the room across the hall in her fairy princess bed.

"I love you," Fionna whispered. Peaceful satisfaction was evident in her tone.

"I love you too, so much." He willed her to understand the depth of his devotion to her.

Suddenly, her cell phone rang on the bedside table. It wasn't even seven o'clock on a Saturday morning, and irritation pulsed through his shield. He'd been thoroughly enjoying a little time all alone with his wife. He wanted her full attention, and he wanted to give her his.

"Great," Fionna sighed as Dan saw his mother's name pop up on her screen.

He pulled the phone from her grasp and narrowed his eyes. "Mom, come on. It's seven o'clock on a Saturday morning."

"Daniel, I thought I might ask Fionna a few things about the invitations. I just got them back from the printers. I don't understand why she has so many middle names. The engraving looks odd, and they need to go out tomorrow."

For the thousandth time, Dan deeply regretted agreeing to this ridiculous reception. "Mom, we told you whatever you want is fine. Just tell us when to be there. Right now, we're in bed."

A warm heat glowed in Fionna's cheeks. Her giggle churned his blood. He fought not to moan.

Dan had phoned his mother and apologized for blowing up at their dinner and had given her the parameters for agreeing to their reception.

He and Fionna were not to be bothered with planning or details of the party. They were spending all of their energy on establishing a firm family foundation for Aida, discussing Dan's future career, and helping Fionna effectively and gracefully end hers. They were also trying very hard to get pregnant, but he'd left that information out when he explained his priorities to his mother.

As planning and executing the reception down to the most minute detail was precisely what his mother wanted, she'd agreed. However, she'd still taken to phoning incessantly to let Fionna know what she was planning in effort to receive praise.

"If she could just leave off Halia, it would look much better. I could rush another printing."

"Mother, leave Fionna's names the way they are," he commanded.

"I could use a little help with all of this." As the martyrdom spewed forth like an erupting volcano, Dan clenched his jaw lest he inform his mother precisely what he thought of her last statement.

"I'm sure you're thoroughly enjoying yourself, but like I said, we're busy. Bye, Mom."

Fionna was still laughing as she laid the phone back on the table by the bed. "I'm glad we were just drinking coffee this time."

Wednesday evening, his mother had phoned six times while he and Fionna had been in the shower doing a whole lot more than drinking coffee. The calls had come after ten at night, so Dan had implemented a curfew when they'd emerged from the shower to find the missed calls lined up on Fionna's phone.

Clearly he was going to have to make a schedule for her. She'd be allowed to phone Fionna once each day between noon and 12:05.

He pulled Fionna back to his chest and they finished their coffee. They discussed everything and nothing and enjoyed the serenity life had afforded them recently.

Just as they were pulling on clothes to lounge around in, a timid knock sounded on their door. Fionna let Aida in and they all returned to the bed.

"Are we still going to get a whole new car today?" she asked excitedly.

"Yep, we're getting a new car," Dan assured her. "What kind should we get?"

"Will it be your car or Fionna's car?"

Fionna's left eyebrow raised as she gave Dan a mocking grin. He'd wanted to sell his Ferrari. He'd argued that he wouldn't ever be able to take her and any of their children in it at the same time, but Fionna insisted that they could have a family car that she would drive and that he could keep his Ferrari at least until they had another child.

"Fionna will drive it most of the time."

"Will my pink flower seat go in Fionna's new car?" She was very attached to the car seat they'd purchased the day they'd adopted her.

"Yep, your pink flower seat will go in my new car just like in Emily's." Fionna kissed Aida's cheek as she wiggled farther down in Dan's arms.

"I think we should let Fionna pick out the car because she picks everything perfect just like my pink flower seat and my fairy princess quilt."

"I think that is a very good idea," Dan agreed.

After taking his girls out to breakfast and watching Aida inhale fried eggs, bacon, and a chocolate chip pancake, Dan drove Emily's Hummer out to Sam's lot.

Fionna had requested that she be able to drive her beloved MR2, Lola, one last time. Dan followed her to make certain that nothing went wrong. Sam had found a buyer that wanted the frame and parts and didn't mind replacing the engine for the deeply discounted price.

Fionna had admitted that she would miss Lola, but that Lola wasn't her anymore and that she was ready to move on with every aspect of her life.

Sam sauntered out of his shop sporting a broad grin. He was wiping his hands on a shop rag, wearing his signature coveralls.

"Well, if it isn't Big Man Vindico and his sweet baby girls. Hello, Miss Aida."

"Hi, Sam. How did you remember my name?"

Sam feigned shock. "I always remember the pretty girls' names."

"You do?"

"Yes, ma'am, I do. And who is this?" Sam touched the top of Phoebe's plastic head.

Aida's eyes lit as she cradled the doll in her arms. "This is Phoebe. She's my baby. Emily gave her to me, and I've never had my very own baby doll before."

Sam let a low whistle slide between his teeth, and Aida grinned from ear to ear.

"Well, Phoebe looks like you must take real good care of her. You must be a very good mommy."

Aida nodded. "I give her a bottle, and I put her dresses on very carefully, and I cover her up with her blanket when she needs to take her nap, and I pat her back like this." Aida flipped the doll over and demonstrated patting her back as Dan and Fionna chuckled.

"Mm-hmm, I knew it. I said to myself, Sam, Miss Aida is just the little girl to take care of Phoebe. Now, should we maybe let Dan and Fionna look at some cars to drive Phoebe around in?"

"And for my pink flower seat."

Chuckling, Sam nodded. "Well, of course. Can't have a little girl and no pink flower car seat."

Sam turned to Fionna. "All right, Mama V, what are we gonna drive Miss Aida and all of the up and comings around in?" He winked at Fionna as she beamed from the thought alone.

"Something safe, but you know, maybe just a little sporty."

Dan chuckled as he kissed her cheek.

"Come over here. Sam'll take good care of you, Mrs. Amazing Wife that doesn't want a minivan." He led Dan and Fionna toward the small gravel lot beside his shop.

"Now, let me tell you, Mama, if you're gonna birth him some boys that are gonna be his size we might as well go ahead and get you a school bus."

Dan and Fionna laughed and gazed adoringly at one another.

Aida lagged behind, picking dandelions as they walked.

"All right, Mrs. Vindico says, *Sam, something sporty.* Big man says, *Sam, I want her in a tank, but you can stick a fancy emblem on the hood if that'd make her happy.*"

Dan nodded his adamant agreement.

"Sam has to try and make Mama and Daddy happy, so here's what I came up with." He gestured grandly to four, brand-new, large SUVs lined up on the lot.

Dan couldn't help but chuckle as he recalled driving Fionna home in one of the Iodex Expeditions and her comparing its size to that of a plane.

"If it didn't get a five-star safety rating before I work on it, I didn't even look. So, we have your Mercedes, your Lexus, your Toyota, and your Infiniti, any of which should make Mama smile and keep Daddy feeling like his sweet girls are safe. They've all got plenty of room for the Big Man and several little ones, along with shopping bags, groceries, and even luggage for taking the babies to the beach."

Dan laughed. "I don't know. You've never seen her shop."

Fionna feigned offense and slapped Dan playfully on the chest.

"Careful now, boy. Don't be saying things like that. She might decide to go out and melt your credit cards."

Aida approached with a small bouquet of dandelions she'd

gathered on her slow journey. Biting her lip hesitantly, she edged toward Sam and presented him with her gift.

"Are those for me, Miss Aida?"

She nodded excitedly.

"Well, thank you, sweet girl." Sam took the flowers and fixed them in the pocket of his coveralls, showing them off proudly.

"I made them for you because you remembered my name, and you said I was a good mommy, and because I like it when you smile and call me Miss Aida."

Sam leaned down and embraced Aida. She squeezed him tight, and Dan knew a very special bond had just been formed. Two souls that the world had taken so much from had just met one another.

After driving and redriving all of the SUVs, Fionna selected the deep-gray Mercedes GLS with all of the upgrades.

After signing the check, Dan agreed to bring it back Monday for Sam to add the enhanced safety features he wanted.

He relocated Aida's pink flower seat from the Hummer to the Mercedes. She was almost as delighted with the new car as Fionna.

"Should we take the Hummer to Rainer and Emily's before we go home?" Fionna quizzed.

Between the Ferrari and his Agusta, they were out of garage space. "Not unless you know how to get it in the garage. I don't want to tip the press off as to where they've moved."

The press was frantic to know where Rainer and Emily were honeymooning. Several papers had been promising location and photographs in the next few days, but Dan was certain they were claims made only to sell magazines.

Fionna sighed. "I can get it in the garage, but I don't want to open their garage door just because it used to be mine. Every paper and tabloid I've seen lately swears they know where they are, but the only pictures are old and obviously taken when they vacationed at Virginia Beach ages ago. We can just leave my car out until they get back. I'm not going to help people hound them relentlessly."

"They'll be back next Saturday, but I really think we need to hide the Hummer as long as we can," Dan agreed.

By the time Dan pulled into the garage and Fionna and Aida spilled out of the Mercedes, they were both grinning ear to ear.

"Tell, Dan," Fionna guided Aida.

"Fionna says because we're girls, we get to name our cars. So we decided to name the new car Lilah because she's Lola's big sister."

"I see." Dan chuckled. "All right, Lilah it is." He brushed his hand on Aida's back as she bound up the stairs in from the garage. "I'm gonna get the paper and mail." He halted Fionna on the bottom step to gain himself a moment with her lips.

"Do you know what Lilah means?" Fionna rewarded him with her naughty grin.

"What's that?" He'd been certain Aida hadn't come up with the name on her own.

"Temptress." Fionna waggled her eyebrows.

"Then I'd say it's perfect for you, my sexy little seductress."

Fionna's energy spun in elation as Dan swatted her backside as she headed in the house.

Finding it oddly satisfying that he could actually receive mail and newspapers at his home now, Dan worked his way through the flash of panic that would sear through his mind as he pulled open the mailbox. *He's dead, and they're all in jail. She's safe. That part of your life is over.* He repeated his daily mantra as he gave a friendly wave to one of their neighbors who was mowing his grass. It was a man that Dan was certain he'd seen dozens upon dozens of times over the last nine years, but had never interacted with in any way at all.

He decided maybe it was high time to cut back the trees and shrubs he'd let cover his home. It was time to live in the light. His girls needed that.

CHAPTER 16
WHAT A TANGLED WEB

He laid the bills and junk mail on the table and opened the paper. Fionna carried in two mugs of the Kona coffee they'd purchased in Kauai, and they settled on the sofa with the large Saturday edition of *The Realm Times*.

"What's my baby girl doing?" Dan quizzed as he flipped through the paper.

"She built a car out of the chairs that go to her coloring table that Daddy got for her in her room. She's pretending to drive Phoebe around. It's adorable. She puts the doll in the back then stops somewhere and puts her in her stroller and they go shopping. She has that old purse I gave her."

Dan tried to listen, but his eyes goggled and his heart seized when he read the headline—"Stories on the Realm's Mind: The Times has Answers."

The stories were broken down into a kind of timeline. Dan's picture was on the front page, the one that had been on his Elite Iodex ID badge. It gave a synopsis of the events that lead to the Tantra takedown.

The next page contained pictures of Dan cradling Fionna in his arms as he raced her into Georgetown Hospital.

What happened inside The Tantra Gentlemen's Club that had Chief of

Iodex Daniel Vindico resigning and making his relationship with Angels Lead Receiver Fionna Styler (Vindico) known to the Realm?

There were then three possible scenarios given by three different reporters.

Fionna sighed as they began to read. One alluded to the fact that Dan might've killed Dominic Wretchkinsides, who they assumed had fired the shot at Fionna. The reporter suggested that the Crown Governor, who was also present, hadn't agreed with Dan's reasoning and had summarily fired him.

Another felt that Dan was vying for Fionna's attention against Garrett Haydenshire, and that they'd fired at one another, and Fionna had gotten caught in the crossfire.

Fionna gasped. She shook her head in outraged disbelief that someone actually believed that either her husband or her best friend would have fired a gun in her general direction.

"Un-fucking-believable," Dan spat.

The third reasoned that someone who'd known about their relationship had phoned Fionna, stating that Dan had been injured in the takedown, and that she'd flown to his side based on the misinformation and had been shot in the confusion.

The next question on the Realm's mind, it seemed, was whether or not Fionna would return for a ninth season with the Arlington Angels.

He started to close the paper, but Fionna stopped him. "No, I want to know what it says, and look, the next story is about Rainer and Emily.

She pointed to a photo of the two of them taken with a long-range lens as they'd said their vows a week before.

It's certainly been an eventful few months for Angels Lead Receiver Fionna Styler now Vindico the story began. *After being named best Receiver in the Realm and receiving a large bonus check for her title, Fionna Styler was involved in the dismantling of the Interfeci Criminal Organization, which culminated at The Tantra Gentlemen's club.*

Fionna was shot and immediately hospitalized where the Realm learned

Rolling his eyes, Dan didn't give a damn why the papers thought Fionna had Adeline all to herself, but he did want to know who had supplied that information.

The Times *learned just a few hours after she'd been admitted to Georgetown that Fionna had suffered a miscarriage of Vindico's child due to the injuries she'd sustained at The Tantra. So, will Mrs. Fionna Vindico continue her successful career with the Angels, or has the notoriously gruff, often militant, and obviously controlling Dan Vindico decided it's time for her to hang up her halo and start him a family? The couple apparently wed on the shores of Waikiki in a private ceremony that even the governor did not attend.*

"They're an island off." Fionna rolled her eyes.

"I ordered you to start me a family!" he spat in infuriated disbelief.

She placed her hand on his forearm and soothed him instantly. "Anyone who really knows you knows that's about as far from the truth as the idea that either you or Garrett shot me."

But the Times *has access to new information on this question that is only being reported here,* was the next ominous statement that had Dan's stomach turning.

to a developing fetus as it can affect the formation of the cells that make Gifted children Gifted.

"Fi, how did they find that out?" Dan was furious. It was no one's business what she'd decided about next season.

"There were a bunch of fans there Wednesday that won a day with the Angels from some sports magazine. That was when they were working on the aegis. Sarrington Sports makes our uniforms and joule meters. It wouldn't have been hard for the *Times* to offer someone a little money to check the orders for next season."

Dan wrapped his left arm over her, giving her a place to hide. The invasion of her privacy had gone several steps too far.

So, though the Times *certainly can't yet tell you if Fionna Vindico is now carrying another of Governor Vindico's grandchildren, it would certainly appear so. We are in constant contact with our sources at Georgetown to find out, and when we know, the Realm will know.*

"Does the *Realm* ever think that you and I might like to be the only ones who know at least for a little while since it is our baby?" Fionna shrieked.

"I'm so sorry, honey." Dan was infuriated with the dogged tenacity of the article but also intrigued with her use of the present tense.

"What does it say about Rainer and Emily?"

Before the shot of Rainer and Emily, Dan read a blurb that stated that Iodex was still working to clean up the rest of the Interfeci. The trials of the members who'd survived the takedown were concluding at the beginning of the week.

Every trial heard thus far had resulted in lifetime sentences in Coriolis, and evidence was flowing like water from sources looking to worm their way out of ties to the fallen men.

Friday afternoon, Governor Haydenshire had assigned Clarence Pendergrath to a two-year rehab work program to take place in New Mexico where a new Gifted prison was currently being dug. It was an exceptionally light sentence, and Dan suspected the Crown Governor had worked a deal with Pendergrath Sr. as Logan's name hadn't even come up at Candor's trial.

There was a statement from Iodex that a significant amount of money had disappeared immediately after the takedown that Iodex was still unable to locate. His brow furrowed. He hadn't heard about any missing money, and he wondered who was leaking information like that to the press.

"That's probably a lie too." Fionna felt his trepidation as he read the line.

He scanned down to the photo of Rainer and Emily's wedding.

It seems Rainer Lawson, who participated in the Tantra takedown that ended with Chief Vindico quitting the force and with Fionna Styler's severe injuries, wasn't thinking too far outside of the box when he booked his and Ms. Haydenshire turned Lawson's honeymoon locale. We have confirmation and upcoming photos of Rainer and the Crown Governor's daughter, Emily, honeymooning on a private island deep in the Florida Keys.

Dan's heart sank. He and Fionna shared a concerned glance.

Emily and Rainer have long been fans of the beach, and it seems Rainer purchased his bride a two-week stay in paradise. But has the honeymoon gone wrong? Has Emily Haydenshire gotten herself in over her head? Did she let her childhood affections for the former Crown's son hide his controlling and abusive ways?

"What?!" Fionna gasped.

Dan shook his head. "You know, *abusive,* like how I demanded that you have me a baby." He was disgusted with everything he'd read thus far.

The paper went on to show numerous shots of Rainer and Emily from their summers at Virginia Beach growing up. There were a few large shots of Emily lying in Rainer's arms recently that Dan assumed were probably from their eventful Labor Day trip.

To prove the point of Rainer's abusive ways, there was a shot obviously taken with an enhanced long-range photo lens of Rainer backing Emily up to the side of the farmhouse dressed in his tux with her in her gown. Though Dan loathed to admit it, Rainer was giving Emily a look that said he would devour her alive if given half a chance.

The last photo was of the very villa on the very island that Dan had checked and rechecked the security of for Rainer. It was from the brochure.

"Dan!" Fionna gasped, "I have to call Emily!" She reached for her phone, but Dan delicately took her hand.

"Fi, baby, wait. We don't know anything yet. Let's not call and ruin their honeymoon when in all likelihood they have a few shots of the two of them on Virginia Beach that they've photoshopped, and then maybe a few more provocative photos that aren't even of Rainer and Emily. If they found them, then the photos will be from a boat a half mile away, and they'd show nothing."

"But you said he took her to the Keys."

"I know," he stated morosely. "But I still think we should wait. I'm certain Governor Haydenshire saw this, and we all know Rainer is taking excellent care of Emily. For now, I think we should just wait and see what comes out tomorrow."

"But I've been having dreams about Rainer," Fionna confessed.

"What?!" Dan demanded.

"Not that kind of dream." She rolled her eyes and shuddered from the thought alone which soothed Dan's panic. "They're really weird dreams where something bad is happening to Emily and he can't save her. They're scary." She willed him to understand how real the dreams had seemed. "Emily is trapped in this weird, mirrored case thing and she can't breathe. I don't know how to describe it exactly, and Rainer keeps trying to get to her but he can't."

"Why didn't you wake me up? It usually helps when we talk about your nightmares." Fionna often had vivid dreams. Sometimes good and sometimes bad, but Dan had always been able to tuck her in his shield and get her back to sleep.

"I don't know, I mean," she hemmed. Her cheeks colored rapidly and she gave him an embarrassed giggle. "I've also had a couple of dreams about Supernova. You know, since Aida started watching the show so much." Her face was now the color of a beet. "I sort of dreamed twice that Supernova hooked up with that pink star girl that plays his luminous assistant Wavelength. He tied her to his lab table, and he did some pretty kinky things with his lightning rod of energy." She managed to explain all of this before they were both doubled over laughing hysterically. "I may never be able to watch that show with her again."

Dan embraced her, still laughing heartily. When he regained his composure, he brushed a kiss on her cheek.

"Baby, when did you start having dreams like these?"

"Just a couple of days ago. I keep waking up either with my heart racing because something horrible is happening to Emily or because Wavelength tells Supernova to make her radiant." She covered her face with her hands as Dan tried very hard not to crack up. He pulled her into his chest, mainly to cover his laughter as he tried to soothe her.

"So, I'm insane, right?" she whimpered.

"You're not insane," Dan vowed in complete honesty. He didn't comment on what he suspected that she *was*, but he couldn't seem to wipe the broad grin off of his face for the rest of the afternoon.

Jean Paul Fitzroy: Captain of French Iodex

"I have extremely good news for you, my friend." Fitz greeted Portwood, whom he was certain was sitting in his new office on a

Saturday, beating his head against the sign on the wall that now declared him to be the new Chief of Iodex.

"I'm listening," Portwood sighed.

"Well, it's sick, but that's Nic Wretchkinsides for you. Apparently, he knew all along about the two operatives that were killed that we'd buried in the Interfeci ranks. We had others, but it seems those were the only ones he was aware weren't actually working for him. This also explains why we would get conflicting information out of them. If he knew, he wasn't going to give them stuff to feed us. Anyway, remember the bizarre codes he sent out from his cell each night?"

"Yeah, I remember. I've been trying to decode the damn things for a week."

"They were to assure a man by the name of Pavel Volkov that he was still alive."

"I'm gonna go with Name a Russian Assassin for a hundred dollars." Portwood chuckled.

Fitz joined his laughter. "Bet it all in Final Jeopardy because the answer is, the Russian assassin I just arrested. Volkov had no dealings with the Interfeci organization. His job was to receive daily texts from Nic, and if he didn't hear from him, to kill our operatives. That was it."

"All right, maybe I'll actually sleep tonight, but what about the missing money?"

"I'm still working on that, but nothing has disappeared in two weeks. Hard to track money that's no longer moving. I think we're ready to officially bury the Interfeci for good. I think it's really over."

Portwood's relieved sigh echoed from DC all the way to Paris.

"And, hey, I'm trying to talk Dan into bringing Fi out here. If you see him, would you tell him he should come? I still don't get the feeling he's really over this." Fitz decided not to mention that he was planning on convincing Dan to move to Paris to work with him again.

"If I see him, I'll tell him, but I'm betting right now he's pissed to hell. The *Times* just ran an article all but proving that Fionna is pregnant again. They also seem to think that Dan might've been who shot her."

"C'est quoi ce bordel!"

Portwood laughed. It seemed Fitz's news had vastly improved his mood. He hadn't laughed in weeks. "Yeah, that was my question as well."

"I bet he is pissed. I'll call him. I just wanted to let you know that we got our last guy."

"Thanks. I think I'll go home and actually spend some time with my wife whom I haven't really seen since I was sworn in."

"Hey, piece of advice—don't do what Dan did. Don't work constantly. There will always be bad guys, but don't sacrifice your whole life trying to catch them a day early. You only get a chance to do it right once, and you're talking to a guy who didn't figure all of this out until I got home one night and realized my kids hardly recognized me."

"Yeah, I'm trying to find a balance. Thanks for that, though. Trust me, I'm not running this office the way Dan did. Ever."

CHAPTER 17

TAKE COVER

RAINER LAWSON

"I think I'm ready to go swimming again." Emily seemed very pleased as she made her announcement Saturday afternoon while Rainer fixed them sandwiches for lunch.

He gave her a wry smile. "I'll have to see what I can do about getting you wet then." The naughty glint in his eye made her giggle. He was thankful she was feeling better, and he felt terrible neither of them had thought to pack painkillers.

He'd had Aldus and Bryna deliver some two days before while Emily lay on the reclined lounge in the sitting area, suffering from cramps.

Trying to answer the repeated questions from Bryna about Emily's health without actually shouting that she was menstruating and to leave her the hell alone had been somewhat difficult.

As soon as they'd gone, Rainer had fixed her tea and cradled her on the lounge in his arms. He'd used a heat cast to soothe her until she was no longer hurting. They'd done nothing but napped, cuddled, and talked for two days straight. She'd set the cast as soon as she'd started, and she seemed back to full health.

He stared at her as he added fruit salad to her lunch plate. She was stunning. Her normally alabaster skin held a healthy golden glow from all of their time in the sun. She was delighted with her lack of tan lines due to the fact that when they'd been on the beach, in the ocean, or out by the pool, she'd been topless.

Rainer was delighted with this information as well but for entirely different reasons. The freckles on her face, shoulders, and arms, that he adored and Emily hated, had made an abundant appearance. He'd taken to kissing each and every one repeatedly.

Emily seemed so happy and relaxed that he hated they only had one week left before they would have to return to work. But he was looking forward to beginning their lives as a married couple. Having a full week without cameras shoved in their faces and their names bellowed everywhere they went had been extremely cathartic as well.

After their late lunch, Emily donned a pair of cutoffs over her bikini bottom along with a white button-down shirt. She tied the shirttails at her waist but never added the bikini top.

She breezed by Rainer carrying her book and seated herself on the lounge by the pool. The unspoken invitation to join her whispered in the humid air.

"So, my beautiful wife wants to go swimming." He paced to her quickly.

With a flirtatious grin, Emily nodded.

He leapt and quickly hoisted her up in his arms. She shrieked. "Rainer, stop!"

"You just said you wanted to swim, baby?"

"Not in my clothes, which I'm running out of because you won't leave them on me, and I don't want those people doing my laundry!"

"Poor thing. You might just have to start going naked."

"Put me down and let me take this off!"

"I think not." He waggled his eyebrows.

"You won't throw me in. I know you won't."

"Oh, really?" He moved to the edge of the pool. "Hold your breath." He couldn't quite do it without making sure she didn't inhale pool water. He tossed her in, but his warning gave her enough time to take firm hold of his T-shirt. She pulled him in with her.

She emerged laughing and threw handfuls of water in his face. He dove under the water, grabbed her around the waist, and pulled her under with him.

They surfaced a moment later. She swam away from him playfully. Everything about the look she gave him dared him to catch her.

As the shirt she was wearing was white cotton, it was now entirely see-through. He wolf whistled as she headed up the steps.

He made it to her quickly, grabbed her around the waist, and spun her around as she shrieked. Instead of dunking her again, he stood and lowered her lips to his mouth.

"See, I did throw you in the pool."

She laughed in his face. "Oh yes, you're so mean. I grew up with seven older brothers, remember? You told me to hold my breath. They never did that. If I swam with them, I was blue for days."

As they climbed out of the pool, he shook his head. "I think I should probably help you out of those clothes, Mrs. Lawson."

"Do you think?" She poked her lip out in a delicious pout.

He grasped the loosened ends of her shirt as he guided her into his arms. "Come here to me, baby." He crushed her mouth to his and peeled the shirt off of her shoulders.

She shivered but not from being cold. The effect made Rainer want to lean her over the lounge chair and make her take him hard and rough.

"But then I'll be cold and naked."

"No,"—he shook his head—"you'll be naked and wrapped around me."

"I do think I need a shower." Her eyes closed in an extended blink as he unbuttoned her shorts.

"I can take care of that." He stopped abruptly, however. He was staring into the villa to check the path to the shower that he was about to carry her to and found Aldus and Bryna staring back at them.

"Oh my God!" Emily choked as Rainer pulled her tight to his chest, keeping her breasts and everything he considered to be his and his alone pressed against him.

"What the fucking hell are you doing here?" he demanded but was unable to move without revealing his wife to the villa staff.

"We've come to deliver your anniversary lunch and your champagne, Mr. Lawson. It's complimentary to our guests who stay longer than one week, of course." He stated this as if Rainer should have known they were coming.

Emily's face burned with her embarrassment, and she kept her eyes shut in her terror. Fury lit through Rainer as he stared Aldus down.

"I never ordered lunch, and I'm getting really tired of your constantly showing up here. And what the hell do you mean anniversary lunch? We've only been married a week!" His argument drowned out immediately.

They'd been married a week. He wondered if that was something he should have remembered as momentous.

Lost in infuriated confusion, Rainer wrapped Emily tighter in his arms. "Leave whatever the hell you came to bring and go!"

"Yes, Mr. Lawson." Aldus looked deeply concerned as they laid a bottle of chilled champagne on the counter with a large platter of food.

"Em, baby, I am so sorry," he pled as he heard the truck crank and drive away.

She nodded against him. Her energy was terror-ridden and frantic.

"Rainer," she finally managed as tears tracked down her face. "Something weird is going on. I can feel it. Please, please believe me. I think we need to go home."

Rainer, please believe me. Don't leave! Please don't go to Norfolk today. Something bad has happened. I can feel it. He heard her almost redundant plea from the past echo in his head.

"Okay, I know. I promise I'm going to take you home." He would never ignore her feelings and intuitions ever again. "You go start packing and I'll call Captain Namphis and see when he can be here." Harrowing defeat settled on him.

"I'm so sorry." Her chin trembled as she stepped away from him.

Rainer guided her back into his arms, back into his shield. "You have nothing to be sorry for. You're right. Something is going on. I should have listened to you when we first got here. We still have a week off of work. We can go anywhere you want or just spend it moving in. I'll honeymoon you in our new house."

Relief flooded through Emily's energy as she nodded against him. He guided her into the villa and pulled one of his Iodex T-shirts over her head, covering her completely.

There had been nothing in any of the extensive research he'd done on the island or the vacation villa about a special week anniversary meal or champagne, and that seemed like something they would have advertised. Rainer pulled his cell from the counter.

Captain Namphis explained that he was flying back from Paris in the next hour but that he could have the chopper there at eight the next morning. He'd need to land it at the Senate to make his next afternoon flight to Paris, so they would need someone to pick them up.

Rainer phoned Logan and gave a hesitant explanation of why they were coming home early. Logan assured him that he'd be there to drive them home and then help them move into their new house.

"I'm sorry, man. That sucks."

"Yeah, I just wish I could figure out what the hell is going on."

"Yeah," Logan choked out. He knew something he wasn't saying.

"What?" Rainer demanded. He'd been best friends with Logan for far too long not to be able to read his tone of voice.

"Well," Logan hemmed. "I kind of thought it was a bunch of bullshit, but now I'm not so sure."

"What's a bunch of bullshit?"

"A couple of papers promised this big reveal tomorrow in the Sunday papers on your honeymoon. But it seemed like this big teaser thing. If they really had something, why wouldn't they have printed it already? Why wait?"

Emily looked pale and terrified as she laid out clothes for her and Rainer to sleep in and to wear home the next day. She piled everything else in their suitcases.

Rainer paced back out to the deck. He didn't want her to hear him. "What kind of reveal?"

"I don't know. It said they were going to tell where you are and what you've been doing. There's no press down there, right?"

"No, there's no one down here."

"Yeah, so it's crap just like I thought." Logan tried to sound reassuring.

"Yeah." Rainer was still watching Emily obsessively. "I sure as hell hope you're right."

He needed to scan the villa for cameras or anything that wasn't supposed to be there, but he didn't want Emily to see him. If he found something, it would be more than she could bear.

Emily laid her head on his shoulder when he joined her at the bed. The sun hung low over the horizon, and Rainer had never felt more lost.

"Will you take a shower with me?" There was no hint of flirtation in her tone, only a haunting fear of being alone.

"Of course, baby."

She wasn't going to leave him, not even for a moment. She was terrified, and he was quite literally her Shield. If there were cameras, he'd make certain they got nothing else, but that would have to be it until they left the next morning.

He guided her into the bathroom and turned on the shower water. He called himself an asshole for what he was about to do. "Hey baby, would you grab me a Dr Pepper?" He had to scan at least this room before he'd allow her to take her clothes off again.

"We're about to take a shower." She was afraid to walk away from him even for a few seconds.

"I know, but I'm really thirsty." He told an outright lie to the woman who meant more to him than drawing his next breath. Her brow tensed. She knew he was lying. He prayed she wouldn't call him on it.

With a deep sigh, she went back to the kitchen. Rainer quickly threw his radar scan all over the bathroom. There was no energy source that shouldn't have been there, at least that he could tell in his haphazard scan.

Emily handed him the drink she'd chill casted for him. "Rainer, what's wrong? I know you're not telling me something. I can feel it." A shivered chill shook through her.

Dammit, Lawson! Get it together! You're scaring her! "I'm just a little freaked by whatever you're feeling and whatever the hell is going on with Aldus and Bryna. And I feel bad I didn't think about this being our one-week anniversary." He left out the rest of his concerns so he was able to tell the truth.

Emily offered him a smile, but it was forced. "I've been in love with you since birth and your girlfriend since I was five. I plan on being married to you for the rest of forever, so one week doesn't really seem all that momentous when we're talking about the rest of our entire life."

"Yeah, that's kind of what I was thinking too." He knew she would see it that way, but he was desperate to do something right by her.

"Come here, baby." Keeping her body as close to his as he possibly could, he undressed her and kept her constantly covered as she entered the shower. He stepped in behind her. She wound her body around his in the streaming warmth. He understood suddenly. In the bathroom, the only room with four solid walls, with a locked door, behind a shower curtain, in his arms, she felt safe.

~

Dan Vindico

"I don't know." Dan sighed as he chatted on the phone with Fitzroy Saturday evening. "I'll talk it over with Fi," he finally agreed. "I'm not saying no. No, no, don't put Maddie on the phone." He drew a deep breath. "Hey Mad, how are you?" He listened to her repeat Fitz's invitation. "I will ask my beautiful bride about it."

Fionna gave him a quizzical grin when he finally ended the call. "Fitzroy thinks I should bring you to Paris next week for a very quick official honeymoon and to celebrate your birthday."

"Oh my gosh, that would be amazing!"

Dan was shocked by her exuberance. "What about Aida?"

"Oh." Her face fell. "Does Fitz not want her to come?"

"No, Fitz and Maddie want her to come. I just didn't know if you'd want to take her on a trip so soon."

"I think it would be a perfect birthday, and that our little girl would love Paris. Governor Haydenshire said we should do educational things with her while she's not in school."

Suddenly, rather excited about the idea of taking his wife and his little girl to the City of Light to see his best friend, Dan called Fitz back to accept the invitation.

CHAPTER 18

THE HIGHEST HIGH, THE LOWEST LOW

Dan's cell phone blared at a quarter of five Sunday morning. While rubbing his eyes, he eased Fionna off of his chest.

"This is Vindico." As he cleared the gravel from his throat, he remembered that he was no longer an officer and no longer had to answer his cell that way.

"I do not care that I fired you! Get up and figure out who did this to my baby girl!" was the Crown Governor's enraged demand.

Dan sat up and rubbed his face. He tried to determine if he was dreaming. He glanced over at Fionna sound asleep beside him. She took his breath away momentarily. Her breasts were swollen once again. They were getting larger by the day, and as Dan thought about what was causing that, he almost forgot that he was on the phone with the Crown Governor.

"What happened to Emily?" He finally formulated an appropriate question.

"Go get your paper!" the governor roared.

Dan crawled from the bed and located sweatpants. He held the phone between his ear and shoulder as he quickly paced down his darkened driveway. The cold concrete bit at his bare feet. He located the paper beside the mailbox. "I'll call you right back."

He rushed back in the house to find Fionna waiting in the entryway. "What's wrong? Who was that?" She was on the verge of tears. "I dreamed about Rainer and Emily again."

Dan was still trying to order his thoughts. He summoned and lit one lamp on the table before guiding her onto the couch beside him and opening the paper.

He extracted a large paper journal with pictures of Rainer and Emily landing via helicopter on Hatchpointe island. *Exclusive Lawson Honeymoon Report* was the title. *What would Crown Governor Lawson think of Rainer now?* was the tagline.

Dan's stomach churned as Fionna's hand flew to her mouth.

"Oh my God!" Dan turned the page to find Emily seated on a reclining Rainer in the oncoming surf. They'd blacked out her nipples, but it was very apparent what they were doing.

"How did this happen?" Fionna began to sob.

"I don't know." Hesitantly, he turned the page, to reveal multiple shots of Rainer and Emily sunbathing. Emily was topless in all of them.

Forcing himself to go on, he read reports that Emily had been sick and Rainer had been denying her food. That he'd thrown her in the pool fully clothed and then pulled her under repeatedly. And that hotel employees had offered help when they'd found Emily sick and lying down in the middle of the day, and Rainer had ordered them away.

There were shots of Rainer and Emily in a large Jacuzzi bathtub together. The positioning of his body coupled with the look of ecstasy on her face made it fairly obvious he was fingering her.

Dan wondered if people would note the look of possessive greed on Rainer's face as support for the claims that he was abusive instead of seeing that she was clearly enjoying the experience.

Another grainy photo of Rainer's right hand around Emily's neck didn't help matters. Dan was certain it had been a gentle caress, but that wasn't evident in the photo.

"I have to call Governor Haydenshire back." He set the paper aside. He didn't want to see any more, and he didn't want Fionna to have to see them either.

The governor answered on the first ring.

"Have you talked to either Rainer or Emily?"

"Yes, they're flying home now."

Suddenly Fionna's face went white as a sheet. "Dan!" she managed just before her hand flew to her mouth, and she raced to the bathroom.

Well, here we go. Dan kept the phone to his ear and raced after her.

"Portwood already has a rapid flight team from Miami heading to the island. All of the rental company's employees are going to be lucky to be alive when I finish with them, but I want to know who the hell paid for this. This was set up long before Rainer and Emily arrived, and I want to know who, and I want to know how, and I want to know now!" Governor Haydenshire shouted louder than Dan had ever heard him before.

Dan rushed into the bathroom and ran a washcloth under cold water. He handed it to Fionna as she stood. He gave her a sympathetic gaze.

As he stood there in awe of his beautiful wife who was most definitely carrying his child, though she seemed confused at the moment as to why she was vomiting at five o'clock in the morning, Dan found the words flowing from his mouth with ease.

"Sir, I'm happy to help any way I can, but I don't have a badge and I'm really not looking to start back at Iodex." He was certain he was about to be on the receiving end of one of Governor Haydenshire's notorious lectures.

"I know that, Dan." He sounded oddly calm and focused suddenly. "But as Rainer's friend, a person who he deeply idolizes and looks to for guidance, as a friend of our family, and a hell of a detective, please be there for him and help us figure out who would do this."

"Of course, but we need to let Portwood run the legal side of this. He can do it. Let me and Fionna be there for Rainer and Emily."

He guided Fionna to him after she'd brushed her teeth. She laid her head sweetly on his shoulder.

"Fine, but if Portwood needs a little guidance?"

"Then I'll be there," Dan assured him. "I promise."

Dan ended the call and wrapped both of his arms around his wife. "Are you okay, baby doll?"

Fionna nodded, but then Dan felt tears leak down his chest. "Fi, what?" He panicked. "Does something hurt, baby? Do you want to go to the hospital?"

"No, I feel fine now. I just kind of wanted to tell you in Paris."

Not certain what to feel in that moment other than the utter joy that coursed through his veins, he chuckled. "I really like knowing right now though." He cradled her face in his hands and wiped away her tears. He gently kissed her forehead. "I love you so much."

Fionna was crying and smiling in equal measure. "I'm not for sure, for sure. I mean I kind of am in the way that I know because I'm a Receiver and I can feel the extra energy, but I'm not sure like I haven't taken a test yet." She stammered and then blushed violently. "I don't even make any sense." She fell back onto his chest as he chuckled.

"Do you want me to go get you one?"

"I don't know. I'm confused, and oh my gosh. Poor Rainer and Emily. This is terrible. We have to do something!"

Dan couldn't take his eyes off her. She was astounding. "Come here to me." He led her to the kitchen. "Wasn't there a box of stuff for this that Tutu sent back with us?" He pulled crates of Hawaiian remedies from the top shelf of their pantry until he located a small box labeled *Hapai, Maylea*.

Overjoyed, Fionna extracted two small canisters of tea bags, a large brown bottle of oil, several smaller bottles labeled *for Maylea's baths*, and two screw-top jars of ointments.

A small, rolled piece of paper fell to the floor. Dan picked it up and handed it back to her. She slowly unrolled it, and renewed tears sprang to her eyes.

She handed Dan a small photograph. He wrapped her up in his arms and studied the photo of Fionna's mother. She looked so much like her it was astounding. Her stomach was swollen rather full of Fionna. She looked ready to pop.

There was a note from Tutu explaining that the photograph had been taken the day of Fionna's birth. It included the prescription that her mother had followed throughout her pregnancy. When she would drink the teas, what she'd done with the oils and ointments, when she'd taken baths and what she'd added, and a few other things that Fionna read and studied intently.

"I've never seen this." She held the photograph and instructions like she'd been given a tremendous treasure.

Dan tenderly kissed the side of her head. "Do you want some tea, baby doll?"

He understood that she desperately wanted to follow the very same regimen her mother had used.

Fionna hugged him tight. "Thank you."

He heated a mug of water with his hands and dropped the ginger root and peppermint tea bag inside. Fionna carried everything from the box to the table, reading and rereading the handwritten labels.

Dan supplied her with the tea after adding Kauaian honey per the instructions. He made himself a mug of coffee and tried to sort through the wide range of emotions the morning had provided.

"I don't know how far along I am because even though I had what I think was that one quick period after the miscarriage, I don't really know my cycle again yet. I don't even know if that was a period."

"Okay, but a medio can tell us, right?"

"Yes, but I don't want to go see Adeline at Georgetown. I don't want the press to know. I just want us to know. Last time..." she choked out. Tears swelled in her eyes again.

Dan knelt down beside her as she sat.

"Hey." He cradled her head on his shoulder. "This isn't last time, and I'm over the moon, Fi, really. I want to do this just the way you want, so you just tell me. I'll do anything in the world to make you comfortable, and safe, and happy, okay?"

"I don't want to tell anyone else just yet."

"Whenever you're ready. I'm just glad you told me."

"But I kind of would like to talk to Adeline soon, because I want her to be our medio."

Dan drew a deep breath. He was overjoyed with their news and horrified over what was happening with Rainer and Emily. "I really think we need to be at the Senate to show our support to Rainer and

Emily, and we'll probably either end up at the farmhouse or at their house, so maybe we could talk to Adeline then."

"I was sick last time too," Fionna confessed in a heartbroken whisper.

"I know, baby." He didn't want to keep anything from her this time. He wanted to work through the pain so they could move on with the joy.

"Would you hold me for just a few minutes before we get ready to go?"

Dan stood and guided her back to the living room. He sank down on the sofa, and Fionna curled up in her ball in his lap. He cradled her tenderly and whispered how much he loved her and how excited he was.

"I'm so excited too, but I feel so awful for Emily and Rainer. I'm confused. I'm still really sad sometimes about…you know."

Dan nodded. "Rainer will take care of Emily, and Governor Haydenshire will take care of the sick bastard that did this." He gestured his hand to the paper folded on the coffee table. "Let me take care of you and of this. It's all been a lot lately, and emotions aren't even my power, so for you this has to be overwhelming." He gently rubbed his hand over her abdomen. Her breath caught as she reveled in the sensation. Had he not been so intimately in tune with her body, he would never have noticed the weight she'd gained in the last few weeks that had slightly rounded her midsection. A broad grin stretched across his face.

"I probably won't be able to curl up in my ball after a few months." She sounded distressed.

Dan kissed her cheek. "Sure you will. We'll just have to form your ball around your belly, because I want to hold all of my babies including my baby girl upstairs. So, we'll just have to get a bigger couch or move it to the bed."

"I don't want to tell her yet. You know, in case something bad happens again." Her fear punctured her elation.

"Okay, but please, for me, let's focus on everything that has gone our way. I spent the last ten years of my life constantly thinking about what might go wrong, and you made everything right. Let's just live, really live in the light, because you're my sweet Maylea. You deserve to live in the bright sunshine not hidden away in the dark anymore."

Tears flowed rapidly down her cheeks as she tucked her head under his chin and let him wrap his shield around her.

"Thank you for loving me," she whispered.

"More than life itself, baby doll."

CHAPTER 19
STAND UP

Three hours later, Dan, Fionna, and Aida stood near the jetway at the Senate among every single Haydenshire, every Arlington Angel, every member of Elite Iodex, friends of Rainer and Emily's from school, and friends of the Haydenshires in an endless crowd of people who'd come out to denounce the media and support the Lawsons.

The crowd of supporters were largely outnumbered by the press, however. Portwood looked morose. Dan slapped him on the back. "You'll be fine. You've got this. You're a hell of an officer."

He was nervous that his first official case was going to involve the Crown Governor's precious baby girl. "Yeah, I hope so. This is a disaster. Hey, if I wanted to call occasionally and run an idea by you, would that be okay?"

Dan nodded. "You can do this, but if you need a little help, I'll be there."

Several reporters neared just then. "Folks, here we have the former Chief of Iodex, Daniel Vindico talking with the new Chief, Landon Portwood. Can you gentlemen tell us what you're discussing in light of all that's happened?" The woman thrust the enhanced mic in Dan's and Landon's faces.

With an audible huff, Portwood and Dan both spat, "No," simultaneously. The woman looked highly offended but decided to move on. "Chief Portwood, can you tell us what we can expect once the plane carrying Rainer and Emily Lawson lands?"

With a cocky grin that made Dan proud, Landon pointed out the windows. "If you want to know what the press can expect if after this sickening invasion of privacy and deplorable act, they decide to print any more photographs of the Lawsons, then watch!" He pointed to a plane that had just touched down.

Dan wondered what he had up his sleeve. A moment later, he laughed and gave Portwood a proud nod.

The plane that landed was not Rainer and Emily's. Instead, numerous rapid response Iodex officers out of Miami stalked into the Senate dragging three men and two women, several of them wearing the rental chain's uniforms, through the crowd of press. They were all sporting enhanced cuffs and shackles as they were humiliated on every Gifted television news network.

"Very nice," Dan complimented.

Portwood nodded. "I thought we'd go ahead and set the precedent that if you want to fuck with one of my officers on his honeymoon, it will not end well for you."

Dan offered him his hand which he shook readily.

Governor Haydenshire glowed crimson in his fury as he glared at the men and women who'd been arrested. Mrs. Haydenshire tried to keep him calm, but it was a mighty task.

"How fucking stupid do you have to be to mess with my baby sister? They're gonna want to rot in Felsink because if they get out, I'll be waiting." Garrett finally made his way through the gridlock to Dan and Fionna.

"Yeah, the thing that bugs me is that this wasn't stupidity. It was desperation." Dan finally confessed the gnawing, plaguing thought that had been with him since he'd opened the paper hours before.

"Fionna, can you give us a statement on the Angels' outcry of rage over what has happened to Emily?" In Dan's distraction, a reporter pounced on Fionna.

"It shouldn't only be an outcry from the Angels," Fionna stated very succinctly. "It should be an outcry from the entire Realm. This is wrong on every level. Not only was it obviously illegal, but you've slandered a good man's character, invaded their intimacy and privacy, and embarrassed the woman who's adored him since she was a toddler. You want to know what Crown Governor Lawson would think of Rainer now? Let me tell you—he would be proud of him because he's a great man just like his dad. I cannot believe the Realm would allow Joseph Lawson's son to be treated this way. Each and every person who pays good money for those ill-gotten photos is just as guilty as the ones who took them.

"Joseph and Rainer both stood up and defended the Realm. Joseph gave his life trying to make this Realm a better place. I think it's high time the Realm stood up for Rainer. The Angels won't stand by and watch you drag Rainer and Emily through the mud, and neither should the Realm!" Fionna spat viciously.

Dan nodded his adamant agreement as he stood proudly beside his wife. "The Vindico household will be canceling their subscription to *The Realm Times* and any other publication that prints the photos, and I would strongly encourage anyone who cares about the things that Joseph Lawson fought and died for to do the same," Dan demanded.

Applause and cheers echoed from the crowds behind him. The cameraman accompanying the reporter eased the camera down, and Dan's eyes narrowed. "You wanna get that camera the hell away from my little girl, or are you looking for yet another lawsuit?"

Visibly shaken from Fionna's diatribe and Dan's threats, the reporter stepped back in front of the camera. "Well, folks, it looks like we are just moments away from Rainer and Emily Lawson's arrival. We are expecting to hear from the Crown Governor himself. He is certainly very disturbed over the photographs and the allegations about his son-in-law, so stay tuned."

Governor Haydenshire stepped to the center of the crowd, glaring furiously at the dozens of cameras surrounding him. "I'm not certain what you want to hear me say," he huffed. "Obviously, I'm furious over this gross invasion of privacy, and the people at fault will be found and punished to the full extent of the law. Let me go ahead and state the only thing any of the members of the press are actually waiting to hear. Any photograph of my daughter or of my son-in-law from their honeymoon that is run in any Gifted news media of any kind will be fined at $250,000 per shot used. Elite Iodex's Chief Technology Officer will be finding every single website that uses the images and charging them as well. Whether Rainer and Emily choose to sue for compensatory damages or not, I will be taking out personal lawsuits against any media organization found in possession of the photographs."

The press reeled from the amount the Crown Governor set on the photographs.

"And let me assure anyone who's interested in the truth, that Rainer Lawson is one of the finest men I've ever had the pleasure of knowing. I could not be more proud that he is my son-in-law, and I can assure the Realm that no one takes better care of my baby girl than Rainer."

Medio Sawyer stepped up. "Let me just add on the heels of the Crown Governor's statement that any photograph of Emily Lawson taken from her honeymoon will not only be considered defamation to her character but also defamation to the Arlington Angels corporation as a whole. The Angels will file lawsuits of their own to recover any amount we feel the photographs have cost either our Junior Receiver or the team."

As reporters turned to their individual cameramen to recap the governor's fury, Portwood's cell rang. He held it up to Dan and Garrett, revealing Rainer's name.

"Hey." Portwood placed his finger over his other ear in effort to hear Rainer over the crowd. "You know what? I can make that happen for you. Give me just a minute, and tell Pete not to make the approach. I'll tap into the radio feed. You just sit tight." He headed toward Governor Haydenshire.

Several minutes later, Portwood stepped to the center of the crowd, sporting quite a smirk. Governor Haydenshire looked somewhat mollified as well.

"I'm not in any way sorry to inform all of you that the Lawsons are a little tired of having their picture taken. In an effort to take care of

Emily, Rainer is having their chopper land at an undisclosed private location."

A broad grin spread across Dan's face. He doubted he was the only one who suspected that the helicopter would be setting down in the Haydenshires' back fields, but the press would not be photographing their arrival.

CHAPTER 20
REGRET

Dan and Fionna joined the Haydenshires at the farmhouse. Rainer looked ten years older. He clearly hadn't slept any the night before, and Dan seriously doubted it was from staying up and honeymooning his bride.

Emily had cried solidly since four o'clock that morning when the governor had phoned them. Her eyes were almost swollen shut. She would move from lying in Rainer's lap, to laying her head on one of her brother's shoulders, and then go back to Rainer.

Adeline and Fionna stuck close by her, willing her to cheer even a little. Aida eventually crawled in her lap and hugged her fiercely. When Aida explained that it made her sad that Emily was sad, she elicited a small smile, which was more than anyone else received.

A knock sounded on the back door as Mrs. Haydenshire was trying to convince Emily to eat something. The Crown Governor pled with her to eat as well. He'd sworn that he'd send out for anything at all, but she'd just broken down in tears again.

Portwood entered carrying several file folders. "We found a wire transfer and the purchase order for the photography equipment in the owner's files, but it's not Langfield, the guy listed as the owner on their website. The actual owner's name is W.E. Bakston Jr. Langfield owns the subsidiary that the island was purchased through, and it seems he makes most of the financial decisions. I'm thinking Bakston has it set up as some kind of tax shelter."

Rainer's brow furrowed, but it was Governor Haydenshire who looked astonished. "You can't possibly mean Wade Bakston owns that island."

Mrs. Haydenshire's eyes closed in what appeared to be defeat.

"Who is Wade Bakston?" Dan finally asked since no one else would.

The governor shook his head. "His father was on the board Joseph and I and your father overturned. He hated Joe above all others when we were at the academy."

Portwood nodded. "So, I'm sure he wasn't difficult to manipulate into agreeing to do this, and he was well paid for this. The cameras were not inside the villa. Miami Iodex is up in the trees trying to find cameras smaller than a pen. Even if you'd scanned the rooms, Lawson, you wouldn't have seen them."

"I don't care." Those were the first words Rainer had spoken in hours.

Portwood gave him a sorrowful gaze as he nodded his understanding. "Well, for what it's worth, the money came from Belgium, and I have a picture of the guy that sent it." He slapped down a black-and-white photo of the back of an average-sized man wearing a baseball cap low on his face.

"The cameras are on their way to evidence. I'm having Miami rapid flight them in. Maybe we'll get some prints off of them. I just wish I understood the reasoning. Surely this wasn't just to get back at Crown Governor Lawson. If they'd taken the photos and tried to blackmail you with them, or they'd gotten more and waited until you were home, that would make more sense. I can't figure out the timing."

"They had everything they wanted as soon as they came in and found Em sick." Abject defeat drowned Rainer's words. "They didn't need to wait. They had plenty of shots by then. They just wanted a good story to go with it. Throwing her in the pool was icing on the cake." His eyes were starting to spin from exhaustion and fury.

"No," Dan uttered the word without meaning for it to verbalize. Every eye in the room turned to stare at him. "Whoever did this needed the money they knew they'd get for selling the pictures, and the papers needed to make back the exorbitant prices I'm sure they paid for them. Neither could afford to wait any longer."

The bitter realization settled on the crowd.

"So, what do they need the money for?" Portwood stated the thought on everyone's mind aloud.

"I don't know yet." Dan continued to ponder.

"Not that it matters after everything else." The governor clearly wanted to change the subject. "I am sorry you were sick on your trip, baby girl."

"I wasn't sick." Emily fumed before turning her entire body so that she was lying in Rainer's lap with her back to everyone else in the house.

Brows furrowed around the room. There had been pictures of Emily on a chaise lounge in the villa looking pale and weary.

"But there was a shot of you…?" Patrick quizzed.

Emily sat up and drew an audible breath. Another round of tears threatened, but she shook her head. "You know what, why not? I was on my period." She returned her head to Rainer's lap. He grimaced but cradled her closely. He draped a quilt over her, trying to let her hide from the world.

All of Emily's brothers shuddered. Dan and Portwood pretended they hadn't heard any of that.

"I'm just gonna go wait on those cameras. I'll let you know what we find out, and I've set up blockades a mile out from around the farm, so you should be left alone," Portwood assured the governor and Rainer.

"Thank you, Landon. I appreciate all of your hard work."

Before he made his escape, Portwood's cell rang. "Hey, man, anything new?"

He was quiet for several long minutes, but a broad grin spread across his face as he listened intently. "No, I'm here now. I'll tell them. Thanks, John."

He ended the call and turned back to the waiting crowd. "It seems both Bakston and Langfield are interested in trying to talk their way out of lengthy stays at Felsink. They turned over the men who paid them to set up the surveillance equipment. As soon as Tuttle got the names, he called Fitzroy. The men were lying low in Arras on the Belgium border. Fitzroy already has them. It looks like there may be a top guy or two who stood to make several million, and I'll find them. I swear, Rainer. But for now we definitely have two major players."

Hope began to permeate the dejected crowd.

"And it seems the *Times* and every other publication who ran the photos this morning have been getting emails and phone calls all day. People appreciate what you gave the Realm, Dan, and when you and Fionna gave the outcry to cancel subscriptions, they listened. Every reputable paper will be running an apology tomorrow and stating that the villa was under surveillance. They're going to vow that Rainer was in no way abusive. I know that doesn't erase what everyone saw, but it's something, and papers, online magazines, and television stations have been turning over their copies readily after you threatened lawsuits if they were found on property, Governor."

Emily regained her composure. She sat up and rubbed her hands over her face. "Really?"

Portwood nodded. "Yeah, like I said, there are obviously a few top guys, and we'll find them. But this isn't how they'd planned on this going. They stood to make millions from the news outlets when the photos circulated. They would've gotten a portion every time they were printed, but the papers are scared. They lost thousands of subscriptions today, so it looks like we put a stop to it."

"And they're going to say that Rainer isn't abusive?" That was clearly the part of the entire scandal that bothered her most.

Portwood offered her a kind smile. "And maybe this will get them to leave you two alone for good."

Fionna and Emily embraced. They both looked relieved to be back together. Emily turned to Adeline next and hugged her sister-in-law. "I'm sorry I was so angry."

"I think if anyone had a right to be angry, it was you," Adeline assured her.

"Landon?" Fionna called sweetly.

"Yes, ma'am?"

"Is there any way at all that we could help them get moved without the press finding out where they are. Maybe, if we did something, it would help get them settled and everyone's minds off everything. And, uh…" She seemed to debate something but went on with, "Receivers need a safe space that's all their own to process everything especially in light of…all of the"—she grimaced—"horrific intrusions."

Landon nodded. He didn't look like he doubted Fionna's explanations in the least. "Are we talking a big moving truck or lots of pickups?"

"Which would be easier? I'll get them whatever they want," Governor Haydenshire vowed.

"Well…" Portwood hemmed.

"The furniture we bought is in a storage place in Alexandria less than a mile from the house." Rainer sounded almost normal again. Dan understood that he needed a purpose. He needed to create the safe space Emily needed to heal. He'd build the thing from the ground up with his own hands if he had to.

"And the wedding presents are already at the house," Logan chimed in. "I took them over while you were gone." He received the next hug from his little sister.

"So, there are just a few boxes in the guesthouse then," Emily concluded.

"If you could get a small moving truck to the storage place, and get someone else to load it without you showing up, then I don't see any reason why you couldn't load the boxes in one of the lesser-known Haydenshire cars and then let everyone take a different path to the new house. I've got blockades up. No one's getting anywhere near the farm."

"That's easy enough." Garrett seemed eager to accomplish something as well.

"Really, you'll help us?" Emily seemed shocked.

"Em, come on. It's us." Garrett rolled his eyes.

Mrs. Haydenshire offered to let Aida help her take care of baby

Abigail and the twins for the afternoon, and Aida had readily asked if she could stay. Dan and Fionna decided to talk to Adeline at the first available opportunity.

❧

Rainer Lawson

"When I think about it, I get sick, like violently ill," Rainer spat as he and Logan walked from the farmhouse to the guesthouse.

Logan knew he needed the distance to talk. "I know, but that one on the beach was the worst of them. You really couldn't see anything but her top half."

"I just don't know how the hell I let this happen. I was so fucking careful!"

"Remember how Dan used to say Wretchkinsides's favorite phrase was everyone has a price. I guess whoever paid for this talked loud."

"She should be furious with me. She should hate me, and she just keeps apologizing." His regret permeated the very marrow of his bones. It sizzled in his shield. "I wish she would scream at me. I deserve at least that."

"Mind if we join you?" Will, Garrett, and Dan caught up with them.

Rainer didn't want advice or anything from anyone except Logan. Why didn't anyone understand that?

"So," Garrett drawled. "Are we more furious that the Realm saw my sister's rack or that people might actually believe that you are somehow abusive when in actuality you worship the literal ground she walks on?"

Turning and narrowing his eyes hatefully, Rainer spat, "You know I'm pretty much pissed to hell over all of it."

Garrett nodded. "They still have the guys Miami arrested this morning down in the Senate holding cells. If you want us to go down there, I feel certain that the guards could be persuaded to leave you alone with them to let you work out your aggressions."

"Don't tempt me."

Will sounded intrigued. "Better yet, maybe all the Haydenshire boys should show them what we think of them picking on our baby sister."

Rainer let the thought of sinking his fists deeply into Aldus's face work through his body. It was a very appealing idea.

"Sure, if you want to go down there and beat the shit out of them, God knows they deserve it, but it isn't going to take back what people saw this morning. Ultimately, it isn't going to make you feel better or make Emily feel better, which I know is what you're really worried about." Dan's tone held no judgment.

Rainer knew if he decided they were all going down to the Senate to work the rental chain employees over, Dan would probably agree to lend his fists, but he wanted Rainer to know what would be at the end of that vengeful journey to nowhere.

"He's right. It won't change what happened," Logan spoke from a knowledge that sounded engrained deeply in his soul.

"You know," Dan offered with a sigh. "I really think people have this idea that we want to know what goes on in other people's lives. That we want to see what happens on their honeymoons behind closed doors. We want our imaginations confirmed." He shook his head. "But I wonder if this time, they didn't push it too far. That isn't what people normally wake up to when they open their Sunday paper. The backlash appears to have been extreme. Maybe things will change. Maybe the Realm will finally demand some morality in news reporting. Or demand the truth or even some facsimile of truth in their papers and on their television screens. Maybe they'll decide that being the Crown Governor's son doesn't give them a chokehold on your life."

"It wasn't worth it!" Rainer defied.

"No, it wasn't," he agreed calmly. "But listen to me when I tell you that vengeance will eat you alive. Emily is in her Hummer with Fi and Adeline crying because you're so angry at yourself. You're out here with the only guy you think might forgive you for what he saw in those photographs when the reality of it is that no one blames you for having sex with your wife on your honeymoon. That's the focus of the trip, after all. Emily isn't going to be okay with this until she knows you've forgiven yourself. I'm married to a Receiver too, remember?"

"One of you has to give in or you're just gonna keep going in circles," Garrett echoed.

Rainer had no intention of forgiving himself today, but he did know that he should listen to wise counsel when it was given. "So you don't hate me?" He finally gave in and let his fear take flight from his tongue. He turned his question on Will, unable to believe that Emily's brothers and her father didn't think him a disgusting jerk.

Will laughed at him outright. "For what, being a good husband to my sister, or being a heterosexual male, and the guy we raised?"

Logan and Garrett nodded their emphatic agreement.

"Did you really think we were upset with you about what's in those pictures?" Garrett seemed truly shocked. "We're upset because no one should have to endure having pictures of that in the papers. Just because something shouldn't be photographed doesn't mean it shouldn't happen."

To prove his point, Garrett slapped Will on the shoulder. "Brooke let you play in the clam shack on your honeymoon, did she not?"

Will laughed. "Uh, and in the limo on the way to the airport, and in the room she got ready in during the reception. And in my old bedroom at Mom and Dad's before the actual ceremony, and we almost got arrested in Paris because we were doing it on an elevator, and I dropped the cast and two old prigs from London almost got a free show."

Everyone cracked up, and Rainer found laughing to be an extremely odd sensation.

Garrett raised his hand to Will as if showing off exhibit A. "Lo, you and Ad did the horizontal mambo in Sydney, didn't you?"

"I am only answering this because you're my best friend," Logan scoffed. "But, hell yeah, and let's see here…on the plane on the way to Sydney."

"We all knew what you were doing. No one thought you were talking," Rainer quipped.

Logan laughed. "And in the castle in the room directly above her father's, and in a dressing room of that mall Lucas dragged us all to."

"What?" Rainer was stunned.

"You got Adeline to do it in public?" Garrett didn't appear to believe Logan.

"Ad's not a prude, and I said a dressing room. We weren't putting on a show, and who could turn me down?"

Garrett shook his head at his little brother. "Trust me, Danny boy had a big ole grin on his face when I got to Kauai and he rented a chalet way out for their wedding night so no one would hear, 'Oh Dan, oh Dan, oh Dan,'" Garrett mimicked in a horrible interpretation of Fionna's voice.

Everyone cracked up. Dan rolled his eyes and shook his head. "It sounds so much better when I get her to say that."

Despite Garrett's best efforts, Rainer was back in the doldrums almost immediately. "Yeah, so you all had sex on your honeymoons, but you don't regret it now, and your wives don't regret everything you did."

"Yeah, well, my girlfriend was pregnant and then got shot because of me. Then she lost the baby which the entire Realm is well aware of, so regret is something I'm very familiar with," Dan reminded him.

"She didn't get shot because of you," Rainer argued.

"Yeah, and Emily doesn't regret marrying you. She doesn't regret what you shared down in the Keys, and together you can regret that there are sick perverts in the Realm, but that isn't your fault either."

Rainer finally laid it on the line. "Look, I really appreciate all of you trying to cheer me up or whatever it is you're doing. But it was my job to protect her, to keep that sacred between the two of us, and I didn't. I didn't keep her safe, which is the only thing in the world that matters to me, so whether it was my fault or not, I still fucked up."

Well aware that concerned glances were being shared all around him, he picked up the pace. He fought the urge to sprint, to have some kind of physical release. He could've run the length of the farm a dozen times and still been furious.

When they reached the guesthouse, Rainer realized that Emily and Fionna had both been crying.

"Are you okay?" He brushed his hand over Emily's shoulder. He wanted desperately to hold her tight, but he didn't deserve the emotional bond.

She wrapped her arms forcefully around his waist and nuzzled her head in his neck.

Unable to stop himself, he cradled her to him. It was where she belonged, and he'd spend the rest of his life trying to make up for letting her down.

CHAPTER 21
LIFE
DAN VINDICO

Dan helped load the majority of boxes from Rainer and Emily's old room into Logan's truck and Garrett's Highlander.

"Why don't you and Garrett go on? I'll ride with either Emily or Dan and Fionna in a few minutes," Adeline urged Logan.

He looked disappointed that she didn't want to ride with him until he realized that the cab of his truck was full of boxes.

"Easier to hide them there than in the bed," Garrett explained. "We're going to the storage facility to make sure no one sees the guys Dad hired to load the truck. We'll meet you at the house in a little while."

"I think we'll just catch a ride with someone else. I'm scared to take the Hummer or the Porsche out at this point," Rainer lamented.

"I'll get them out for you." Dan let his Visium Predilection take over and work through different scenarios to make that possible.

"Will you come here for a minute?" Emily took Rainer's hand.

"Sure," Rainer agreed but looked like he didn't deserve the opportunity to be alone with his wife.

Dan shook his head. Rainer was an absolute disaster.

"Dan," he heard Fionna call.

"Yeah, baby doll?"

She motioned for him to follow her into Logan and Adeline's bedroom. Adeline was standing at the door waiting on him.

His heart thundered as he rushed to follow them.

Fionna's energy was spinning in nervous jagged twists as Adeline closed the door. Dan seated himself beside her on the bed and held her hand. He tried to supply her with calm, but his own nerves were much easier to access at the moment.

"Well, congratulations." Adeline grinned at both of them.

"Thank you," Fionna replied.

"We will have to do this at the hospital whenever you're ready, just to make it into your official file, but I can do a few things here and at least tell you what I can read from the fetus's energy."

Dan and Fionna nodded their understanding.

"And, I just want you to know that I would never, ever tell the press anything. I don't know who talked to the papers, but please know it wasn't me."

Fionna gave her a sweet smile. "We know that. If we thought you had, we certainly wouldn't be asking you to be our medio."

While willing his heart to beat in rhythm, Dan seated himself at Fionna's head and held her hand. Adeline sat beside Fionna's abdomen and eased her jeans past what Dan considered the promised land. She pulled her shirt up to her breast line.

He watched Adeline draw deep breaths and suppress her own rhythms so she could lock on to Fionna's more easily.

"You think you had a period after the miscarriage?" she quizzed quietly.

"Maybe." Fionna shrugged. "If it was, then it wasn't anything like what I'm used to, but you said they might be different now, so I'm not sure. I didn't set the cast because you said not to for the first one, but it only lasted a couple of hours. There wasn't much blood."

Adeline offered Fionna a knowing smile.

"I don't think that was a period, but we'll find out." Adeline turned to Dan and gave him an apologetic look.

"What?" Dan tried not to sound demanding of the woman who was going to get his precious child out of his wife.

"I'm sorry, but would you mind sitting over there?" She pointed to a chair on the other side of the room. "I'm going to be trying to read the energy off nothing more than a tiny cluster of cells. Your energy is really, really potent, and you have a lot of it. It's hard to work around." She tried to explain without sounding offensive.

Fionna giggled. "You're telling me."

"Oh, uh, yeah. I guess." Dan kissed Fionna's forehead and then moved to the assigned chair. He'd wanted to be right beside her for the entire process.

Fionna gave him his smile as he fumed.

"It's just that you're a Double-Predilect, so it's kind of like trying to read four sets of rhythms at once, and the one I'm interested in is the very quietest of them all."

"It's fine." Dan wished she'd get on with it.

"All right, Fionna, you're going to feel me lock on to your energy and then move to the cells in your uterus. Just try to relax."

With one last nervous glance to Dan, she let her eyes close.

While fighting the desperate urge to stand and pace, Dan watched Fionna intently. Adeline's hands were on her lower abdomen, and she was concentrating hard.

"There it is," she whispered. Dan saw Fionna visibly relax which allowed Adeline a deeper read. "Good. Try to ease your rhythms for me. I'm locked on now, so just tell me what you want to know."

"Everything," Dan and Fionna vowed at the same moment.

Adeline chuckled. "Always good when Mom and Dad are in agreement. When you come into the hospital, I can do a full energy scan of the cells, but I don't have the equipment to do that here." She slid her hands closer to Fionna's mound. "The placenta is strong. The fetus is a little bigger than a pea. It's more the size of a tadpole now."

Dan tried to envision that but found it mildly disturbing.

"You're right at seven weeks exactly. So, that wasn't a period. That was just your body getting rid of everything it didn't need so that you could develop this one the way it's supposed to be."

Fionna gasped suddenly.

"What?" Dan leapt from the chair. Tears began flowing down her cheeks. "What's wrong?"

"Dan, we made her on our wedding night in Kauai."

"Her?" He swallowed back tears of his own.

Adeline nodded her agreement. "And her rhythms are almost identical to Fionna's."

She is a child of the land, Dan could hear Tutu's voice echo in his mind.

He couldn't stay away any longer. He flew to the bed. He kissed her forehead.

"I'm sorry." He pulled away when he remembered that he was hindering Adeline's read.

"It's okay. Here, give me your hand, and try to suppress as much of your energy as you can."

She placed his hands low on Fionna's abdomen. "You know Fionna's rhythms better than anyone. Right now their rhythms are almost identical, but the fetus's are tiny and run much faster. Try to move through Fionna's and lock on to what will eventually become your little girl's."

Dan had never concentrated so hard in his entire life. He closed his eyes and worked through Fionna's rhythms.

"Do you feel them?" Adeline whispered.

"Is that her heartbeat?" He felt the tiny rhythmic pulses.

"Kind of. It's the pulse of her energy."

Adeline removed her hands and let Dan fully lock on to his wife and his child.

"This isn't medical knowledge that you'll find in a textbook, but I can promise you there's a reason little Abigail loves the governor so much."

Dan kept both of his hands formed in a loose circle around his developing child while he listened intently.

"She needs to feel your energy regularly. She needs to feel the way you two work together. It will make her stronger. She can feel the bond between you through your rhythms. As she continues to develop, let her hear your voice and feel your rhythms as often as you can."

Adeline chuckled at Dan as he stared dumbfounded at Fionna's stomach, unable to look anywhere else. "Basically my patients' partners all really like me, because I'm telling you to have sex and to keep your hands on Fionna as much as you can for the next seven months."

Dan and Fionna laughed through their tears.

"Is there anything we should or shouldn't do?" Fionna asked.

"No smoking, no alcohol, obviously stay out from under the field aegis, and I assume you won't be signing your new contract."

"Definitely not," Fionna assured her. "Can I have coffee and tea?"

"Yes, but limit your caffeine intake. Drink lots of water, and tea is fine, but decaffeinated fruit or herbal teas that state that they're safe for pregnant women are probably best."

"We're leaving for Paris on Friday. That's okay, right?" Fionna continued to fire off questions.

"Sure. The rhythms are very healthy and embedded strongly. Your uterus recovered nicely. Thankfully, the placenta isn't attached near where you were injured. We will need to keep an eye on the scar tissue as she grows, but I don't foresee any major problems."

A million thoughts seemed to settle in Dan's mind all at once. When he felt his little girl's rhythmic energies, his entire world settled into perfect accord, and he knew precisely what he wanted and needed to do.

"And sex is good for her? It won't hurt her?" Fionna's cheeks were still blazing.

"Sex is good for your relationship and not something the baby will feel in any way other than she'll probably pick up on your emotions from it when she's much more developed. Right now, her energy will just recognize Dan's rhythms joining with yours. You may have to come up with some creative positions for the last trimester, though."

"I'll take care of that," Dan assured Adeline.

"Okay, but please don't tell me about them. For some reason, my patients think I want to know that, and I really don't."

"When will I be able to feel her move?" It seemed Fionna wanted to change the subject.

"It's different for everyone, but at least another two or three months. Try to rest. The first and last trimesters are extremely taxing on your body. Naps are excellent, if you can take them. Low-key exercises like walking, yoga, that kind of thing, are also really great and will help with the birth. If you're comfortable with it, then I'm happy to not see you in the hospital until you're twelve weeks along. You can hide it until you're showing if you want."

"Thank you," Dan and Fionna both vowed.

"And your little girl should be here sometime in the last week of November."

"Wow." Fionna was suddenly overwhelmed.

Dan leaned and kissed her forehead. He caressed her face tenderly. "I love you so much." He elicited more tears.

"Your mom's going to be disappointed in me again." Fionna shivered.

"I'm just gonna let you two talk. If you have any other questions, I'll obviously be with you for the rest of the day." Adeline offered them a kind smile before she eased the door shut.

"My mother can be disappointed all she wants. I'm so excited I can't even see straight. Besides, shouldn't she be disappointed in me? Wasn't that one of my parts of the deal?" His mother could just get over the fact that the Vindico name wasn't going to be passed down unless Fionna wanted to try again in a few years.

"Yeah, well, the whole thing is really your fault." A mischievous grin made the tears on her cheeks gleam in the sunlight from the window.

"That's right, baby doll. All mine." He winked at her, as she grinned ear to ear.

"I need new bras. My girls are kinda getting huge." She folded her head down to examine her own breasts.

Dan laughed. "I wasn't going to comment, but I was trying to be really careful with them the last week or so."

"It feels better when you massage them, as long as you're gentle." Renewed heat colored her cheeks.

Dan slipped his hands from her still exposed abdomen to her breasts. They were indeed fevered, swollen, and heavy. Her nipples pulled taut immediately, and he had to remind himself that they were in Logan and Adeline Haydenshire's bed. He fought the ardent desire to soothe his wife's tender pain, to make her feel him, and to let the baby feel his energy.

"So far I really like this pregnancy thing."

Fionna giggled. "You aren't the one that puked this morning."

"That is true."

"How do you want to tell our sweet girl that she's going to be a big sister?" Fionna managed her next question just before her eyes closed and her rhythms began to roll in craving pulses. Dan continued to rub and massage her breasts. He lifted their weight with his hands. She wanted more. He could feel that, but he wasn't certain how to grant her wish.

"Do you want to go home, baby? We could tell Aida and then I could take good care of you."

Fionna shook her head. "No, we promised to help Rainer and Emily move but tonight after my bath."

Dan tried to will away his sudden erection.

"You have to rub this oil and ointment that Tutu makes all over my belly and my boobs every night, so I don't get stretch marks."

"I'm gonna take care of every single thing you need. Don't worry," Dan assured her in a husky growl.

∼

Rainer Lawson

"Please talk to me," Emily finally begged after Rainer had watched her pace in what had been their bedroom before they'd officially become the Lawsons.

He closed his eyes in effort to keep the tears from leaking out of them. He already felt weak and hopeless. Tears would only add to the effect. "I don't know what to say except how sorry I am."

"I know that." She pushed him down onto the floor and seated herself beside him. "I know that you blame yourself for all of this, because you always do, even though none of it was your fault."

Rainer wanted to scream. He wanted to roar. It was his fault. It was all his fault, but he wouldn't yell at her, not about this, not ever. As long as it was his fault, maybe he could somehow fix it. If it wasn't, he'd lost all control and that was terrifying.

"Dad isn't mad at you."

"I'm mad at me! You should be mad at me!" His tone rose viciously, but he forced away his fury.

"But I'm not mad at you," she whispered. "I'm mad at the people who did this," she shrieked suddenly. The difference in her volume from one statement to the next was dramatic. It caught Rainer off guard.

"But you know, the more I think about it, the more I just want to remember all of the great parts and forget the horrible parts. It was an amazing week right up until the point they showed up and I felt that last night, and then Dad called this morning. It was awesome. I got to spend every waking moment with the guy I somehow convinced to marry me, with my very best friend, and we had fun, and we had some amazing sex." She grinned at him, and a slight chuckle echoed from his lungs.

"I loved spending the week with you too, but I let you down. I let everyone down, and I will never forgive myself for not protecting you and keeping you safe. You've given me everything, and I know what that must have cost you. I let someone else take that from you and plaster it all over the news. I don't give a damn if they apologize, or if new laws are passed, or whatever. I let you down. You—the most important person in the entire world to me. I'm supposed to be your Shield."

"I know what happened! But you didn't give someone permission to take and print those. You had no idea what was happening. You didn't let me down, and you never could. It isn't even in you to be able to.

"I fussed on the plane that my eyes were swollen and that I was about to be bombarded with more cameras, and somehow magically you got Pete's flight to Paris moved and had him land us here so no one would see me. Don't you see? You don't always get to be in control, and sometimes really shitty things are going to happen because that's life. But the very first opportunity you had to do something to protect me, even from my own vanity, you moved heaven and earth to give me that. You cannot always protect me, but the fact that you always want to means the world to me.

204

"I don't want to let this ruin my memories of the most important day of my life or the most wonderful week of my entire life," Emily continued. "It was like this huge thing that's really just a small part of really getting to be your wife, of getting to relax with you after the season, and Wretchkinsides, after everything that's happened this year both good and bad."

Rainer was desperate to do whatever she wanted though misery and fury fought for stronghold in his shield.

"Look at me," she whispered. He met her emerald-green eyes, just beginning to clear after all of her endless tears. "I want to move into our new house today, and I want to begin our life as a married couple. This is what I've wanted from the time I was a baby. There aren't many girls who get to marry the guy they've been in love with their whole entire life. We're going to fight this, and I'm going to walk around town and just accept the fact that the entire Realm now knows what an amazing rack I have and how hot you are in bed. And I'm eventually going to get used to the idea that people besides you have now seen my orgasm face," she managed before she cracked herself up.

Not certain how she'd done it, Rainer suddenly found himself joining in her laughter.

When they quieted, she was grinning at him. She leaned to brush a kiss across his jaw. "But I'm going to hold my head up high, because I'm Mrs. Rainer Lawson, and there is nothing that makes me prouder than that."

He gave her a begrudged nod of acceptance.

"Can we talk about something else for a while?" Emily begged.

Perfectly willing to do anything she wanted, he nodded. "Of course."

"Fionna's pregnant. She told us on the way over here, but Aida doesn't know yet. Adeline's in there reading her." Her terror was evident in her tone.

Rainer willed everything to quiet in his mind so he could focus on what Emily was telling him. "Baby, you're going to be a fantastic Lead Receiver for the Angels, and that's really great for them. Don't you think?"

"It is great. They were trying, and Fi really wanted to get pregnant again, after everything. I'm just scared, and I'm really gonna miss her."

He reveled in how naturally it felt to cradle and comfort her, to kiss her forehead, to shut out the rest of the world for just a little while.

"You and Fionna are really good friends. I don't think you have to work with her to still get to see her all the time."

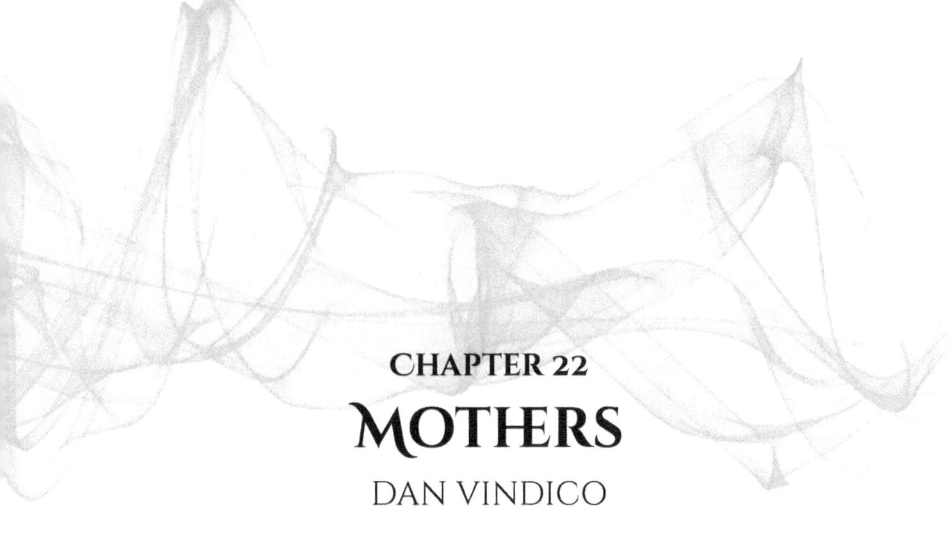

CHAPTER 22

MOTHERS

DAN VINDICO

Dan kept his fingers laced through Fionna's as he followed her out of the bedroom. Rainer and Emily emerged from their room at the same moment.

Whatever Emily had said or done, Rainer did look more relaxed. "I hear congratulations are in order." He offered Dan his hand.

"Thanks." Dan shook Rainer's hand. "And I think I know how to get the Porsche and the Hummer to your new house without the press finding you, but it will require you giving me the keys to your Porsche."

"You got it." Rainer tossed the keys to him.

"What are you going to do?" Fionna gave Dan a wry grin.

"I'm gonna see if I can't get myself followed."

Several hours later, Dan and Garrett were positioning a television on the wall according to Rainer's directional guidance. Logan had already screwed the brace to the wall.

Fionna was trying to hide her disappointment that Rainer had the hardwoods throughout the house replaced before the wedding. She and Adeline were helping Emily arrange the kitchen.

Once the TV was hanging properly, Garrett switched it on and summoned. "Oh, oh, here it is!"

Dan chuckled as he watched himself be chased by numerous news vans. The women joined them. Fionna stood in front of him, and he wrapped his arms tenderly around her midsection. She shot him a pride-filled grin as she watched the screen.

Dan spun the Porsche in an empty parking lot, forming two perfect donuts before he exited feigning irritation. "Why the hell are you following me?"

"Chief Vindico, why are you driving Rainer's car? Did Rainer loan you the Porsche?" The questions preceded reporters tumbling frantically out of the vans.

"No longer Chief Vindico, and yeah, Rainer let me use the Porsche while he and Emily are out of town."

As the reporters began setting up cameras to announce that Rainer and Emily had decided to go on another trip after the debacle with their last one, Dan leapt back in the Porsche and flew away.

As the numerous pizzas Rainer had ordered were devoured, the women began opening the hundreds upon hundreds of wedding gifts that occupied every available surface of the room.

"We have to write six hundred thank-you notes," Emily whimpered.

"Well, this is the tenth coffee maker I've opened, so maybe you could scan and copy them and just change the names," Fionna offered. "But you should keep this one." Fionna held up the coffee maker in her hands. "This is the new Cuisinart one that can be casted, and comes with a grinder, and a percolator, and a double filtration system, and the hot tea maker!"

Emily slid over to Fionna, took the box from Fionna's hands, and then immediately handed it back. "Rainer and I didn't get to give you a wedding present. So, congratulations on marrying your dreamboat, and tell the baby that Auntie Emily is keeping her caffeinated."

"Are you serious?"

"As long as you don't mind me regifting."

"Are you kidding me? Thank you!" Fionna threw her arms around Emily.

"Wait? What?" Garrett's eyes goggled.

Emily's hand flew to her mouth. "I'm so sorry. I thought you'd told him first."

"It's okay," Fionna assured her. "I just don't want Aida to find out yet. I was just about to tell Garrett."

"Are you freaking kidding me? You two work fast." Slapping Dan on the shoulder, Garrett offered him his hand. Then he moved to Fionna and lifted her up in the exuberance of his embrace.

"Speaking of my baby girls, we should probably go relieve the Haydenshires of the elder of the two and take her home and put her to bed," Dan urged, but his gaze must've lingered just a moment too long on Fionna.

"Uh-huh, I think you want to go home and put Fi to bed." Garret laughed.

"Well, she is mine, and she is drop-dead gorgeous."

Fionna rolled her eyes as blood pooled in her cheeks. She clung to the large box containing her new coffee maker, as she stepped over piles of unopened gifts to make her way to Dan.

"Careful, baby." He panicked as he took the box from her hands and then guided her over the stacks of presents.

After they'd given Aida her bath and read her a story, Dan and Fionna tucked her in. She was almost asleep. Her day of playing with the twins on the farm and helping with Abigail had worn her out.

"Can I call Malani before my bath?" Fionna quizzed as they made their way into the living room.

Dan chuckled and studied her incredulously. "Sure, baby, but not too long. You need to get your homework done."

"Yes, sir." She waggled her eyebrows and gave him a naughty smirk.

Dan growled in her ear as he swatted her backside when she shook it for him. "I think I'd like to hear that several times tonight."

He watched her eyes display her intrigue. She shoved Dan down in the chair and crawled in his lap with her phone. Before she could touch Malani's name, her phone rang.

Fionna whimpered and showed him the screen.

He rolled his eyes. "Just don't answer it."

"Then she'll just keep calling." She drew a deep breath and then answered, "Hey, Mrs. Vindico."

Dan began to rub Fionna's shoulders and back. He dragged his fingers softly through her long chestnut tresses. As the heavenly scent of vanilla, coconut, and her own sexy musk reached his nostrils, he inhaled deeply.

His hands slipped to her backside as she listened to his mother drone on about some reception detail that had her eyes rolling.

Dan yanked her shirt out of her jeans and cradled his hands around to her swollen breasts. He traced his fingers along the lines of her bra. He tried to relieve the heat and tender ache as he released them.

Fionna twisted in his lap to study his face. Intention lit his hungry eyes. Her lips spread in a broad grin of challenge. She was clearly intrigued to see just how far Dan would go while she talked to his mother.

"All mine, baby doll," he whispered in her other ear. He cupped the swollen flesh and lifted their weight, giving her relief. Her breath tangled in her throat, but she tried to keep up her end of the conversation.

"Oh, uh, yeah. Tomorrow night should be fine," Fionna agreed, but her body was trembling, and she was beginning to pant.

Dan let her nipples, drawn tight in need of relief, glide between his thumb and the side of his index finger. He gripped her breasts again. She laid back against him, giving her body over to his pliant touch.

With his right arm supporting her breasts, his left glided to her jeans and unbuttoned them quickly.

"Mrs. Vindico, I need to run," Fionna pled, but his mother didn't even hear her request as she continued her incessant chatter.

Dan let his finger delicately trace over her satin panties. She trembled from the sensation.

The storm in her eyes was mixed with heady relief. Her body

clearly wanted more, so he pushed farther, homing in on her clitoris. It was throbbing but hadn't yet bloomed.

"Oh god," she gasped as he began to stroke over it through the satin.

"Uh…uh…I meant, gosh. Gosh, I don't know that all of that is necessary, Mrs. Vindico."

A dark, greedy chuckle escaped Dan. "Your sweet little clit needs to be sucked, baby doll. It aches, doesn't it?"

A slight moan escaped her, but she covered it well.

Slowly Dan edged his fingers under the thong as Fionna shot him desperate looks. "Mrs. Vindico…I…uh…Dan's calling me!" Her voice shook in her need.

With a mischievous smirk, he shook his head. He let his fingertips spread her lips. Her mouth fell open and her eyes closed from the sensation.

"So wet, baby," he whispered in her unoccupied ear. "My good girl. So hungry for me. You need to come, don't you?" He brought his fingers to his mouth and sucked them before returning them to her panties.

She shuddered and tried to quell an all-encompassing moan as he continued to tease and torture her. He dipped his fingers deep inside of her, gathering her dew. Her entire body tensed as she writhed.

"Oh… uh… I don't think…we'll need that," Fionna managed though her eyes rolled back in her head momentarily.

"I've got just what you need, and I'm gonna make you take it all as soon as you shut my mother up," he promised in a husky growl.

"I've really got to go. Yes, we'll see you then." Fionna forced the end of the conversation. Her words turned breathy and uneven as Dan's fingers coaxed her.

She tossed her phone on the couch beside her and shot Dan wild, untamed looks that threatened to make him combust. She turned in his lap and straddled herself over his crotch. She ground fiercely against his erection as he devoured her mouth.

"You are in so much trouble." She panted as he directed his lips to her throat.

With a defiant growl, Dan grabbed her hand and forced her to feel the intensity of his strain.

"What are you gonna do about it?" He kept his hand over hers, showing her exactly how he wanted to be rubbed.

She pushed up on her knees, hoisting her swollen cleavage in his face. "Make you suck me."

With a fervent groan, Dan dispensed with her shirt and the loosened bra completely.

"That's just rewarding bad behavior, sweetheart. Now, bring me those gorgeous tits." He grasped her waist and pulled her breasts toward his mouth.

He bathed her nipple with the heat of his tongue. As her moans grew in intensity, he began to suck. Her body writhed above his strain.

"Yes," hissed from her deliciously.

Dan moved to her left but continued massaging her right with his hand as he suckled and consumed her.

He gasped for breath with his mind full of all the luscious things he wanted to do to her. He dragged his teeth over her nipple delicately.

"Oh god! Yes!"

Dan locked his hands around her waist and guided her body up and down over his cock.

"You feel that, baby doll. You feel how hard you make me? Such a naughty girl. It's gonna feel so damn good when I bury it deep inside of you."

A long, needy moan quaked from Fionna's lungs.

He kept his mouth tending her swollen need. Dan tugged her jeans farther down. He laid her out on the couch and jerked them all the way down her long legs.

"There's something else I want to suck, baby. Spread your legs like a good girl."

Her energy spiked hard. His fierce commands almost pushed her over. "I'm gonna fill you so full," he warned as he dragged his fingertips up and down her slit. "But I want to taste that sweet cum first, then I'm gonna fill you so full of me you'll beg me to set you free."

He spun his tongue around her clit, priming her before he drew it in his mouth and began to suck. Her entire body trembled and her thighs locked tightly against his jaw. Her energy unfurled around him.

She went wild. She climbed up on her knees and pressed her stomach to the back of the couch. Her body rolled in invitation. "Take me. Make me feel it. Nothing will ever feel as good as you inside of me."

Every cell in his body quaked and vibrated in need. Dan unbuckled his belt and dropped his jeans enough to give her what she wanted. "My good girl likes it like that, don't you, baby?" He crowded behind her, and she let her backside slide up and down his throbbing cock.

"Now," she demanded.

With a furtive groan, he grasped her breasts and thrust his cock deep into the depths of her heat, the only relief to his desperate need. "You feel so fucking good. Take it all," he ordered as she met his every thrust, and their energy spun in perfect accord. The erotic vibrations of the two rhythms becoming one drove them to the brink of ecstasy.

That slick wet heat of her body pressed in around him. He pounded into her and then pulled away, coated in her perfection.

"You feel that? You feel us together? You feel how deep I am, how much of you I own."

Her back arched as Dan kept his hands holding her breasts as her body contorted in an erotic display.

"You want more? You beg me like my good girl."

"More! Please!" Her begging nearly ended him. He began riding her again, spinning his hands around her breasts, lightly twisting her nipples, and then kneading the swollen, fevered mounds.

"That feels so good," spilled from her lips in lust-driven passion as she placed her hands over his, showing him how to satiate her needs. It drove him wild.

Her body shook. He kept one hand on her breasts and slid the other to her clit. Her body rhythmically milked his strain. "You're gonna make me lose it, baby. My good girl needs to come with me." Dan felt her swell and her body tense.

With another stroke of her clit as he drove into her from behind, she let go, calling out his name. Unable to fight it, the sensations too overwhelming, too perfect, Dan buried himself deep inside of her and drowned her body in his potent climax.

He fell to the couch beside her and guided her into his lap. He cradled her lax body in his fierce strength. "You are amazing," he vowed reverently.

She gave him a very satisfied grin and giggled. "I'm glad our little girl didn't decide to come find us."

"Me too, 'cause you know once I get you going, you're kinda loud."

Fionna's mouth fell open, and she swatted his chest.

"I love you." Dan laughed and brushed a tender kiss on her cheek that was now glowing crimson from his teasing.

"I love you too, and I am not loud."

Dan smirked. "If you're not making those sweet noises that drive me wild, I'm not doing something right."

She tucked her head under his chin and let him cradle her. "Let's go take a bath."

She stood and Dan pulled the T-shirt he'd been wearing over her head before he closed the snap on his jeans.

"Don't guess we'll be leaving clothes down here like we used to," Fionna pointed out as Dan gathered everything he'd pulled off of her.

"That might be difficult to explain." He followed her up the stairs.

A few minutes later, he helped Fionna into the tub of warm soothing water and then slid in behind her. She reclined against him with a replete sigh. Her eyes closed. Dan could feel her entire body give over to concentration.

"She feels you," she whispered.

His heart stuttered and then flew. Dan was desperate to know what she was feeling. "How do you know?"

"I don't know how to explain it. I can just feel it. But I mean she's just a little bundle of energy so maybe it's more like her energy is responding to yours."

"Here,"—she took his hands and settled them low on her abdomen —"I'll try to suppress mine, so you can feel hers."

Dan let his eyes close in deep concentration as he carefully moved through her rhythms. After several minutes, he felt the tiny quick pulses of what would someday become his little girl.

"Do you feel her?" Tears of joy fell from Fionna's eyes as he nodded. "Does it feel different to you than this afternoon?"

Using every ounce of willpower he could muster, he couldn't feel the slight difference that she could.

"I'm sorry, sweetheart." He was defeated.

Still smiling, Fionna allowed her energy to move back into place. "It's okay. It's not that different. She just feels sort of safe, I think. That's what it feels like. I could also be projecting my emotions onto hers though. She…doesn't really have emotion yet."

"It's amazing. You're amazing. I'm so happy, and I love you so much." He was completely overwhelmed by what he'd felt from his little girl and from his wife.

"Will you still take baths with me when I'm huge?"

He planted a kiss on her head. "Even if I have to have a bigger tub installed."

They sat in soothing silence for several long minutes. Fionna relaxed and suppressed her rhythms again so that Dan could continue to lock on to their baby girl's.

"Oh no!" she groaned.

"What?"

"Uh, well." She giggled. "When someone was distracting me while I was on the phone with his mother, I think I agreed that we would have dinner over there tomorrow night."

Dan laughed and couldn't hide his smirk. "And, I suppose now you're going to tell me that's my fault."

"Obviously."

"It's not my fault you're so damn gorgeous that just the thought of you carrying my baby makes me completely incapable of keeping my hands off you."

Fionna shook her head at him. "You just remember that tomorrow night when we're eating soggy corn flake-covered frozen chicken casserole."

"Okay, no." Dan gagged. "I cannot allow you and both of my precious little girls to have to try and digest that."

"I haven't even told you the worst part," she confessed as the recollections of her conversation with Dan's mother seemed to perforate the memories of their lust-filled lovemaking.

"What's worse than that casserole?"

"She wants to have some guy over that she thinks you should go and work for."

"Dear God," Dan whimpered as he envisioned his mother's pick for his future employer. "Did she say who?"

"Maybe?" Fionna wrinkled her adorable nose.

"It was definitely worth it."

"I'm glad you think so."

"Trust me, baby doll, that was all I'd been able to think about since Adeline told me that the baby needs to feel my energy often, and you told me that these felt better when I massaged them." Dan slipped his hands to her breasts, cupping them in the warm water. He massaged their heavy mass tenderly.

Fionna trembled against him. Dan's body responded, but he doubted she was up for another round just yet. He'd take care of that after their bath.

"Do you think your parents would mind if we walked around their house with your hands on them because it feels so much better when you do that?" She cracked herself up.

"Hold on, I'm trying to envision the governor and Marion's reaction to me telling them that I knocked you up and then explaining to my mother's choice for my prospective employer that helping to support your tits is the only job I'm currently interested in for the next several months." He laughed heartily before continuing. "You know, Mom, I can't eat. I have to keep my hands here." He squeezed her breasts. She laughed hysterically.

Dan reheated the water with his hands, and then moved them back so she could relax against him.

"But don't worry, baby. We've had quite enough of my parents lately. We're not going over there. I'll call them in the morning and bow out. I think I probably should tell them about our next addition." He caressed her belly again and wondered what she would look like in a few months. "Then I'll call Chancellor Wilshire and accept the position so my mother will shut it."

"Are you sure that's what you want to do?" Fionna lost all sense of teasing banter as she leaned back to gaze up at him.

"I'm not sure, but I'm taking the job. I would be in charge of recommendations to Iodex, so I would still be connected there. And I have this completely incredible wife, and I'm gonna have this amazing little girl. And they both need to go back to where they were made on a regular basis. I already have this precious, amazing, seven-year-old who I want to be there to see grow up. I want to be at every recital, every birthday party, every single thing, so if I teach, then I'll be home when Aida's home. Every summer after graduation, I can take all of my girls to Kauai, and we can spend several months relaxing, and resting, and being a family." He explained all of the many reasons he was going to take a job he was fairly certain he was going to hate. The time he wasn't at work was all that was going to matter.

Tears flowed rapidly down her face as she hugged him. "Are you certain? I don't want you to do something you don't want to do just so the baby and I can go back to Kauai."

"Fi." Dan swallowed back the emotion that had come on him suddenly. "A lot of innocent people lost their lives at my hands whether I pulled the trigger or not. I want to give back. Maybe, somehow, I can teach these kids how to really build a Realm that doesn't allow people like Wretchkinsides and organizations like the Interfeci to get a foothold. It means a lot to me to feel like I could better the Realm instead of damaging it. So, I'm certain this is what I want to do, and I was thinking there's really no reason we shouldn't leave for Kauai after Paris and this ridiculous reception."

"Oh my gosh!" Her energy flew, and Dan reveled in her overwhelming bliss. "We can live on the farm in one of the guesthouses, the one where you and Garrett stayed. The girls can have one room and we can have the other. Tutu and Papa will be thrilled."

"Good, because I'm really thrilled to be able to do this." It was incredibly cathartic to finally look forward to everything his future held.

"And you know our little girls can even spend the night with Tutu and Papa sometimes, so I can show their daddy just how much I love him and what he means to me."

Dan gave her the moan she was after. "Sounds like a plan, but we may just have to quiet you down a little because I plan on spending most every night of my summer vacations wrapped up deep inside of my beautiful wife." Her excitement and elation mixed in equal doses in her rhythms.

She turned in the water to indulge him in a fervent kiss. As they eased apart, she grinned. "And you're sure you're not doing this just so you'll be there to terrify all of the boys away when Aida starts dating at the academy?"

"There really are a lot of advantages to this job, but I'm confused by this *Aida starts dating* concept." He feigned mystification as she laughed at him outright. "If you stupidly decide you wanna date one of my baby girls, you fail." He shrugged flippantly.

He helped Fionna step out of the tub and dried her off. He located the ointment and oils, made of kukui, shea, and coconut, that Tutu had prepared. He guided Fionna to the bed, lathered his hands, and tenderly massaged everywhere she instructed.

"I'm still hard for you, baby. You up for another round?"

She gave him a needy nod.

"I'll be gentle this time," he promised.

"I don't want you to be gentle," she begged.

When he finished with the ointment, he lay beside her, giving a prayer of fervent thanks for all they'd been given as he took his wife yet again.

CHAPTER 23

RESTORATION

RAINER LAWSON

Still horrified over everything that had been in the paper, Rainer refused to stop working.

"I'm kind of tired," Emily hinted.

He gazed at her sweetly. "Go on to bed, baby. I'll finish this, and then I might try to get my office sorted out." He gestured to the new dishes he was frantically loading in the dishwasher.

Emily shook her head and continued to unload the box she was working on. Rainer heard the slip of metal and rustle of the papers. He didn't raise his head. He was too busy willfully shutting down the images that haunted him.

His wife topless on a beach with him right beside her. His hands on her breasts, making love to her in the quelling tides displayed for all the Realm to see. That was his. Those images didn't belong to anyone but him and Emily. It just wasn't fair. How could he have let this happen? He shuddered and worked faster.

"Rainer, we never went through this box. Look, there are letters from your parents." Emily looked like she was to blame for him never going through the safety deposit box that Governor Carrington had given him on his twenty-first birthday so many months ago.

He shrugged. "Yeah, we don't have to keep them." He couldn't stand to even consider what his father would think of what had been in the papers.

"We are not throwing these away." Emily stared at him like he'd lost his mind. He was fairly certain he had. Defiantly, she picked up one from the top of the stack and unfolded it.

He went back to work.

"Oh my gosh!" she gasped as more tears escaped her tired eyes.

"What? What's wrong?"

"Just read it, please."

Rainer took the notebook paper and stared down at his mother's handwriting.

Joe,

I took Rainer over to Stephen and Lillian's today. You've been gone for so long I can't remember which city you're in now, but I know that you're doing all of this for me and for our precious little boy. He's growing up so fast. You should have seen him and Logan playing with little Emily today. She's adorable and already has Stephen wrapped around her finger.

Today, while Lillian and I were baking, Emily followed Rainer into the bathroom. Lill found them with Rainer's jeans and Superman Underoos down around his ankles, and with Emily's little sundress up around her neck.

Emily requested that she be able to touch it to which our son replied that he had to ask his mommy. When we stopped laughing, I realized that it's like watching my son's future unfold before my eyes.

They're kismet. I just know it. He's barely four, and he already looks after her constantly. He told Patrick not to be mean to Emily after he'd pulled her little pigtails. The older boys found the bathroom story hysterical, of course. Rainer told them that she is sweet and soft. I'm not certain whether or not she let him touch, but I suspect that might be what he thought was soft.

I can see the look on your face and hear your laughter as I write this. He reminds me so much of you. You're always so protective of me and willing to do whatever it takes to make certain that nothing bad ever happens to us.

They ran that photo in the paper again today. The one of us protesting at the academy. I never realized when I pulled my bra and blouse off that day that when you actually became Crown Governor, they would print it constantly. But just think, everything we worked so hard to end, you've ended.

You rewrote the constitution, and I'm married to the Crown Governor. You've made the world a better place even if your wife got a little carried away trying to prove a point at a protest so many years ago.

Anyway, I'm rambling, and that picture usually upsets you even though I still say they were so much perkier then I don't mind the Realm still thinking I look like that.

I wish I could hear you laughing at me. I wish you were here to tell me that you still think I'm beautiful even if our baby is almost five and I haven't lost one ounce of the weight I gained carrying him. I love you so much. I'm counting the days until you'll be back in my arms.

Love, your Magpie

More emotion than Rainer was capable of sorting through flooded his mind. He tucked the letter from his mother behind the following piece of paper.

Emily moved closer. She'd only read the first page.

Rainer's chest physically ached as he ran his hands over his father's even balanced script. The reply to his mother's letter was dated a few days later and had been written on hotel stationery.

My baby Magpie,

I saw the picture in the paper Monday, sweetheart. I bought every copy in the newsstand just to torture myself as to what I'm not getting to see and feel because of my own absence. That picture has always driven me mad. It's a horrible tidal wave of confusing emotion. When you whipped off your bra to protest the abuse of women by the Realm, that's when I knew you were it for me. But when I see other men buying the paper, all of my work for peace and negotiation, my speeches on cooperation and tolerance, go right out the door. I want to sink my fists into anyone who's ogling my beautiful wife, who is still just as beautiful today as she was baring it all at eighteen years old for the causes she believed in.

You tell Rainer I said to behave. It takes quite a bit of pluck and grit to go after a redhead with Stephen Haydenshire for a father and seven older brothers. I'm certain it won't be too many years until Rainer won't be informing Miss Emily Anne that he has to ask your permission before letting

Emily was sobbing, and Rainer couldn't make sense of any of his feelings. *A horrible tidal wave of confusing emotion* summed it up very well. He read and reread the correspondence between his parents.

Rainer shook his head and forced his heart and then his soul to believe the fact that his father loved him no matter what. That he was proud of him, and had, to some degree, lived Rainer's deep regret and then gone on to become Crown Governor. He'd even joked about the photo with his mother.

"He loved you so much," Emily vowed.

Nodding, he waged a futile war against tears of his own.

"And you know what, you are here to tell me you love me and that I'm beautiful, and to feel me deep in your soul, and you keep shutting me out."

"I'm sorry." He refolded the letters, knowing he'd been given one of his most treasured possessions. He set them aside and pulled Emily tightly into his embrace.

"And I'm totally telling all of my brothers that you touched me first," she declared as they both began laughing through their tears.

After convincing Rainer to take her to bed in their brand-new home, Emily emerged from the bathroom wearing a delicate, white lace nightie. It barely skimmed her backside and was completely see-through.

Rainer's breath seized in his lungs as he took in the innocent white lace that obscured nothing at all.

He was unable to take his eyes off her, as a deep guttural groan reverberated from his lungs. "You're not gonna make this endlessly punishing myself thing easy are you?"

"You didn't do anything wrong." Her face held no traces of makeup. She'd cried too hard that morning to ever apply any. But her cheeks held a healthy, rosy glow from their hours in the sun.

Tiny, adorable freckles dotted her cheeks, shoulders, and nose. She was perfect. Her long, thick, auburn mane hung over her shoulders, slightly tousled from their day. Her skin glowed pink where she was flushed for him. Her nipples were already puckered and dark under the tiny lace design of the gown.

She wound her arms around his neck. Rainer moaned as he let his hands slip up the hem of the tiny nightgown. He needed to feel her flesh in his hands. He needed to cling to his saving grace.

"You wanna touch it? Apparently, I'm sweet and soft."

A genuine laugh overtook him. "Oh, I know, baby. Nothing could ever feel as good as you do." Against his best efforts to continue his self-torture, the relentless terror he'd felt for the entire day ebbed away in the healing power of her.

"I want you." Her whispered plea made his heart race as his trousers restricted uncomfortably.

"God, baby, I don't deserve you."

"That isn't true. Now kiss me."

Her intoxicating energy moved through him as she slipped her hands up the back of his shirt. Rainer groaned his defeat.

He traced his hands up over the lace and leaned to devour her mouth. He wanted her. He wanted her desperately. He added to the intensity of his kiss. He longed to consume her. She was his, and no one else's. His need to claim her took hold. He throbbed in desperate need to restore her, to restore them.

"No one knows we live here," she whispered furtively. "No one even knows we're in DC. No one will ever see any of that ever again." She soothed his debilitating pain.

"And you know what," she continued as he kissed down her neck and grasped her backside. He kneaded it firmly, plying her flesh, feeling her meld into his touch.

"There is so much more to this, to us, than what was in those pictures, because they didn't show how much you love me. How you always know the perfect spot to kiss, and lick, and touch, or the way you always take my breath away when I feel you inside me."

He groaned from desire to hear her breath catch and the quaking moans that he elicited.

"No one will ever know those things except for the two of us." She slowly popped the snap on his jeans and lowered his zipper. She dropped to her knees in front of him, and he groaned in dire anticipation.

"No one knows that you like it when I do this."

The heat of her breath as she slipped her tongue deliciously around his ridge made him weak. His body shuddered from the overwhelming sensation.

She shoved his jeans and boxers down and drew him in. A growl thundered from his chest as she sucked.

She worked her way back up, kissing along his cut lines, and then pulled off his shirt. She flicked her tongue over his nipples, making him pant.

She was astounding. When he'd felt hopeless, she'd restored him. When he felt the harrowing grief of the loss of intimacy, she'd supplied more without end.

"Take me to bed." Desperate need perforated her plea.

His eyes flashed in voracious hunger. Rainer pulled off everything he was still wearing and eased the lace up over her curves. "You are so beautiful. I can't stand that other people saw you. You're mine," he demanded futilely.

She led him to their new bed. "All yours, and you're the only person that knows where my birthmark is."

A slight chuckle escaped him. He leaned and kissed just behind her right ear where she had a small red mark in the shape of a slightly misshapen heart that had been there her entire life.

Heat crept seductively up from her breasts and settled in her cheeks as she went on. "No one knows that I have dimples on my butt that I hate, or which side of my lip I bite when I'm nervous. No one makes me laugh the way you do or smile just because they came into the room. No one makes me feel like the most beautiful girl in the whole world. No one but you."

As Rainer let her tidings wash over him in a soothing balm, she crawled in the bed, took his hand, and guided him with her. "I need you."

He let his hand glide from her neck over her breasts. His fingertips teased over her abdomen and then traced her delicate mound, swollen ripe for him.

He shut out everything else and sought only to soothe their pain. "I need to touch you, sweetheart. Spread your legs for me."

His gravelly commands had her writhing. She did as she was told. He dipped his fingers gently between her folds, feeling the wet heat begin to prepare her for him.

He reveled in his knowledge of her. No one else would ever know the sweet hidden-away spots that drove her wild at his touch, or the way she felt as she clenched tightly around his fingers and then around his cock. The heady spasms that quaked through her body when he brought her. The way she tasted. The delicious moans she made for him. The way she called out his name when she was close. That was all his, and no one could ever have that.

He worked her over with his hand, adding to the friction and the force as she began to grind against him.

"Yes!" Her body arched as she pulled him deeper.

"Let it go for me, baby. Give it to me," he commanded.

With another fervent stroke, he pushed her over as she moaned his name.

He sealed her off immediately as her energy unfurled in potent arcs. He covered her with his body and pushed his shield over them both as he slid his throbbing cock against her clit.

She moaned and bucked underneath him.

"Please," she begged in desperation. "Please, I want you inside of me."

She trembled underneath him. His need was far too great to draw it out. He longed to own her, to bury himself inside her, and to drown out the world that was simply more than he could handle. It had him pushing inside of her hard and fast. He formed her around his throbbing length and made her all his own.

"Yes," spilled from her lips as she arched her back, taking him deeper.

He pumped her full, filling her, feeling the tight, hot perfection open for him and then nurse away everything that had gone wrong.

She was his. Made for him alone. He felt the depth of their energy spinning and casting in ecstasy as he made them one.

Her moans were unending. She clenched tightly around him as she swelled with each fervent thrust.

"Come on, baby. Just give it to me. You're all mine," he urged as she writhed under him.

Her breath caught, and she grasped the sheets under her and clung to them as he pushed her over.

Her orgasm drove his, and he buried himself deeply inside her. He drowned the tedium of the world in the mix of their releases.

CHAPTER 24

OF INTIMATE IMPORTANCE

Sun drenched the bedroom, and Rainer gazed sweetly at Emily sound asleep on his chest. He didn't want to awaken her. He was thankful she was sleeping so peacefully after everything they'd been through the day before, but he missed her. He wanted to talk to her, have coffee with her, and listen to her laugh at his stupid jokes. He wanted to flirt with her and watch her grin and roll her eyes. He wanted their life back.

He couldn't undo what the Realm had seen in the papers the day before, so he tried to think of what his father's advice would be if he'd been there to give any.

Life's not fair. And, *If you can't change it, what can you learn from it?* echoed in his mind, two of his dad's favorite quotes.

He let his thoughts drift to what was supposed to be in the paper that morning and wondered how he might go about getting one or two without letting anyone know where they'd moved and alerting the press to the fact that they hadn't flown to an undisclosed location to continue their honeymoon.

Suddenly, his heart hammered to the tune of someone knocking on their front door.

After debating chambering his pistol, Rainer eased away from

Emily. She was exhausted and barely stirred as he pulled the covers back over her.

He located a pair of jeans and shoved his pistol in the back before he closed the bedroom door. He edged to the windows beside the front door. The pent-up air escaped his lungs.

Quickly stowing the pistol in his holster hung in the hall closet, Rainer opened the door for Governor Haydenshire.

"I'm sorry, son. I didn't mean to wake you. I wanted to bring you these before I went to the office, and I figured you and Emily might not want to be out and about today."

"Thanks." Rainer took the large stack of newspapers from his father-in-law. He still couldn't bring himself to look Governor Haydenshire in the eye.

"Do you want some coffee or something, sir? Emily's still asleep." His voice was abashed and childlike. He cleared his throat but doubted that would help.

"Sure." The governor studied Rainer as he edged into the entryway.

Rainer slid packed boxes, wedding presents, unwrapped but not unboxed, and packing blankets to the sides of the hallway so the governor could get through to the kitchen.

"We got like seventeen coffee makers. I think this is the one she wanted to keep." Rainer lifted a duplicate coffee maker to the one Emily had given Fionna and began unpacking it.

Chuckling, the governor gave him a wry smile. "It's all right. I'd take you looking me in the eye and understanding that I'm not upset with you over coffee anytime."

With a defeated nod, Rainer raised his eyes to meet the governor's.

"She is my baby girl, and I know that's a drum I beat way too loud way too long, but you're her husband. As much as I might not have really wanted to see photographic evidence of your honeymoon,"—he chuckled as blood pooled in Rainer's cheeks—"you and Emily did precisely what you're supposed to do on your honeymoon. And as much as I will try desperately not to think about it, that is a large part of what makes a marriage strong, so I do sincerely hope that you and Emily make intimacy a vital part of your lives."

Rainer tried to be mature and to stop wishing that he could melt into his brand-new hardwood kitchen floor.

"Though I don't yet know who would have done this, I really don't believe you could have been more studious or careful. I also believe that unless you and Emily had honeymooned in her loft in the barn, they were going to find you."

"Then that's where we should have stayed," Rainer defied.

The governor drew a steadying breath and shook his head. "Lillian has given birth ten times. She's been pregnant thirteen. All my doing. We may not have had to endure someone photographing our sex life and putting it in the papers, but we do have numerous examples of the fact that we have an extremely healthy physical relationship.

"And people have talked for years. I usually just smile because I always assume if you want to denounce another man's wife and children, if you want to drag his marriage through the muddy pits of gossip, then perhaps you should spend a little more time working on your own.

"That's awfully crass, I know, but you're talking to the guy who's accused on an almost daily basis of not getting anything done in the Senate because I'm too busy in my bedroom," the governor urged vehemently. "Recently, the Senate was working on purchasing new heat and bullet energy syncs for the vests and coats Iodex officers wear." He gestured his head to Rainer. "Obviously, they're extremely important, and several companies were vying for the business as the Senate contracts generally provide quite a bit of money due to the vast order size."

Rainer nodded his understanding.

"It came down to two different companies who both make the latest, greatest heat sync. One company marginally outbid the other, so Governor Willow and I called the CEO into my office to award him the contract and place the large order. He and his CFO sat across from me and began telling me that they would have the syncs ready quickly because they would work their crews around the clock to fill the large order. Then the CEO began bragging and joking about the fact that because of his dedication to his work, he and his wife hadn't slept together in years. He said this with a great deal of pride." Governor Haydenshire shook his head.

"I gave the contract to the other company. Not being intimate with your wife is not okay, and joking about it with me is disrespectful to her. It tells me there are numerous problems with the marriage that need to be healed. He was obviously a man with his priorities so far out of whack, he somehow thought I would be pleased with his work ethic.

"There's a lot going on inside of that marriage, and there's a reason he threw himself into his work. I have no idea what might be going on between him and his wife, but he needs to stop working, go home, and communicate with her until they figure out how to solve whatever has come between them." He opened the copy of *The Realm Times* that he'd brought and slid the front page toward Rainer.

"All I'm saying, son, is that people are always going to talk, but the more you're happy with your decisions the less you need other people to be happy with them. No one makes my baby girl smile the way you do. She lights up when you walk in the room. She soothes when you hold her hand. She always has, so I'm gonna tell you like I told Dan a few days ago—try focusing on keeping her happy and doing things that build a firm foundation for this marriage. And yes, that means being intimate on a regular basis with Emily." He kept his eyes locked on Rainer's without so much as a grimace. Rainer had to smile.

"Worry less about what the Realm is chattering about because next week it will be something different, and I certainly hope that you and Emily will be married for the rest of your lives."

Rainer pulled the paper toward him. "If I knew how to work this coffee maker, sir, I swear I'd make you some."

Governor Haydenshire laughed heartily. "Read the paper, son. I have to go to work."

"Oh, you're not working at home today?" Rainer teased.

Sporting the original version of the Haydenshire smirk, the governor shook his head. "That's what my lunch hour's for. Now read."

"Wow." Rainer shook his head in disbelief.

"It's a day late and several dollars short, but maybe we're getting somewhere." Governor Haydenshire shrugged.

"Yeah, maybe."

The governor stood. "It's a new day, and you have a week off in your new house, so maybe spend the rest of your honeymoon making a home with my baby girl. If you play your cards right, just like your old man taught you, you'll find this home with my baby girl inside of it will be better than any island paradise you could ever have found."

"Thank you." Rainer knew Governor Haydenshire was correct. He always was.

He pulled Rainer into his embrace. "I love you, son. I always have."

Rainer nodded his acceptance of that. "I love you too, sir."

"Let her sleep. She gets cranky if you wake her up." The governor gestured up the stairs on the way to the front door.

"Oh, I know."

They laughed together. "Call if you need anything at all."

"Yes, sir. We will." Rainer watched the man who'd raised both him and his wife give him his kind, reassuring smile and then slip out the front door.

Rainer eased back into bed. Emily immediately crawled back on his bare chest, making him chuckle. "Hey there, baby."

"Were you talking to Daddy, or did I dream that?"

"He brought the papers by, and I can't even figure out how to put that coffee maker you picked out together or I'd make you coffee."

She sat up and rubbed her eyes before giving him his favorite smile.

"We have a whole week and no one knows we're here, so we can hang out, unpack, and have lots of sex, and you can give me baths, and then we can have more sex, and we can get everything in the house arranged, and make it our home, and then have more sex." She beamed.

"That sounds perfect. The only problem is we have enough dishes and cookware to feed an army, but we have no food other than leftover pizza."

Rainer was captivated by her replete smile. It was a new day, and she was in his arms. That was all that mattered.

"Well then, we'll go out and get food, I guess. We can't hide out forever."

"Or we could have leftover pizza for breakfast, and then we have several friends who would be happy to bring us some groceries. Maybe, in a day or two, we'll venture out and see how many flashbulbs go off in our faces."

"Perfect." Emily leaned up to kiss his jaw.

CHAPTER 25

LIFE IS FOR THE LIVING

DAN VINDICO

Dan sauntered into the living room, yawning and rubbing his eyes. He found his beautiful wife curled up on the sofa with their precious little girl.

Fionna was sipping coffee, and Aida was drinking what Dan assumed was probably juice out of a matching mug. He chuckled as he took in his girls watching TV with clear, throwaway shower caps over their dark brown hair which was slathered in a green eggy mixture.

"I like it," he teased.

"We're going to have a beauty morning, and then we're going to get Fionna new clothes and maybe me some too, but I don't think I need any more. I have more now than I've ever had, and they don't pinch," Aida explained.

The child had very few outfits. It still made her uncomfortable when they bought new things for her to wear, so they'd eased up. Dan assumed that Fionna's buying new clothing was probably a strategy to get Aida shopping, so he nodded his understanding of the day's plans.

"How you feeling, baby doll?" He kissed Fionna's cheek as the top of her head was covered in avocado, egg, and olive oil. He brushed a kiss along Aida's cheek as well.

"Better." She'd been up at five vomiting, but Dan had gotten her back to sleep after that. "That tea really helps, and Aida made me a bowl of cereal."

"I would have made more, but I'm not allowed to touch the oven," Aida lamented.

"You took excellent care of me."

"I'm sorry your tummy hurts."

"Oh, it's okay. It only hurts when I first wake up."

"Maybe Medio Hendricks could make you some medicine and then you won't be sick anymore." Medio Hendricks was the pediatrician Adeline had recommended for Aida and all of the upcoming Vindico children. She'd given Aida all of her shots the day after the wedding.

Dan and Fionna shared a glance. He was eager to tell Aida about the baby. Fionna was hesitant, but she smiled and turned off the television.

Dan seated himself on the sofa with his girls.

"Aida, we have something that we've been wanting to tell you," Fionna began. Aida nodded, but she looked worried.

Dan stepped in immediately. "The most important thing for you to know is how much Fionna and I love you, and how special you are to us, and that we always, always want you to be our little girl."

"That's good because I always, always want to be your little girl." Dan's heart swelled rapidly. "I would be very sad if I wasn't anymore."

"Sweetheart, you will always be my girl," he assured her.

Aida crawled into his lap. "What did you want to tell me?"

"Well." Fionna drew a steadying breath. "What would you think about being a big sister?"

Aida's eyes goggled. "Are you going to adopt another little girl?"

"No." Fionna chuckled. "Well, not right now, but I'm going to have a baby, and that means you get to be the very special big sister."

Fear shadowed Aida's entire face. She clung tightly to Dan's chest. "Do you want me to go back to the orphanage?" she asked in a heartbroken whisper.

"Aida, no, never!" Fionna pled.

"No, baby, not ever! You are our baby girl just like the new baby will be," Dan immediately vowed.

"Are you sure you want me and the baby?"

"Yes, sweetheart, we want you and the baby very much, and just because you have a little sister doesn't mean that Fionna and I love you any less, okay?"

Aida studied Fionna closely. "I had lots of big brothers, but I was always the baby."

Fionna cradled her chin in her hand. "And now you get to help, and you can show the baby how to do all kinds of things."

"Can I hold her when she gets here?"

"Of course."

She tucked her head in Dan's neck as he wrapped her tiny frame up in his arms. "We love you so much." He prayed she would believe what they were telling her.

"And I still get to be your girl?"

"You will always be my girl, no matter what."

"And Garrett's girl?" she insisted.

Dan grinned. "And Garrett's girl. Always. I promise."

Slowly, she curled up in her ball in Dan's arms as tears leaked down Fionna's cheeks. "I was kind of hoping you'd be excited."

"Oh." Aida sat back up quickly. "I am excited. I love babies, and I get to be the big sister. I promise I'll be a good big sister and help the baby, but sometimes I like to get all snuggly like that when Dan holds me cause it makes the sunshine come back to my tummy if it gets nervous."

"I don't want you to be nervous," Fionna whispered as Aida reformed her ball, and Dan's heart fissured.

"Will we still have beauty mornings?"

"Yes."

"And I can still have my tea, and you'll still read to me?" She turned her pleas on Dan.

"Every night, baby."

A sweet smile spread across her face as she nodded. "Okay, then, let's have a baby."

"She won't be here for a long while. She still has to grow a lot," Fionna explained.

"Is she inside your tummy?" Aida moved her face inches from Fionna's stomach to study it. Dan and Fionna tried not to laugh.

"Yep, she's in there."

"How did she get in there?"

Their laughter halted abruptly. "Uh," Dan stammered as Fionna's eyes widened. Thinking back, he recalled the last time he'd been asked that by three-year-old Keaton Haydenshire.

"God!" he announced much louder than he'd intended. "God put the baby in Fionna's tummy."

Aida turned to stare at him in shock. "Wow! Is He going to take her out when she's all done growing?"

"Uh, no," Fionna offered with a slight whimper. "Adeline will help Dan and me get her out."

"Is that going to hurt?"

Fionna grimaced, and Dan's shield gave a slight tense. He'd been trying not to think about Fionna going through the pains of childbirth to get his baby girl here.

"It might hurt a little, but Dan will be with me, and after she gets here, you can come give me hugs and make me feel all better."

"I will give you lots of hugs," Aida assured her.

"Can I have one now?"

Aida wiggled from Dan's lap and squeezed Fionna tightly. "I love you so much!"

Renewed tears tracked down Fionna's cheeks. Her tears still crushed him. He rubbed her shoulder and tried to tell himself that Receivers were often emotional. The pregnancy certainly wouldn't help.

"Does that make you sad?" Aida panicked.

"No, sweetheart. It makes me so happy that you're part of our family."

"Can I ask a question?"

"Sure, baby."

"Can I take this off of my hair? It's kind of itchy."

"Oh, I forgot we had this on." Fionna giggled.

She washed Aida's hair and instructed Dan on how to dry it while she showered.

He assumed he hadn't quite achieved the goal when Fionna decided to French braid her hair after his attempt.

"Sorry," he lamented.

"You're gonna have a house full of girls. There's gonna be a lot of hair."

"I'll learn."

While Fionna rectified the hair situation, Dan phoned Chancellor Wilshire to accept the position as the head of Ioses order at Venton Academy.

The knot that twisted in his stomach whenever he considered becoming a mentor constricted with every word he spoke. *This is for my girls. They're all that matter.* He repeated the mantra in his head.

The pay and benefits were lucrative, but all he cared about were the vacation days and paternity leave. He agreed to look over the classes and the schedules that were listed online. He would assign all other mentors in the Ioses department their requested number of classes and hours, but he would be in charge of all senior-level courses. The planning and curriculum development would fall to him. Despite his encouragement, Wilshire was less than enthused with Dan's acceptance of the position.

When his Visium Predilection shifted his shield out of the way, Dan knew something was going on at Venton Academy. Maybe there was something he could do that wouldn't involve college seniors.

After ending that call, Dan phoned his father to get out of the dinner Fionna had unwittingly agreed to the evening before. He tried to rid his voice of the smug arrogance that came from thinking about why Fionna was so distracted.

"Hey, Dad, listen, we've got a lot to do today. I don't think we can make dinner tonight."

"Daniel," the governor sighed. "I already rescinded the invitation your mother gave Cad Larrington."

"Who is Cad Larrington?"

"He's the guy your mother wanted you to meet and work for. His company is barely holding on, and he was hoping your name would save them. I also don't think you'd be too impressed with his loose interpretation of fidelity. She didn't know any of that. She's worried about you. I don't ask for much, but please come tonight. Let's try to mend a few fences."

He couldn't argue his father's point that he didn't ask for much. A sudden thought occurred to him. "Hey, Dad, do you know if there's anything weird going on at Venton?" Governor Vindico was the governor over all Gifted Academies. Maybe he knew what had Wilshire acting oddly.

"I know that the rumor mills are at full capacity, but I have no proof of anything. What does that have to do with you coming for dinner?"

"Nothing, and we'll be there tonight, but we can't stay too late. We're leaving for Paris Friday. I'm taking Fi there for her birthday, and I want Fitz and Maddie to meet Aida."

"Good. I'm glad you're going. I'm glad you're finally living."

"Yeah, me too."

On the way to the mall, Dan and Fionna discussed things they would need to get for the new baby.

"She can share my room. I'm used to having lots of girls in my room," Aida offered from the back.

Dan shook his head. "You keep your fairy princess room, and we'll give the baby her own room."

"But if she gets scared or has a nightmare, she can sleep with me."

"Absolutely," Fionna agreed.

"Can I ask another question but not about my hair this time?"

Dan chuckled. "Sure, sweetheart."

"When the new baby comes out of Fionna's tummy, what will she call you?"

Dan shared a quick glance with his wife.

"She won't be able to talk for a while," Fionna placated. "That's one of the things you can help teach her."

"But when she can talk, what will she call you?"

"Well, she'll probably call me Mommy and Dan Daddy."

Dan was certain his heart couldn't contain all of the love he felt for his precious little girl in her pink flower seat right behind him when she asked, "If I wanted to call you that, would that be all right?"

"Oh, Aida, of course!" Fionna's elated energy was so powerful in that moment Dan felt it flood through him without being in contact with her at all.

"I used to call my other mommy and daddy, before they went away, that wasn't you and Dan, Mamãe and Pai, so I think my heart wants me to call you and Dan Mommy and Daddy just like the baby, because when I think about calling you that, it makes it happy."

Dan was certain he was going to have to pull the SUV over on the interstate as he tried desperately to blink back his tears.

"It makes our hearts so happy too." Fionna tried to choke back a deluge of her own.

"I might forget at first."

"It's all right, baby. You just do it whenever you want to," Dan assured her.

"What are we going to call the baby?"

While trying to wipe away her tears and restore her eye makeup, Fionna hemmed. "Dan and I will have to think about that."

"I can help!"

"Okay, what does my girl think we should name her baby sister?" Dan took his eyes off the road just long enough to wink at Aida.

"Maybe we could name her Wavelength like Supernova's assistant. She's pink!"

Dan choked back laughter as Fionna cringed. "We will definitely think about Wavelength," he finally managed.

Several hours, a few new summer outfits for Aida, numerous bras that would contain Fionna's new cup size, and sandals and sundresses for both of his girls later, Dan begrudgingly loaded his family in the car to go to his parents' home.

Aida gnawed on her lip as she buckled in and clung to Phoebe. She looked terrified. Still feeling deep remorse over the way he'd stormed out when his parents had come over the last time, Dan blamed himself entirely.

"Aida, baby, I promise you I'll be right there the whole time," he vowed for the third time.

"We're just going to have dinner, and you get to play with Olivia. It will be nice, and then we'll come home," Fionna assured her.

"But sometimes I don't know that I'm doing something wrong and it is wrong. What if I do that, and Grandma gets mad at me, and then Dan, I mean Daddy, gets mad at her because she gets mad at me? It will all be my fault. I don't like it when everyone yells. It scares me. I think it would be better if I stayed with Garrett," she insisted. "Please."

Dan swallowed down another knot of raw emotion. "I'm not going to get mad at Grandma, and I won't yell. And you're not going to do anything wrong, baby, because you're such a sweet girl."

"I will try very hard not to. I promise."

"If we get there and you want Garrett to come get you, I'll call him," Fionna promised. That seemed to give Aida peace.

Dan pulled in his parents' driveway to find his father grinning ear to ear and awaiting them. Tim and Meredith were in the driveway with Oliver and Olivia. Kara and Zach seemed eager for them to arrive as well.

"Oh no! Maybe we're late. I thought she said six but I was... distracted," Fionna panicked.

Dan was unable to contain his chuckle.

"Aida!" Olivia buzzed excitedly as Dan opened the doors. "Gramps has a surprise for us!"

"You do?" Aida took Dan's hand. She was uncomfortable receiving gifts.

"I do, sweet girl." Governor Vindico winked at Aida.

"What are you up to, Dad?" Dan had a feeling this was his father's olive branch for what had happened the last time they'd all been together and whatever might be coming tonight.

"I saw these, and it reminded me of the girls. It's spring, so I thought they could use them now." With that, the governor summoned and raised the garage door.

There, where the Land Rover was normally parked, sat two brand-new, pink and purple bicycles complete with tassels on the handlebars. Instead of a basket on the front, there was a baby doll seat in the back, which would hold the girls' most prized possessions. Both bikes had hot-pink training wheels.

"Oh wow!" Aida gasped.

Very nearby was a tiny Harley-Davidson tricycle for Oliver. He clapped excitedly as he toddled over and needed no instruction before he climbed on.

"Thank you, but you didn't have to get me a bike," Aida assured the governor.

He knelt down and beamed at her. "I know, sweetheart, but sometimes Gramps likes to spoil his grandkids." He popped a kiss on top of her head.

"Today has been so many surprises," Aida announced as she let Olivia pull her toward the bikes.

They strapped their dolls in the back as Dan and Governor Vindico strapped helmets on both of them.

"And when I first woke up I didn't even know it was going to be a surprise day. I thought it was just going to be a regular day. But every day here is so great because you get to have breakfast always. And you get to get hugs whenever you want them, and you can have snacks, and play with Phoebe, and read all the books you want. And if you're cold at night, there are more quilts, and Dan will lie down with me if I have a nightmare and hold me like this." She gave herself a tight hug as Kara and Meredith swooned.

"But today was even better because I found out that I can call Fionna and Dan Mommy and Daddy, and Dan held me so my tummy had sunshine, and I got a headband with a purple flower that I can wear tomorrow when my hair isn't braided, and I got new sandals, and I found out that I'm gonna be a big sister, and now I get a bike!"

Fionna covered her mouth, trying to hide her broad grin. She and Dan had decided that telling Aida to keep the baby a secret would be more than a seven-year-old could handle, so they hadn't given her any instructions on the topic. They'd decided to wait and see if she would say anything.

Meredith and Kara were on top of Fionna in a half second.

"Oh my gosh! I'm so excited! How are you feeling? Do you know what you're having yet? Are you going to find out? We should go through Dan's baby book. I just bought the cutest maternity dress at this new store downtown!"

Dan took Fionna's hand and eased her back so he could wrap his arms around her. "Let's let my wife breathe, please."

The governor looked extremely pleased. "Congratulations, son. I had a feeling that might be happening soon."

"Yeah, well, we're over the moon about it, so if it's gonna upset Mom…." The challenge was implicit without him finishing the statement.

"I'm sure she'll be thrilled. Do we know what we're having?" He tried to sound nonchalant, but Dan and Fionna knew if they were having a boy, Mrs. Vindico would be far more pleased.

"It's a little girl." Fionna blinked back another onslaught of tears.

"And we couldn't be happier," Dan spat.

"Of course. I'm thrilled for you. Maybe let me tell your mom. You all stay out here with the girls." Governor Vindico looked relieved with his own plan as he rushed back inside the house.

"Mom will be happy." Meredith lied outright, desperate to soothe Fionna's tears.

"No, she won't." Fionna kept her head buried on Dan's chest. "I don't ever seem to make her happy."

Dan shook his head to protest, but Kara stepped in. "But you know what, you make Dan happy. You and Aida gave him a family and a real life. You don't know how much I used to worry about him. Ask Zach. I cried myself to sleep some nights because he was so miserable, and then he met you, and it was like all of my prayers had been answered. I got my big brother back." She grinned at them. "I still don't know how this happened. I've been married for three years and just have one on the way. You've been married for, like, six weeks and already have two!"

Dan kissed away Fionna's tears as he chuckled. "We work fast."

"But you work." Meredith stepped in. "And it doesn't matter what Mom thinks or what anyone thinks because it works for you."

"They're right, Fi. I don't give a damn what my mother thinks because you and Aida and this little one,"—he gently slid his hand over her stomach—"you're my whole world, and you make my life worth living."

Fionna turned to Kara, and they embraced, both crying together. Dan shook his head in defeat.

Meredith laughed at him outright. "You'll never really understand pregnancy hormones."

A few minutes later, Dan was standing with his sisters and Zach watching the girls ride circles around little Oliver in the very same cul-de-sac where Dan, Kara, and Meredith had learned to ride their bikes.

Tim had gone inside after declaring that the pollen from the cherry trees was giving him a headache.

"Mommy, watch me!" Olivia urged.

"I see you, baby."

Aida seemed to consider as she slowly followed Olivia's path. She bit her lip and was visibly distressed. Dan raced toward her, worried she'd forgotten how to stop.

"Are you okay, baby?" He positioned himself to catch her as she went by. Aida pressed back on the pedals, halting the bike beside him.

"Yes," she assured him as he knelt beside her. "I wanted to say, watch me too, Daddy, but I was scared with all of these people around."

Dan lifted her off of the bike and into his arms as she wrapped her body around his chest.

"Okay, clearly, I have no hope of not crying all night," Fionna whimpered.

"I'm watching you, baby girl. You don't have to be scared."

"Okay, put me back on so I can say it!"

Dan set Aida back on the bike. He stepped back and wrapped his arms around Fionna.

"Watch me, Daddy!" She beamed at Dan as she picked up pace and began flying around the cul-de-sac. Fionna turned into his side and cried in earnest.

"Always, sweetheart, always." Dan was certain he'd never heard anything so sweet.

Zach slapped him on the back as Kara attempted to hug him and Fionna simultaneously. The size of her stomach combined with Dan's sheer width prevented her from her task.

"Well, it's been quite a while since I've seen so many Vindicos playing in the cul-de-sac." Gerald Richmond, Amelia's father, joined everyone outside.

Dan's heart went numb from the sheer emotion of the evening. "Gerald, uh, how are you, sir?"

Fionna pulled away and tried desperately to wipe her eyes.

"I'm all right. Faith and I just received the invitation to the reception." He offered Fionna a kind smile.

Her eyes goggled as Dan stood utterly astonished on the cement. How could his mother have invited Amelia's parents to his and Fionna's wedding reception?

"Mr. Richmond, sir, please don't feel like you have to come. Dan and I completely understand." Fionna's voice was choked and harried. Dan nodded his adamant agreement.

"What was Mom thinking?" Kara whispered in shock.

"We'd like to come, but Faith was worried it might make you uncomfortable."

"If you'd like to come, we'd love for you to be there," Fionna assured him. Dan was still unable to speak.

"Daddy, watch me again!" Aida called, and Dan immediately turned his attention back to her. Confusion and terror spiraled into a maelstrom in his gut.

"I see you, sweetheart."

Gerald looked completely stunned.

"Dan and Fionna adopted Aida about a week ago." Kara appeared bereaved as she gestured timidly to Aida.

Gerald managed a half nod. "Arthur and Marion didn't mention that you'd also become parents."

Aida pulled to a stop right in front of Fionna. "Did you see me? Was I fast?"

Fionna guided Aida closer. "You were fast, baby. You be careful."

Aida gave Mr. Richmond a sweet smile.

"Aida." Fionna drew a deep steadying breath. "This is Mr. Richmond. He's a very, very dear friend of ours." She held Gerald's eyes steadily with her own.

"Hi! It's nice to meet you, sir."

Clearly moved by Fionna's vow, Gerald gazed down at her sweetly. "It's nice to meet you too, Aida." He lifted his eyes to meet Dan's bewildered expression. "Daniel, life is for the living. Faith and I both know what Amelia meant to you. We don't blame you for anything that happened to her. I'm thankful you finally decided to really live while you're here, because life is precious."

"And you should never take any day for granted." Fionna completed the sentiment for him.

"Precisely." He held up the mail that he'd come to retrieve from the mailbox and smiled. "Enjoy your evening and your family."

"I still can't believe she invited them." Kara was distraught.

Fionna turned to Dan. "You promised Aida you wouldn't yell." Her reminder was vehement as they followed the girls back to the garage.

"I will not yell," he vowed more for himself than his wife. "But I will talk."

"Nicely."

"Not likely," was the best Dan could offer her.

"Well, I hear we've decided to rush into something else," was Mrs. Vindico's bitter greeting.

"What the hell were you thinking inviting the Richmonds to our reception?" Dan kept his voice low but menacing. "Did you not think that might make them extremely uncomfortable?"

"I really don't think that we need to tell everyone about *this* until after the reception." Mrs. Vindico gestured her hand to Fionna's abdomen.

"It's like you're having two different arguments." Meredith sighed.

"This!" Fury began to pulse acridly through his veins. His shield tensed red.

"Dan, please! You promised Aida," Fionna begged.

He swallowed down his volatile anger. "*This* is my wife, the woman who means everything to me, the woman who quite literally pulled me out of the depths of hell. Whom, by the way, I have already married. She is carrying my child, just like Aida, my baby, your granddaughter. Please, for once, respect something that I want even if it isn't just how you planned it."

"The Richmonds have been our neighbors for thirty years. I had to extend them an invitation. They are aware that you've moved on. It would have been rude not to invite them."

"Did you ever think that having my late fiancée's parents there might make my wife uncomfortable, or that it might make me uncomfortable? Of course you didn't. It doesn't matter what I want. It never has! As long as it's all about you, that's all that will ever matter." It took all of Dan's massive strength to keep his tone a notch under shouting.

"Olivia, why don't you and Aida come up to my old room, and we'll play Barbies." Kara attempted to guide the girls out of the storm of tension barraging the kitchen.

"No! We're eating now!" Mrs. Vindico flung a massive casserole dish of some kind of rice concoction onto the dining room table.

Nervous glances shot around the room like a lit fuse.

The shrill ring of the house phone shattered through some of the choking tension. The governor shot Dan a warning glare before answering.

"Hello?" He rolled his eyes. "Since you are currently speaking with the governor, let me assure you and any other media organizations that I have no comment on whether or not my daughter-in-law will be signing for another season with the Angels. Let me also assure you that if you phone me at home again, it will not end well for you."

As he slammed the phone down, Fionna's head sank. "I'm so sorry, sir."

Governor Vindico gave her a reassuring smile. "Sweetheart, this certainly isn't your fault. It's none of their business. They'd planned to run those honeymoon pictures of Rainer and Emily for the next couple of weeks. When Stephen made that impossible, they scrambled for news."

"Oh, that reminds me, I intended to phone Lillian and request that they return the place settings and linen napkins we gave them." Mrs. Vindico drew herself up into a pursed-lip, craned-neck monument of righteous indignation. "I need to put that on my lengthy to-do list."

Incensed fury catapulted through Dan. "What!?"

"Dan!" Fionna glanced at Aida.

"Marion, you are not requesting that they send our gifts back.

That's ridiculous. Stephen and Lillian have been friends of ours since the academy. Joe and Maggie as well. If Joe were still with us, he would have dismantled the entire Gifted Associated Press over this. His son did nothing wrong." Governor Vindico appeared to agree with Dan this time.

"Arthur, did you *see* those pictures? I don't hold with such things."

"Yes, I'm aware, but they had no idea they were being photographed."

"If they had more decorum and decency there would have been nothing to photograph. Stephen and Lillian were far too lax with Rainer and Emily, just like all the rest of them. I think we've seen where their liberal parenting has gotten them." Mrs. Vindico seemed to decide to continue setting the table as she spouted off her injustices.

"Mother! My God! It was their honeymoon! And, yes, we've seen the products of the Haydenshires' parenting. They currently have ten biological children and two non-biological children who are all phenomenal human beings. Will is a Vice President of the Senate bank, the youngest by a decade. Garrett has been named Officer of the Year three times now. He gave up a high-ranking position in one of the DC precincts to come help me train Logan and Rainer because he loves his brothers. Connor was just hired on as the youngest city planner in DC. Cal gave his life serving this Realm. Levi is an extremely talented architect. He could design most anything, and he just signed a massive contract to design buildings that will alter the DC skyline. Patrick owns his own real estate investment company. Logan is one of the bravest men I've ever known, and he will follow in both Garrett and Cal's footsteps. His wife is one of the top medios at Georgetown. Emily is about to become the Senior Receiver for the Angels, and mark my words, Rainer Lawson will run Iodex one day. He'll be Chief of Elite. On top of all of that, they give of themselves to make other people's lives better on a daily basis. What more do you want?"

"Let's just eat!" his mother shrieked. Aida and Fionna's simultaneous shudders kept Dan working his molars instead of matching his mother's volume. He lifted Aida up into his right arm and wrapped his left around his wife. The emotions in the house were getting to both of them.

"Come on." Fionna drew in a fair amount of resolve and directed Dan to the table. Tension thickened the air in the already stuffy dining room as everyone took a seat. Dishes were passed. The occasional muffled clink of silver on porcelain was the only sound willing to wage war against the deafening silence.

The severely overcooked chicken and undercooked rice did nothing to improve Dan's mood.

"Uh, so you're going to Paris." Kara shared a pleading gaze with Fionna. "Are you excited?"

"We're very excited." Fionna glanced uncomfortably at Dan's mother. "The Angels played in an international exhibition there several years ago, but I didn't get to see much of the city. Dan even made us a reservation at the Eiffel Tower for my birthday."

In an effort to be civil, Dan joined the conversation. "It's good to be friends with the Captain of French Iodex."

"Are Fitz and Maddie keeping my grandbaby or are you taking her with you to the tower?" Governor Vindico winked at Aida and tried to ease her visible distress.

Dan braced for her to ask for Garrett to come rescue her. He appreciated everything Garrett always did for his girls, but God, he wanted to be the one to rescue them at least occasionally. Given the pained expressions on both his wife's and his little girl's face, Dan knew what he should do was call Garrett himself and ask him to take both of them away from his parents' home.

"She's going to play with Alex and Alfred, so Fi and I can celebrate that evening."

"Good. That's important, and you two really didn't stay in Kauai very long after your wedding."

An exasperated huff from his mother was her contribution to the conversation.

Dan rolled his eyes. "What, Mother?"

"Not that my opinion ever matters to you, but do you intend to just gallivant around the globe forever, or are you planning on returning to work at some point, Daniel?"

Dan tossed his napkin down on the inedible meal. "I've accepted Chancellor Wilshire's offer to replace Mentor Sullivan as the head of Ioses Order at Venton Academy next school year."

"Mommy," Aida whispered hesitantly, and Dan was certain he knew what was coming. He pulled his phone from his pocket as defeat tensed in his shield. Fionna leaned down. "This rice makes my tongue feel funny."

Dan turned to attend to his daughter while his parents stared at him in bewilderment.

"You don't have to eat it, baby. How about if Daddy takes you and Mommy out for pizza after this?" Maybe, just maybe, he could rescue them this time.

His mother was too distracted with his announcement to bitch about his offer to Aida.

"Son, do you really want to teach?" Governor Vindico sounded like he couldn't quite believe what he'd heard.

"Why didn't you tell us that you'd decided to teach at Venton?" his mother demanded.

"I didn't really get a chance," he came right back.

"Come on. You're never very forthcoming with information when it comes to your mother and me," the governor reminded.

Fionna offered Dan her sweet smile and a look that said his father was right.

Mrs. Vindico fought tears. "He's right. I mean you called us an hour before your wedding, you didn't tell us about Aida, and you didn't tell us about the baby—Aida did. If Fionna hadn't asked to meet your family, we probably wouldn't know about her either."

"I'm…sorry," he stammered though he wasn't entirely certain the statement was the truth.

Governor Vindico handed his wife a handkerchief from his pocket then turned to Dan. "You've always wanted to be independent. From the moment you could walk, you never wanted anyone else's help, and you did that at ten months old." He shook his head at the memory. "And I know most of the time you think we're interfering in your life, but your mother and I love you. We want to help you and be a part of your life again. We want to be a part of our granddaughters' lives."

"Okay, fine, but I don't need your help finding a job. I am perfectly capable of handling my life."

"I only want what's best for you. I was only trying to help." Mrs. Vindico shuddered through her abashed tears. "Your father kept telling me that you were going to have a baby soon, and I knew you needed a job."

Dan let his eyes close in defeat. Fionna laced her fingers in his to supply him with soothing calm.

"Okay, you're right. I did shut you out. I shut everyone out. But Mother, you have never listened to me, really listened to anything I said. Did you think I would just get married, adopt a child, get my wife pregnant, and never go back to work? Is that really who you think I am? Do you really have that little faith in me?"

This brought his mother up short, and in the silence, Aida's brow furrowed. "I thought God put the baby in Mommy's tummy?"

Nervous chuckles went around the table as Dan grimaced.

"He did," Zach assured Aida and then provided her and Olivia with some Skittles from a pack in his pocket.

"Well, no," Mrs. Vindico admitted. "But you just always seem to have everything figured out. You never needed me. Sometimes, it would be nice for you to ask for your father's or my opinion. It might not have been the way I would have liked for you to go about it, but we should have at least been given the option of seeing you and Fionna marry, of being there. You're my only son."

"Fine," Dan sighed. "You're right, and that was my doing not Fionna's. But I never felt the need to ask your opinion. You've shouted them at me at every available opportunity my entire life." He was willing to accept his part of the extremely tenuous relationship, but he wanted to be heard as well.

The governor squeezed her hand. "He's right, Marion."

She forced a slight nod. "I suppose I'm sorry that you felt that way. I will try to listen to you, but I do not agree with the way you choose to conduct your life."

"I know that, but if you want to be included in our lives more often, then you need to learn to keep your opinions to yourself." He stood. "Right now I think Fi and I are going to take Aida on. This evening has been enough."

The words forming in his Mother's mouth appeared to taste very bitter. "I suppose I understand that, and I will try."

"Thank you." He forced his feet to move toward her and embraced the woman who'd given him birth.

"Lindley is getting out of the healthcare facility spa at the end of the month. Perhaps when you get back from Paris, we could let her meet Aida."

While trying not to laugh hysterically at his mother calling his youngest sister's stint in drug rehab a visit to a healthcare facility spa, Dan shook his head. "We're spending the summer in Kauai on the Ionas' farm. We'll be back just before school starts, and we're leaving after this reception you're throwing."

"You're spending four months in Kauai?" Now his father sounded as offended as his mother.

Two for two. Dan fought another eye roll.

"Yes, we are."

The governor considered for a split second. "Fine. I think your mother and I will vacation there this summer. We can spend several weeks together."

"Oh, you know Jim and Bev vacationed there two years ago. They stayed at a lovely resort. I believe it was a Grand Hyatt. I'll find out, and we'll get the kids reservations there with us."

Dan rubbed his temples, still trying to keep his temper in check. "We are not staying at the Hyatt. We have a house there on the farm."

"But you'd be welcome to stay on my grandparents' farm as well if you'd like." Ever the peacemaker, Fionna made the hesitant offer.

Dan shot her a pleading glare. He wasn't certain he could stand having his parents so close for weeks on end.

"We'll get it all worked out, sweetheart, but thank you." The governor stood to walk them out.

A half hour later, Dan and Fionna were tucked up in a corner booth of the local pizzeria watching Aida select songs on the old-school jukebox with the money Dan had provided her.

"I'm exhausted." Fionna laid her head on his shoulder.

"As soon as we eat, I'll take you home and put you to bed, baby." He was still unable to believe their evening.

"What a night." Her sigh turned into a deep yawn. Their pizza arrived, and Aida devoured two pieces of pepperoni.

When they'd finished and Dan had paid, he loaded Aida up in the car. Fionna was yawning constantly.

"Let's go get my girls in the bed."

Fionna wrinkled her nose. "I'm sorry I'm so tired."

"Baby doll, tonight was insane, and you're growing my little girl inside of you."

"Dan." Fionna glanced back to make certain that Aida wasn't paying them too much attention. "When we go to bed, I want you to feel her again. I want her to feel you before I go to sleep."

"I want to feel her. It's absolutely incredible. She feels so much like you."

After they returned to the calming serenity of the home that Fionna had created for them, Dan gave Aida her bath. Fionna helped her with her kukui oil, and they pulled on her purple pajamas. They tucked her in and kissed her good night.

Dan followed his wife to their bedroom and slowly undressed her. With constant kisses and vows of how much he loved her, he laid her gently in the bed and massaged the shea, coconut, and kukui ointment slowly and tenderly into her breasts, all over her stomach, and into her mound.

He lay beside her, holding her with nothing between them. She relaxed, completely content in his arms as he concentrated. His eyes closed as he moved through her energies until he locked on to his little girl.

Fionna smiled against him as he pushed soothing energy through her womb, supplying both of them with his all-encompassing love and his ardent protection.

CHAPTER 26

HIDE-AND-SEEK

That week the press was ravenous. They'd gone so far as to track Fionna and Aida down at the grocery store. Fionna hadn't dared enter a maternity shop, not that she was showing much. She was desperate to browse a new baby boutique that she'd been drooling over, but she'd stayed away. As the Angel contracts were due back to the owners by noon on Friday, Dan decided that perhaps getting her out of the country was an excellent idea.

She was putting on weight, he noted with a smile. Her face was slightly swollen and her breasts were spilling out of every bra she owned. This had been pointed out in the newspapers and tabloids constantly along with debate over whether or not she had a pooch, much to Fionna's horror.

As the majority of her jeans, which she'd always preferred to wear tight, were now just a little too tight to button, she'd taken to wearing long, loose, flowing sundresses when she went out. Just the day before, a tabloid showed her in multiple shots of different sundresses with the headline "What's famed Angels Receiver hiding now?"

The article went on to point out that if Fionna and Dan had hidden their relationship and the first pregnancy for so many months, they were certainly capable of hiding another pregnancy.

Fionna had come home from her trip to Starbucks and the drug store in tears. The article had hit just a little too close to home.

"Can I ask you something and you swear you'll tell me the truth even if you think it'll hurt my feelings?" Fionna asked as Dan located her in their bedroom Thursday evening. She was packing for Paris, and her rhythms were strung tightly. He'd been correct in his assumption that a pregnant Receiver's emotions could get the better of them relatively quickly.

With the same level of caution he would use to work through a minefield, Dan nodded. "Sure, baby doll."

"Am I too big to wear lingerie for you?" Her tone held a volatile combination of fear, fury, and frustration.

Since this question was easy to answer honestly, Dan breathed a sigh of relief and shook his head. "Hell, no. First of all, you are gorgeous always. As I am the guy who not only knocked you up, but that gets to rub you down with oil and ointment every night, I can definitely say the only place that's changed at all is here." He reached and let his right hand slide tenderly over her breasts. Her delighted grin righted his world.

"And if you strap something black, lacy, and sexy as hell over those, it might just drive me over before I even begin."

She loved lingerie, and he was pleased she wanted to continue the finer points of their lovemaking into her pregnancy.

"And you promise to still think I'm sexy even when my belly is huge?"

"Baby." Dan wondered if he should just go ahead and begin every day with this same answer as he was asked about that often. "I keep telling you that thinking about you—the most beautiful woman in the world, swollen full of my baby girl, that I put in there—drives me wild. Just thinking about it makes me crazy. I've jacked off several times recently with that on my mind. Why don't you believe me?"

A sexy giggle over his admission seemed to boost her confidence. "I keep telling myself that, but then I don't know. Adeline weighed me when she came over to check on the baby yesterday, and those numbers were higher than I've ever seen before in my life. I kind of freaked...and then the tabloids."

"You are gorgeous. You take my breath away on a daily basis. Adeline told you that your weight was perfect." He'd been standing in their bathroom with her when she'd looked down at the scale and promptly burst into tears.

"If you want to put on some lingerie for me tonight, I'll be happy to show you just how sexy you are."

"So, if I put on something kind of dirty and want you to do all the stuff I like for you to do to me, then you will and it's okay that I'm pregnant?"

A hungry groan lit the air as Dan breached the small distance between them. "Let's take our little girl to get burgers and fries and get her into bed. Then I'm gonna bring you home and take you dirty, baby doll. Make you beg me for it. I'm gonna drag it out for hours until you ache. I'm gonna make you earn it, baby. Make you so wet you drown my cock in that tight little pussy that I'm gonna own. I'll take you so fucking hard you can't walk."

His trousers tented as he envisioned what he'd described. That seemed to do the trick. Fionna shivered her desperate approval.

"You promise?" Her darkened eyes lit in challenge.

With a great deal of intent, he slapped her sexy ass. "Ask me again."

A half hour later, Dan kept Aida's face buried in his shoulder and shielded Fionna with his body as two reporters spotted them heading into Big Buns.

"Get the hell away from my wife!" he growled as they began calling in camera crews.

Quickly tracking to a booth in the back, Dan placed their orders and requested that the press be kept out of the restaurant.

"Good grief!" he sighed. "This is ridiculous."

"Why do they want to take Mommy's picture so much?" Aida fussed dejectedly. "I haven't talked to anybody about my baby sister except for Garrett, and you said that was okay."

Dan's heart sank. He hated that she thought it was her fault. "Baby, we know you didn't tell. They just want to know about her so they want to take Mommy's picture and talk to us. Don't worry about it. Daddy will take care of it."

His father had been correct. Every news organization in the Realm had been planning to run the photos of the Lawson honeymoon for weeks. When that had been removed as a viable option, they'd turned back to Dan and Fionna.

"Everyone's going to know tomorrow anyway." Fionna tucked herself into Dan's body. He cradled her close as they waited on their food to arrive.

She tensed and shot a concerned glance to a man seated in a booth nearby. Dan had already spotted him. "What do you feel?" he whispered.

"Deception and excitement but it's dark," she explained.

"I'm betting he's going to try to walk without paying. Do you want to leave?"

She shook her head. "No, it'll be okay. Maybe we should offer to pay. Maybe he's short on cash."

"I'll keep an eye on him, but I doubt that would make him excited," Dan reminded her. "And tomorrow, we'll be on the other side of the world. Just you and me and both of our sweet baby girls, so I don't want you to worry about anything at all."

She gave him another one of his smiles, the ones that warmed every darkened, cold place in his soul, and kissed his jaw. "You always know just what to say to make me feel better."

Dan reveled in her declaration, but he knew this pregnancy was likely to be on the front page and on every available Gifted press outlet for months on end.

Their burgers and shakes arrived, and Fionna dug in feverishly. Aida took great delight in slurping up her chocolate shake, but Dan had to coax her into finishing her cheeseburger.

He kept Fionna cradled under his arm as she sipped the last of her mocha shake. "Ready, baby doll?"

He threw away their trash and scooped Aida up into his arms as they headed out of Big Buns.

Suddenly, microphones, cameras, and reporters surrounded them.

"Fionna, can you confirm the pregnancy?" chanted reporters as they buried them.

"You heard it here first, folks. A channel 456 reporter inside the popular burger joint Big Buns overheard the Vindicos' daughter state that she was going to have a little sister. Mr. Daniel Vindico, Fionna's husband, confirmed that tomorrow they would be on the other side of the world with their baby girls. Yes, folks, it was plural, and we have confirmation that the Vindicos will be traveling to Paris tomorrow morning, meaning that Fionna will not be in Alexandria to sign her contract to return to play for the Arlington Angels. It seems she's hung up her halo and is going to give the former Chief of Elite another girl."

"No comment!" Fionna yanked on Dan's hand and they rushed to the car.

"Get away from her now!" Dan shoved a reporter out of his way, furious with himself as he blocked her entire body with his own as she climbed in the car. He quickly settled Aida in her car seat.

"I'm so sorry," he lamented as soon as he slammed his own door.

"It's fine. They'd be doing this tomorrow anyway."

"It was the guy you sensed. I just wasn't thinking."

"It's fine, really."

After driving for almost an hour to lose the press and make certain they weren't being followed, Dan finally pulled into the garage. By this point, Aida was asleep. They'd fielded a few questions, but had managed to assure her that everything was fine.

He scooped Aida up and laid her head tenderly on his shoulder.

She stirred. "Is it time to go to Paris, France?"

Fionna kissed her cheek. "No, baby. Let Daddy carry you to bed. When we wake up, then it will be time to go."

Aida pressed her face into Dan's neck. She hid from the world and soothed his soul.

CHAPTER 27

LITTLE EARS

After tucking Aida in her bed, Dan pulled her door closed and eased toward his and Fionna's bedroom. She'd already closed their door. His brow furrowed.

The evening's events had driven them from one end of the spectrum to the other. Before they'd left, she'd had more carnal pleasures on her mind, but that was before he'd stupidly confirmed her pregnancy to the entire Realm.

Uncertain if she was upset and wanted a little time alone or if she wanted to surprise him with something, Dan debated knocking. After praying she wasn't furious with him, he tapped on the door gently.

"Come in." She didn't sound upset. As soon as he turned the knob, he realized just what she was eager for.

A shuddering growl echoed from his lungs. "My god, you are so fucking sexy." His eyes goggled, and the real estate in his jeans became nonexistent as he took in his gorgeous wife wearing a strapless corset. Her heaving, fevered cleavage was spilling out of it deliciously.

It laced up the front with an extremely enticing black ribbon and attached with black straps to her thigh-high, black, lace stockings. There was nothing between the bottom of the corset and the top of the stockings except the elastic straps that drove him wild.

Her backside was on luscious display along with her mound which she'd just had waxed clean for him the day before. She'd completed the ensemble with sky-high, black stiletto heels.

Kicking the door shut and locking it instantly, he made it to her in two long strides. She wanted to feel just a little less like a mom for a little while, and a whole lot more like the hot sex goddess she was. She wanted to shut everything else out except for the erotic all-encompassing sensations he was determined to bring her.

"Looks like you forgot something there, baby doll." Dan traced his index finger over her mound as she began to pant.

"Oops." Defiant challenge stormed in her darkened eyes. It drove him wild.

"You have to be careful. I might take advantage of what you've left uncovered for me." He breathed the warning in her face.

"I'm hoping."

A hungry growl tore from his lungs. "You are a naughty girl, aren't you, baby doll? You need to be fucked like a naughty girl, don't you?"

He grasped her ass with one hand and kneaded it with greed. He kissed her fiercely then swirled one finger just inside her lips before plunging it deeply inside of her. Her body swayed against his strokes.

"Is that what you wanted, baby doll? Or do you need something more? Tell me."

"Oh, God, yes. Fuck me hard, please."

"My naughty girl's so wet for me. I could make you take it right now. You've been thinking about me haven't you?"

Her body convulsed. Her head fell back from the pleasure he was bringing her, but she backed away suddenly.

His eyes flashed in irritation. "Come back here to me. I didn't tell you to move. Don't make me turn you over my knee, baby, because I will."

Spinning away from him in abject defiance, she moved to the wall, placed her hands against it, and hoisted her backside out.

A thundering growl tore from Dan as he watched the erotic display.

"I want it. Give it to me now!" she demanded.

Pulling off everything he was wearing in seconds flat, he moved to her.

He cupped her ass with his right hand and then slapped it hard enough to pinken her skin.

"I said not to move. Now you're gonna get it rough and dirty, baby. I'll make you mind."

"Yes!" She shook her sexy ass all for him, stroking her lush cheeks against his cock.

"There, that's my good girl. You know what I like. Behave."

"I want it, please. Please give it to me." With a sexy pout and abandon lit in her eyes, she begged.

"Take it!" He pulled her back over his throbbing cock. "Take it, baby. You take it all. Be a good girl for me." His order thundered from his lips. His eyes rolled back in his head from the exquisite sensation of plunging her depths with little to no foreplay. She was so tight he was certain he was going to lose it all in moments.

"Give it to me, please." Her lips and her body made the same plea to be filled full of him. "Harder!"

"Fucking hell, you are so damn hot!" He pounded into her. "That's it. Good girl. You want it? You take it hard. Take everything I give you." He grasped the elastic straps of the corset and pulled her back as she encased him in the heavenly perfection of her sweet little pussy.

His right hand popped the strap against her ass and then wound around to her throbbing clit. He stroked up from where his own cock was straining inside of her and gathered the mix of the two of them together. When his fingers were slicked, he rolled them over her clit, making her whimper and groan in need as he devastated the tender bundle of nerves.

"Ask me, baby. Say please like a good girl. Ask me to let you come."

"Please, please, give it to me now," she cried out.

But suddenly he stopped. He heard something.

"Don't stop!" Her desperation shook through her body, but then she heard it as well. Aida was crying and knocking on their door.

"Oh shit! Get out!" Fionna panicked.

Dan gasped for breath and withdrew instantly.

"Dan! She cannot see me like this!"

"I know, baby, but you're gonna have to give me a minute." He gestured down to his painfully swollen erection then squeezed his eyes shut and tried to will it away.

"Go get in the bed," she commanded.

Dan climbed in the bed, pulled the covers over him, and turned on his side as to avoid creating a tent out of their sheets. Fionna flung on a robe and opened the door.

Aida was sobbing. "Why are you crying, and why are you fighting?" she managed through her heartbroken tears.

"I'm not crying, baby." Fionna drew her in tenderly and tried to wipe away her tears.

"Yes, you were, and you were fighting." Her entire body convulsed in fear.

Certain he'd never felt so horrible for anything in his entire life, Dan didn't know what to do.

"We weren't fighting. I promise. We were...uh...just playing," Fionna stammered.

Aida pulled away from Fionna and rubbed her eyes. "I heard Daddy say *take it* a bunch of times, and I heard a sound like this." She clapped her hands together forcefully. Dan cringed in horror. "And you said *give it to you,* and you were crying."

"I promise I wasn't crying. See, I love Daddy very, very much." Fionna kept the robe tied tightly around her as she moved toward the bed.

Realizing what she was doing, Dan sat up and hugged Fionna tightly.

"See, we're not fighting, baby. I love you and Mommy more than anything in the world," he vowed adamantly.

Aida's brow furrowed. "Why are you wearing your very high heels to bed?" Her curiosity dried her tears.

Fionna was the shade of the crimson corset she was wearing under the robe. "Uh...I was just trying them on to see if I wanted to take them to Paris." She lied rather well under the circumstances.

"I like your pretty tights." Aida timidly touched the intricate nylon covering Fionna's knee.

"Oh, uh, thank you."

Dan squeezed his eyes shut.

"You know, I think I'll just leave these home." Fionna kicked off the heels. "So, why don't we get you back in bed and then we're going to go to sleep, so we can get up early tomorrow and go to Paris."

With that, Fionna returned Aida to her room and sat with her for a few minutes. Dan could hear her reassuring Aida that she was fine and that she and Dan hadn't been fighting.

She slunk back into the bedroom, sank down on the bed, and let her head fall into her hands. "Oh my gosh!"

Dan nodded as he wrapped his arms around her. He was certain his face was just as red as hers. He helped her dispense with the corset and stockings.

"Okay, this may be a horrible time to say this, but"—he held up the corset—"this is the hottest damn thing I've ever seen, and at some point when our child or children aren't home or are completely asleep, I'd really like to see you in it again, and I'd really like to peel it all off of you."

Fionna succumbed to an abashed mix of laughter and tears. "Dan, we've had her like two weeks, and I've ruined her."

"You didn't ruin her. She has no idea what we were doing, and for future reference, we'll remember that the wall right across from her room might not be our best choice."

With a deep breath of regret, he went ahead with the speech he'd prided himself on never having to have made. "Sweetheart, do you need me to do anything for you? I know I didn't really get you where you needed to be."

Fionna cringed and shook her head. She brushed a tender kiss along his five o'clock shadow. "I don't think I got you where you were going either, but in light of my horrendous embarrassment, maybe we'll just pick this back up in Paris."

Dan was thankful that they were in complete agreement. He kissed her sweetly. "I'm sorry."

"Me too. I was really horny." She tucked her head on his chest as she made her confession as if that hadn't been obvious.

"Don't worry. I'll take care of you tomorrow night after we put Miss Aida to bed and make certain she's completely asleep."

CHAPTER 28

PROFFERED OFFER

The next afternoon after Captain Namphis had come out of the cockpit to tell Dan how much better he looked than the last time he'd flown on his jet, he let Aida go into the cockpit and see how they flew the plane.

"He flew me back from Paris after the incident in Russia," Dan begrudgingly explained to Fionna.

She chuckled as Aida delighted in the way the Gifted flight was flown.

"She hasn't said anything about last night," Fionna whispered in relief. Dan nodded. He'd been relieved as well.

They landed at Charles de Gaulle and were heartily greeted by the Fitzroys.

"Maddie, this is my beautiful wife, Fionna." Dan made introductions as Maddie embraced Fionna, kissing both of her cheeks twice.

"I had to see you for myself," Maddie gushed in her heavy French accent. "The woman who saved Daniel from himself. You are a queen among women!"

Laughing, Dan kissed Fionna's cheek. "She is that, and this is my little girl, Aida. Aida, this is Mr. and Mrs. Fitzroy and these are my godsons, Alex and Alfred." He scrubbed the boy's heads.

"Aida, it's so nice to meet you." Fitz winked at her.

"Isn't it, boys?" Maddie demanded.

"Bonjour, Aida," Alfred offered politely. "It is very lovely to meet you."

"Thank you. It's very nice to meet you too," Aida managed though she was clinging to Dan's hand and hiding most of her body behind his leg.

"I speak French and English," Alex boasted.

"I speak English and Portuguese," Aida combated Alex's bragging. Dan swelled with pride.

"All right, Alex. Let's get them settled, and then we'll go exploring," Fitz guided his eldest son.

Fitz drove everyone to the two-bedroom apartment he'd secured for the Vindicos. It was owned by the French Senate for use of visiting foreign dignitaries from other Realms, but it wasn't needed for the week, so Fitz had booked it for Dan.

It was only two blocks from the Fitzroys' home, and though Dan had offered to get a hotel for them instead, Fionna was thrilled that they would have a full kitchen. She wanted to shop at the markets and cook French food.

Fitz helped Dan carry in all of the luggage as Fionna eased Aida inside and tried to coax her out of her shell.

"She's adorable, and Fionna is just as lovely as Fitz promised." Maddie seemed very pleased.

"I happen to agree."

"The baby, she is doing well with the pregnancy, yes?"

"Yeah, I guess as well as can be expected. She throws up every morning at five. I make her tea and get her back to sleep until around seven, and then she's fine. Little tired, but that's it."

"I will take care of that. She needs to relax. She's been through enough." Maddie took care of everyone and loved doing it. Dan thanked her for letting Fionna into the relatively private family life she conducted like a master of a symphony.

"Jean Paul, where are our children?" She sighed.

"I thought they were behind me." He headed back out of the apartment to locate Alex and Alfred. After finding them outside playing on the sidewalk, Fitz dragged them upstairs and into the apartment. "And you better play nice with Aida."

"Oui, Papa. We will, we will." Alex wriggled out of his father's grasp.

"It's all over the papers and sports blogs this morning," Fitz lamented. Dan nodded his regret-filled agreement.

"I thought the guy was going to walk out without paying. I knew he was up to something. I had no idea he was a reporter. I was an idiot."

"Would you stop?" Fionna joined everyone in the living room. "Everyone would have known by noon anyway. I didn't show up to sign next year's contracts."

Dan guided Fionna into his arms. He still felt terrible that he was the one who'd confirmed their pregnancy and even the sex of their baby to the press.

"Aida's room has two twin beds, so she's making one for Phoebe," she informed Dan. They tiptoed to spy on their little girl. She was explaining to her doll how to sleep in a big girl bed without falling off.

"This apartment is perfect, and I'm so excited to be here. Thank you for having us," Fionna vowed to the Fitzroys as they moved back to the sitting area.

"We're glad you're here. Dan's never come to visit except to work."

"Yeah, that sounds about right." Fionna shot Dan a mischievous smirk.

"No working this week. You two relax. We will take care of the sweet little Aida and you just enjoy Paris," Maddie insisted.

Aida raced to Fionna. She looked bewildered as she cupped her hand over her mouth. Fionna leaned down and Dan heard, "There is something that isn't a potty in the bathroom, and I don't know what it is. I have to use the potty bad, please!"

"Oh," Fionna giggled, "come here, sweetheart. That's a bidet, but there's a potty also." She led Aida back to the bathroom near her room.

~

A little while later everyone headed out onto the streets of Paris.

"It's so pretty." Aida held Dan's hand and really began taking in the city.

"There's this great place I want to take you to dinner tonight," Fitz urged. He was up to something. Dan knew. He could tell as soon as they'd gotten off the plane.

"Great."

After a few quick tourist attractions and a stop at a bakery for a croissant and coffee, which Fionna had declared they would be doing on a daily basis for the rest of their trip, the Vindicos returned to their apartment to get ready for dinner.

"I think my tummy is confused," Aida informed Dan and Fionna. Chuckling, they agreed the time difference took a little getting used to. Dan tried to explain it to Aida, but she still seemed confused by the concept.

"Okay, Miss Aida, I think you need to go get your book and lie down and read for a little while. You're going to be up late tonight." The Gifted pediatrician who'd given Aida her physical was concerned with her height, weight, and her sleep deprivation. A nap every day had been strongly suggested to recover her health by the time she started school the next year.

Fionna was tired as well. She laid her head in Dan's lap on the sofa as he played with her hair.

"What are we thinking?" She gave him his smile. She knew him far too well.

"Fitz is up to something."

"Yeah, I noticed that too. I'm sure you'll figure Fitz out, but this is amazing. Thank you so much for bringing us."

"Hey, I'm thrilled to watch you two have fun." He gestured his head to Aida's room. "Making my girls smile is all I'll ever need."

"She's pretty worn out. I don't think she'll be waking up tonight." Fionna cringed.

Dan couldn't help but laugh. "Did you bring the corset for me, baby doll?"

Giggling, she shrugged. "You'll have to wait and see, Mr. Vindico."

"I love you." Dan was overcome suddenly with the need to tell her.

Her energy spun in elation. "I love you too."

"Fi," he whispered. "Can I feel her again?"

She gave him a look that said he'd just made her entire world fall into place as she edged her jeans down, lifted her shirt, and closed her eyes to suppress her energy.

Each time he locked on to the baby's developing cells, he was able to perform the task faster and easier. Their baby girl was growing rapidly, so her energy became stronger with each passing day.

His heart always paused momentarily as soon as he felt his little girl's rhythms.

"She feels you," Fionna assured him in a breathless pant.

Dan concentrated and counted each tiny rhythmic pulse of her energy.

A little while later, they followed closely behind Aida as Fitz led them through the seventh arrondissement. He stopped and offered Maddie his arm as he guided everyone up a grand staircase to what appeared to be an old home.

A maître d' opened the door and welcomed Fitzroy heartily.

"Monsieur and Madame Fitzroy, so good to see you zis evening!"

Dan wondered why the man chose to speak English.

"Dandre, nice to see you." Fitz shook the man's hand. "These are some dear friends of ours." He stepped back to introduce the Vindicos. "This is Dan and Fionna Vindico and their little girl, Aida."

"'Ello, Monsieur Vindico and the lovely mademoiselles. How are you this fine evening?" the man announced with just a little too much gusto.

Dan narrowed his eyes, kept Fionna tucked under his arm, and gently eased Aida closer to him. She didn't argue. She wanted away from the restaurateur as well.

They were led to a table on the second floor with a stunning view of the tower.

Fionna was nervous about whatever she'd picked up on from the maître d', but she was taken with the restaurant and the view.

"Look, Aida." She knelt down and pointed out the Eiffel tower. "Isn't it beautiful?"

Aida nodded but was still unsure about her surroundings. "And

Daddy is taking you there tomorrow for dinner, and you're going to wear your pretty new dress because it's romantic, and I'm not allowed to go because I'm little and not romantic yet," she lamented as Dan pulled her chair out for her.

He popped a kiss on top of her head. "Daddy will take you next time, okay?"

"Ah, Aida, you don't want to go with them to eat at the tower," Fitz assured her. "It's boring, and no one there can do this." He waved his hand behind Aida's head and made it appear that he'd pulled several French coins out of her ear.

She giggled. "Those weren't in my ears."

"That's true, but you can have them." He dropped the coins in her hand.

"Wow! Thank you!"

"We are going to have lots of fun tomorrow night, my sweet Aida," Maddie assured her.

Well aware that Fitz had strategically seated everyone so that the boys and Aida were tucked away on the far corner of the table against the wall, with Maddie and Fionna in the middle, and the men on the end, Dan narrowed his eyes. "All right, spill it. Now!"

"Damn, you're good." Fitz and Dan kept their voices low so the kids couldn't hear them.

"Let me guess. The restaurant is a front for something. Gambling, drugs, money laundering, whatever, and the guy down there that has deviant written all over him, he's what? Obviously not the big player or you'd be down there arresting him, so he's a little player in a bigger league."

"How did you figure that out in five minutes?"

Dan rolled his eyes. "First of all, I am married to the strongest Receiver of our generation. If my hands are on her, I know something is wrong instantly. Second, I have another little radar screen right down there." He gestured his head to Aida. "And, come on, it's me, so before I start shouting about the fact that you not only brought my wife and my baby girls up here, tell me what the hell is going on."

"Jean Paul!" Maddie sniped as she began telling him off in French.

Dan and Fionna had no idea what she was saying, but they were certain he was getting an earful.

Fitz waved her off with, "Désolé, désolé!" before turning back to Dan.

"He knows I'm onto him, but I can't figure out who he's working for. I need some help."

"Dammit, Fitz. My girls are here with me—little, tiny, helpless!" Fionna scowled.

"In my defense, two of them are traveling together for a while." Fitz threw his hand out to Fionna, making her laugh.

"I am not helpless, Mr. Vindico, and unless you'd like to have a slumber party with Fitz tonight, you'll take that back. Now."

"Fine, but our little ones are."

"Look, I know you already signed on with Venton, but just hear me out." Dan immediately knew where this was going. "I want to offer you a job. Governor Haydenshire was an idiot to force you to resign. You're the best damn officer out there. If you don't want to move here, then just be an advisor. Fly back and forth. I could really use your help."

Fionna's energy spiraled in terror. It shocked Dan. He wrapped his arm around her and tried to assure her with his body that he wasn't getting back into law enforcement. Clearly, everything that had happened lived there just under the surface of their marital bliss and the elation of having another child.

"Thank you, but no. I want out. It isn't good for me, and there's no end to it. Just like I said, you aren't arresting him because you want the guy he's working for, and it just keeps going.

"I don't want to fly back and forth. I want to be home with Fi and my girls. I want to see them and be there for them every single day. I will not live out of a hotel in Paris wondering what they're doing and worrying about them."

Fionna leaned and kissed Dan's cheek. A whispered, "Thank you," caressed his ear.

A waiter appeared with a selection of breads. He suggested several wines, which everyone agreed to save Fionna who ordered a sparkling water.

"Fionna, you'll have to come back when you can really enjoy everything Paris has to offer," Maddie fussed.

Fionna smiled. "It's okay. I'm pretty excited about the reason that I can't have wine."

"Yes, and Mommy's tummy is going to get really big like when you have a ball in your dress," Aida was informing the boys with a great deal of knowing sass. The adults laughed quietly as they listened. "But my tummy will not get big, but when my baby sister gets out of Mommy's tummy it will be normal sized again."

"Ah, if only it were that easy." Fionna sighed.

Dan gazed at her as he kissed her cheek. "You will always be the most stunning woman in the room, in the city, in the entire world to me."

"Yeah, I remember that 'cause I'm bigger than Alfred," Alex assured Aida.

"Oh yeah, he remembers at ten months old." Fitz rolled his eyes and brought on more laughter.

"How is your sister going to get out of your mommy?" Alfred seemed genuinely fascinated.

Aida's lips pursed to the side, and her brow furrowed. "I'm not exactly sure, but I think Daddy will do it."

"But how will Uncle Dan get your sister to come out of your mommy?" Alfred restated his question. His tone rang with disbelief.

Aida shrugged. "Maybe he'll just say *Aida's baby sister, you can come out and play with Aida now.*"

"He's Uncle Dan. He can do anything," Alex scoffed.

Dan shook his head. He was thoroughly abashed by the admiration.

"Aww, I think so too." Fionna only furthered his embarrassment.

"I'll have to give that a try." He laughed.

"Yeah, I'm pretty sure *Daddy*,"—Fitz laughed—"is more into the delivery not the retrieval."

Dan and Fionna laughed.

"So, you're sure?" Fitz leapt back on the previous topic.

"I'm sure."

"Jean Paul, no more work. Dan and Fionna are here to relax," Maddie commanded.

She immediately engaged Fionna in a conversation about pregnancy. Maddie explained how American women become so frantic about rules for pregnancy and which products are best for them and the baby, that they not only make their babies fussy, but they don't enjoy being pregnant.

Fionna was fascinated, and Dan smiled as he listened intently to Maddie's advice. Fionna asked dozens upon dozens of questions.

"It is a magical thing, no?" Maddie urged. Fionna nodded adamantly. "You are a powerful Receiver. You feel her, yes?" Maddie quizzed again as the main courses were served.

"I do. It's amazing!"

"So, relax and enjoy her. Enjoy each and every part of having what you have created together inside of you. Men certainly cannot do this. We are the only ones. Don't ruin it with what you can eat, and whether or not the newest pillow is all right to sleep on, and if I have a piece of chocolate will my baby's IQ be half a point lower."

Fionna was beaming as she continued to intently pick Maddie's brain. Every time she began a question with, "I read on a pregnancy website," Maddie would shake her head and roll her eyes.

"Fionna, darling,"—she finally reached across the table and held Fi's hand in her own—"you are her mother. You will know what is best for her, but if you don't trust your abilities, neither will she. Women have been giving birth since the beginning of time without the Internet. You must trust yourself to know what will be best for your little girl and, perhaps more importantly, what will be best for you and the entire family.

"My sister told me that some American medio was warning women against enjoying the art of love with their husbands while they are pregnant. This is ridiculous!" Maddie's tone picked up in her fervor. "Jean Paul and I had amazing love while I was pregnant with both of our boys, almost every day. It was required. I needed it."

Fitz turned the shade of his heirloom tomato salad.

"Did ya now?" Dan laughed heartily.

"Really?" Fionna was too intent on learning every single thing she could from Maddie to find her rather loud declaration humorous.

The children were caught up in a conversation all their own. Aida was asking the boys all about school as she had never attended one before and was already nervous about starting in September.

"How did you learn to read if you didn't go to school?" Alfred asked.

"My brothers were bigger than me, and I wanted to learn so they taught me when I was little-er and then Sister Mary Francis finished teaching me."

Dan flitted back and forth between the conversations as he ate the delectable meal. The restaurant might have been a front, but the chef was outstanding.

"And you wore lingerie and everything?" Fionna urged Maddie on.

"Naturally," Maddie scoffed. "Who does not wear lingerie?"

"I don't think I'll be able to wear mine much longer."

Maddie's brow knitted deeply. She shook her head. "Do they not sell lingerie for maternity?"

"Not in America anywhere that I know of."

Maddie gasped. "Preposterous! We are going shopping! You do not stop being a woman just because you are a mother." Maddie gestured to Aida. "You become more of a woman, and Dan wants to see this. Balance, my dear. You don't give up one for the other. You make them all work together. It is the only way. I will teach you."

"Oh my gosh! I love you!" Fionna gushed.

"Yeah, she's taken, but I'd be willing to trade you her for Dan, for a little while I guess," Fitzroy offered.

CHAPTER 29

FOR ME AND YOU

They walked back to their apartment slowly, still enjoying each other's company. Aida was yawning, and Dan scooped her up. She laid her head on his shoulder and cuddled into him as he walked.

Fionna gave her a quick bath and helped her into her pajamas before kissing her good night.

"So." Dan freed himself of his tie and belt and then unbuttoned his shirt. "Should I be concerned that you're going to run off with Maddie, leaving me and Fitzroy mere shells of the men we used to be?"

Giggling, Fionna shook her head. She changed out of her dress, seated herself on the bed, and patted the spot beside her. He removed his shirt and joined her. She laid her head against his chest and drew from his ample energy supplies.

Vulnerability permeated her rhythms. He wrapped his shield around her and spent several long minutes soothing her. "What's wrong, baby?"

"You don't know what it's like. I never talked to my mom about being pregnant, obviously. It's been a long time since Tutu had a baby, and Gretta never had kids of her own. Having a professional career in Summation kind of meant that everyone I hung out with was most definitely not pregnant. None of my friends have kids. I feel completely lost. Some of those websites on what you should and shouldn't do if you're pregnant are scary and crazy. Every social media post about pregnancy and motherhood are posted with so much authority even if the person posting doesn't know what they're talking about.

"Maddie is the only person I know who's done this before, and she's willing to help me. And I love what she said about me still being a woman. That makes sense to me, and nothing else seems to. Everyone has an opinion about everything. Nurse, don't nurse, stay home, go to work, public school, private school, homeschool—it's never ending. People become very adamant about their opinions, especially online. It's just a lot to take in."

"Baby, there will always be a million things that the rest of the world is doing or saying that aren't going to work for us because we're not them. And this is our baby." He slid his hands to her abdomen. "Let's take it a little at a time, and Maddie was right. You're her mother. You're kind and you're completely brilliant. You're going to know what to do. You need to listen to you, and if you can't figure something out, Aida's baby sister's daddy would really like to help with all of this."

"Thank you." She whispered a kiss across his chest. "Can I ask you something now?"

"Of course."

"There was an offer in my email this morning. They must have sent it as soon as the story broke last night. It's hardly any money at all, and I don't want to take the money they did offer, but I would kind of like to take the offer."

Dan studied her closely. Her excitement lilted in her energy. "What's the offer?"

"Since we both had high-profile careers, they would like for our family to pose for a few paper ads for the Auxiliary International Adoptions in the Realm program because we adopted a child who isn't an infant even though we could have our own and because we're determined to make us all a family even if Aida isn't our biological child.

"They even said in the offer that if we didn't want the girls' faces photographed that they could work with us however we would agree. It's such a great program. There are so many kids in the orphanage in Brazil, and there are so many other orphanages."

Though he was adamantly opposed to his children being in commercials, Dan suddenly felt like he'd been given an opportunity to give back to the Realm that he felt he'd taken so much from.

"If you want to, I'm in."

"Really?"

"Really. Still not crazy about the girls' pictures being everywhere, but maybe we could figure something out."

"They really just want us. Our pictures and our story, but they said they could take carefully placed shots of us with the girls so you can't see their faces."

"That sounds perfect."

"I'm so excited. I can't wait to tell them!"

"Hey baby." Dan had been thinking about this for a while, and it seemed like the perfect time to bring it up. Her brow rose in expectation as she gave him his smile. "I was thinking we should name the baby something besides *Aida's little sister*."

"I know. And I name everything—my cars, my boobs, everything. I even named my vibes, but I can't seem to come up with a name for my baby." She cringed into his chest.

He laughed outright. "Okay, I don't know which I want to know more."

She dissolved in a fit of giggles. When she finally regained her composure, she gestured her head downward to her breasts. "June and Bonnie."

Joining in her laughter, Dan shook his head at her. "And how did June and Bonnie earn their names, Mrs. Vindico?"

"The original Pointer sisters," she scoffed.

"Of course." Dan continued his laughter.

Fionna's energy soared as they lay in the bed laughing and cuddling.

"And your vibes, baby doll?"

She blushed violently which made him all the more curious.

"Whenever I got a new one, I would name it after a crush I had. It's usually actors and singers, stuff like that. But I will admit that my very favorite is named Dan."

"I hope I lived up to my name." He was awkwardly honored by her admittance.

Still giggling, she nodded against him. "You do, but occasionally I use Dan and think about how having both of you together would be oh so good."

"I will take care of that fantasy as soon as I get you home, baby doll, unless you brought my namesake with you, and then I'll take care of it tonight."

"Dan Jr. is at home. I once had a TSA guard go through my bags at an airport. They pulled it out of its bag, and I was mortified. I don't bring them on trips too often anymore."

Dan cringed on her behalf as they both laughed again.

When they quieted, she sighed. "But I can't seem to come up with anything perfect enough for the most important thing I'll ever name."

He brushed a kiss on her forehead. "Would you be up for any suggestions?"

"Yes, definitely! Why didn't you tell me you wanted to pick?"

"I want us to pick."

"Okay, what is your suggestion?"

"How about Halia Elisabeth after you and your mom?"

"Dan," she gasped as tears sprang to her eyes. "I love that, but I think it should be Halia Elisabeth Amelia Vindico."

"Fi, no, you don't have to do that." Emotion, thick as syrup, settled in his throat.

"I know," she soothed. He felt her dizzying powers, her ethereal light, fill him. Her warmth flooded through his soul, healing and binding him. "But I really want to. That's perfect. That's what Halia means—in remembrance of those who have gone before us."

"You're sure?"

"I'm positive."

They lay there in the calming serenity, letting their energy pass from one to another within Dan's shield.

Suddenly, she grinned. "You know, June and Bonnie are really sore." Her lusty, mischievous smirk made him ache.

With a deep groan, Dan eased his arms down her sides and let his thumbs brush her breasts.

"Are they, baby doll?"

She gave him a heavy nod.

"I can't have that." He unclasped her bra. A quaking moan gasped from her lips as he began to massage.

"Does that feel better, sweetheart?" He added to the intensity as he groped her. Breath panted from her lungs as she slipped her hands down his abs and over his crotch.

"Tell me what else hurts my girl. What else do you need?"

"Make me wet." Her eyes flashed in ardent desire.

Dan's body shuddered from her touch and her plea. He longed to be inside her again. The images of her stunning display from the night before, leaned up against the wall in a corset and heels begging for it harder, had driven him wild all day.

He needed relief, needed to feel her pulse around him as he brought her, needed to hear her call out his name as he opened her wide.

"I'm gonna go make certain Aida's asleep. While I'm gone, take everything off for me. Spread your legs. I want to see you touch yourself. Let me see that gorgeous body ready for me. When I get back, I'll make you wet, baby doll, and then I'm gonna make you suck me, and then I'm gonna fill you full. I'll take you so hard and so deep I make you scream. Why don't we see just how many times I can make you give it all up for me?"

"Oh, God, yes." Her body trembled from pent-up desire. Dan slipped from the bed quickly. He checked to make certain Aida was sleeping, pulled her door closed, and switched on the bathroom fan. He wanted to hear the sweet noises Fionna made for him, wanted her sultry island scent to cling to his skin. He wanted to own her, and he didn't want to be interrupted.

His trousers tightened to the point of pain as he took in his wife, naked on the bed with her eyes dark and ravenous. Her breasts were swollen, pert, and anxious for his touch and his tongue on her nipples.

Her knees were bent, and her hair was splayed out over the crisp white sheets. Her eyes were locked on his. He watched her lick her fingers and then stroke her clit rhythmically.

"So fucking sexy, baby doll." He quickly dispensed with his clothes and knelt over her. Every time her fingers slipped away from her pulsing clit, he granted it a stroke from his tongue, keeping her wet and whipping her into a frenzy.

He grasped her calves and spread her legs farther as she quaked in anticipation. Her hands flew to the bed. "Let me help you, honey. You're so wet I know you need to come. It hurts, doesn't it? Let me make it better." Separating her lips with his thumbs, he leaned and swirled his tongue up her slit. "Watch me."

She leaned her head up to follow his commands as his tongue stroked back and forth over her clitoris. Her sweet little pussy glistened in the moonlit Paris night, slick and ready.

"That feels so good," fell from her mouth in a desperate plea.

"I know, baby. I know everywhere my good girl likes to be sucked, and licked, and bitten." He let his teeth slide along the tender folds. Then he sucked her inner thigh, branding her all for him.

She went wild. Her entire body writhed as she gripped the sheets under her and spread her legs wide. She wanted to be owned.

"That's my good girl," Dan coaxed as her entire body tensed deliciously. Her temperature shot upward. Her body fevered for him. "Come for me, baby doll. Fill my mouth like a good girl." She lost it all. Her energy flowed around his tongue as he groaned against her. Her body contorted. Everything she'd needed, everything she'd wanted, since the night before was fulfilled.

"Such a good girl, but I'm just getting started." He watched her body convulse and tremble from the strokes of his tongue. He dipped his fingers inside the slick heat he'd just elicited.

Her abdomen clenched as she pulled him deeper. Unable to wait, desperate to have her attention, Dan grabbed her hand.

"Yes," she gasped as he wrapped it around his throbbing cock.

"Feel it. Feel what you do to me before I bury it inside of you." He kept his strokes deep and rhythmic in the perfect spot.

She cried out for him, but he kissed her, quickly quelling her sweet moans. He didn't want to silence her. He wanted to hear her pleas, but he wanted to feel her tremble around him more.

"Is my good girl ready for me to make everything better?"

"No," she sassed defiantly as she leapt. She crawled up on all fours and dragged her tongue up his length. Her heaving breasts brushed his sac as she swirled her tongue around his head.

A deep thundering groan rang from his lungs, as his body responded with a mimicked thrust. He pulsed hot and heavy in her face.

"You take it then. Suck my cock. Right fucking now," he demanded in a lust-driven growl as he wrapped her hair up in his hand and guided her mouth over his head. With deep sucks, she pulled the erotic energy from his body in heavy doses.

He was hot-wired to detonate. He'd needed to get off for the last twenty-four hours. He had to stop her. Cradling her face tenderly in his hands, he guided her back. "I want you to just lie there and take it for me, sweetheart." He turned her over, laid her out on her stomach, and penetrated her in one deep advance.

"Yes," hissed from her as he began to thrust rhythmically.

"Nothing will ever feel as good as you do," he vowed in a reverent groan of supreme satisfaction. He pounded into her, listening to her demands to be taken harder and faster.

"I'm gonna..." Her back arched up as he continued to plunge her depths.

"I know, baby doll. I feel it coming. Just let it go. It'll feel so much better when you give it up for me."

She unfurled around him and surrounded him in the very essence of her love, her trust, her needs, and her desires that he was soothing and fulfilling.

His release gathered fiercely in his groin. He strained inside her so tightly he couldn't stop the imminent explosion. She was too perfect. The love passing between them was far too overwhelming. He felt her tremble again. He groaned in ecstasy and filled her full of everything he was.

After regaining the ability to breathe and move, Dan eased out of her and pulled her onto his chest.

"So much better when our little girl isn't knocking on the door." Fionna leaned up and brushed a sweet kiss across his lips. "Maddie was right. It's a requirement. I need it."

Chuckling, Dan turned to cradle her in his arms and to block out the sights and sounds of Paris coming through the window. "I've got everything you need, baby, and I will always take care of you."

"Okay, cuddle me up so I can dream about that. I have to be up to puke in a few hours."

"Maybe with the time difference, Halia will let you sleep a little later."

Fionna's entire body swelled with pride and elation. "I love her name, and you're the most amazing dad in the world."

"I've been calling her that in my head for a while."

"Why didn't you tell me?"

"I wanted to see if there was something you liked first."

"Dan, she's your little girl, and we have to do this together."

"Do you want me to put the oils on you, baby?"

"I almost forgot." Her weary body managed another yawn.

"That's what I'm here for." Working quickly, he lathered his hands and made circular motions tenderly over her stomach and mound as her blinks grew heavy. When he finished, he held her on his chest and waited until she fell asleep.

Easing his hands back to her lower abdomen, Dan closed his eyes in concentration. His heart flew as he felt Halia's rhythms, strong and contented, as Fionna slept soundly. He pushed his loving protective bands through to her.

Suddenly, something shifted. Her energy spun differently. She could feel him.

His breath panted as he understood what he was feeling. "Hey there, baby girl," he whispered. She could feel his energy from inside Fionna and coming through her womb from his hands. "We love you so much, sweetheart. I promise I will always keep you safe." He lay there locked on to his tiny baby girl until he fell into a deep sleep.

CHAPTER 30

GLASS HOUSES

Gasping for breath, Dan wiped the sweat pouring from his brow.

"Daddy!" Aida pled in terror.

"Dan, wake up! I feel someone!"

"Fi!" He couldn't understand what was happening. His brain fought the images of Fionna screaming convulsively on the operating table. The metallic scent of blood hung in the air. But he heard Aida crying and trying to awaken him.

"Dan!" Fionna grasped his shoulders, effectively shaking him from his hellish nightmare. His heart thundered out of rhythm.

"Daddy, I heard something in my room and Phoebe heard it too!" Aida wailed.

Blinking rapidly, he tried to understand where he was.

"I felt someone, but they're gone." Fionna's voice shook in her terror.

"Okay." He managed to stand, thankful that he'd pulled on boxers. "Get in bed with Mommy, baby. I'll make sure everything's okay."

He discreetly handed Fionna one of his T-shirts, which she slipped into as Aida crawled into bed beside her and curled up in her waiting arms.

Dan eased his pistol from his suitcase and slid out of the bedroom.

He closed the door behind him before turning on the lights in the hall. Years of training and instinct kicked in as he methodically studied the apartment.

He cleared the hall and the bathroom before moving into the room where Aida had been sleeping. He flipped on the light. Shattered glass was on the floor. His heart hammered as he backed along the wall to the broken pane in the window. There was no one on the street, and all of the streetlights were glowing brightly. Half of a broken brick lay at the foot of his daughter's bed.

He methodically swept the rest of the apartment. No one was there. The doors were all bolted tight. It was four in the morning. While debating what to do next, Dan checked and rechecked every room and every window. Nothing was awry save the window in Aida's bedroom. He unlocked it and eased it upward. The bushes outside were crushed. Someone had been outside recently. That's why Fionna had felt them.

Harrowing guilt took him over as he recalled closing her bedroom door and turning on the bathroom fan to block out noise the evening before. He closed the window and pushed a blanket around the casing before returning to Fionna and Aida.

They were huddled together. Aida was in Fionna's soothing cast and clinging to her fiercely.

"Please don't make me go back to my bed."

"No, baby. Of course not." Dan climbed back in bed with them. "You stay right here with me and Mommy."

"Thank you." She effectively shattered his heart.

"Her window is broken. I'll stay up. You go back to sleep. Fitz will be up in an hour or so. I'll call him then."

Fionna was on the verge of tears. She cradled Aida tenderly to her chest and ran her fingers through her long, thin, brown hair.

"I want Daddy to hold me, please," Aida begged but was clearly afraid she was going to hurt Fionna's feelings.

Fionna nodded her understanding. "I like it when Daddy holds me if I'm scared too."

Aida crawled into Dan's lap but kept one hand in Fionna's. Dan pushed his shield out over all of his girls. She was asleep moments later with both Fi and Dan watching over her obsessively.

～

"Honestly, I have several ideas as to what might've happened. None of them are great," Fitz admitted as he and Dan moved around the outside of the apartment building looking for any sign as to who might've shattered the window. He pointed to the crushed shrub and shook his head.

"Let me guess," Dan huffed. "Some die-hard Angels fan took it way too far last night and wants to let me know what they think about Fionna not playing next season."

Fitz offered him a sorrowful nod as he held up a crumpled piece of magazine paper. A page out of an old Angels program. "I'm thinking this was supposed to be around the brick. The only thing with this is that even though it got out that you were bringing the girls here," he eased as Dan continued to lambaste himself for discussing their trip and their children in public, "no one knew where you were staying. I didn't reserve the apartment in your name. Old habit, I guess, but even if I had, the only people who know you're here work for Parliament. On the other hand, if you have friends who are Angels fans and you know Fionna Styler is going to be here, you'd talk. People are stupid. Nonetheless, I can't have my best friend's family waking up in the middle of the night because people are throwing shit through the window."

"Aida's terrified. She actually thought we were going to send her back to bed." Dan still felt the heartbreak of his baby girl begging to be allowed to stay in her mother's arms.

Fitz chuckled. "She'll be all right. You, however, are a hopeless case. She's got you wrapped so tight you'll never be able to straighten yourself out, and you've got another one on the way."

"I don't want to be straightened out. I like it right where I am."

"Yeah, I know, and I'm really happy for you, but let's go get you packed. Maddie won't be happy until she has you all at our house anyway."

"Are you sure?" Dan quizzed. "I could get a hotel room, or maybe we should go home. What if this gets worse?"

"You're not going home. The boys will double up. Aida can have Alfred's room, and you and Fionna can have the guestroom. It's fine."

Fitzroy had purchased his home, about twenty minutes outside of Paris, under an alias, and very few people actually knew where he lived. Dan knew Fionna and Aida would be safe there, so he agreed.

"Besides, we need to get going. Maddie's already alerted every lingerie house in Paris that she's bringing Fionna shopping today, so by the time they're finished, you won't have money for a hotel room or an earlier flight."

Dan grinned. Fionna would be thrilled to spend her birthday shopping for French lingerie. "There are much worse things she could spend it all on besides lingerie."

"Well said." Fitz laughed.

"Fi will be thrilled. I just have to convince my baby girl to hang out with me and the boys all day."

"She seems pretty taken with you, Daddy-o. I thought I was going to have to pry her out of your arms with a crowbar when I got here, so I'd say you've definitely got yourself a daddy's girl. We'll take the kids out to the boys' favorite children's park." Extremely pleased with Fitz's assessment, Dan nodded his agreement.

An hour later, Dan and Fionna were settling Aida in Alfred's room. She seemed pleased she wouldn't have to sleep in the apartment anymore, but she stuck close to Dan for most of the morning.

"I wasn't sick this morning. That's something," Fionna allowed.

"I think the time difference threw you off, and then you'd eaten before you're normally up being sick."

"Yeah, I was thinking that too, because I feel better as soon as you make me my tea and I eat a little something. I think it was Halia's birthday present for me." She chuckled.

She knelt down in front of Aida. "All right, my sweet girl, you have fun with Daddy today, and tell him to take lots of pictures of you so I can see when I get back."

"What are you and Mrs. Fitzroy going to do?"

"We're going shopping."

"I like to go shopping. Daddy and I could come with you."

"You and Daddy are going to a super fun park, and I'll be back later this afternoon. You can tell me all about your day."

"What if someone throws another hard thing?" Tears formed on her eyelashes.

Dan's heart stuttered. "Baby, remember, Mr. Fitzroy and I are pretty sure that was an accident." He gazed into the innocent, tear-filled eyes of his precious little girl and lied to her. It made him sick.

They guided her out of Alfred's room, and Alex finally convinced Aida to play a game in his room as Fionna was getting ready to leave.

"Fi, please be careful for me," Dan begged as he led her to the door. He was terrified some idiot out there was going to try and take out his disappointment that the Angels would be getting a new Receiver on her.

"I'll be fine. We'll be in public the entire time, and I'll text you all day so you know I'm okay."

"Just watch everyone around you. If you see or more importantly if you *feel* anything strange at all, leave wherever you are and call me."

"I promise, and I really, really want to do this. I'm so excited that Maddie's taking me under her wing. There's so much I want to ask her about. Please."

All of his mental debate about forbidding her to go melted in the light of her pleading gaze. Dan nodded. "I know, baby. Just please be careful."

"I promise." She brushed a kiss across his lips. That was all it took to catch the very essence of her energy.

"Come here to me, Mrs. Vindico." He pulled her back and engaged her in a deeper, far more intense kiss. She responded heatedly and soon they were consuming one another.

Fitzroy cleared his throat, and Dan pulled away, gasping for breath.

Aida giggled as the boys pretended to gag loudly. Dan wasn't aware they'd come to the door as well.

"They do that a lot," Aida informed everyone.

"Do they?" Fitz egged her on.

"Yes!"

"That's so gross, Uncle Dan." Alex stuck his finger in his open mouth and made another gagging noise.

"Talk to me in a few years, kid."

"We'll be back around four, so you two can get ready to head to the tower," Maddie explained. "Have a good time, and Alex, mind your father and your Uncle Dan."

"Oui, oui, Maman." Alex rolled his eyes.

A little while later, Dan buckled Aida into Fitzroy's car between Alfred and Alex. As they were driven to the northernmost end of Paris, the boys began regaling Aida with everything she would see at the park.

"There's a huge playground, and lions, and monkeys, and sometimes there's a puppet show," Alfred explained.

"Yeah, and you have to be careful because lions eat girls," Alex sneered.

"Alexandar," Fitzroy scolded.

"My Daddy won't let a lion eat me," Aida retorted.

"Yeah, definitely Daddy's girl." Fitz chuckled.

"Can we ride the train please, Papa?" Alfred begged.

"A train like in Anne, Daddy?" Aida sounded thrilled.

"Kind of."

"Sure." Fitz turned to drive to the train entrance at Pointe Maillot. Soon, Dan was holding Aida's hand and guiding her onto a miniature train. He squeezed into a seat and felt badly as she tried to wedge herself beside him.

"I've never ridden a train before."

Dan was pleased she didn't seem frightened. She was excited, but she kept his hand tightly in her grasp.

The train lurched, and her entire little body tensed, but as it pulled away from the station she relaxed and smiled. Dan pointed out landmarks as they rode.

When his cell phone chirped, he had to stand to pull it from his pocket, but he reseated himself quickly.

Just checking in... was the text from Fionna. It also contained a selfie taken in a lingerie store dressing room mirror. She was wearing a loose, sheer, purple nightie that scalloped up over the tiniest G-string Dan had ever seen. Both of her lips were visible to his prying eyes. There was delicate cream lace that formed a delicious curve over her nipples, but they were on full display in the see-through nightie.

He couldn't seem to recapture his breath or calm his hammering heart. He understood that the loose fabric that currently hung off of her slender waist would one day fall around her baby bump.

The G-string had tie sides with satin ribbons that hung down her thighs, begging to be untied.

Buy that now! was his reply.

"We're here." Alex's announcement shook Dan from his erotic fantasies and reminded him that he was supposed to be giving all of his attention to his little girl and his godsons.

Over the next hour, Dan had a ball watching Aida experience so many things she'd never seen before. He took pictures of her petting goats and feeding birds. They rode water rides, the carousel, and other carnival-style rides, much to her delight.

As Dan carried her on his shoulders to find some lunch, his phone vibrated in his pocket. After deciding to wait until Aida wasn't directly above him to read the text, he listened to her squeal in delight as he hoisted her to the ground.

Fitz guided everyone into one of the restaurants on the property. As they found a table with a view of the lake, Dan pulled his cell from his pocket.

"What kinds of things do you like to eat for lunch, sweetheart?" Fitz asked Aida kindly.

"When I lived in the orphanage, I ate stew almost every day, so I don't think I like stew anymore. Sometimes there was other food, but I didn't want to eat it in case someone else wanted it."

Fitz and Dan shared a heartbroken expression as she went on. "But now I like it when Mommy makes me a peanut butter and jelly sandwich with strawberry jelly that makes my tummy smile, and I eat carrot sticks with,"—her brow furrowed—"what do I put the carrot sticks in?"

"Ranch dressing." Dan winked at her.

She beamed up at him. "With that and sometimes she makes me cucumbers that I hadn't ever had before I came to live with Mommy, but I like them very much. And I get to have a few potato chips, and a glass of milk. And if I want more milk, then Daddy says 'sure, baby girl' and he pours me more. And when you live in the orphanage, you can only have one of everything because someone else might need the others."

Fitz clutched his chest. "Okay, she has to stop talking now. I can't cry in front of my boys."

"Yeah." Dan nodded his understanding. "Did I tell you that we're going to be the poster family for the Auxiliary International Adoptions in the Realm program?"

"Yeah well, if they need money, call me. If they have two more of her, I'll take them too."

As Fitz explained the dishes on the buffet to Aida, Dan opened the text from Fionna. He had to stifle the groan that threatened to thunder from his chest.

The text read, *Thought this was cute.* It contained a picture of Fionna once again in a dressing room mirror. She was wearing a black see-through nightie with a ruffled bottom that didn't cover her backside. He could see it on full display in the mirror. The nightie tied deliciously between her tits with a hot pink bow. But what had Dan's eyes goggling and him panting for breath, were the slits in the fabric over both of her nipples. The back of the flyaway nightie ruffled over her backside, and she'd completed the ensemble with a black thong that had a matching hot pink bow at the top of her lush cheeks.

Baby, you are driving me wild... he responded immediately.

CHAPTER 31
SOMETHING TO LOSE

After lunch, Fitz and Dan watched the kids climb all over a massive playground. Suddenly, a man Dan recognized sauntered over to the bench where they were seated.

"Le Capitaine Fitzroy, comment allez-vous, monsieur."

"Malden, I'm doing well. How are you?" Fitz offered the man his hand. "You remember Dan Vindico, don't you? He's the former Chief of Iodex in America. You've met him several times."

Switching to English with a great deal of ease, the man nodded. "Chief Vindico, so nice to see you again. I did hear that you recently married zee Fionna Styler of the Arlington Angels, and I used to just admire your casts," he joked.

Dan had never liked Malden. He'd worked with him on a few occasions when he helped Fitzroy slowly and methodically dismantle the hub of the Interfeci that had taken over Paris. He was pompous and irritating. Dan kept one eye trained on Aida as she slid down a long tube slide.

"Yeah, I definitely married way out of my league."

"Daddy, watch me!" Aida attempted to cross the monkey bars. She got stuck two rungs in. Terror formed on her face as she looked to the ground. Dan bolted toward her.

"I've got you." He wrapped his massive hands around her waist and lowered her gently to the ground.

"It was too much higher from up there."

"I know, baby. It's okay."

She hugged him. A man pedaling an ice cream cart pulled up in front of the playground. Dan lifted Aida back into his arms, not certain why he so desperately wanted to hold her. "Want to get a popsicle?"

She nodded. "I haven't had dinner yet though."

"I think since it's a special Aida-Daddy day, it's okay."

With her eyes sparkling, she picked out a strawberry fruit pop. Dan ordered a chocolate one for himself.

They headed back to the bench. Aida crawled up in his lap as she unwrapped her popsicle.

"Who's zis?" Malden gave Aida a kind smile.

She cringed, and Dan's heart flew. His muscles tensed fiercely as he wrapped her up in his arms.

"This is my little girl." He supplied no more information.

"I didn't know you had children?"

"Well, I do." Dan glared at Malden.

"It was so nice to see you, Capitaine Fitzroy. I'll see you at work Monday."

"Yeah, I won't be in much next week since we have company, but I expect you all to get all of that paperwork done while I'm gone." Fitz sounded mildly threatening.

"Yes, sir. Of course," Malden agreed. "So nice to see you again, Chief Vindico."

"You too." Dan kept his cold glare leveled on Malden as he walked away.

Aida began eating her popsicle. She sat contentedly in Dan's lap with her head cradled between his chin and his chest.

"How's the tummy?" Dan asked the question he already knew the answer to.

"It was nervous a minute ago, but now it feels better. Maybe strawberry popsicles work like the strawberry jelly Mommy puts on my sandwiches. It makes my tummy feel better too."

"Very strange." Fitz turned his body to watch Malden walk away. "What?"

"Malden doesn't have any kids, so what the hell is he doing out here?"

"Yeah, my littlest Receiver picked up on something."

Fitz ground his teeth. "If it has anything to do with kids, I'll be short a lackey officer, and his family will be short a son."

Fitz left Dan with all of the kids to acquire tickets to the puppet show before they headed home. He returned a few minutes later empty-handed.

"Were they sold out?" Dan hoped the kids wouldn't be disappointed.

"No." Fitz grimaced. "The show today is about a little French orphan girl who's not taken care of by the family who adopted her so she runs away."

"Good call." Dan was sick from the thought alone.

"Let's take them home. You have to get ready, and they can play in the courtyard."

Dan headed toward the slide where Aida had been a moment before.

"Aida, it's time to go, baby."

He searched the large playground as his stomach twisted uncomfortably. "Aida!" he called again frantically. "Aida!" He started to run but couldn't see her in the huge crowd of swarming children.

His heart pumped frantic terror through his body. His stomach seized. Where was she? "Aida!"

"I'm right here!" He heard the sweetest voice in the entire world, and breath tried to return to his lungs. "I'm sorry. I tried to get through all of those kids when you called, but then I moved and I couldn't see you."

Dan rushed to her, lifted her into his arms, and held her tight. "It's okay. You just scared me." The words stunned him. He was Daniel Vindico, and for many, many years nothing had frightened him because he'd had nothing worth living for.

As he held her in the safety of his embrace, he'd never had so much to lose.

"I'm sorry." Aida looked crestfallen as she wrapped her arms around his neck. "I wouldn't have left without you. I know I'm not supposed to."

"I know, baby." He tried to sound reassuring, but it wasn't her leaving of her own accord that worried him.

Dan carried her back to the train, terrified to put her down, but he couldn't reason why. Seeming to sense his need to keep his hands on her, Aida crawled in his lap on the train. "I'm right here." She sweetly quoted his reassurances to her the night before just as she'd fallen asleep tucked safely on his chest.

Dan kissed her cheek. With a deep yawn, she wiggled until her head was tucked in his neck, and he kept his arms wrapped around her.

Fitz gave him a genuine smile as he shook his head and chuckled. "Been ten damn long years, man, but it's nice to have the real Dan Vindico back."

By the time they arrived at the Fitzroys', Aida was yawning constantly. "I think it's time for you to say, 'Aida, it's time to lie down and read for a little while,'" Aida informed Dan making him and Fitzroy laugh.

"Why don't you go get Phoebe and bring me Anne and I'll read to you both?" Dan offered.

"Really?" She tittered ecstatically.

Dan nodded and watched Aida race up the stairs.

"It has to hurt," Fitz goaded. "I mean her fingers are so tiny to be wrapped up so tightly around one."

Joining in his laughter, Dan couldn't deny the charges. His cell phone chirped again, and he pulled it quickly from his pocket.

Heading back now, was the first message. *Look, room for our little Halia,* was the next and was accompanied by Fionna wearing a sheer black top that came over her shoulders and dipped down, showing off most of her cleavage. It tied between her breasts and was accompanied by a tiny skirt that tied on the side at her hipbone. The entire ensemble was see-through.

Dan stared at her for a long drawn-out minute.

"Don't drool on your phone, man." Fitz chuckled.

"That obvious?"

"Oh, yeah. You don't go all slack-jawed and stare stupidly at your phone for anyone but her."

Aida returned, and Dan quickly stowed his phone as she climbed beside him on the sofa.

The boys, tired from their excursion as well, ended up listening to Dan read the story though they'd never have admitted to enjoying the chapters they heard.

Aida fell asleep against Dan, and the boys switched on the television.

Dan eased Aida up onto his chest, covered her in her blanket, and fell asleep almost instantly.

A gentle kiss awoke him from his deep slumber.

"Hey, baby doll." He tried to clear the gravel from his throat.

"Sweetest thing I have ever, ever seen." Fionna gestured to Aida who was sprawled over Dan.

He yawned and tried to determine the time.

"Maddie's making coffee and a cheese tray. Do you think you could lay her down without waking her?"

He rubbed his eyes for a moment and then turned and eased out from underneath Aida. He laid her gently on the sofa. She stirred, but Fionna casted her and she fell back asleep, breathing in the warm serenity and the peaceful calm that Fionna brought both of them.

The boys had regained their energy quickly and were playing outside as Dan and Fionna joined Fitz and Maddie at their kitchen table.

Aida awoke and located them in the kitchen as they were finishing their coffee.

"Hey, sweet girl. Did you have fun with Daddy today?"

Aida crawled up in Fionna's lap. "Yes, ma'am. I rode on a train like in Anne, and I saw goats, and I got to ride on a river over water that splashed me, but Daddy said I wouldn't fall out. And I ate a very yummy lunch, and played on the biggest playground I've ever seen, and Daddy got me a strawberry popsicle, because he said it was okay because it was a Daddy-Aida day and I think those days are very special. And Daddy took lots of pictures of me and that way we won't forget Daddy-Aida day."

Fionna swooned.

Dan kissed her cheek. "We'll have lots of Daddy-Aida days."

"Okay, but this was my very first one, so I want to remember not to forget everything we did together."

"It sounds like you had a sunshine tummy day!" Fionna tickled her stomach. Aida folded forward and giggled.

"Except for when Daddy got lost," she fussed a moment later. "And when the man came."

"Daddy got lost?" Fionna glanced at Dan.

"I heard him say, 'Aida it's time to leave,' but I couldn't see him, and I looked everywhere. He was only a little bit lost though, I guess."

"I, uh, found myself very quickly."

Chuckling at his verbiage, Fionna nodded. "And the man?"

"Malden?" Fitz whispered hesitantly. Dan nodded. "Don't worry. I've been keeping a close eye on him."

Aida laid her head against Fionna's shoulder. "I didn't like him, and I missed you."

"I missed you too, and I was just talking to Mrs. Fitzroy, and we decided that maybe one day while we'e here we should have girls' day where we take you and maybe get our nails done, and our hair fixed, and a few other fun things. We'll let Daddy and Mr. Fitzroy play with the boys."

"I get to have an Aida-Mommy day too?" Fionna nodded. "Oh, wow!"

A little while later, Aida was seated on the bed while Dan and Fionna got ready to go eat at the Eiffel Tower.

"What do you and Daddy do on romantic dates?"

Fionna sat beside her with her hair pinned up in large curls.

"Daddy pulls my chair out for me because a gentleman always pulls out the lady's chair."

"That's right," Dan agreed as he tied his tie. If at some point in the very distant future, preferably after she turned thirty-five, Dan allowed her to date, then the guy better treat her like a princess.

"And then we talk, and we laugh, and we eat yummy food, and then Daddy brings me home, and then the best part comes."

Aida's eyes danced. "What's the best part?"

"Daddy kisses me."

Aida shook her head. "Daddy does that all the time."

Dan headed to the bed and kissed Fionna sweetly. "That's because I love her so much," he informed Aida before he kissed her cheek. "And I love you so much."

"When I grow up, maybe I should marry Daddy too or maybe Garrett?"

Fionna bit her lips together to keep from laughing as she nodded. "Daddy and Garrett are the very best choices."

CHAPTER 32

DAN AND FITZ

As the sun began casting its last vestiges of light over the Paris skyline, Dan watched Fionna check her lipstick one last time.

"You are breathtaking, honey." He was unable to take his eyes off her. She was stunning. Her hair fell in loose waves over the top of the short, figure-hugging tan-and-black dress she'd picked for their evening. The tan was the precise shade of her skin. It gave the illusion that the black swirls danced up her naked body, and Dan was already drooling.

She'd pulled on a pair of strappy, stiletto heels, and the effect was overwhelming.

Fitz and Maddie complimented Fionna as well as they headed toward the door.

"We'll be back late, so you and Phoebe go on to bed, and Daddy and I will come kiss you when we get back," Fionna guided Aida. She nodded dejectedly and clung to Dan's hand.

"Come on, Aida. Let's go play," Alex ordered.

"Go play, baby. You'll have fun," Fionna soothed. "Here." She gently kissed Aida's cheek. "You keep Mommy's kiss safe until I get back and give you another one."

Aida placed her hand delicately over her cheek and looked up to the task. "Okay."

"Do you think you can keep two safe?" Dan teased her.

"I can!"

He knelt down and kissed her other cheek. She held both sides of her face in her little hands. Fitz and Maddie gazed at her adoringly.

"Have fun with Alex and Alfred." Dan wrapped his arm around Fionna and guided her out of the house.

After a quick ride on the Metro, they were walking arm in arm through the streets of Paris. The city came alive under their feet, and Dan watched his beautiful wife as she took in the stunning architecture and all of the city's secrets held deep within its steadily flowing river and each and every historic landmark.

Fionna beamed as Dan led her to the elevator to begin their ascent up the Eiffel Tower.

"Have you ever eaten here before?" she whispered in awe.

"No, baby doll. I only ever came to Paris to work or to see the boys."

"It's so beautiful."

"Yeah, the view is stunning." He was staring at her and not at the Paris skyline.

Fionna smirked and rolled her eyes at him. They exited the elevator and stepped into the Jules Verne restaurant. Dan gave his name and they were immediately escorted to a secluded table in the back corner that gave them an outstanding view of the city and as much privacy as a restaurant surrounded on all sides by windows could offer.

"How did we score the best seat in the house?"

"Have to give Fitz all the credit for that." Dan had thanked Fitz profusely for getting them the reservations on her birthday, but clearly he needed to thank him again.

"This is amazing." Fionna sighed in replete satisfaction after Dan seated her. The waiter arrived immediately and offered them wine and asked which menu they would prefer, the five or seven course.

"Could I just get some seltzer water, please?" Fionna requested.

"Certainly, madame," the waiter assured her with a nod. He

returned with their drinks, and they selected the seafood for their first course.

Fionna gave Dan that smile that lit his entire world. The one that she reserved for him alone. "So, I have something I want to tell you."

Quite certain that his wife laughing and gazing up at him with her sweet smile had to be the most beautiful sight in the world, Dan took her hand from across the table.

"Okay." He played along with a wry smile.

"I'm pretty sure that I'm pregnant, so we're gonna have a baby."

They both laughed.

"That's amazing, sweetheart. I'm thrilled. Do you feel okay?" Dan supplied all of what he assumed would be standard replies for being told that your wife was expecting.

As their first course arrived, they scooted closer together. They wanted the rest of the patrons, the rest of the world, to melt away just for a little while.

"I felt her last night, Fi," Dan confessed in a choked whisper. "I mean, I felt her feel me after you were asleep."

Emotion shone in her beautiful sienna eyes. "It's amazing, isn't it? That's what she always does whenever you lock on to her. Her rhythms change. I can feel it."

"It was incredible."

She studied him closely for a long minute. Dan smiled at her, curious to know what she was thinking about.

"You're just amazing." She sounded overwhelmed.

"No, baby doll. That's you."

"I just…" she choked out.

He scooted closer to her and offered her his hand. She regained her composure by drawing from him. He allowed himself a moment to supply her with his love and his protection and to revel in the sensation of her taking from him.

"I still hate everything that happened."

Dan drew a deep breath. "I know. Believe me, I do too."

Offering him a smile through the tears that had escaped, she nodded. "I know, but honestly, I can't imagine ever being any happier than I am right now. It's like everything I've ever wanted—even the things I was too afraid to wish for—I have, and you gave them all to me."

He couldn't understand how she couldn't see that she was the one who'd given him everything. "I think we both just finally decided to start living, and I somehow managed to get lucky enough to get to share the rest of my life with you. All that matters to me is getting to wake up beside you every morning and getting to hold you in my arms as you go to sleep every night."

Their ravioli course arrived, and Fionna dug in. "This is delicious."

"It's not as good as what I plan on devouring later," he informed her shamelessly.

Fionna smirked. "And what might that be, Mr. Vindico?"

"You, baby doll."

She trembled slightly. The effect made Dan's trousers begin to tighten.

"Is there something else I get for my birthday besides this amazing dinner? Something you might be craving?"

Giving her a cocky chuckle, he grinned. "I'm seated across from the most stunning thing I've ever laid eyes on, and see, baby, it's not just that. She's wearing my ring. She's all mine, and unlike every other guy in here who keeps throwing glances your way and would gladly pay the tab for this meal ten times over to be sitting where I'm sitting, I know how gorgeous you are when I get you out of the little black dress. I know how delicious you taste. I know how tight and sweet you are, and I know just how you like it. So, yeah, I'm definitely craving something. I want you."

Fionna's eyes danced from his explanation. They darkened with need flaming in their depths.

A little while later, the waiter arrived with their bowls of bouillabaisse, effectively interrupting the mood around them that was drowning in their passion and in the lust that was coursing rapidly between them.

"You're certain you won't be having the caviar this evening?" the waiter asked again.

Despite Maddie's assurances that Fionna take her pregnancy in stride and indulge occasionally, she'd decided against the caviar course as it wasn't a food she particularly enjoyed anyway.

Dan winked at Fionna and took her hand. There was nothing to lose at this point, so he grinned. "Not this evening, sir. My beautiful wife has just informed me that she's expecting our second child, much to my delight. Caviar might be a little rough on her stomach."

"Ah, oui, oui! Congratulations, Mrs. Vindico, Mr. Vindico! It is a special night then." He nodded to Fionna with a kind smile.

"Oh, thank you." Fionna looked truly touched.

A man accidentally bumped into Fionna's chair as he headed toward his table. Dan scowled, but he apologized. It was because of Fionna's bristle that Dan studied the man more closely.

"What did you feel?"

"I think it's just a devious thought or two." She shrugged.

While she was distracted with the waiter refilling her water, Dan slid the long velvet box he'd pulled from his jacket in front of her plate.

"Dan, you brought me to Paris. You weren't supposed to get me anything."

He shook his head. "My wife is turning twenty-nine again tonight," he chuckled, "and Paris or no Paris, she gets presents on her birthday. She should get them every day just for being the phenomenal woman that she is."

Her eyes danced as she lifted the box.

"Aida helped me pick it out."

"This is the best second twenty-ninth birthday I've ever had." She laughed.

"Open it."

She popped open the hinged, velvet box and gasped. "This is so beautiful!" Her hands shook as she grasped the box.

Steadying her hands, Dan lifted the diamond and pearl tennis bracelet from the box. She cradled the dangling sapphire pendant hung from a diamond drop in her hand as tears made their way down her cheeks.

"It's Aida's birthstone."

Dan pulled a handkerchief from his pocket. He'd come prepared.

"Here." He clasped the bracelet around her wrist. "When Halia arrives, we'll add hers as well." She leaned and threw her arms around him. "You are amazing, and this is amazing! I'm just completely overwhelmed."

"See, thirty's not so bad."

"Shh." She giggled through her tears.

They continued chatting as they were supplied with the roasted chicken course.

"So, I had fun shopping with Maddie today."

Dan laughed. "I had fun seeing what you were shopping for. I'm hoping I get to try my hand at getting you out of some of it tonight."

"You do have amazing hands."

Dan arched his left eyebrow in intrigue and let his fingers stroke over her inner thigh just under the hem of the dress.

"And," her voice stuttered slightly as she reveled in his pliant touch. "Maddie says I have to stop feeling ashamed of my own desires, that I have to embrace them. She says it's perfectly natural, and if I want to have wild sex and feel a little more like I'm twenty-one and less like I'm twenty-nine for the second time, she says I should just tell you."

Dan promptly choked on the hunk of delectable chicken he'd just put in his mouth. He downed a sip of water. "Baby, if you want to be a bad girl for me, or you want to go wild for the night, you just say the word and I'll make it happen. Anything you want I'll take care of."

"Maddie also told me that you coached Fitz before the first time he asked her to stay over."

"I might've done something like that." He chuckled.

"You must've been a pretty good teacher. She didn't know it was his first time until he told her several months later."

Dan shrugged. "Fitz taught me a lot, so I figured I owed him. I tried to think of everything I wished I'd known before my first time." His recalled the night he and Fitzroy had stayed late at the French Senate. They'd been the only two officers still in the Iodex department. Fitz pled for information before he met Maddie at the Moulin Rouge where she was a dancer. He'd invited her to his flat that night.

"How did you and Fitz meet? He didn't go to Venton with us."

Dan recognized the excitement that colored her tone when she was learning something new.

He continued to let his mind move back in time. "Fitz is a year older than I am. My senior year at the academy, all I really wanted was out so I could go into Iodex." He left out the fact that at the time, the driving force had been so he could marry Amelia and get away from his mother. "I pled with Mentor Sullivan to let me go into a special ops training that year instead of the year after. He agreed. I was a good student, I guess."

"You were head of Ioses order and graduated with a 4.2," Fionna bragged.

Dan scoffed over her admiration. "Anyway, my Dad got me in the class I wanted, and Fitz had come back to America to go through American Special Ops that year. His mom is French, but his dad is American so he grew up in Columbus. His parents divorced when he was sixteen. He moved back to Lyon with his mom and attended a Gifted academy here. He spent his summers with his dad. He'd wanted to study Special Ops in America, so we partnered up in the classes. I guess the rest is history."

Fionna glanced back out the windows to the stunning Paris skyline as the waiter brought their cheese tray. "I'm really glad you and Fitz met, because I'm sitting here with you on my birthday. Thank you so much for bringing me here. This is amazing."

Bored with his and Fitz's history, Dan returned his hand to her thigh. He edged the hem of the dress just a little higher as he plied her skin.

With another sexy smirk, Fionna leaned to the side and brushed a kiss along his chiseled jaw. "You're making me wet, Mr. Vindico." Her hot breath on his ear set every nerve ending in his body on high alert.

He turned to gaze into her hungry eyes, giving her a look that said he'd devour every last drop of her and then make her beg for more.

"And that's kind of a problem," she continued in a throaty whisper.

"I've never found it to be a problem I couldn't take care of, sweetheart."

Fionna slid away from him and took a long sip of her water before she moved back in. "Yeah, I know, but the panties I'm wearing are crotchless." She shot him a grin that threatened to set him on fire.

"My God, baby." Dan fought the deep desire to demand the check immediately.

"Yeah, so all of the important things are uncovered just like the matching bra I'm wearing with them."

His muscles vibrated in ardent desire. He stifled the thundering moan threatening to tear from his lungs. His shield lifted with desperate arcs.

"Do you really want the dessert? Because I suddenly find myself wanting something else entirely."

With a wanton smirk, Fionna giggled. "Be patient, honey."

She was going to make him work for each and every inch he gained, and he was more than up to the task.

Eventually their waiter supplied them with a soufflé covered in chocolate.

"Oh, yum!" Fionna's eyes closed in ecstasy as she licked the spoon. Then with another naughty smirk, she dipped the spoon back in the chocolate confection. She kept her eyes locked on his and brought the spoon to her mouth and proceeded to lick it seductively. She let her tongue spin precisely the way she moved it over his cock when she took him in her mouth.

"Don't worry, baby doll," he assured her in a low growl. "I've got something I'm gonna make you lick and suck until you swallow everything I give you, and then I'm gonna show you what happens to naughty girls who wear extremely sexy lingerie when their husbands rip their clothes off and make them take it until he's satisfied."

Her chest rose and fell in quick gasped breaths. "I want to leave now."

"Be patient, honey." He quoted her before taking another bite of their dessert. She narrowed her eyes in spite.

After Dan paid the bill and thanked the waiter for their meal, he led Fionna back to the elevator.

CHAPTER 33

MARKED

Frustration surged through Dan's veins as they waited in a large crowd to access the elevator. His mind painted him stunning artwork of Fionna's nipples peeking through an open-tip bra and her lower lips caught up in crotchless panties. By the time they entered the elevator and headed down to the streets of Paris, his cock had taken over all rational thought processes.

He fought not to order the hordes of tourists out of his way as they exited the elevator. People pressed around them as they tried to navigate to the more open lawn.

"Buy the lady a Louis Vuitton." A pushy black market seller thrust a large handbag in Fionna's face. She shrunk back, and Dan deeply lamented no longer having a badge. "Look! Look! Only fifty dollars American. Real leather!" Dan's Visium Predilection stirred in his shield. She was carrying a real Louis. Black market sellers typically knew how to pick their buyers. Someone carrying a real one wasn't likely to purchase a fake. Something was off.

"No, thank you." Fionna's voice shook.

"Get the hell away from her!" Dan bared his teeth and glared at the offending salesman. He drifted back into the crowd looking for his next victim. Sellers with Eiffel Tower trinkets tried to bait tourists all around the tower.

"Dan." She trembled in his arms. "I need to get out of this crowd. Something's happening."

Panic replaced every ounce of sexual frustration he'd felt just a few minutes before. He used his sheer size to push through the crowd and got her to the opposite side of the tower base away from the throngs of people.

"What's wrong, baby? Is this better? Here, I'll get a cab." He turned to determine the best way to hail a cab without having to drag her back through the crowd. Occasionally, Receivers' rhythms would plummet in a large crowd. It was too many emotions to work through, and they would panic.

She was as white as a ghost. Her rhythms were frantic as her heart raced. A cold sweat dewed on her forehead and arms. Before he could cast his shield around her, he saw the man approach. In one quick move, his hand was in her purse. He paused one moment too long, and Dan had him on the ground.

"Bad plan, motherfucker." He pressed the man's face against the cold concrete and forced the air from the would-be pickpocket's lungs.

"Fi, baby, give me that scarf around your purse and call Fitz, please." She managed to follow his requests though she was still thoroughly shaken.

Dan tied the scarf tightly around the guys hands, casted the scarf, and kept his foot on the guy's back. "Don't move."

～

"I am so sorry!" Fitzroy continued to apologize as Dan fixed Fionna a cup of water at the Iodex station an hour later. The guy was being processed.

"It's not your fault." Dan sighed. "He's obviously Paris's lousiest pickpocket. Her wallet was right there."

Fionna shook her head. "I was so stupid. I just wasn't thinking. I could feel something coming. There were so many people. I couldn't tell where it was coming from. I should never have taken my purse with me. I know better."

"No." Fitz shook his head. "This happens all the time. We've tried to clean it up, but I can't seem to keep them from the big tourist locales. It is never the victim's fault. He's the asshole. He's the one going to prison. You should be able to carry your bag wherever you want."

"Are you feeling better, baby? You still look a little shaken up." Dan drew her back into his arms. She'd been there for the better part of the last hour, but her color hadn't returned and her pulse was still out of rhythm.

"I'll be okay. My radar is a little jumpy after all of that, I think."

Fitz was sick over what had happened. "Let's get her home."

Before they could leave, Eric Oliver, Fitz's top officer, came in carrying a file folder and shaking his head. He offered Fionna a kind smile and then spoke quietly with Fitz.

"Yeah, fine, turn him over. Tell them I want him off of French soil tonight, though." He turned to Dan. "Guy's got two outstanding warrants. Seems he's expanded his business from Brussels."

The next morning, Dan's eyes flashed open, and he sprinted across the hall.

"Baby," he soothed. It seemed the time difference had caught up with her. She was pale and drawn as she stood weakly from the toilet.

Dan gently wiped her face with a cold rag and supplied her with her toothbrush. He helped her back to bed and held her. He sent a heat cast through his shield. She was shivering from being sick and still seemed off from the evening's events.

He flooded his shield with his own energy, essentially making her drunk on his love and protection. She fell back asleep almost immediately.

They spent most of Sunday relaxing with the Fitzroys. The kids played while the adults talked and laughed.

They all thoroughly enjoyed Maddie's cooking. She taught Fionna to make coq au vin that they all devoured for dinner that evening.

Fitz regaled Fionna with tales of some of Dan's more idiotic stunts in their days of training. Alex begged Fitz and Dan to retell the story of the night the two of them had led two teams into an old, abandoned house well outside of Paris and had taken out ten of Wretchkinsides's men.

Fitz retold the story, but Dan didn't add much. He tried to enjoy Fionna's pride as Fitz heralded Dan's amazing shot where he took out two guys with one electric cast through a window, but he would never qualify that night as a success. That was the night Cascavel had somehow escaped him again. He could have had him years before he finally ended the repugnant evil that was Cascavel.

Dan tried to shake off the emotions of that night. He wished Fitz would stop talking about it. He didn't want to revel in his glory days. They were nothing but an endless, hellish abyss, and he'd been given a chance at heaven. He had everything he'd ever wanted, and he was never going back.

When he awoke for the second time the next morning, he was alone in the bed. He'd gotten Fionna back to sleep after she'd been sick again. With a deep yawn, he realized it was already close to ten.

He pulled himself from bed, shrugged into a pair of jeans and a polo, and went to locate his family. Fionna was refereeing an argument between Alex and Aida while Maddie worked in the kitchen.

Dan studied the kids. Aida was wearing a paper sack that Fionna, he assumed, had fashioned into a kind of jacket.

"Princesses do not rescue the prince!" Alex spat. "The prince rescues the princess and kills the dragon!"

"But that's not the way it is in my book!" Aida defied. Her little face held a mixture of fury and frustration. "Sometimes the prince needs the princess to rescue him!"

"Hey!" Dan scooped Alex up and promptly turned him upside down.

"Uncle Dan!" He wiggled his legs while Fionna and Aida watched.

"Trust me, little man. There are a whole lot of times the prince needs the princess to rescue him, and if you find a princess willing to rescue you then you are one lucky, lucky guy." Dan winked at Fionna as she beamed at him.

"Put me down!"

Giggling, Aida looked quite proud of herself as she narrowed her eyes in on Alex. "Daddy, will you please put Prince Alex down," she requested in her best princess voice.

"Why, yes, my little princess, I will." Dan flipped Alex up and over his back.

"See, I just saved you."

Alex scowled at Dan. "A princess never saved you."

"Oh, buddy, you have no idea how wrong you are. You're looking at my own personal saving princess." He gestured his head to Fionna.

She chuckled. "Aida, you know, sometimes the prince needs the princess to save him, but he still kills the dragon. If you two want to play Paper Bag Princess, maybe Alex could slay the dragon after you save him," Fionna offered as Dan willfully fought the memories of his own dragon slaying.

"You can slay the dragon if you say I'm pretty in my paper bag," Aida negotiated.

"Fine, you're pretty in your paper bag," Alex mumbled spitefully. "The dragon's in my room! Come on!" He raced through the house.

Dan sank down on the couch and pulled Fionna into his lap. "Besides dragon slaying and teaching my godson a thing or two about women, what else did I miss?"

Fionna kissed his cheek. "Fitz went into the office for a little while, but as soon as he gets home we're going to the markets. I'm so excited, and Maddie's even going to let me cook tonight."

"Why didn't you wake me up, baby?"

"Because Halia gets you up every morning at five, and you take such good care of me I wanted you to sleep."

Just as Dan was finishing up leftover croissants with chocolate sauce, Fitz made his way back home.

"Can I talk to you for a minute?" He headed toward his home office.

Dan followed him. "What's wrong?"

"Probably nothing. I hope it's nothing." Fitz sank down in his leather chair.

"What the hell happened?"

"The pickpocket had reservations at the tower. He was there when you were there and presumably left when you left."

Tension twisted up Dan's spine. He tried to think like a cop instead of an insanely overprotective husband. "Okay, that's not odd. High-end pickpockets do that. They pick out their targets and follow them."

"I know," Fitz agreed. "And like I said, he has two outstanding warrants, so clearly he's been in this game for a while, but you said he didn't grab her wallet. It's just odd. I can't shake the feeling that something else is off. He didn't follow you. Like I said, he had reservations already."

"I don't want Fionna worrying. I want her to relax and enjoy Paris. She's been through enough," Dan demanded hotly. "Our relationship was a disaster before the takedown, and then the hospital, and working through everything that had fallen apart. Besides marrying me and adopting Aida, this is the second time she's been pregnant in just a couple of months. Not to mention the fact that she was shot, and now all of this shit with the Angels and the press."

Fitz visibly softened. "I know, okay, and I'm not saying there's anything wrong. You may have struck upon some crappy luck as of late, but does it not strike you as odd that first a brick flew through the window of the apartment where you were staying, and then you were targeted at the tower and her wallet was almost taken?"

Dan wondered if he was in denial. What if he was so exhausted from living a life in the darkest shadows that he was ignoring some unknown danger right in front of him just so his precious girls could live in the light? He fought the vomit that swirled in his stomach. He refused to believe that. Wretchkinsides was done for.

He loathed to admit what he was about to say, but it was the only conceivable conclusion. "You will repeat none of what I'm about to say to you," he commanded.

Fitz nodded readily.

"My wife made a shit-ton of money playing for the Angels. She was the highest paid Receiver in Summation. Think about what I'm telling you. She has very high-end taste, and that's apparent in the clothes she wears, the bags she carries, and the jewelry she likes. She's also very sweet and always chooses to see the good instead of always suspecting that people don't have her best interest at heart. She would make a very appealing target, and I stupidly gave her a rather expensive diamond bracelet last night at our dinner table. Maybe I'm losing my edge. I don't know, but when he saw that bracelet I'm certain he was foaming at the mouth for us to leave. We were marked from that moment on."

"Okay, you are an idiot, but that makes me feel a hell of a lot better." Fitz's body slumped in relief. "For the sake of my sanity, maybe try to talk her into leaving the jewelry here, save her wedding rings, of course. Although the sheer quantity of diamonds on those rings would give every pickpocket in Paris a hard-on." He shook his head. "She obviously doesn't look French. Her Hawaiian heritage marks her as American, and French thugs know what to look for. That bag she's carrying around had to cost several thousand, easy."

CHAPTER 34
OUT OF THE MOUTHS OF BABES

That evening, Fionna, Maddie, and all of the children were in the kitchen happily creating dinner. Maddie had been letting the boys help prepare food for quite a while, and they were eager to show Aida everything they knew.

Fitz asked Dan to help him go through some evidence on the gambling ring the restaurateur was a part of that he was trying to take down. Dan knew he was hoping to bait him into accepting a position with French Iodex. He had no intention of doing that, but he gave in to the temptation to go through evidence and figure out what might be going on. It was in his blood. He couldn't deny the ardent desire to put his fierce shield to work.

"I can still remedy the fact that you no longer have a badge if you're interested," Fitz tried again as they settled in.

Dan shook his head. "No."

"Hey, Fionna loved the lingerie shops and the markets today. She loves Paris. That's all I'm saying."

Dan directed him back to the problem at hand. "So, you've been working on this guy at the restaurant. What else do you have?"

"They've got a gambling ring and money laundering deal going on there, but there has to be more to it. That's what I can't figure out. I've been working the cleanup of the few guys left around Paris that found themselves lacking work since Uncle Nic's no longer signing paychecks. The timing of this tells me they might be related, but that's the only thing that makes me think it has anything to do with the Interfeci."

"Let's start with the guys you have names and records for that are on the take with the gambling rings."

Fitz pulled several thick file folders from his large briefcase and slapped them on the desk. He'd grabbed one too many. Three mugshots skated out of the top folder. Dan shuddered as he stared down into Nic Wretchkinsides's black eyes. Just under that was a mugshot Dan had never seen before. He read the name Pavel Volkov and the murder charges listed under his picture.

"Sorry." Fitz shoved the documents back in the folder.

"Who is that guy?"

"Nobody. Don't worry about it."

"Fitz, come on. You want to bring me back on, but you won't tell me who the hell that is? What's going on?"

"He was an assassin for Nic. We didn't know about him. I located him a few weeks ago and arrested him. It's over. Let it go."

"Yeah, I wish I could." Dan finally gave voice to the fears that haunted his soul. He'd tried so hard to bury them deep in his shield, so Fionna wouldn't feel them, but she still could. He knew.

"What the hell does that mean?" Fitz's tone softened.

"I threw it off of me, or I tried to. I didn't want any part of him in my energy, but sometimes I swear I still feel him. It scares the fuck out of me. And I did what I did. I killed him that way for her. Receivers are able to read intent off of energy. According to Fionna, a great deal of what makes a person who they are is in their intent. She doesn't seem to feel anything black from me, but what if what I did affects the baby? What if it makes her sick or something? What if I'm hurting Fionna, and she doesn't know it?"

"Hey,"—Fitz shook his head—"didn't you tell me if she's around dark energy she vomits her disapproval?"

Dan nodded.

"She loves you."

"Yeah, I know. I'm not sure how the hell I got lucky enough to be able to say that, but somehow she does."

"It takes a hell of a guy and a hell of a lot of strength to be able to throw off that much black energy. That was a dark soul you took on. Of course you feel it. How could you not? But that doesn't mean that any of it will affect Fionna or the baby."

"If I hadn't been coming completely unglued over Fi bleeding out at my feet, I would have vomited. That was the sickest, most vile thing I've ever felt inside my energy for the few seconds it took me to kill him." The relief was instantaneous.

The cathartic consolation of talking about what he'd done and what he'd felt as he pulled every ounce of energy out of Dominic Wretchkinsides made him woozy with relief.

"Yeah, well, you've been through hell. Not just with Fionna and the baby you lost. All of that was after Amelia. I guess I'm not the man who gets to make the final judgment call, but to me, you did the world a tremendous service. For what it's worth, thank you that my sons don't have to live with that kind of despicable power as a presence in their life anymore."

Dan nodded meekly. "That's kind of what I feel whenever Aida crawls up in my lap or when I think about the baby. Maybe all the hell we went through is going to mean something to them."

"Of course it will. Take Aida. Think of all you and Fionna have done for her after what Pravus did to her family. What kind of sick bastard does something like that? These were not wealthy people. They had nothing, and he took what little they had."

"Yeah, I know." Dan's stomach churned. "I can't think about it, honestly. It's too much." He couldn't go there. It was a new day, and he'd never allow his baby girl to be hurt again.

"You just remember that you're the hero in this whole shit storm. You took him on, but you won. If any part of him is still in you, you're strong enough to kill it off too."

Fitz flipped open a different folder on the top of the stack.

Dan forced Wretchkinsides out of his mind. He didn't want to think about him anymore. He studied the information set before him and Fitzroy's notes.

"How many guys do you have something on?"

"Only seven, and they seem completely inept. It's like they're trying to set up a big ring but don't know how. I have to stop myself from giving them tips, so I have something to really arrest them for."

Dan lifted some of the evidence. "They do seem to be fairly petty crimes. Vandalism and getting caught with a few cell phones and traveler's checks won't amount to much in jail time, but I agree there has to be more to all of this."

"Precisely. So, maybe I should have the guys I've got something on picked up. Maybe scare them straight or scare them into talking. A few weeks in Bertereau might have them rethinking their current business venture."

Bertereau was the Gifted prison in France. It was positioned out near the Le Puy mines, and the rare combination of cerussite and aragonite surrounding the prison made it particularly unsavory for any Gifted person. The energy drain was dramatic.

Dan had taken several Interfeci members out to Bertereau. As long as you didn't stay long, it wasn't too bad. The effects took several hours to set in, but once it happened it would take weeks to recover from.

"Other than your restaurateur, this seems like a bunch of bratty kids. Taking a few of them in might get the message out to anyone who's thinking of joining them."

"Agreed. I'll call Oliver and have him file the warrants. We'll start picking them up in the morning."

At seven o'clock, the children presented their dinner to the adults with a great deal of pride. Everyone raved over their work.

Aida grinned from ear to ear as Dan helped her carry the platter of chicken to the table. Alex slopped the asparagus spears down while Alfred carefully managed the hollandaise sauce.

Fionna and Maddie supplied bread while Fitzroy poured wine. Dan followed Aida's instructions on bringing the potatoes to the table as they were much too hot for her to carry.

As everyone seated themselves and dug in, Maddie smiled at the kids. "Aida, why don't you tell us about DC." She seemed to be trying to teach her boys about proper dinner discussion and not to just inhale their food and leave the table.

Aida swallowed down a bite of chicken as she nodded thoughtfully. "Do I live in DC?" she asked Fionna.

"That's the big city near our house," Fionna reminded her.

"I remember now." She turned back to Maddie. "Living in my new house with Mommy and Daddy is the best wish. I didn't even know to wish for it, but if I had I would've."

Maddie swooned as Dan kissed the top of Aida's head.

"I got to pick my very own room, and Daddy painted my walls purple. And I have a fairy princess quilt. And I have a special baby bed for Phoebe and my drawers and my closet have clothes. More clothes than I ever had before. It's wonderful. I don't have to share with the other girls at the orphanage anymore. And I have shoes that don't pinch my toes. When I first got to my new house, Mommy had a hurt tummy so I took care of her."

Fitz and Maddie gave Fionna sorrowful gazes, but she shook her head.

"Did you know about her hurt tummy already?" Aida quizzed Fitz.

Dan wasn't certain if she didn't want to be repetitive or if she was hoping Fitz could tell her more about Fionna's ailment.

"Uh," Fitz glanced at Dan not knowing what Aida had been told. "I came to visit your Mommy when she was in the hospital, but she's better now."

Aida turned a crestfallen gaze on Fionna. "I didn't know you had to go to the hospital."

"Sorry," Fitz mouthed but Dan shook his head. He certainly hadn't known.

"It was just for a little while, and Daddy stayed with me and took good care of me. The medios made me all better."

Aida seemed to agree that Fionna was all better. "Everything is better than at the orphanage, and I'm going to have a baby sister that I get to hold and help take care of." She continued to spew forth information rapidly.

"And I have my very own books, and when I want my hair braided like Anne's, Mommy braids it. My skin isn't itchy anymore because after my bath Mommy puts on my oily stuff that makes it not hurt anymore."

Maddie was on the verge of tears and giving Fitzroy looks that said to impregnate her with a little girl immediately.

Bewildered, Fitz turned back to Aida. "Have you gotten to see any of the cool buildings in DC yet? Have you gone to the Senate?"

Dan shook his head. "We've been sticking close to home."

Aida nodded. "And at my new house,"—her eyes lit suddenly—"when Mommy and Daddy do laundry and chores, I get to help. Mommy's always happy. When she walks by Daddy, he does like this." She made a scooping motion ending with a slight squeeze of her hand, and Dan choked.

"Right here on Mommy." She pointed to her own backside with a giggling grin. "And then Mommy does this." She plastered on a huge smile and batted her eyelashes.

Fitz guffawed, and Maddie fought very hard not to join in.

"Aida, that isn't really a story we need to share," Fionna urged.

Furrowing her brow, Aida nodded. "But all of the nuns in the orphanage never smiled like that. It makes me happy when you smile."

Unable to bring himself to scold her after her explanation, Dan willed his face back to its original color. Fitz was still laughing at him outright.

"Is there anything you don't like about DC?" Alfred asked. He seemed genuinely intrigued in the conversation. Maddie beamed proudly.

Aida's brow furrowed and then she shook her head. "I don't think so yet. At the orphage if I had a nightmare, I had Davy the bunny stuffed animal that was my favorite with me, but no one could lay down with me. Sometimes, if I have a nightmare here, Daddy lies down with me and makes the sunshine come back to my tummy so then you don't have any more nightmares."

Fitz's earlier amusement melted into a heartbroken expression.

"Maybe you won't have those anymore," Maddie suggested.

"I can't remember if my nightmare woke me up or the brick the other night, but I hope they're going away. They're scary," Aida confessed with a slight shudder.

Devastated gazes went around the table as Aida continued to eat.

"It was probably the brick," Alfred offered Aida sweetly. He didn't want her to have nightmares either it seemed.

"Before we came to Paris, France, I woke up because I heard Mommy crying."

Panic broadcast from Fionna. "I wasn't crying!"

Dan shook his head but his mouth was full of potato, and he couldn't speak. Fitz and Maddie nodded confusedly.

"She wasn't crying I don't think because she said she wasn't, but I heard loud noises and I heard Mommy tell Daddy to give her something. She said it a bunch of times, and it sounded loud." Dan and Fionna looked at one another completely horrified.

"Aida, Mommy wasn't crying, remember!" The look on Dan's face gave him away.

Fitz smirked as he studied both Dan and Fionna. It didn't take him long to figure out what Fionna had been asking for.

With a delighted, mischievous look, he urged Aida on. "So, then what happened?"

Dan glared at him hatefully. Much to her parents' chagrin, Aida went on. "I heard Daddy say take it, and he sounded kind of mad, and then Mommy made that funny noise again."

Fionna's head fell into her hands.

"Jean Paul! No!" Maddie demanded when she realized what had been taking place, but he wasn't going to be dissuaded.

"Uh-huh," he urged her on.

"And I heard a sound like this…" Aida clapped her hands together rather loudly, and Fitz lost it. He roared with laughter, shocking Aida.

In her confusion, she seemed to decide to speed up the story. "But she wasn't really crying, because when they opened the door, Mommy was okay and she was wearing her purple, very silky gown that's my very favorite. It has black lace up the sides here and here." She gestured to her own sides. "And it feels so soft."

She continued to inform as Fitz was doubled over, laughing hysterically.

"But she also had on very, very high heels in her robe and very beautiful tights that had designs in them and bows at the top right here." She pointed to the upper midsection of her own thighs.

"And she was wearing that before bed, so that was funny, so she wasn't sad, I decided."

This brought on raucous laughter from Fitzroy. He wiped away tears, unable to catch his breath from laughing so hard.

"Boys, why don't you and Aida go out and play. I'll clean up and then we'll have the strawberry tart." Maddie began damage control.

Excited by that idea, Aida turned to Dan. "May I please be excused?"

Dan nodded as he was unable to speak as he tried to soothe Fionna who was on the verge of tears.

"I am going to kill you!" he growled as soon as the children were in the courtyard.

"Apologize!" Maddie demanded.

"I'm sorry." He was still chortling and didn't look sorry at all. "Oh, come on. It's not like we don't do that. You coached me through our first time, and believe me, Alex and Alfred have interrupted more than a few sessions."

Fionna's head lifted as she took in Fitz's apology. "Really?"

"Hell yeah." Fitz drew a quick sip of his wine. "At least she knocked. Alex just busted in one time. That wasn't easy to explain away, trust me. For what it's worth, he took in quite a show. For weeks, he kept asking why I was hurting Maddie. It was horrible!"

"What did you tell him?" Fionna relaxed with Fitz and Maddie's reassurances.

"I don't remember exactly. It was few years ago," Maddie explained. "I know that I kept assuring him that Fitz wasn't hurting me. Americans are very hung up about sex. It's part of life. Children need to know that their parents love each other."

"Don't worry about it," Fitz insisted. "Kids are resilient. She'll forget about it. It's not as big a deal as it seems. I do remember thinking that after Alex stormed in."

Dan was shocked that Fitz's promises seemed to soothe her.

"Alfred always knocks." Maddie glanced out the window to check on the kids. "But I think it happens to everyone. All of my friends have stories as well."

"None of my friends have kids." Fionna seemed happy to be able to confide in Maddie once again.

"You have us," Fitz vowed, and Dan was suddenly able to remember why Jean Paul Fitzroy was his best friend.

After the strawberry tart had been consumed, Fionna gave Aida her bath while Maddie tucked the boys in.

Dan joined Fitz with a bottle of beer they'd purchased at the market. Fitzroy was on the phone with Oliver discussing the warrants he was putting out.

After chilling the beer with his hands, Dan sank down in one of the chairs. Fitz ended the call and grabbed his own beer.

"Best part of the whole damn story was the sound like this." Fitz set his beer down long enough to clap his hands together, copying Aida.

"I'll just point out that I know seven ways to kill you with this beer bottle, and you have never out shot me."

Fitzroy continued laughing. "Heels, huh?"

Dan shook his head and refused to answer.

Obviously sensing that he'd pushed it far enough, Fitz retreated. "She's amazing, Dan. You're a lucky guy."

"Yes, I am." He was still irritated with Fitz, but he did finally admit that if it had been Alex telling the story, he would have done the same thing.

CHAPTER 35

MUSÉE DE L'ÉROTISME

In an effort to make up for his stunt the evening before, Fitz and Maddie offered to take the kids to see the Louvre Museum. The museum was hosting a children's event. Fitz had assured them that he would gladly translate anything Aida might need help with, but that she would have a ball with the hands-on art displays in the Gifted Sciences area and playing with the boys.

They'd insisted that Dan and Fionna enjoy an extended afternoon in Paris taking in the sights.

"Okay, have fun!" Fionna called as they waved goodbye.

Dan was pleased that Aida seemed excited to go off without him and Fionna and had only asked once if they would be back when she arrived home.

"What might my beautiful wife like to do today in Paris?" Dan took Fionna's hand and spun her into him as they stood on the front stoop of the Fitzroys' home. Her energy would still tense occasionally like her radar was sensing something. She hadn't brought it up though.

She feathered kisses across his cheeks. "Mrs. Vindico would like to spend the day with her husband getting lost in Paris."

"I think I could probably handle that. Would Mrs. Vindico like to get lost inside one of the many stores on the Champs this morning?"

Fionna giggled and then gave him a moan. "Stop it. You're turning me on."

Dan laced his fingers through his wife's as they proceeded to the Metro station. "I'm shocked you didn't come to the Champs when you challenged out here." He was hardly able to believe Fionna had never been to the mecca of Parisian shopping.

"It was an exhibition, kind of like the one in Vegas. We challenged all day, partied that night, and then left the next morning."

Dan caught the deeper regret in her voice. "You party with anyone in particular?" fell from his mouth without him really meaning to ask.

"Kind of." She sounded confused.

"Kind of?"

"You don't want to know."

With a nod, Dan worked through his possessive chauvinistic reactions as the train pushed them rhythmically farther into Paris.

Twenty minutes later, he was laughing outright as Fionna gazed longingly up at a department store with names like Louboutin, Lola, Versace, and Valentino advertised on the signage.

"Don't drool, baby doll." He led her inside.

"I've died and gone to heaven." They headed to the shoe department. She spied a pair of high-heeled mules that she grasped lovingly. They were made of folded black leather with an open toe.

Quickly deciding not to point out that as she continued to expand the heels might not be so easy to wear, Dan just grinned at her as she gazed at them. She'd be able to wear them long after little miss Halia made her appearance, so there was no reason he couldn't spoil her to his heart's content.

"Oh, Louboutins!" She rushed to a center display table.

"I met him once. He's actually a really nice guy," Dan commented as he watched her admire the shoes.

"You know Christian Louboutin?"

He laughed. "I said I met him once. You know he's Gifted?"

"Obviously." She pointed to a patented, red-bottomed heel. "I just didn't know you knew him." She seemed irritated he'd never mentioned that before. "Can you get me shoes?"

"Fi, baby, I met him once. He's a nice guy. Wretchkinsides tried to extort money from him." He grimaced as he recalled the details of the situation. "I really don't know him well enough to get you shoes from him. I will, however, be only too happy to buy you some Louboutins if you want them."

Fionna continued to gaze longingly at the seven-inch stiletto sling heels. The bottoms were signature Louboutin red. Everything about the heel said *fuck me.* Her favorite kind to wear, and his favorite kind to see her in.

"They're expensive, but they're so completely fabulous."

"Oh, I don't know. I'd say if you wear these for me with nothing else then they're worth every penny."

She gave him a naughty grin and waggled her eyebrows.

"Fion-na?" drawled from a heavy French accent.

"Oh shit." Her face fell into a horrified grimace.

Dan spun and narrowed his eyes.

Fionna turned much slower and drew a deep breath. "Pierre, hi." She made no effort to hide her disdain.

Instantly aware of exactly who Pierre must be, Dan glared at him hatefully.

"Wow, Fion-na! You look amazing, stunning, a vision." He was working his accent a little too hard in Dan's opinion. He tried not to think how satisfying it would be to break the guy's jaw.

"Uh, Pierre, this is my husband, Dan." She quickly offered Dan an awkward glance.

"Oh, you're married?" he lamented but then began to try and calculate if she was happily married. Dan could tell by the way he studied the rings on her fingers and then her eyes.

While clenching his jaw so tightly it ached, Dan put his arm around Fionna possessively, daring Pierre to make a move.

He was a little shorter than Fionna even and not in great shape. Dan shot him a cocky glare.

"What brings you back to Paris? You said you didn't think you'd be back."

Dan chuckled.

"Yeah." She sighed but then a devious grin came over her. "Actually, we're on our honeymoon. We're just in here looking for something for our little girl."

"Oh, you have a baby?" Pierre seemed thoroughly shocked.

"Well, we'll have another one here in a few more months." Fionna pushed her stomach out and arched her back as she rubbed her nonexistent bump. "But we were shopping for our oldest."

Dan ran his hand over his mouth to hide his chuckle. Fionna pulled her phone from her purse and supplied a picture of Aida and Dan lying on the couch watching TV.

His eyes goggled. Judging by the look on Pierre's face, whenever Fionna had played the exhibition game in Paris had been in the last seven years.

Pierre was speechless, and Dan fought not to guffaw as he added, "Yep, that's my baby girl. She's beautiful, isn't she? Just like her mama." He proudly kissed the side of Fionna's head as Pierre nodded with his mouth hanging open stupidly.

Finally regaining the ability to speak in English, Pierre gasped, "But you never said, and I mean, you don't look like you ever, and I didn't know. How old were you when she was born?"

"Well,"—Fionna was thoroughly enjoying herself—"she's seven, so I was twenty-three when she was born."

Pierre nodded. "And you're on your honeymoon?"

Fionna leaned and kissed Dan's jawline. "Yes! He's amazing. I'm the luckiest girl in the world."

"And she's yours?" he pointedly asked Dan.

"What the hell is that supposed to mean? Of course she's mine." He had no trouble letting the menace he felt leak into his voice.

Pierre seemed to suddenly take in Dan's sheer size and his strength. "Sure, whatever. I hope you can keep her happy." His voice cracked slightly as he handed Fionna's phone back.

"I certainly plan to."

A store manager walked by and ordered Pierre to go to the stockroom. Dan caught that much in the quickly spoken French.

He pointed to the shoes Fionna had liked. "She'll take those in an eight, that's in a US size, of course. I feel certain you can do the conversion, right, Pierre?"

"Of course," Pierre huffed indignantly. "This just came in, actually. Louboutins. Very popular."

"I didn't know you worked here." Fionna draped herself across Dan.

"I worked at that bar when we met, but that was several years ago. I just started working here last week."

"The shoes!" Dan demanded. He enjoyed watching Pierre's eyes goggle.

"I'll get them."

Dan shook his head. "Okay, first, that was a little bit mean, Mrs. Vindico, and second, him, really?"

Her face was the color of the bottom of the Louboutins he'd just sent away with Pierre.

"His friend was way cuter, but Chloe wanted him, and he was such a tremendous jerk. There was a reason I told him I was never coming back to Paris." She shuddered disgustedly.

"And did he do anything that I should remind him about now with my fists?"

"Uh, no, darling, but are we a little bit jealous?"

"You could say that." He would never lose his overly possessive desire to injure anyone she'd ever been with before him, but he tried to make it dissipate long enough to buy her the shoes.

"Do you want to leave?"

"Nah, this is kind of fun, actually."

With an abashed giggle, she leaned in and whispered, "I didn't sleep with him. We started to, but he didn't quite make it past the kissing. He never even got his pants off, but he acted like it was my fault, so I threw him out. I don't know why he's being nice now. He was such an ass."

"I suddenly like Pierre a whole lot more." Dan smirked. "And he was being polite because for a few hopeful minutes there he thought you might let him have another shot."

"I'm a very happily married woman to the man of my dreams with a seven-year-old little girl and one on the way. I'm not a party girl anymore, and even if all of that weren't true, hell would freeze over first."

Before Dan could respond, Pierre returned with the shoeboxes. "Here you go, Fion-na. Jus' sit there. I'll help you put them on."

Dan shot Pierre an extremely cocky grin. "I got it, Pierre. Wouldn't want you to get ahead of yourself there."

Fionna covered her mouth to hold in the laughter.

Defiance cast Pierre's face. "I can do it. It's my job," he bragged like putting on a pair of shoes was a major accomplishment.

"Nah, Quickdraw. Don't worry about it. I'll get the job done."

"Dan." Fionna stood. "I'll do it." She reached for the boxes, but Pierre jerked them away. Fury seared through Dan. He narrowed his eyes and stepped in front of Fionna.

"Sit down, Fion-na," Pierre ordered angrily. Dan clenched his fists. His eyes flashed dangerously, and he felt his biceps flex in anticipation. "How about this, Pierre. If you touch her foot, I'll put mine so far up your ass you'll be tasting boot leather. Now give her the damn shoes."

Pierre shoved the shoes toward Dan with a huff of disdain. He quipped several words in French that Dan was certain weren't kind before turning and stalking away quickly.

"I told you he was a jerk." Fionna rolled her eyes as Dan handed her the shoeboxes. He caressed her back while she slipped on the shoes. He didn't want Pierre to ruin her day.

"Well, let's see them, baby doll."

Her smile returned immediately. She squealed slightly as she stood and modeled them for him.

"Very, very nice. I can't wait to see them later."

"Really? You like them?"

"Oh yeah. I like them." He swallowed down the lust building rapidly in his body.

They exited the store hand in hand after Fionna shot Pierre a derisive glare and waved with her left hand. She let the large diamonds on her finger sparkle in the sunlight before she planted a kiss on Dan's jawline.

"All right, Mrs. Vindico, where shall we go now?"

"Is there anything you want to see?" She turned back into his sweet, empathetic wife once they were out of Pierre's line of sight.

Dan wrapped his arm around her. "I want to keep doing things that make you smile like that all day, and then tonight I want you to put on these heels and let me make you smile all over again."

"I'm kind of in a naughty mood."

Dan let a low growl sound in her ear as they walked. "Does that mean I should take you back to the Fitzroys' and take you on their kitchen counter while they're out?"

"No, because every time I walk in their kitchen, I'll laugh, and they'll know what we did."

"But I like to take advantage of each and every naughty mood I get."

He let his right hand slip to her backside and squeezed it discreetly. He forcibly ignored the fact that her Receiver's radar was still pulsing erratically. He wondered if she was feigning horny to hide what she was really feeling.

"I'll be naughty for you tonight, but right now I had another kind of naughty thought." She gestured her head to a passing city bus.

Dan turned his head to see the advertisement plastered along the side. "Musée de l'érotisme" was scrawled in red letters over the black background with a picture of several fertility goddesses underneath. "Ever been to the red-light district, Mr. Vindico?" He gave a slight chuckle. "Yes, I have." She scowled. He knew that was coming. "Not for that, and you've also been to the red-light district, sweetheart. He'd crossed a lot of lines in his wilder years, but prostitution was not one of them.

"I have?"

God, she was adorable. He couldn't contain his laughter. "Yes, baby. You were there a few nights ago. That's where the Gifted Parliament is along with the Iodex precinct."

"Really?" She was intrigued.

"It's been there for centuries, so I'm not certain it was the red-light district when they built the Parliament there, but this is Paris so anything is possible. And the red-light district really isn't dangerous here."

"Will you take me to the museum?"

Hesitant to tell her no, Dan hemmed. "I don't think you're going to like it."

"Please, it'll be fun. We don't have to stay long. I just kinda want to see it while we're here."

"All right, I'll take you, but you have to promise me if we get down there and you don't like something you see, you'll tell me so we can leave."

"Dan, I'm not a baby. Plus, I bet they have a gift shop."

His breath tangled in his throat. Maybe Fionna's libido really was in overdrive. He was extremely pleased with this pregnancy-related hormone.

"You don't have to go to the erotic museum for that kind of shop, baby doll. They're all over Paris. I'd much rather take you to those."

"Come on. The museum will be fun. Have you ever been?"

They headed toward the Metro station. "No, anytime I was down there I was either working with Fitzroy or after one of Wretchkinsides's guys. He had quite a setup in Pigalle. So, I never stopped to take in a phallic display or to see pagan sex statues."

"I really want to go. Do you mind?"

"I don't mind. Let's take you to see the original vibrator." He guided her onto the train. "It's not far from here."

After they exited the train, Dan walked her to the steps that headed out of the station and led to the street level. She noted the advertisements for show girls, brothels, and peep shows but didn't comment.

Dan studied her closely. He could have taken her off of the train one stop closer, but he'd wanted to make certain she was comfortable before they began an exploration of eroticism.

They passed by a heavily graffitied building with several women leaning on the front stoop. He whisked her to the other side of the street.

On the next block, there was another grouping. They were calling out their prices in euros and then in dollars.

"Wow," Fionna gasped.

"Do you wanna leave?"

She shook her head. "They're not doing anything wrong. Who did you chase through here?"

"Wretchkinsides used to have quite an installation here until Fitz slowly and methodically took them out. After that, Nic moved operations back to Russia temporarily. That's why I was here so often. Do you remember that story Alex wanted Fitz to tell about that old, abandoned house? It's about thirty miles from here, actually." He pointed back down the street in the direction they'd come from.

"The one where you took out two guys with one shot through a window."

"It was a lucky shot."

"I doubt that." She always made him feel like a king though he'd never admit that to her. "Does it bother you to be here?" She stopped suddenly, and he almost chuckled. She was just as worried about him in the middle of the red-light district in Paris as he was about her.

He shook his head. "I'm fine, baby, as long as I'm with you."

The museum was flanked by sex shops, X-rated movie houses, and a brothel on both sides.

"Nice."

"Just say the word and we're gone," he offered again.

"No, I want to see it, and it's not like we can just drop Aida off with my parents and go to an erotic museum in DC for an afternoon. While in Paris...."

Dan tried to envision what kinds of things he was going to be exposing his wife to inside the museum. He knew Fionna definitely had a sex-goddess side, one he loved to indulge on a regular basis, but she was also demure. She was definitely not inexperienced, but Dan had no interest in corrupting his sweet baby.

She was the perfect mix, nine parts heavenly angel with that one part hellcat that drove him wild. He never wanted her to change. He also knew that she might like him to leave a hidden hickey a few places for their eyes only, or for him to slap her ass occasionally, when she was in a more carnal mood. She had one hell of a submissive praise kink that drove him wild since he was a Dominant praiser by nature. She was definitely willing to explore different sexual avenues, but it wouldn't take much of the licentious side of the act to turn her off completely.

He paused at the darkened entrance doors, but before he could ask again, she giggled. "I'm sure. I'm fine, and if I decide I want to leave I'll just whisper something dirty in your ear. No, wait, I'll just say I want to leave—that way I can whisper naughty things in your ear anyway."

"Got it." After purchasing their tickets, they queued up behind a church tour group, which they both found hysterical.

The first display was individual photos of the two men who'd founded the museum. They were both dressed in suits and ties and looked thoroughly normal.

Dan kept a close eye on Fionna. He knew she intended to slowly torture him throughout the entire museum in an effort to make him so turned on he could hardly walk, so he braced for the incoming comments.

She pulled him away from the church group as they moved into the main floor of the museum. "I'm a fairly dirty girl. I don't want to corrupt the church group."

"I'm very fond of your dirty side, baby doll." He found it adorable that she qualified herself as a *dirty girl,* though he would never tell her that he thought otherwise. They turned a corner to take in a frosted glass sculpture of a life-sized female tigress. It was actually an oil lamp. The oil remained ever burning in the loins of the tigress.

"Aww, poor thing," Fionna drawled. "I get that. Sometimes you just need somebody to put you out." She delightedly watched his body seize against his will.

He wasn't going to make it through seven floors of comments like that. He'd take her in the bathroom.

He held her eyes with his own. "You need somebody to put out the fire, baby doll, you let me know. I'll take care of it." He raised his eyebrows suggestively.

She shivered, but then seemed to will resolve as she moved to the next display of stone sculptures of women having sex in many varied positions, all with men portrayed as demons.

Shuddering slightly, Dan wondered why the men were the demons. He'd met several women he'd qualify as such.

Fionna leaned up on her tiptoes and brushed a kiss across his jawline.

"Don't worry, baby. I've never thought of you as a demon. I think of you more as my sexiest fantasy come true only better."

He couldn't halt the cocky grin that spread rapidly across his face.

They moved on to a display of fairly normal looking cherrywood dining room chairs all set around a table. Each chair was equipped with a rather large dildo in the seat. Fionna cracked up as Dan shook his head.

"Oh my gosh! The Angels should get a set of those for the boardroom." She guffawed. Dan lost it as well. He found it odd that he was enjoying the afternoon with her in the erotic museum.

I shouldn't be surprised. It never matters what we're doing as long as she's beside me.

They walked by a large display behind glass of female mannequins all dressed in pinup-style costumes of the more common male fantasies. There was a nurse, a teacher, a dominatrix, a submissive, and women in general states of undress.

Dan wasn't surprised that Fionna didn't spend too much time on any of the mannequins. He followed her to a large dollhouse-styled display with figurines in each and every room in numerous sexual acts. Dan shifted his eyes to Fionna as she took in a blindfolded woman fully bound in ropes in one of the bedrooms. Her male counterpart was fully dressed, holding a belt as he stared at her.

"Yeah, I just don't think so." She shuddered.

Dan recalled a conversation they'd had after Eric Kent had broken into her house about whether or not she'd want to try out cuffs and a blindfold. He chuckled to himself.

The next area had her far more intrigued. There was a table set with foods and flowers that all naturally resembled vulvas, breasts, and penises.

"That's really cool. They're beautiful." She pointed to the seeded fruits with fleshy centers that looked very much like an aroused female vulva.

"Makes me hungry," Dan growled in her ear.

She giggled as they took in a display of nutcrackers with the portion that was used to crack said nuts being either between the legs of a woman or a man. "Come on. That's a little funny."

He grimaced in mock pain. "It really isn't."

They climbed the first set of stairs to the next floor and followed another cluster of tourists to see a large grouping of phalli. They varied in size from a few centimeters to several feet high.

"Seems like that might get lost." She pointed to a few of the tinier sculptures.

"Wouldn't know. Never had that problem." He smirked.

"I know." She waggled her eyebrows.

The next display was a grouping of male genitals where the testicles were actually female breasts. Dan laughed at her outright when she rolled her eyes. "What? That's one of my favorite places for it to be." He discreetly grabbed her ass but made sure no one saw him. "So, when Aida asks what we did today?" He teased her as they headed up another flight of stairs.

"We went to a museum," she stated but then broke out in laughter again. "I hope I'm not corrupting Halia!" She covered her abdomen with her arms.

This had Dan laughing again. "I think she's fairly safe."

"Oh, look, honey, they have a whole display of your favorite position." She held her arms out to paintings, sculptures, and mannequins all having doggy-style sex.

"Yeah, but it looks way better when I get you on all fours, baby doll." If she was going to flirt dirty, he could too.

The next floor was dedicated to early porn. A large portion of this floor was a movie theater showing examples of early motion pictures in black and white. There were silent, dirty film clips that showed in succession.

"Wanna see the show?" she teased.

"Yeah, I'm gonna go in a dark theater with you. A man can only take so much, sweetheart."

She poked her lip out in a delicious pout.

"Fi, baby, I know you're thoroughly enjoying torturing me, but think about what might be on those seats."

She grimaced with a shuddered, "Yuck."

He took her hand and led her around the few displays of early magazine porn.

They ventured on to the next few floors that contained more contemporary art displays of sex. Nothing held their interest very long, so they moved on.

The next two floors were quite interesting. The nude artworks of many varied couples were breathtaking. Fionna took in a painting of a man and woman in the act. The name of the painting was *Her husband, His wife.*

"It really is beautiful," she commented thoughtfully, and he nodded his agreement.

"I'm a big fan myself," he teased, but as he thought about the painting, he knew that it was a truly beautiful act when it was shared by two people in love with one another.

There was a temporary display on the female clitoris and G-spot. There were graphs and pictures of the locations of both and then research done on the areas suggesting that the G-spot is actually where the sides of the interior bulbs of the clitoris attach to the vaginal wall.

"The only area on the human body whose only function is pleasure," Fionna read on one of the printed studies that had been enlarged and displayed beside the model.

She was instantly fascinated and moved farther into the temporary display room. There were numerous scientific research papers denouncing the existence of the G-spot, and then examples of ancient religions that had denounced sexual activity altogether.

"Those scientists should have just asked you because you're so good at finding mine."

"I make it my business to know all of your hotspots, baby doll, and all of the delicious ways to get you going."

She beamed up at him but then gasped as she read the next display. "The first major published study on the clitoris wasn't until 1998! How is that possible?"

Dan read the research associated with the display. "I would say it goes back to a lack of women's healthcare and lack of research on what makes a woman orgasm. So the patriarchy," he summed up.

She sighed and moved on to read a study on sexual stigmas from the past. "You were only allowed to do it to procreate?"

Dan nodded as he read the same studies. Those rules seemed destined to fail.

"What's wrong with pleasure?" She seemed to genuinely want an answer.

"Well, these people"—he gestured to an article that he assumed must have been written by the very early Gifted people, though the article wouldn't have appeared odd to any Non-Gifted individual—"believed the man was giving away all of his energy, and I think some religions thought if it felt that good it must be bad."

Fionna was thoughtful for a few minutes. "We need to hurry. I don't want to be too much later than Aida getting back."

"We can skip the last floor if you want."

"No, it's just one more. I want to see it."

They climbed the stairs to the top floor of the erotic museum. The entire level was dedicated to brothels and the way they'd shaped the Parisian cultural landscape for centuries.

One entire wall was pictures of rather famous individuals who'd frequented the Parisian bordellos in the past. Suddenly, Fionna gasped.

"What?" Dan's brow furrowed.

She pointed to a small black-and-white photo. Swallowing harshly, Dan felt the icy hands of evil gripping his soul again as he looked into Dominic Wretchkinsides's malignant eyes.

He would have been barely eighteen years old, seated at a table right beside Pendergrath in a brothel long before Dan had even been born. The placard stated his name and told that he was the son of famed millionaire Hadrian Dietrech Wretchkinsides. Apparently the picture was taken just days after his father had cut him off. It stated that he had traveled from Moscow to Paris to drown his sorrows in the local bordello.

The picture was taken on the same street Dan and Fionna were currently standing on. The ladies employed by the brothel were draped around both of them and were wearing very little.

Fionna spun. "Do you want to leave?"

"I'm fine, baby." He clung to her hand and wished Paris would stop thrusting pictures of Nic Wretchkinsides in his face. *As long as you're here, I'm fine.* He pulled her closer to ward off the terror and the malice he saw when he looked into the blackest eyes he'd ever gazed upon. He tried not to recall their depths as he'd stared into them as they'd died.

After a few more displays, they made their way out.

"Thank you for enduring my perverse side for a little while." She laughed.

"Anytime."

They grabbed a late lunch from a bistro.

"This is where Fitz chased Rainer and Logan when they were here, and he was convinced they weren't officer enough to bring home the evidence I needed." Dan shook his head.

"Yeah, I heard about Rainer and Logan barging in on Adeline and Emily dressed up in some pretty racy lingerie."

"The fact that Logan didn't kill Rainer then and there just shows you how good friends they are."

Fionna chuckled. "Emily was pretty embarrassed her brother saw her like that."

"I'm sure she was. I sure as hell don't want to see any of my sisters dressed up like that."

When they returned to the Fitzroys', they were greeted excitedly by their little girl. She rushed to them as soon as they entered.

"Look!" She held up a large canvas she'd painted a full floral display on.

"Wow!" Fionna gushed.

"That's beautiful!" Dan was certain no artwork hanging in the Louvre or anywhere else was prettier.

Aida rocked up on her toes as she showed off her artwork.

"We'll have to get it framed and hang it up when we get home," Fionna assured her.

"And I got to look all around at the museum, and Mr. Fitzroy showed me how if he touched a balloon and then touched it to my hair it would stand up like this!" She lifted her hair straight up away from her head.

Fitz seemed pleased that Aida was so impressed.

"What else did you see?" Fionna seated herself on the sofa and pulled Aida into her lap.

"I saw lots of pictures, and there were some of people that didn't have any clothes on. I think they were going to get in the bathtub."

Dan bit back a chuckle as he refrained from stating that they'd seen lots of pictures of people lacking clothes as well.

"Alfred said that Mrs. Fitzroy said that it was art, so they weren't really naked, but I'm pretty sure they were."

Dan and Fionna tried not to double over laughing as they nodded their agreement.

After they ate and put the kids to bed, they confessed what they'd done with their afternoon. Fitz and Maddie informed them that the Erotic Museum was one that they frequented every time the displays were changed or a lecture was being held.

Several hours later, Dan crawled into bed as Fionna headed into the bathroom. She exited wearing nothing but the Louboutin heels they'd purchased, a black ribbon tied up in her hair, which was slicked back in a ponytail perfect for pulling, and a naughty smirk.

Dan swallowed down desperate desire. "Hey,"—he caught her hands—"you look fucking phenomenal, but before I indulge, tell me what's wrong?"

Her rhythms still tensed oddly. They'd been doing it off and on all day. She was trying so hard to ignore it, but Dan couldn't. He had to know. He wouldn't survive her shutting him out again.

She shook her head. "I'm not sure. My radar is still a little ragged, I think. I'm sure it's the pregnancy hormones."

Dan bit back the question he so desperately wanted to ask.

She shrugged. "I was so depressed last time I don't know what I felt," she answered his unspoken question. "But since I'm here in heels, could you just please make me forget everything else."

Dan set out to grant her wishes.

CHAPTER 36

BAITED BILLS

RAINER LAWSON

"You're certain?" Rainer sat stunned in his desk chair. "No, no, I'll tell him," he assured the bank manager from KBC in Brussels. "Thank you."

"Who was that?" Logan quizzed.

"Claud Janesson. Come here. You have to hear this." He turned and knocked on the already open door to Portwood's new office.

"What's up?" Portwood gave Rainer a kind smile.

"I just talked to Janesson from KBC in Brussels where we traced the money that went missing from those accounts after the takedown. Some of the money was taken in from the last bank job Pendergrath pulled, and some of the bills from the Bellingham job were baited. They were hot!" Rainer was ecstatic.

"And when they were planning to attack our shower at the farm, they didn't bother to clean the money. They needed it to pay for the weapons Pravus was bringing up from Colombia. Anyway, the money was taken by someone and deposited in Brussels in KBC several weeks after the takedown, but here's the thing." Rainer drew a deep breath. "Some of the money was used to pay for the cameras set up on my honeymoon."

"What?!" Portwood's mouth hung open.

"Yeah."

"Is he certain?" Logan asked in abject disbelief.

"He gave me the account numbers." Rainer held up the slip of paper where he'd taken notes on his phone call.

"Whoever took the money right out from underneath us is the same person that set you and Emily up?" Portwood gasped.

It didn't sound possible. Rainer wasn't certain if he was thrilled that they'd gotten a break in the case or horrified that it appeared some piece of the Interfeci might still be in existence.

"What do we do now?" Logan took the paper from Rainer's hands and studied the account numbers.

"Give me a minute." Once again, Portwood appeared to be questioning whether or not he was really the man for the title he'd been given. "All right, I take it there's no money left in the account that the KBC traced it to?"

"They took $240,000 from one of the accounts that we didn't know about until after the takedown. The wire was $225,000 for setting up the cameras, but we don't know what the media paid for the photos and where all of that money went or where the other fifteen thousand is now. I assume that's about what the equipment cost to take the long-range photos," Rainer lamented.

Portwood nodded. "Call the KBC back. Tell them I want any information they have on who set up the accounts. Wretchkinsides used to pay top dollar to guys who worked for banks all over the world to keep him informed of the serials on marked bills. Whoever took the money either thought it was already cleaned or forgot that step."

"Janesson was going home. He's emailing me any other information he has. It's almost eleven o'clock in Brussels."

"Yeah, and we arrested most of his cleaners when we got their names from the information that poured in after the takedown," Logan said.

Portwood stared thoughtfully at the pictures on his desk. "Maybe whoever is behind this knew we'd taken out all of the cleaners. He needed the money, so he just hoped it had been cleaned after the bank job."

"No." Rainer shook his head. He disagreed with Portwood and Fitzroy's insistence that Dan not know anything, but he also wasn't going to defy orders so he did the next best thing. He tried to think the way Dan always thought. "Think about Wretchkinsides and what Pendergrath did for him. They were both vindictive about everything always. They had no idea that Dan would do what he did with Marlisa. They thought they were going to make the weapons buy and then attack the farm." The thought still made him short of breath. "Nic Wretchkinsides believed that the gun runners would end up with the marked bills. I'd go so far as to bet that Nic planned to report them to get them caught with the money."

Portwood and Logan both looked deeply impressed.

"Nice job, Lawson," Portwood complimented.

~

Dan Vindico

"Dan, get up now!" Fionna shrieked.

Dan's chest vibrated in his terror as he leapt from the bed. "What? What's wrong?" The world spun momentarily as he tried to awaken. It was three fifteen. His brain took in that information as he stared at Fionna.

She was pacing frantically. Her energy was erratic and terror-filled. She was sobbing and tugging at her own hair. Her eyes spun disconcertingly.

"Go get Aida! Something is wrong!"

"Fi, what? What is it?" He tried to keep his voice calm. She convulsed and he panicked. "I feel it. Something bad is happening! There are people here! All around! I feel them. They're everywhere! Go get Aida!" she screamed in his face.

Suddenly, she flew from their room and raced across the hall. Dan sprinted after her, throwing his shield over her and Aida as Fionna lifted her small sleeping body from the bed.

A bullet flew through the window. Dan felt the air vibrate as his shield deflected the bullet headed straight for his chest.

"Get down!" He shoved Fionna and Aida, who was now screaming, to the ground and covered them with his body.

"Dan!" Fitz threw a revolver end over end his way.

Dan dropped the east end of his shield from his right hand and caught the gun. He fired at the man crawling through the window, knocking him back out of the house.

Fitz low crawled into the room. "Fionna, take Aida and go with Maddie. She's taking the boys to the basement. There's an enhanced fallout shelter from the war. I casted it myself. Go!"

Fionna and Aida both sobbed in harrowing terror as Dan kept them shielded all the way into the shelter. He raced back up the stairs, meeting Fitz in the center point of the hallway.

"Do you have a count?" Dan demanded.

"No." Fury cast Fitz's face as they stood back-to-back, guns drawn, scanning the house. Shattering glass rent the air in a thundering crash, and another gunman moved in through Alex's window.

Fitz threw electricity through the air, and the man fell with a deafening thud to the floor. Dan crept to the guy.

"His heart's still beating." He took the rifle from the man's hands carefully.

"Good, I want to talk to as many of them as we can. Here!" Fitz hurled a pair of cuffs toward Dan.

Catching the cuffs and keeping his gun on the intruder, Dan cuffed the man's hands around Alex's bedpost.

Head snapping to the right, Dan and Fitz heard the front door fall into the entryway.

Slowly they low crawled toward the foyer. Fitz pointed to the light cast from the street lamps now over the hardwood floors with no door to block it. They took in the two shadows, one male, one female.

Dan held up two fingers then flashed a one and one, with Fitzroy nodding the same count.

Fitz pointed up to the light mounted on the wall near the male's head. Nodding, Dan understood what he was to do. Drawing a steadying breath, he summoned and then shot a violent stream of electricity into the lamp, momentarily blinding the intruders.

As they attempted to cover their eyes, Fitz threw his powerful shield out and knocked them backward onto the brick front steps. They leapt simultaneously. Fitz pulled another pair of cuffs from the front hall table and cuffed them together. Dan bound them back-to-back with duct tape. He was certain they saw nothing more than ghost spots from the light flare he'd blown a foot from their faces.

Something moved in the bushes. The man Dan had shot crawled back toward Alfred's window. He was bleeding badly and moaning. Dan moved to him and heard the gun chamber click.

"You just won't give it up, will you?" Dan stomped his bare foot hard on the guy's face, feeling his nose and cheekbones crunch under the force. With that, he pulled the pistol from his hands, uncocked it, and emptied the bullets into his hand.

"You go back through the house. I'm going around," Fitz ordered.

Dan kept his gun up as he cleared the house all the way to the backyard. There were two more near the large bushes on the edge of the lake.

He couldn't fire. He was too afraid he would hit Fitz in his sprint. "Two by the lake!" he bellowed loudly. There was no response, and Dan had given away his position.

A bullet ripped past him. Dan caught the bullet in his shield, drained its momentum, and then let it fall to the ground.

Dan narrowed his eyes, forced all thoughts that Fitz might not have made it to the backyard from his mind, and slid alongside the house. He shouted, "Firing now," as he pulled the trigger. He took out one at the thigh.

Another shot fired and the man beside him collapsed on top of the one Dan had felled. While keeping in the shadow of the house and low to the ground, Dan met Fitz by the bodies.

"Dan, move!" Fitz shoved Dan to the ground and fired at the same moment. The last gunman didn't get a shot off.

"Thank you." Dan panted as they moved the third guy to the pile and began draining them of energy. "Got anymore cuffs?" He was still unable to think beyond getting the intruders detained.

"Yeah." Fitz tried to chase down his breath. "There are several pairs in my bedside table." In a few hours, Dan was certain he'd be able to process that information and would find it humorous, but currently, he sprinted into the house and pulled numerous pairs of handcuffs from Fitz and Maddie's bedside drawers. He took them gingerly back out to Fitzroy and helped him cuff the men lying in the backyard.

"At some point I'm gonna want to hear about that." Dan sank to the ground with his mind reeling over everything that had happened.

Fitz nodded. He appeared shocked he was also chuckling.

They dragged all of their captives inside the living room as Fitz called in his Elite team.

As he raced down the stairs, Dan tried to find the words to explain to his girls what had happened. He sprinted to Fionna huddled in a corner. Aida was sobbing and wrapped in an old quilt, sitting in Fionna's lap.

"It's okay, baby. We've got them. Don't bring her upstairs yet."

"Daddy!" Aida reached her hands up. Dan lifted her into his tender embrace. "It's okay. I'm right here. You're safe," he soothed rhythmically.

Fionna stood, and he held them both tightly.

"Boys." He shook his head. "Stay down here with me. Your dad's all right, but you don't need to go up yet."

Suddenly, Alex and Alfred were clinging to him as well. He knelt down to cradle all of the kids in his massive embrace.

"Fitz is all right?" Maddie's voice was ragged and terror-ridden.

"He's fine. I promise. Just give the team a minute to get here."

She tried to draw steadying breaths.

Fionna broke down in convulsive sobs. Dan shifted Aida to his right hip and held her tightly. "Shh, baby. It's okay. You were so brave." She'd tried so hard to fight the terror, to stay calm for Aida, and the mighty task had been more than she could withstand.

Dan heard the thunder of boots rushing into the house from above.

"That's Iodex." He let his shield encapsulate Fionna, Aida, and the boys. Maddie kept her distance while trying desperately to regain her calm.

CHAPTER 37
INCOMING

Fitzroy appeared, ragged and weary, a few moments later. Maddie rushed into his arms, and he held her tight, waging war against tears that would ultimately be his victor.

Dan released his shield to allow Alex and Alfred to rush to their father. Fionna seemed unable to calm her energy. Her rhythms spiked and dipped rapidly. She slumped against Dan and shook violently.

He handed Aida to Fitzroy and carried Fionna upstairs. He set her on the couch and located his cell from the guestroom. He touched Logan's name on his phone and continued to soothe both Aida and Fionna. "I'm sorry I don't even know what time it is there," he managed.

"It's just after eleven. It's okay. We weren't asleep. What's wrong?"

"I need to talk to Adeline."

"Sure."

"Dan, what's wrong?" Adeline demanded.

He recounted the story, Fionna's reaction, and her energy's erratic pulses that were getting worse by the minute.

"The fetus is too young to react to her emotions yet, but the pregnancy is affecting her energy's ability to recover. It sounds like her blood pressure is spiking, and we can't have that. I'm going to call the American Hospital in Paris. Do you know how to get her there?"

"Yeah." Dan moved in a trance. His brain wouldn't allow him to consider what had happened. Making sure the baby was safe and Fionna was okay was the only thing that made sense to him.

"She's going to be fine, but you've got to remain calm. I'm going to need you to cast her for the next several hours," Adeline guided him.

"Okay." Thankful to have the next steps, he began drawing steadying breaths.

"Get Aida and Fionna. Take them to the hospital. I want you to eat as much as you can before you arrive. I'll give them all of my instructions, but I want you to cast her as soon as they have her admitted and begin giving her the medications that will stabilize her blood pressure. We're going to use your energy to regulate hers because she'll respond to you faster than anyone else. Once she's back to normal, you can take her back to wherever you're staying. She'll need to rest for several days. She might not do well on a flight, if you're planning on coming home. I'm going to call the hospital. You get her there."

"I will. We'll leave right now."

Twenty minutes later, Dan and Fionna rushed into the American Hospital in Paris. The Fitzroys were right behind them. The press was out in force having heard Fitz's call go out over the radio, but Dan was astonished as soon as they entered. Several medios met them with calming smiles and guided Fionna into a wheelchair and then to a room in the obstetrics ward.

"Medio Haydenshire has given us our instructions, and you'll be just fine," a woman, who'd introduced herself as Medio Bridgette Capusan, soothed. "Now," she guided Fionna into the bed. Her rhythms were still ragged and varying rapidly. She was panting for breath, and all of the color washed from her face suddenly.

"Dan!" she choked.

"She's gonna be sick!" Dan hoisted Aida into Fitzroy's arms as he sat Fionna up.

Medio Capusan miraculously caught everything in a large dish. "Her blood pressure is dropping and spiking. We'll get it taken care of." She remained steadfast and calm.

Dan eased Fionna back against the pillows. Her head appeared too heavy for her to hold upright. He guided it back gently with his hand and fought the relentless voices, the constant buzzing of his mind, that said he'd let her down yet again.

"Let's start with this." The medio crushed two pills into what appeared to be seltzer water. "Drink that while I get everything set."

Without warning, she hoisted Fionna's T-shirt up and her sweatpants down.

"We'll just wait outside." Fitz handed Aida back to Dan. He held her in his lap as he sat beside Fionna.

Suddenly, they heard the sounds that brought air back to their lungs. Fionna's face immediately regained some of its color as she gave Dan a slight smile and reached for his hand.

"See, she's fine," Medio Capusan assured them as they listened to Halia's rapid heartbeats over the monitors. Dan watched her tiny rhythmic pulses. "She doesn't have any idea you had yourselves quite a night."

"My baby sister is okay?" Aida pled in a heartbroken whisper.

"She's fine, sweetheart. Do you hear that? It's her heartbeat."

Aida's frightened eyes lit as she nodded. She placed her little hand on Fionna's stomach. "It's alright, Halia. Don't be scared. I'm right here."

"Mr. Vindico, the medicine I just gave your wife will settle her rhythms and blood pressure. Her Receiver's radar is spiking violently. Her energy is struggling to settle. You need to keep her casted for several hours. The fetus will recognize your patterns and allow you in."

"You're certain all she needs is my shield?" It didn't seem it could be that simple.

The medio nodded. "The fewer clothes either of you are wearing the faster it will work, but I understand if your daughter wants to stay with you. Just keep what I said in mind as you cast her. Might I also suggest that after we get Mom settled here,—she gestured to Fionna— "we might want to see if your daughter would like to talk to one of our Auxiliary counselors about what happened."

Dan nodded. "That would probably be good."

Fionna settled Aida beside her, and Dan removed his shirt. Not only was it the nicest hospital room he'd ever seen, the bed was large enough for two.

"Dad, the more of you that you can push through to her, the faster she'll recover and sleep. We'll be monitoring her and the baby constantly. The results are being fed to Medio Haydenshire in the States." Medio Capusan placed her hands on Fionna's stomach and closed her eyes to read her rhythms intently.

"Are you a Double-Predilect, Mrs. Vindico?"

"No," Fionna managed though she'd begun shivering again and couldn't seem to hold her jaw still. Her teeth were chattering violently.

"Why did you ask that?" Dan demanded. He was wondering if somehow something else was wrong as he tried to comfort Fionna.

"Because your wife currently has four energy streams, so I'm assuming you are the Double-Predilect."

"Yes." Apparently Fionna still had enough of his energy inside her from their lovemaking session hours before to be read by the medio.

"It's perfectly fine. It's good. The more of your energy we can get to her the faster we can heal hers. So,"—Medio Capusan set her iPad on a table in the room—"we'll stay away for an hour or so and see if you can get her calmed. If she can sleep while you keep her casted, that's even better. We'll bring you as much food as you need. Use a low level of heat and as much soothing energy as she can stand."

He tried desperately not to recall the last time he'd casted Fionna lying in a hospital bed after receiving those same instructions.

"Just press the button if you need me." She pointed to a call button near Fionna's head, then lowered the lights in the room as she left.

Dan slid into the bed. He wrapped his shield around all three of his girls and forced as much of his energy as he could manage into theirs.

Aida's hand went slack on Fionna's stomach. She fell asleep almost instantly. As soon as she was out, Dan helped Fionna remove her shirt so he could push more energy through her.

"Fi, baby, I'm so sorry." He let his tears of abject defeat fall into her hair as he held her tightly. She was too weak to argue, but she shook her head and buried her face in his chest.

"Go to sleep, baby. I'm right here." He wondered how him being beside her could possibly make her feel safe anymore, but she relaxed and a few minutes later was sleeping soundly.

~LOGAN HAYDENSHIRE~

"Hey, have you talked to Dan?" was Logan's greeting to Portwood as soon as he answered his cell.

"No, but I just talked to Fitzroy." Portwood sounded heartbroken.

"Ad says the baby's gonna be fine. She's reading the scans coming off Fionna. She says they look good."

"I know," Portwood sighed, "but my God, are they ever gonna get any peace?"

"Yeah, I know." Logan had to agree with his frustration. "Hey, you don't think this has anything to do with the money and what the bank manager told Rainer?" Logan thought Portwood really should tell Dan about their findings. They could all be in danger.

"I really don't." Portwood said the words that allowed Logan's lungs to release the pent-up air he'd been holding. "Fitz says the guys who attacked his house were people he'd put out warrants for. I don't know how they knew he'd decided to go after them, but apparently they were stupid enough to think they could take on Fitz and Dan and survive. Two of them didn't, by the way. The rest are quickly making Bertereau their new home."

"Did you tell Fitz about the money?"

"I started to, but his kids were with him and his wife. They've been through enough tonight. I'll call them next week when we have more information. They have to move now. He's got a full plate, and Fi's back in the hospital. Little Aida's a disaster, and Dan can't even bring them home yet."

Logan hadn't even thought about Aida being in the house when it was attacked. Who would do such a thing?

Dan Vindico

Dan awoke at eight to the ring of his cell phone. Panicking, he immediately reset his cast over Fionna, but her rhythms had soothed in his shield.

"I'm okay. I soothed you to sleep," she whispered as she kept Aida cradled on her chest. She was still sound asleep.

"This is Vindico," Dan managed on the fourth ring.

"Dan, it's Stephen. Are you all right, son?"

"Yes, sir. I'm sorry. I just woke up." He apologized and moved from the bed to try and let Aida sleep.

"I've been in contact with Adeline and the hospital for the last few hours. They both assure me that all of your girls are fine."

Dan studied Fionna and Aida. "Well, Halia's fine. I'm not sure about Fi and Aida. I just can't seem to keep them safe." He was desperate for Governor Haydenshire's calming rhythmic intonation and for his wisdom.

"Halia is a beautiful name, and you did keep them safe, all of them."

"Why does this keep happening?" His voice shattered as he forced his emotion back with sheer strength of will.

"Do you want me to come out there?"

"No, sir. I just want to get them home."

"All right, listen to me. You won't get yourself or your family anywhere if you start making rash decisions, so take it down a notch or two. Adeline says Fionna isn't ready to fly yet. I'm going to send my plane out there in a few days and make certain that you all get home safely. But don't push her or Aida. They need to work through this at their own pace. Jerking them up out of a hospital bed and flying them home may not be the best thing for any of you. Listen to your wife. Follow her lead. She knows what's best for your little ones, and to be frank, she knows what's best for you. You're a better man when you're with her."

"Yes, sir." He clearly needed to listen. Thus far he felt like an utter failure as a father and as a husband.

"Aida will recover as soon as she's certain that you and Fionna aren't going to fall apart."

Dan gazed down at his precious little girl with her head lying placidly on his wife's chest. He moved back to the bed and laced his fingers in Fionna's.

"I'll do whatever she needs me to do."

Fitz knocked as a hospital attendant wheeled a breakfast tray in for Fionna. Dan shook his head, and he moved back out until Dan helped Fionna pull her shirt back on.

The hospital brought food for him and Aida as well. Dan let Fitz and Maddie in as Fionna began plying a very sleepy Aida with some fruit.

"No, thank you." She yawned and promptly fell back asleep in Fionna's arms.

Fitz chuckled though his expression was morose. "I'm so sorry." He looked utterly broken.

"Jean Paul, it was not your fault," Maddie consoled him.

"No, it certainly wasn't," Fionna agreed.

"Look, I don't know how the hell this happened, but obviously, we can't live there anymore. I'm certain you're about to tell me you're taking them home. I'll get you a plane. I'll do anything, but you have to be here for the trials. Parliament set them all for Friday morning," Fitz concluded dejectedly.

Dan let the information try to work through his brain. He felt hung over. The exhaustion of keeping Fionna casted and of all that had happened began to make him lightheaded and weak.

"Here, Dan, eat something." Fionna panicked as he stumbled forward.

"Sit down." Fitz stepped in and helped Dan sit on the bed.

"I'm fine," he insisted but that was far from the truth.

Fitzroy pulled a high-powered protein bar, only available to Iodex officers and Gifted military members, out of his pocket. "Here, I picked some up at the office last night. I figured you might need them."

"Thanks." Dan tore open the packaging and began inhaling the protein. As his brain received the nutrients, his breath steadied. "As soon as you're ready to fly, you're going from here to Kauai."

"No, I'm not." Fionna shook her head. Her tone was perforated with fear and sorrow. She handed him a small plate containing several pastries.

Without arguing, he began inhaling the sugar and carbs.

"I'm not going home without you, and I'm certainly not going to Kauai without you," she demanded with more vigor that Dan thought she had in her at that moment. "We'll just stay in a hotel, and I assume Aida and I can go to the Senate with Dan for the trials?" she asked Fitzroy.

"Of course, but we call it the Parliament, and I may have a much better option."

Dan downed a shot of espresso so he had energy to argue with his wife and his best friend. "Fi, baby, if you don't want to leave without me, I'll take you and the girls on to Kauai. My mother will get over the reception. You'll actually be able to recover there. I'll come back here, do the trials, and then I'll go home, get all of our stuff, and meet you out there. I'll be gone two nights, max."

"What was your option?" She turned back to Fitz.

He cupped his hand, summoned a brilliant green shield, and threw it over the door. Dan saw the glow of a sound cast cover the shield. No one outside the room would be able to hear him.

"This was supposed to be a surprise for our anniversary, but I already told Maddie about it while we were coming back over here. I purchased us a vacation house on the Mediterranean. It's near Camargue. No one, not even any of my officers, know that I purchased it. Only the guy I bought it from has any idea, and I bought it under an alias, so he doesn't even know who I am. He's almost ninety-five and a complete curmudgeon. He's never left the town of Camargue, so I'd say he's probably not a risk. We're going to move in there for a few weeks until I can figure out what the hell happened. Obviously, we're selling our place."

Maddie blinked back tears of frustration.

"You're more than welcome to stay with us. It's a big house right on the water, very private, and mostly furnished. There's an enhanced express from the little town there, so it'll be an hour or so trip both ways to come into the city for the trials. Like I said, no one, not even my mom, knows I bought it. I wanted somewhere way out of the way that no one knew about. Fi and Aida could stay at the house with Maddie and the boys and be completely safe while we're gone. After the last trial, I'll get you a jet. You can go home, or to Kauai, or wherever you want."

Dan was quite certain that he no longer believed anywhere was *completely safe.*

"Let me talk to Fi for a minute, okay?"

"Of course." Fitz pulled his shield from the door and guided Maddie out of the room.

Fionna stared up at him sweetly and held her hands out for a hug. He guided her into his embrace and allowed himself just a moment to feel her tucked in the safety of his arms.

"I'm okay. I feel all right. My radar is still a little ragged, but Halia is perfect. I'm starting to be able to feel her energy without even having to concentrate."

"I know, but your radar isn't okay. I can feel it. I can't keep letting this happen."

"I do not want to go home without you. I would be terrified. We still don't know if these people were after you, or Fitz, or me. My energy is just a little off. It'll settle down. I need our family together, and your mom has invited the entire Realm to our reception. We can't just call it off. It's this weekend."

"Eat, please, baby doll. For me." Dan slid another plate of eggs and croissants her way. "I don't give a damn who my mother has invited. I understand that you're scared. Please just take Aida on to Kauai. No one but the Haydenshires and my parents know you're from there. Even the press thought we'd gotten married in Waikiki. They never made the connection. You'll be safe, and I'll come as soon as this is over."

"We can't teach Aida that the way we deal with our problems is by separating and running away. A private beach house in the south of France doesn't sound too terrible."

"I just don't understand this." Dan finally let the terror and the grief flood through his shield.

Fionna hugged him and tried, with her weakened capabilities, to soothe him. "I know, but I also think Fitz could really use your help figuring all of this out."

"Dammit, I don't want to figure it out. I want it to stop happening! I ended him. I killed him with my bare hands, so that you wouldn't have to live through something like this ever again, so that my babies would be safe, so that we can have a real life. It just doesn't seem like I'm asking for too much."

"I know," she whispered. Her intoxicating warmth and her love moved through his chest. His shield tried desperately to block her out. He wanted to be mad, but it just felt too damn good. He couldn't deny himself the healing salve that soothed his every pain.

Listen to your wife. Follow her lead. She knows what's best for your little ones, and, to be frank, she knows what's best for you. You're a better man when you're with her. Governor Haydenshire's command seared through his anger and frustration.

Medio Capusan knocked and then entered. Dan backed away and slipped his shirt back on. He moved to the other side of the bed as the medio checked the baby monitors.

"Aida." He kissed her cheek.

Her eyes fluttered open hesitantly. "Hi, Daddy."

"Hi, baby." He smiled against his will. "Come sit with me in the chair, so the medio can check on Mommy."

"Mrs. Vindico, your blood pressure is stable, but your rhythms are still jagged. The fetus appears to have suffered nothing from the episode, so you are free to go, but I'm going to write you a prescription for something to help you relax. Dad, she's going to need lots of rest over the next few days and to be casted every few hours until her radar rhythms sooth on their own. I don't recommend her flying until those have stabilized."

"Thank you." Fionna was visibly relieved.

The medio offered Dan a knowing grin. "A little of the medicine you administered a few hours before you arrived here would ensure that there was a stabilizing energy available for several hours."

Fionna giggled and blushed as she nodded her understanding. Dan found himself chuckling despite the desperation permeating his soul.

Medio Capusan waved her goodbye, and Dan moved to the bed. "You sure you're ready to leave?"

"I'll be fine. I promise. I'm looking forward to the medicine that will help me calm down. The bad stuff has already happened. I wish my body would stop thinking it's incoming."

"And you want to do this seaside thing?"

"Yes, I do."

"Fine," he acquiesced. "But you are relaxing for the next day or two, just sleeping, or lying out, or something that requires no effort." Dan laid out his orders.

"Or maybe just a little effort." Fionna attempted to flirt to show Dan that she'd made a full recovery. But he saw the weary exhaustion in her swollen eyes, and her normally vibrant magenta Receiver's rhythms were crackling and tensing with anxiety.

"Yeah, well, I'll take care of that too." Dan refused to admit to her that he knew she wasn't quite as healthy as she wanted to pretend to be.

CHAPTER 38

THE BEST-LAID PLANS AND COFFEE

As all of the logistical planning for the move had to be done and executed carefully to make certain no one knew where the Fitzroys and the Vindicos were heading, everyone ended up at Fitz's mother's home in Nanterre.

Taking a page from Rainer and Emily's playbook, Dan called and booked a suite at the Ritz Paris. He returned to Fitzroy's home while Fitz stayed with Fionna, Maddie, and the kids.

After packing all of their things as quickly as he could, Dan lugged their suitcases into the waiting cab. He halted the cab a mile before the Ritz and slowly walked along the sidewalks. He only needed a few people to recognize him.

When he turned the corner near the hotel, he saw them. They'd been looking for him since the night before.

"Are you planning on moving to Paris? Are you and Fionna separating for her safety? Did she kick you out? What about the baby? Can you tell us what happened last night?" The questions rang out quickly, most in English and a few in French. Dan ignored each and every one.

He paced silently to the hotel check-in desk, acquired the keycards, and disappeared up the elevator. He entered the suite, collapsed in a chair, summoned, and changed one of the complimentary American papers he'd picked up on his journey. He kept close watch out the windows of the suite as the press began to dissipate.

"Emily Lawson (Haydenshire) named Senior Receiver for the Arlington Angels," was the headline.

Certain that today was not the day for Fionna to see that, Dan left the paper in the suite and carried the luggage back down the elevators once the reporters had gone. He met another cab near the back kitchen entrance of the hotel and was driven back to his family.

Fitz moved next. He made quite a show of packing numerous suitcases and then driving his car around town until it was recognized. He then drove to the apartment complex owned by the French Parliament and unloaded.

Fionna and Aida joined Dan in a third cab a couple of hours later and were driven to the train station.

Dan pulled on a baseball cap and his darkest sunglasses. He moved through the station warily. Fionna and Aida entered through another door and headed away from Dan. He located a ticket-teller who was wearing thick glasses, meaning she was not Gifted, so he stepped up and purchased a ticket on the enhanced express to Camargue.

Fionna had donned one of Maddie's pashminas, covering her hair and a good portion of her face. She'd worn her sunglasses along with ragged jeans and an old T-shirt. Besides the expensive sunglasses, it certainly wasn't something Fionna Styler would ever have worn out of the house. She moved to a different teller and purchased two tickets on the same train that Dan would be on.

Aida was sporting one of Alex's baseball caps with her hair in a bun underneath it along with one of Alfred's button-up shirts. Dan hardly recognized her.

An hour later, Dan breathed a sigh of relief as he stepped off the train and into the car he'd rented using one of his aliases. Following Fitz's directions, Dan located the house, which he had to admit was rather well hidden.

"This is beautiful." Fionna offered to Fitz as she took in the expansive house and the sandy seashore that was completely unpopulated.

"Not bad, right?" Dan knew Fitz still felt terrible about what had happened.

"Very nice." Dan gave him a genuine smile. They entered the home. The relaxation his weary body pled for began to seep into his veins.

Fionna rushed to the large deck along the back of the house and took in the teal-blue Mediterranean waters. She breathed in the salty air like perhaps it would carry her home.

Aida stuck close to Dan as Fitz showed them around the house. There was a large sitting room and a reading nook, which Aida eyed. There was a simple kitchen and master bedroom on the main floor and four additional bedrooms on the upper level.

Two of the bedrooms had sliding glass doors that led to another deck that overlooked the ocean. They contained large queen-sized beds.

There was a room with bunks for the boys and another smaller room with a double bed and a purple coverlet that Aida asked if she could sleep in.

Fionna joined them upstairs as did the boys who were already asking if they could go swimming.

"Sorry, boys. No one is going out to the beach until Uncle Dan and I figure out what's going on." Fitz sounded morose, and Dan was surprised when even Alex didn't argue.

"Why don't Aida and I make some butter cookies for later this evening, and you and Dan go rest," Maddie urged Fionna.

"I think that sounds like a great idea." Dan was unwilling to negotiate.

"All right, fine." Fionna sighed.

Maddie did an outstanding job of distracting Aida and the boys as Dan led Fionna up the stairs.

"Are you going to keep being mad at yourself the whole time we're here?" Her tone held no judgment, but it rang with disappointment.

"I'm sorry." Dan sighed.

"Will you hold me? You're starting to shut me out again." Her voice broke and tears pricked her eyes.

"I'm not. I swear. I'm just trying to figure out how this happened."

"Fitz said that when he put out the arrest warrants, they all panicked."

"I know that, but what I want to know is how they found out the warrants had been issued? Only Iodex officers and the one minister who signed them should have known that. Fitz has a leak, and I'm not certain he's willing to admit that yet."

"Okay, he has a leak, but he didn't tell any of his officers that he bought this house. Why don't we sort of relax and enjoy just being together where no one knows where we are? Please."

"Yeah, okay." He had to get it together. His girls weren't going to really relax until he did.

He tried to remember everything Medio Capusan had instructed and forced a smile. "How much talking would I have to do to get you to take a nap in the buff with me?"

She grinned at his attempt at flirting. "Does that door have a lock?"

Dan checked it and gave her a nod.

"Then you probably wouldn't have to talk too much." She granted him one of his smiles. The effect eased the terror that had permeated his soul.

"But I am looking forward to hearing the talking part." She threw the pillows off the bed, eased the sheets and quilts down, and moved toward him.

He wrapped his arms around her, squeezing and plying her backside. "I want to hold you naked in my arms, baby, with nothing between us. I want to wrap you up in my shield. I want to feel you, all of you, and I want to feel Halia. I need to know you're both safe in my arms."

With a heavy nod, she dispensed with the jeans and T-shirt. He watched the panties slide down her legs and her bra slip as it was relieved of the weight of her breasts.

He undressed and guided her into the soft, cool sheets. She curled up on his bare chest.

Just as he'd begun running his hands over her body, caressing and adoring his wife, Dan's cell rang. "Dammit."

"Who is it? Didn't you already talk to your dad?"

"Yeah, and your Dad and Gretta twice. It's Portwood." He answered immediately. "Hey, you okay?"

"I called to ask you that." Portwood chuckled.

"Oh." Dan supposed that was fair. "We're all right. Fi's radar is still off. She's just lying down for a nap." He hinted that he'd like to join her.

"Is Aida all right?"

"For the moment. I'm sure there will be lots of questions in the next few days. She talked with an Auxiliary counselor at the hospital, but I'm sure that will need to keep happening once we get back home."

"Tell Fi we're thinking of her and little Aida too," Portwood stalled.

"Did you want to ask me something?" Dan fished around in his mind until he landed on Portwood asking if he could call if he had any work-related questions.

"That obvious?"

Chuckling, Dan was glad they were getting somewhere. "Nah, just a guess."

"Are you sure you don't mind? I'll be quick."

"It's fine. Go ahead."

"We traced some money that's been bounced around from one of the Interfeci accounts that ended up in Belgium. Something about it bugs me. It's not like Nic. Lawson had an idea, but I wanted to see if you agreed."

"Okay." Dan tried to think back over all of Wretchkinsides's moneymaking ways.

"He took marked money, I mean hot, straight from a bank job, to purchase those guns from the supplier that Pravus had in Colombia. Why wouldn't he clean it? He was so meticulous about everything."

Dan drew a deep breath. It seemed his past would forever haunt him.

"My guess is that he did it because he was trying to take the gun running ring down. He wanted them to be caught with the marked bills. He always had to have the last word, and he loved to stick it to someone who was making money off of him. The guns we confiscated in Vegas were most of his storehouse, so he was probably paying top dollar to get the ones up from Colombia. That would have irritated him."

"That's precisely what Lawson said. I shouldn't have doubted him."

"It's okay to ask for confirmation. You've been doing this for a few weeks. I did it for years."

"I know, and thank you. Enjoy wherever you are, and tell Fionna I hope she gets to feeling better soon."

"What was that all about?" Fionna yawned deeply. The medicine had somewhat muted her anxious radar rhythms, and her body was relaxing before his eyes.

Dan reformed his body around hers and cradled her back to his chest.

"They're still dealing with all of the money they took in from the Interfeci. Portwood just doesn't trust his own gut enough yet. He knew everything I just told him. Apparently, Rainer even explained it to him, but he wanted to hear me say it. He'll simmer down. He needs to get a few cases under his belt, and then he'll trust himself more." Dan found himself yawning as well.

"Aida still hasn't said anything about what happened last night other than that it was scary. I wonder what she told the counselor." Her voice was sluggish now, and she couldn't hold her eyes open without great effort.

Dan kissed the top of her head. "Governor Haydenshire said we have to let her deal with it at her own pace."

"He's right," she agreed. "I just wish I knew what was going on in her little head."

"Our sweet girl usually gives very detailed descriptions of what she's thinking about. I'm certain, when she's ready, she'll lay it all out there for us. But you, my beautiful bride, and my tiny baby girl, need to get some sleep."

"Do you want to feel her?"

"I'm going to while you sleep. Just relax, baby. I'm right here." He somehow needed to know that Halia was all right, that she was strong and vital, and that she still recognized his rhythms.

The fight in Fionna's body gave out, and she closed her eyes.

Dan slid his hands to her abdomen and closed his own. He had it a moment later. His heart raced as he felt his baby girl's rapid pulses. It shifted again, and Dan felt his breath pick up pace.

A sleepy smile spread across Fionna's face though her eyes remained closed. "Do you feel that? She feels you."

Dan nodded but didn't speak. He was afraid he'd affect the connection.

"I can't wait to hold her," he confessed in a pleading whisper. Restless murmurs in the back of his mind kept him frantic that they would lose her too, that he'd never get the chance to have her in his arms.

Fionna was asleep before she could formulate a response.

What felt like only a few moments later, Dan awoke suddenly.

"No!" Fionna shook in her sleep. "No, stop!" Her entire body attempted to push something away.

"Fi." Dan tried not to awaken her too abruptly.

"Dan! Make them stop!" Terror shot through her rhythms as her body tried to awaken.

"Fionna, baby, wake up." Dan sat up and tried to rouse her. "It's all right. It's just a dream."

She gasped for breath, and her eyes flew open. She began sobbing. His heart shattered as he wrapped his arms around her.

"It's okay. I've got you. It was just a dream." He rubbed her back and wiped away a few of her tears.

Shuddering against him, Fionna nodded as her breath began to steady.

"You want to talk about it?"

"Halia!" She panicked again.

"She's fine. Lie back. Let me feel her."

Dan casted her quickly and flooded his shield with soothing warmth. When she managed to calm, he locked on to Halia.

"See, she's fine." He felt the same strong, steady rhythms. As Fionna calmed and her own heartbeat steadied, she was able to pick up on Halia once again.

Dan felt her body ease slightly as the panic subsided.

"I'm sorry. I thought the medicine would help. I just can't get my radar to stop freaking out."

"What on earth are you sorry for?"

"These pregnancy dreams are crazy."

"Our life has been completely insane. You've been through a lot lately."

"You were right. Maybe this wasn't a good idea. Maybe I should go on to Kauai. I can't seem to calm down. I'm a disaster. I'm afraid all the time. I can't get my radar back to normal. I have this constant sense of dread, like something else terrible is going to happen."

"I already checked the flights, baby. There isn't a flight into Lihue until tomorrow afternoon. If you want to go, I will get you there, but I don't think even on Gifted flights I could be back out here by Thursday afternoon. If you want to go now, maybe Garrett could meet you in DC and fly on to Lihue with you." Defeat pulsed through him. Once again, some vicious, felonious pricks were keeping him from his family.

"I don't want to go without you. Even Kauai isn't home unless you're there. And I am going to your mom's thing Saturday night."

If he couldn't get her home, maybe he could bring some piece of home to her. He knew precisely what she'd meant. He would be happy on any street corner of the world as long as she was beside him.

"Hey." He lifted her chin gently with his hand. "If you could do anything in the world right now, what would you want to do?" He wouldn't let her fall again. He wouldn't let her walk the fraying tightrope of fear and vulnerability. He would hold her tight, and he would never let her go again. "Anything at all."

"Surf the North Shore off of Princeville." She let her eyes close. He knew she was trying desperately to tap into her own rhythms to soothe her own soul and her own spirit.

"You're not gonna make this easy, are you?"

A genuine laugh echoed from her, and Dan felt his tension ease from the sound alone. "How about a second choice? Maybe one that you and Halia can do together."

"I don't know." Her shoulders drooped in wearied fear.

"How about if I see if I might be able to rustle us up some American style coffee, big cup, lots of cream and honey. And Fitz has this place all wired up with Wi-Fi, so how about several romance novels to get your mind off everything."

"No, Dan, that would be rude. Fitz and Maddie invited us out here and have been so nice and hospitable, other than when their house was under siege." She tried for a joke.

Dan shuddered from the memory of their harrowing night.

Suddenly, she couldn't keep it locked inside anymore. She turned and buried her face in his chest and began to sob.

"It's okay," he whispered as her heartbreak washed through his weary veins. "Talk to me." He wouldn't let her shut him out again. He couldn't. They wouldn't survive. Determination set in full force.

"Tell me anything. I want to know. Tell me you were terrified, and that you're mad it happened, and that you're mad at me. Believe me, you can't possibly say anything worse than what I've been thinking all day. Just tell me you hate me and you hate what I've done to you."

"No!" she convulsed. "I would never hate you. I'm not mad at you." She continued to sob. "I just…" She dug her nails into his skin in desperation to cling to something that wouldn't let her go.

"I hate basements!" she finally spat. "I hate being in basements when I'm pregnant! I hate them! I really, really hate them!" She fumed in fury and fear as they mixed in a volatile combination deep inside of her rhythms and then spewed forth violently. "I was so scared!" fell from her lips in a heaving outpour of emotion.

"I know, baby." He held her. Her nails tore at his skin. He deserved the pain.

"I never thought anything could be worse than what I felt when you were at The Tantra and I wasn't with you, but it was. It was worse. I couldn't go to you because of Aida, and I felt like something was ripping me apart. Everything inside of me came apart."

He finally understood even just a modicum of what made his wife the extraordinary person that she was. Her greatest strength, her ability to love and to see the good all around her, was also her greatest weakness. Her inability to be with him when he was in danger and also to be with their girls to keep them safe had frightened her more than even the thought of losing her own life. She'd needed the vast power of the only Shield on the planet capable of protecting her, and he hadn't been with her.

Not certain what to say, he held her and let her cry as he kept her tightly casted in his shield. She was the greatest Receiver of their generation, and he needed to be more than a Shield. He needed to filter the world for her.

Receivers need to feel safe. She'll make you a better person if you let her. Rainer's words from the hotel in Sydney, so long ago, seared through his mind.

"Fi, I don't know what happened last night, baby, but I will figure this out. I will make our family safe if we have to move to an island all our own."

"I know." She scrubbed her hands over her face. The tears seemed to have been cathartic. They washed away a little of her fear and pain.

As he continued to tell her how sorry he was and vowed to do anything at all to keep her safe, a semblance of a smile made a return.

"Maybe let's go downstairs and visit with Fitz and Maddie and check on Aida. If you can really make coffee appear in a big fat American mug with lots of cream and honey then you will forever be my hero."

Dan gave her a loving smile. "Even if I have to drive back to DC, I'll get you coffee, baby. I will take care of you. I will take care of all of my girls." He prayed she would believe in him, believe in them, and that she might find peace.

CHAPTER 39
DREAMS OR NIGHTMARES

As it turned out, Fitz was able to supply Fionna with a large mug of American coffee, as he preferred it to the stronger, richer, albeit smaller French roasts.

Dan made a quick trip to the small local market, donning his hat and glasses again to acquire real cream, some honey, a few things Maddie wanted for dinner, and a few French coloring books he hoped Aida might like.

After he returned to the beach house, he enjoyed a large mug of coffee with his wife while Aida methodically colored. She was overjoyed with her surprise.

Fionna sat with her and let Aida tell her all about the story that was taking place in her mind as she colored the pictures, and Fitz used the opportunity to discuss what he'd learned from the men and women they'd arrested last night.

"They all turned on the girl we took down in the entryway. Said she was the ringleader trying to get something started here, make some quick cash, and then spread it across Europe.

"She heard if she could get past Paris Iodex she'd have it made. I didn't know anything about her before she showed up in my foyer. As far as I know, we took the burgeoning organization out."

"Yeah, but I still want to know how they knew you'd put out the warrants." Dan was tired of Fitzroy's excuses. He had a leak, and they needed to find it quickly.

"I've got three guys I'm watching, Dan. I'm not an idiot."

"I know that."

Fitz felt bad enough about what had happened. He didn't need any more guilt. Dan commanded himself to shut it.

Thunder rumbled in the distance and lightning fractured the sky out over the sea. Aida frowned and left her coloring book to retrieve Phoebe. She crawled into Dan's lap.

"Even little Receivers don't like storms," Fionna whispered as Dan nodded his understanding.

Fitz tousled Aida's hair and she gave him a slight grin, but the storm had her worried.

"Anyway, the girl's name is Vythica Dietrech. She has a Russian accent, but licenses, birth records, everything says she's from Belgium. She's a piece of work, let me tell you. Oliver had her in the tank for two hours. She never cracked. She did, however, spit in his face."

Fionna looked horrified, and Dan grimaced. "Maybe we could talk about this later." He gestured his head to Aida who was curled up in her ball in his lap.

They ate a relatively low-key dinner while watching the storm wash over the house. With every clap of thunder, Aida shuddered. Dan couldn't stand it. He seated her in his lap and slid her plate beside his.

"Fionna, you still look tired," Maddie fussed.

"I'll be all right. I think the baby just amplifies my radar. The medicine helps, but it wears off quickly. I'm on pins and needles. I just need to relax. I might take a bath tonight."

"Of course. There is one in the bathroom upstairs. And I know precisely what you need. This will be perfect. Jean Paul, this will fit with your plan as well."

"What's that?" Fitz's hand hadn't left his wife's. She was drawing from him while they ate. Dan and Fionna pretended they didn't notice.

"We will take the boys to Maman on Friday while you and Dan are at the Parliament. Then Fionna, my sweet Aida, and I will go to see Cosette."

Whoever Cosette was, Maddie was thrilled with her idea.

Fitz smiled and nodded. "That is a good idea."

Maddie smiled at Fionna. "Cosette is a Gifted massage therapist. She gave me massages every week all through both of my pregnancies with the boys. She works at one of the best spas in Paris. They will take care of you while our husbands deal with this little disaster. You will feel like a whole new woman. After your massage and makeup, we'll have lunch and go shopping."

Fionna looked excited, and Aida lifted her head. "Is that what will be Mommy-Aida day?" she quizzed.

"Sure, baby. You can get your fingernails and toenails painted," Fionna assured her.

The first broad, beaming grin he'd seen all day appeared on his daughter's face.

Not wanting to rain on the proverbial spa parade, Dan debated how to explain to the two women who made his world spin that they were under no circumstances going to a spa and then to traipse around Paris completely unprotected while he was in a courtroom all day.

Fitz gave him a knowing grin. "How about if I assign them an entire Elite team? They'll be the best protected people in all of Europe."

"Please," Fionna begged.

"All right, but a full team. Four officers, only Elite," Dan commanded.

"Come on, Aida. Let's go play," Alex requested.

To Dan's shock, Aida wiggled out of his lap. The kids seemed to have bonded over the ordeal the night before, and they'd stuck by each other playing for most of the day.

Thunder rent the sky once more, and Aida shuddered. "Don't worry." Alex pulled his arms up into a lifted flex. "I'm gonna keep working out like Uncle Dan, and my arms are gonna be as huge as his," he informed her with a great deal of certainty.

Fionna and Maddie broke out in giggles. Fitz rolled his eyes. "When exactly did Alex start working out?"

Fionna quieted quickly as the children disappeared up the stairs. "Have you talked to the boys about last night?"

"A little." Maddie offered Fionna a reassuring smile.

"We talked after we left the hospital last night," Fitz soothed. "It's probably easier for them because they've known what I do for a living since they were little. They know there are bad guys, and that I try to put them in prison. By the way, we all owe you a tremendous thanks, Fionna. I heard you crying when you raced into Alfred's room. That's how I got Dan the pistol so quickly."

"Oh." Fionna tried to force a smile. "It's okay. I guess that's sort of what I do."

"Let's hope you don't have to do that ever again, and I also need to say thank you because I know you're the reason Dan agreed to stay here with us. If it'd been up to him, you and Aida would be on a plane to Kauai right now, and I'd be here with angry Dan. You've never seen angry Dan because you are the reason anti-angry Dan exists, but trust me, he isn't fun."

Fionna cracked up. It was a sound that delighted Dan, who certainly couldn't argue with Fitzroy's assessment.

"I really think it's best to just let the boys ask the things they want to know." Maddie brought the conversation back to Fionna's concerns. "Let Aida know that if she wants to talk, you want to listen, but try not to force too much information on her."

"Yeah, I think you're right."

An hour later, Dan and Fionna gave Aida her bath. "You know, Daddy, what happened last night was pretty scary." Fionna helped Aida dry off and rubbed her down with kukui oil.

"It was really scary." Dan guided Aida's feet into her pajama bottoms.

"I didn't know you got scared," Aida whispered. She'd been gnawing on her lip and staring at her feet.

Dan lifted her sweet face with his hand so he was staring into her deep brown eyes.

"I was scared, and it's okay to be scared, baby. I'm so sorry about what happened."

"Alex said his daddy will get the bad guys, so they won't be bad anymore. And I said I don't want my daddy to get bad guys, and Alex said I was a chicken." Her chin trembled. "But I don't understand what that means."

"I think maybe Alex was afraid, but he didn't like how being afraid made him feel," Fionna explained. "When people are afraid, sometimes they say and do unkind things."

"Because it makes your tummy hurt?"

"Right."

"Maybe he should talk to his mommy and daddy because they'll make it better."

"I'm sure he will," Dan consoled her.

"I don't want to think about it. I want it to go away."

"I know." Dan and Fionna both wrapped themselves around her. "We'll keep talking about it until you feel better, and when Daddy gets you to Kauai, I think it will start to go away."

"What if I had been in my bed, and Halia hadn't been in your tummy? What if she'd been in the baby room?"

Assuming that the baby room had been the nursery at the orphanage, Dan cradled Aida tighter.

Fionna soothed, "Then Daddy would have gotten Halia, and I would have gotten you, or I would have gotten Halia, and Daddy would have come for you. We would have made certain that you and Halia were safe. We always will."

"I was worried about her," Aida confessed.

Fionna tenderly brushed an errant hair behind her ear. "That's because you're such a good big sister."

Dan lay down with Aida and kept his shield tucked around her until she was fast asleep.

He peeked in the room Alex and Alfred were sharing. Both boys were in the top bunk.

As he returned to his and Fionna's room, he let a few ideas of how he might help his wife relax run quickly through his mind. He was greeted with Fionna's tender grin, but worry plagued her eyes. Sliding into bed beside her, he wished for the hundredth time that he could just take them on to Kauai where he was certain her rhythms would reset, and she'd be able to really relax.

"How about a bath, Mrs. Vindico?"

"I don't want to wake everyone."

"The kids are exhausted, sweetheart. I checked on the boys on my way in here. They're all out, so for a little while let me take care of you."

She nodded hesitantly. "Maybe that would help."

Dan guided her up and into his arms. "You don't have to hide it from me, baby. I can feel it. I know you're not okay."

Fionna nodded against him. "It's like in my head I know that I'm safe and my girls are safe, but my energy just won't calm. I know there's not some kind of horrible danger, but my rhythms are so agitated. They flare constantly. It's exhausting."

"I'm sure it is."

"But I didn't want to tell you because it makes it worse when you keep blaming yourself."

Dan drew a deep breath and tried not to let her confession add to his guilt. "How about this? I'll try to stop blaming myself if you'll let me help you get to feeling better, but you have to stop pretending that you're okay."

A whispered, "Okay," slipped from her lips.

"How about that bath?"

Dan ran hot water in the tub in the Fitzroys' guest bathroom. There was no showerhead, so the tub was well equipped for adults. He lifted the small, wooden crate from Fionna's toiletry kit that contained all of the oils Tutu prescribed for baths.

He helped her undress and then lifted the small, brown glass bottles and read the remedies on each.

"Want some help?" Fionna offered.

"I'm trying to learn."

She picked up four bottles from the box. "I've been doing this since I was a little girl, remember?"

"Lavender helps you relax. Geranium helps balance crazy hormones. Rosewood and frankincense help with anxiety. And jasmine helps if you're overwhelmed or depressed." She added the oils together into a carrier oil and then methodically to the water.

Dan's body seized. Thoughts of her eyes red and swollen, of the hollow sorrow that had been her only expression for the weeks before he'd killed Wretchkinsides, of her inability to eat or even carry on a conversation, of her sleeping, not only because she was pregnant, but because she was shutting out the world and shutting out him, made him sick.

"Fi." He caught her hands. "If this doesn't work, if you aren't feeling better by tomorrow, I'm putting you on a plane to Kauai."

"Dan." Fionna shook her head. "Tomorrow is Thursday, and we're going home Friday evening. I'll be okay. This isn't like last time where I couldn't see my way out. And would you stop trying to get out of our reception." She smiled.

Her ability to joke with him restored him more than her insistence that she was staying in Paris.

Refusing to agree, Dan held her hand as she stepped into the warm, soothing water. He crawled in behind her and felt the relaxation set in almost immediately.

The tub wasn't quite as large as theirs at home and certainly not as big as the tubs Tutu had in all of the cottages on the farm, so Dan shifted until Fionna's body was submerged between his legs and reclined against his chest.

"Why does Tutu always have to be right?" She sighed as her muscles eased their constant strain.

"I want you to relax for me, baby." Dan began to massage her neck and shoulders using the slick water to let his hands work through her knotted muscles.

She groaned and let her head fall back as he began to unfurl the knots that had set in the night before. He tried to rhythmically soothe her stress as he moved down her back.

When her body was lax and languid, he decided to massage other things. He cupped the warm water in his hands and gently groped her breasts.

"I was really hoping you'd get to those."

"I'm gonna take care of each and every part of your gorgeous body, baby."

She turned her face and hid against his neck. He understood precisely what she needed. She wanted to be held, to be surrounded in the safety of his arms, to be hidden away, buried deeply inside of his shield, as he buried himself deeply inside of her.

She could draw from his release for hours. It would soothe her ragged energy and her overly agitated radar.

"I love you," she pled suddenly.

Overcome with the identical emotion, Dan squeezed her tighter. "I love you too, and I meant what I said. If this gets worse, I'm putting you on a plane to Kauai."

"If you hold me like this for the next two days, I may never leave."

"I'm serious." He refused to let it happen again. He couldn't watch her sink into the depths of depression. It was simply more than he could stand.

"I'll be okay. I promise. The baby just sort of makes everything a little more exaggerated. It's taking some getting used to, but I won't ever shut you out again. That's why I was so miserable last time, because I didn't have you."

"I'm right here, baby, and I'll always be right beside you."

"Best shot buys the beer tonight," Fitz goaded.

"You're on." Dan watched the paper target displaying the top of a human form joggle on the line as it was brought into place.

Raising his brand-new Glock .22, he let the feel of the grip course through his veins.

He'd earned it. He should enjoy it.

His arms rose and tensed into place. He narrowed his eyes. He steadied his breath, lowered his heart rate, casted the weapon, and fired a straight line down the target from the center of the forehead, through the neck, through the heart, through the stomach, and then through the groin. Dan beamed as he lowered his weapon.

"He's done it again, gentlemen! You all let the kid not only beat you but scrub the floor with you." Sarrington slapped Dan on the back.

Fionna shifted and awakened Dan. He raised his head to make certain she wasn't having another nightmare. Cool night air had settled in the room. He pulled a blanket from the end of the bed and spread it over them. He heated the blanket and sealed the warmth around her tranquil, beautiful body. Her energy soothed again a moment later, and he fell back asleep.

"First of all, you need to calm down, and maybe clean the pipes so you don't go off when she takes off her coat."

"Fine, be an asshole!"

Dan grimaced. "All right, fine. Sit down."

"Thank you!" Fitz seated himself on the desk Dan had been using at the French Iodex office for the week.

"Take it really slow. Start out somewhere other than your bedroom, and you'll be able to tell if she wants to take it further."

"I invited her to spend the weekend with me, and she said yes. I'm thinking she's thinking we're taking it further."

"Okay, if she hasn't had guys beating down her dressing room door, so to speak, it's gonna hurt her, so don't get carried away." Dan tried to remember everything Will Haydenshire had told him before he'd taken Amelia to the freshman formal at Venton.

"Yeah, but it doesn't hurt bad, right?"

Dan offered him a sorrowful look and watched all of the blood drain from Fitzroy's face.

Thunder shook the window casings in the office as rain cascaded down the streets of Paris.

"I have to pick her up from her last show in like a half hour, so talk fast." Fitz seemed to strengthen his resolve.

"Warm her up a lot first. Start with kissing. Make sure she's comfortable and as relaxed as she can be. When your hands get where you want them to be, go slow. You'll feel her open more or whatever. Go down on her. Make sure she's really slick. Try to get her to come before your dick is anywhere near her. Just take it slow and easy. Tell her she's beautiful," Dan added at the end.

"She is beautiful." Fitz seemed momentarily shocked that he was being given the opportunity to take Madeline Durand to bed with him.

"Yeah, but tell her and make her feel loved even if you haven't said it yet. It kind of makes them vulnerable to do that. She needs to feel safe with you. She needs to know you're not gonna break her heart. Now, if I'm allowed to leave, I'd like to see if I can get home in time to take Amelia to bed and keep her awake for a while."

Fitz checked his watch for the tenth time in a four-minute block.

"Yeah, I want to get her flowers before the show lets out."

He slapped Fitz on the back as they headed toward the exit doors. "You'll be fine, but you look scared to death. Confidence is key, my friend. Make her believe you know what you're doing, and she'll let you do a hell of a lot more."

"I am scared to death." Fitz pulled his set of keys out of his pocket and opened the door into the pouring rain.

"Please, I need your help!" An extremely attractive woman who spoke with a Belgian accent was standing under the awning. She was trembling in the freezing cold.

Dan and Fitz both stepped back into the office, eyeing each other concernedly.

Dan eased his pistol from his holster.

"Who are you, and why do you need our help?" Fitz watched the woman closely. She was tall and curvy with wavy blonde hair. She was wearing a short black skirt and a hot-pink sweater that clung to what Dan was certain was a very cheaply done boob job.

"Please, you have to help me. He's going to kill me," the woman pled.

"Who's going to kill you?"

"Dominic."

Fitz looked like he might actually cry as he discreetly checked his watch again and grimaced.

"My son, he's just a little boy. I thought I had hidden him, but he found out I had him. I wasn't supposed to. I was supposed to get it taken care of."

"Are you saying Wretchkinsides wants to kill your kid?" Fitz gasped.

Dan agreed that even for Nic Wretchkinsides that sounded harsh.

"Maybe, but me as well!"

"Where is your son now?" Dan asked.

"With his aunt in Belgium, but Dominic is coming here. He found out about my little Hadrian. I don't know what he will do." She began to cry.

"Okay, the Auxiliary department handles kids and Non-Elite handles witness hiding," Fitz sighed.

"You go on. I'll call Mrs. Vincent and Lambert back in. They'll know how to get them taken care of." Dan didn't want Fitzroy to miss his big night.

"Thank you! Thank you! I love you!" Fitz stopped short of kissing Dan.

"Go on. I'll leave as soon as we get this taken care of."

Fitz sprinted out into the cold rain.

"What's your name, ma'am?" Dan asked as he dragged his feet back to his desk.

"Vivianna Malden." She wiped away her tears. "You have to save my children."

"Wait, I thought you said your son?"

~

"Daddy," Aida whimpered.

Dan jerked upright, gasping for breath. He tried to remember the dream he'd been having. "What's wrong, baby?" He rubbed his face and head trying to massage his memory into compliance, but he had no conscious memory of the dream.

"Phoebe had a bad dream, and I think Mommy forgot to put on her pajamas." Aida pointed to Fionna whose breasts were on full display as the covers had lifted with Dan.

"Okay." His ability to formulate logical thought returned to him slowly. "Why don't you and Phoebe go get your blanket, and I'll remind Mommy to put on her pajamas. You can sleep in here with us for tonight, okay?"

"Thank you." She sounded so relieved it broke Dan's heart.

The Haydenshires had warned them about allowing Aida to sleep with them. They'd vowed that it was an easy habit to get into and then a hard one to break, and that it wasn't good for the marriage. Dan decided he'd allow it for the night since numerous gunmen had never attacked Haydenshire Farm in the middle of the night.

"Fi." He hated to awaken her. She was sleeping so soundly.

He grabbed the T-shirt he'd had on earlier in the day and coaxed her body upward. She stirred as he pulled the T-shirt over her head.

"Aida's gonna sleep in here, just for tonight."

"My poor baby girl." She yawned as Aida crawled into their bed and scooted down between them.

"My fairy princess bed makes me feel safe and snuggly, but the beds in Paris, France, make me hear scary sounds."

"When we get home you need to sleep in your room, but we've kind of had a rough trip so it's okay for tonight, all right, sweetheart?"

Aida turned on her side so Fionna could cradle her tenderly.

"I promise not to wiggle, and I won't take up too much room."

"You're fine, baby. Just go to sleep. We're right here." Dan could see her sweet smile in the moonlight as she reached and pushed her tiny hand into his. He kissed her forehead as she fell back asleep almost instantly.

As sunlight bouncing off the Mediterranean began to dance across the walls of the bedroom, Dan rolled to his side. He smiled at his girls cuddled beside each other sound asleep.

They were perfect. He stared at Fionna's beautiful face. It was starting to swell from carrying his little Halia. He let his eyes trace down her body and tried to envision what she would look like in a few months' time.

It took his breath away. He wanted it so badly. He wanted to feel Halia move inside of her, wanted to hold his baby in his arms, wanted to walk the halls with her in the middle of the night and give her a bottle so Fionna could sleep. He wanted it all.

His eyes moved to Aida's sleeping form, languid and relaxed in her mother's safe embrace. Her blanket was tucked by her face as she clung to it.

Something plagued him, some fear he couldn't access, the details of something he was missing lost in the labyrinth of his mind.

His cell phone blared on the bedside table. His heart thundered in his chest. He answered it before moving quickly from the room.

"This is Vindico." He heard the Fitzroys in the kitchen and wondered what time it was.

"Dan, it's Roy Stegman."

Dan turned the phone quickly to see the time. It was ten in France, so it would have been the middle of the night in Vegas. He eased from the bed and moved to the hallway.

"What's wrong, Roy?"

"I meant to call Portwood, truthfully. I forgot you ain't the man no more."

"Okay." Dan wondered what had gotten Stegman out of bed in the middle of the night.

"Anyway, I s'pose this might still concern you."

"What might concern me?"

"I just came from Latimer."

Latimer was the limestone fault prison out in the Mojave desert. The limestone fields probably had more to do with Stegman's forgetting that Dan was no longer an Iodex officer than his lack of sleep or his age.

"Did you just take somebody out there?"

"Nah, but it seems they had themselves a quake. In the middle of the chaos, Quentin Vitrio got himself knifed."

"What?" Dan gasped. "Are you certain?"

"Yeah, one of the Non-Gifted food suppliers had a scuffle with him earlier in the week, and he brought a knife to the fight this time it seems. Guess you can only escape death so many times if Uncle Nic put out the first hit."

"Did you catch the guy?"

"Nah, but we will. Suspicious though. Couple of his buddies said he got a big mouth a few days ago, and he just went and bought himself a brand-new Audi. Course that was also his getaway car, so shouldn't be too hard to find. In fact,"—Stegman paused—"that's my guys on the radio. They just got him. Talk to ya later, Dan."

Dan reeled as he tried to sort through everything he'd just been told. He moved back into the bedroom. Fionna and Aida were awake and snuggling under the covers.

"What's wrong?" Fionna asked.

Dan shook his head and gestured to Aida.

"Come back to bed, Daddy. I want to be an Aida sandwich!"

Dan laughed and slid back into the bed. He squeezed Aida between him and Fionna, then began tickling her until she was giggling hysterically.

Their little girl's laughter was probably the sweetest sound in the world. The warmth only his girls provided flowed through his veins and soothed his troubled soul.

"Can I go play with Alex, and then can I have Anne braids in my hair?" Aida asked when she'd settled down.

"Sure, baby. You go play," Fionna urged.

She slid into the space Aida had occupied previously. "Who called?"

"That was Roy Stegman. He's…" Dan began but Fionna supplied, "The Commander of Nevada Iodex."

"Yeah." Dan wrapped his arms around her. He needed to hold on to his saving grace. "Do you remember the guy that showed up at our hotel in Vegas? The guy that handed over Adderand?" Fionna nodded. Dan drew a deep breath. "He was murdered in prison last night."

"What?"

"Yeah." Dan was still unable to fully process the information.

"I'm so sorry."

The statement struck him as odd. "We weren't particularly close or anything, sweetheart."

"I know, but you didn't hate him either. I could tell you felt sorry for him."

"You're amazing. Did you know that?" Dan was in awe of his wife's tremendous powers.

She blushed violently, and he brushed his thumb over her fevered cheeks. "He came from a bad neighborhood. His dad drank all the time. Used to do some pretty terrible things to his kids. Wretchkinsides offered him a way out when he was barely sixteen, and he jumped at the chance." Dan explained Vitrio's past and why, of the many varied members of the Interfeci, he was one that he felt genuinely sorry for.

Fionna's cell phone chirped. She retrieved it from the table on her side of the bed. A delighted smile formed on her beautiful face as she giggled.

"Who's that?" Dan was desperate for anything that made her smile.

"Malani. She's going to bed, and she's texting me the number of days until we arrive. She's so excited. I haven't had the heart to tell her we'll probably have to delay our arrival."

"What?"

"We were supposed to go home yesterday, but now we can't until tomorrow. I just don't think we'll be ready to move to Kauai for over three months with only one day to pack."

"Hell no." Dan shook his head. "I used to work days at a time with no sleep. I'll pack everything. I'll do whatever we need to do, but we're leaving Sunday afternoon."

"Are you sure?"

"I want you and the girls on that island as soon as I can get you there. I'm not waiting. You're too important, and Halia needs to be there."

Another broad grin spread across her beautiful face. "I guess we could just pack all day Saturday, then go to our reception, and finish up Sunday before we leave."

"If we forget something, I'll buy it for you when we get there." Dan wasn't certain why he was so adamant, or why he was ordering Fionna around, but every cell of his body needed to know that his girls were safe in Kauai. They had to be away from the insanity they'd been living lately.

CHAPTER 40
ALEX AND AIDA

A little while later Aida appeared and crawled up in Dan's lap as Fitz and Maddie settled in the living room with them.

"Alex taught me some words in French," she announced.

"Oh no." Fitz closed his eyes in defeat, and Maddie looked horrified.

Fionna took in the situation with a slight chuckle. "Are the words he taught you nice words, because it's not okay to say unkind words even in another language?"

Aida nodded her understanding. "He taught me to say bonjour which means hello. And how to say another word that means something you do in the bathroom, but I told him I didn't think we should say that word because it isn't nice, but it was a little bit funny." She blushed, but it was the delightedly impressed look in her eye as she informed Dan of all of this that had him reeling.

"Alex!" Fitz roared.

"Fitz." Maddie shook her head. "He's acting out because of what happened."

Alex appeared and Aida grinned at him. A sudden sense of panic came over Dan, but he couldn't quite reason why.

"Let's go play ball on the deck, Aida."

Aida's eyes sparkled as she nodded and leapt out of Dan's lap.

"I want to be on your team," she admitted to Alex in an almost flirtatious drawl.

Alex looked thrilled. "Of course," he assured her arrogantly.

Dan turned to Fionna. She was biting her lips together trying not to laugh.

After they ate breakfast, Fionna braided Aida's hair into two long braids on either side of her head just like Anne's.

Alex appeared just as they were all sitting down again. "Watch this!" He performed a handstand and then proceeded to walk the length of the kitchen on his hands before flipping back on his feet. "Neat, huh?"

"That was really good!"

Dan's coffee began to twist uncomfortably in his stomach.

"It's cause my muscles are way bigger than Alfred's." He flexed his scrawny arms once again.

Fionna's hand covered her mouth as she tried hard not to laugh.

"You can touch them if you want." Alex held his nonexistent bicep out for her to touch.

Dan's eyes goggled in horror as his own biceps began to tremble. Aida reached and squeezed Alex's arm and then giggled.

Fitz and Maddie were both biting their lips together as Fionna continued to fight hysterical laughter.

As soon as she pulled her hand away from his arm, Alex dealt the final blow.

He took firm hold of one of her braids and yanked.

Aida looked shocked momentarily, but then a knowing grin formed on her face.

"I pulled your hair. That means you have to chase me!" Alex chanted excitedly.

Dan clutched his chest as Aida laughed. She took off chasing him out the back door and onto the deck.

Fionna began laughing with Fitz and Maddie but halted as she took in Dan's horrified face. "Okay, now, don't freak out."

Dan was way beyond being calmed. He shoved back from the table with fury pulsing through his shield. "He just pulled her hair! Are you just gonna let him get away with that?" he demanded angrily of Fitzroy who looked thoroughly bemused.

"Dan!" Fionna warned. "Would you come upstairs with me, please?"

He started to pace as she grasped his hand and attempted to drag him toward the stairs.

He followed along in her wake as he drowned in fury and confusion. This couldn't be happening. She was a little girl, his baby girl. Thoughts raced through his head as his stomach twisted into violent knots.

Fionna led them to the guestroom they were using and closed the door.

"Sweetheart," she soothed, but he shook his head and marched to a window to see if he could still see Aida. "This is perfectly normal. She's seven. He's eight, and he's your godson."

"Not Alex," Dan demanded furiously. "Definitely not Alex!"

She fought hard to keep from laughing as she gave a knowing nod. "Because Alex reminds you a little bit too much of someone else I know?"

"Yes!" He didn't understand how she didn't see this as a disastrous problem.

"Come on. Calm down. She doesn't even understand why she feels like that and neither does he. He just wants to impress her, and she just wants him to like her, nothing more. Okay?"

"She's way too young for all of that."

Fionna rolled her eyes. "No, she isn't."

"And why does she want him to like her so much? She's perfect! Who the hell wouldn't like her?"

"So, Alex has good taste."

"Oh my God! Alex! Why does it have to be Alex?" He continued his relentless pacing.

"They've been through a lot together. He makes her feel safe because he was with us in the basement the other night. They've bonded over the last few days. She had a crush on a little boy in the orphanage. They used to eat together. His name was Leo, and I think she misses him."

"What?!" He was enraged again. How could that have been? He hadn't been there to protect her.

"Would you please calm down? No one has done anything to her. This is perfectly normal. It's completely healthy. Of course she likes him. He's an eight-year-old version of you!"

That did nothing to calm him. "Oh my God!" He sank down on the bed. "If he hurts her…."

That was met with another eye roll. "He's eight. He just wants to show off for her. He wants her to think he's cool, because again, he's eight. And she's only too happy to show him how impressed she is, because she likes playing with him. Did you really think she'd never have a crush?"

"No! I just thought she'd be much older, you know, like well into her thirties."

She doubled over laughing, and he continued to pout and to try to look out the windows to spot Aida.

"He pulled her hair!"

Fionna bit her lips together and nodded. "Sometimes you pull my hair, and I really, really like it."

His eyes flashed in fury. "No! No, no! Do not go there! I can't take that. I cannot think about her and Alex. My God, Fionna! What is wrong with you?"

"I was only teasing. Listen." She took his hand and forced calming energy into his fury. "I know this is hard for dads, but just try to hear me out. She was probably a little bit surprised that he did that, but she was also delighted because she can feel that he wants her attention. Since she also wants his attention, she likes that. If it had upset her, she would've come to you. I promise. And we will tell her that under no circumstances does allowing someone to hurt you mean that they are trying to communicate affection. But you have to remember that she's a little Receiver. She can, to some degree, feel what he's feeling."

"I should not want to kill one of my godsons." He added guilt into the volatile cocktail of confusion and fury swirling in his stomach.

"Yes, that's true. You kind of flipped, but I think that's normal, since this is the first crush she's had that you've witnessed."

"Did I yell at Fitzroy?" The whole, horrific scene replayed in his mind.

"You did."

He had no idea what to do. He prided himself on always having a contingency plan, but he was completely unprepared for this.

Fionna brushed a tender kiss on his jaw. "Are you okay?"

Dan shook his head but allowed her to guide him from their room.

Aida and Alex were playing in the room Aida was staying in. "Let's play house. I'll be the mommy, and you can be the daddy, and Phoebe will be our baby."

"Are we gonna have another baby in your stomach like Uncle Dan and Fionna are?" Alex quizzed.

Bile flooded Dan's throat. He spun in the hall and glared at Fionna.

"Wow! You've had a really rough week." She cringed.

Eventually, Dan sauntered down the stairs to find Fitzroy flipping through papers splayed all over the coffee table.

"Are you gonna be all right or should I go ahead and take Alex to the gun range?"

"Talk to me when you have a little girl, asshole," Dan demanded indignantly, earning him another round of laughter from Fitzroy.

Suddenly, Dan remembered the phone call from Stegman. "Hey, have you talked to Portwood?"

"No, should I have?"

Dan sank down on the sofa and glanced over the paperwork. "Quentin Vitrio got himself killed last night out in Latimer. It looked like a hit."

"What?"

"And I don't want Portwood to think I'm checking up on him," Dan urged.

"Ah." Fitz pulled his cell from his pocket, checked the time, and phoned the American Senate Iodex office.

"Hey, Landon, it's Fitz." He laughed. "Nah, he's not checking up on you. We were just curious about Vitrio."

Dan tried to hide his chuckle. Fitzroy cast his phone, projected the speaker out, and they listened intently.

"I'm still not certain it was actually a hit. Stegman doubts it,"

Portwood supplied. "According to the cafeteria staff, Vitrio was mouthing off about the guy's sister. He identified a rather well-hidden birthmark that he apparently would have to have done the things he was bragging about to have seen. I can't figure out where the car came from, but sounds like the guy was pissed and thought he'd get away with it."

Dan and Fitz shared a doubtful glance. "Let me know if you hear anything else," Fitz commanded.

"Will do," Portwood agreed. "Good luck tomorrow. Hey, is Dan there with you?"

With a mischievous smirk, Fitz lied. "Nah, he's upstairs with Fionna. I swear they're like rabbits. He can't keep his mitts off of her."

Dan rolled his eyes and anxiously awaited Portwood's response.

He laughed. "Yeah, I know, but good for him. He deserves to be happy."

Dan was truly touched.

"Leave 'em alone. It's nothing. I'll ask him later."

Fitz ended the call.

"Okay, you and I both know there is more to it than he banged the guy's sister," Dan quipped.

"Yeah, but we need to let Portwood figure that out."

Dan lifted a stack of papers from the coffee table. A photograph of an attractive blonde that he recognized but couldn't place was on top. "Who's this?"

"One of Nic's mistresses. Vivian or something like that. I can't remember. She got mouthy about Lucinda. He shut her up permanently a few years ago. The Auxiliary department just handed all of this back after you ended him. It's their case files on the Interfeci. I found them at the house when I was grabbing everything from my office. I'm trying to sort through it and take most of it to the precinct until I find us a new place."

"Want some help?"

"Thanks." Fitz accepted the offer with a sigh. "Hey, how's Fi really? She still looks a little off."

"She is, but she refuses to leave. I've got to get her home. I can't let her get like she was before."

"I know you're worried, but she's probably just freaked about tomorrow. Once the trials are over, I'm sure she'll be fine."

Dan studied the photograph again but couldn't figure out why he was so intrigued with it.

"You might not want to let Fionna catch you drooling over that," Fitz teased him.

Dan rolled his eyes. "She just looks familiar for some reason."

"She looks like all the others to me. Blonde, custom-made top, fawning all over him, just how he liked 'em."

Dan had to agree. Wretchkinsides had mistresses at every port, and they all fit the same playbill.

"What time do we have to be there tomorrow?" Dan tossed the picture back on the table. All that mattered was getting Fionna home.

"They start at ten. I tried to book them back-to-back. I know you want her home."

"Thanks. Truthfully, I'm a disaster. I hope I make it through the trials. I'm worried sick."

"They should be open and shut. They were caught in my home with guns. Basically, we nod our heads that they're the people, and the Prime Minister hands out punishments, which won't be pretty."

"Good."

CHAPTER 41

KALEIDOSCOPE TURNS

The next morning, Dan paced. His breakfast was on the constant verge of making a dramatic comeback as he read the Elite team Fitz had assigned to Maddie, Fionna, and Aida the riot act.

He watched the officers, two men and two women, who would be responsible for bathroom and spa room accompaniments, escort Fionna and Aida into an extremely posh salon in the middle of Paris.

He glanced at his watch fretfully. In six hours, the Crown Governor's jet would be at Charles de Gaulle. He was putting her on a plane and taking her home.

He began his countdown as he followed Fitz onto the Metro and toward the French Gifted Parliament building.

He fell onto the prosecution bench with a fitful huff. How the hell was he was back in yet another courtroom? How had he put his wife and baby girls in danger yet again?

Fitz slapped him on the back though he was also pale and weary. Fury flooded his shield as he scowled at the defense attorney.

The Parliament Board glided into the room, and everyone stood. The Prime Minister read the charges and gave an account of the attack on the Fitzroys' home.

Vile revulsion coursed through Dan's veins as he recalled Fionna waking him, sobbing, screaming in his face, and racing to Aida. Images of her inability to do anything more than gasp for ragged breaths as she sobbed after it was over raced through his mind. Her lying in the hospital bed with Aida trembling beside her made vicious rage seep from his pores.

"The first trial will be of Ms. Vythica Dietrech," the translator stated.

Dan's blood ran ice cold. It seemed to freeze in his veins. All of the heinous pieces of the puzzle that had plagued him for days began to sear into place in his mind.

Like the turn of a child's kaleidoscope, Dan's heart vibrated in his chest. *"What's your name, ma'am?"* He heard the frustrated question fall from his own lips ten years before.

And the answering reply shot through him like a blazing bullet.

"Vivianna Malden."

Realization tore through him as the woman was led into the room. She looked just like her mother. Blonde hair, blue eyes, curves, only there were no frightened tears. No, she wore the hate-fueled scowl of her father.

The son of famed millionaire Hadrian Dietrech Wretchkinsides. Dan gasped in horror as he saw the picture from the Erotic Museum with the placard underneath. That was the clue his brain had been unable to locate for the past several days. It had eluded him just like his prey.

"Where's Malden?" he demanded of Fitzroy.

"What?" Fitz glanced around the room nervously as all eyes fell to Dan in disdain. He continued to reel.

"So, what do they need the money for?" Dan heard Portwood's question echo in his mind as he glared at the answer before him.

"Whoever did this needed the money they received for selling the pictures, and the papers needed to make back the exorbitant prices I'm sure they paid for them. Neither could afford to wait any longer." His own words pounded against his skull.

He'd had every account, every dollar tracked except the ones Nic so often sent to Belgium in odd amounts, the ones he sent to his son. Difficult to track money when it was immediately being hidden by another Iodex officer.

"Guess you can only escape death so many times if Uncle Nic put out the first hit." Stegman's quip had bile rising violently in his throat.

The money for the setup of Rainer and Emily. Dan shuddered in horror. *"Well, for what it's worth, the money came from Belgium."* He could still feel the confusion he'd felt as Portwood rattled off the evidence.

His phone call to Fitz several months before. *"Hey, I've been over this all a million times, but would you check the place Lawson is planning on bedding his bride for two weeks. Just make sure Nic has no way of finding them for me."*

Fitz's chuckle. "Will do. Just send me the address."

"Vivianna Malden! My God, Fitz! Where the hell is Malden?" Dan shouted loudly.

"We traced some money that's been bounced around from one of the Interfeci accounts that ended up in Belgium." Portwood's words allied with his own. They joined the war in his brain.

"Oh my God!" Dan grabbed Fitzroy's collar. "Where the fuck is Malden!"

"Dan, what the hell?" Fitz glanced around the chamber room. Every eye was on Dan.

"Is he speaking of the Officer H. Malden? He was not called for testimony today, Mr. Vindico." The court clerk tried to soothe him.

"What is his real name?" Dan demanded.

"He goes by Richard, but H. is his first initial." Fitz stared at Dan like he'd lost his mind.

"How's the tummy? It was nervous a minute ago."

"Oh my God, Aida!" Dan recalled Aida's tiny body curling up in his lap at the children's park. He'd followed them there. He'd been watching her.

The brick through the window. *"The only people who know you're here are people who work for the Senate."* They were trying to get in. That's why the bush outside was crushed. He'd stood close enough to try to keep it from being too loud. It was the best he'd come up with in the limited time he'd had to plan when Dan himself had alerted the press to the fact that they were traveling to Paris.

As he recalled holding Fionna in the bed, Dan heard her frightened intonation. *"It's like in my head I know I'm safe and that the girls are safe, but my energy just won't calm. I know there's not some kind of horrible danger, but my rhythms are so agitated. It's exhausting."*

The pickpocket. He hadn't wanted her wallet. He wanted her phone. That's what he was searching for in her bag. Malden wanted to tag her phone to follow her. *"Guy's got two outstanding warrants. Seems he's expanded his business from Brussels."*

His body trembled. He'd never felt the need to move or such acrid terror in all his life. Every hair on his body stood as his temperature fluctuated rapidly.

"There's nothing wrong with her radar! She was right all along! Fionna, oh my God! Why didn't I listen?" Dan swallowed back vomit and turned to the Parliamentary board. "H is for Hadrian! He named him after his father to piss him off! His name is Hadrian Dietrech Wretchkinsides! Malden was his mother's surname!" Dan seethed. "And that is his sister!" Dan pointed to the woman on the stands, just before he bolted from the courtroom, sprinting outside with Fitzroy hot on his heels.

"Enfermez-la et trouvez-moi Malden!" Fitz shouted the orders to detain Vythica and to find him Malden.

Officers sprinted out of the courtroom without any idea where to begin looking, but Dan knew.

Every strike of his foot against the pavement reverberated in his skull. Dan shoved through a crowd of tourists photographing the windmill over the Moulin Rouge. He pulled out his phone as he sprinted toward the train station.

Fitz leapt onto the train right behind him. "Answer, baby, please! Please!" Dan pled to the pitiless air around him as he heard Aida's sweet voice on Fionna's voicemail message. "Hi, this is my mommy's cell phone. She'll have to call you back." His heart sank to the ground.

The malice and hatred that had been gone for so long returned with a vengeance. It filled him. It narrowed his eyes, blackened his heart, and permeated his soul.

"You are a motherfucking son of a bitch, and when I find you, Hadrian, I will end you myself!" Fitz spat into his own cell leaving a message as Malden clearly wasn't taking his calls.

After ending that call, Fitz touched another name. "Oliver!" He panted for breath. "Are you still with Maddie and Fionna? NO!" Fitzroy pounded his fist into the metal pole beside him. "My God, no, get over to Maddie's mom's and make certain my boys are all right. Bring them to me at the spa!"

"Malden told them to leave." Dan already knew what Oliver had informed Fitzroy of.

"Told him I needed him at the trial!" Fitz spat furiously.

Dan shoved four people into one another to make certain he was the first one off the train. He dodged through the crowded Parisian streets and headed back to the spa. Fitz continued to try and call the female officers who were to have gone into the massage room with Fionna and Maddie as he ran beside him.

The wind burned Dan's face in his fevered sprint. He threw the glass door to the spa open with enough force to shatter the pane as it hit the brick building.

"Eu quero meu pai!" He heard Aida sob before he turned the corner to take in the scene. In her terror, she'd reverted back to Portuguese.

I want my daddy! Dan translated it.

"Get away from her!" Fionna shrieked. He saw her throw a more powerful shield than he'd ever have thought her capable.

Fury like Dan had never felt before seared through his veins. He swung, but Malden ducked and threw Aida hard against a wall as he spun. Fitz leapt but Malden jerked to the left and raced out the shattered door.

"Daddy!" Aida sobbed.

Dan reached and lifted her into his arms. Her little hands flew to her head where she'd hit the wall.

"Are you okay, baby?"

"He hurt my shoulder. He said I had to go with him or he would hurt Mommy!" She convulsed in her harrowing terror.

Fionna moved toward him. She was pale and weak, wearing a spa robe and nothing else. She trembled in her walk as she tried to keep it tied around her.

"He told the other officers that he'd been sent to replace them, that Fitz had ordered them back to the precinct. He said you'd been hurt, but I knew he was lying. He took my phone. I couldn't call you," she tried to explain before the tears overtook her.

Fitz was already back on the phone calling in an ambulance as the rest of Iodex entered the spa, securing everything as they went. Maddie rushed into Fitz's arms.

The ambulance he'd called arrived moments later. Dan raced Aida and Fionna out to the ambulance, sealing the doors closed behind him.

Aida's shoulder had purple, finger-shaped bruises forming on it rapidly, and Fionna's cheek was blazing red. Dan hadn't seen it at first, but she'd been backhanded.

"Mommy!" Aida tried to sit up on the gurney. Her face went white as a ghost. "I don't feel good," she managed before she folded over her stomach.

Fionna held out her hands in an effort to catch the vomit. One of the many medios immediately stepped in and cleaned them up.

"Baby." Dan shook from the effort of not driving his fist into the side of the ambulance. He tried to help clean Aida up.

She lay back and gasped for breath. Her tiny hand found Dan's.

"Are you going to find the bad guy?"

"Oh, I'm going to find him, baby. Don't worry." Vengeance spiked his blood. It was a poison, a drug, he recognized all too well. He craved it.

"Dan, we're safe. Please don't," Fionna pled, but he shook his head.

"No!" he demanded. He would make her no promises, not now, not after this.

Acrid fury rose in his throat. His eyes flashed dangerously. Tears leaked down Fionna's face as she gave him a haggard nod. He grabbed a flannel blanket, tore the plastic off of it, and covered her body.

"Get her clothes. Heal them, and take them to the Parliament!" Dan ordered the ambulance driver and medios as he opened the back door and stepped out onto the street.

He grabbed Oliver's collar and jerked him forward as he delivered Alex and Alfred safely to Fitzroy. "If anything happens to them, I will kill you after I kill him! You got that?"

"Yes, sir." Oliver managed a half nod before he climbed in the ambulance with Fionna followed by three other officers that Fitz ordered as his backup.

"Dan, please be careful!" Fionna begged. "Just please don't…." She started to beg again but stopped. She knew better. Her eyes closed in defeat. "I love you."

"I love you too, and I will be right back."

"I put a tracer on his phone two weeks ago. I know where he is." Fitz held up an enhanced radar map of Paris with a pulsing red sonar dot moving out of the city. It took them less than a full second to know precisely where Malden was heading.

"He's got a guy with him. Do you want backup?"

"No." Dan ordered an officer out of his car and took it for him and Fitzroy.

His cell rang as Fitz drove like a bat out of hell.

"What?"

"Sir, it is Oliver. They're taking Mrs. Vindico to the hospital to check the, uh, enfant," he managed through broken English. "It is precaution. I am going with her. Madame Fitzroy and the children and Elite are as well."

"Tell her I'll be there as soon as I take care of this."

"Yes, sir. I will."

"Is she okay?" Fitz swerved around an oncoming bus.

"They're taking her to the hospital to check on the baby." Dan used most of his control to keep from vomiting, as he recalled his wife's beautiful face glowing red and his baby girl's tiny shoulder swollen and purple.

They roared through the red-light district with sirens blaring and lights blazing alerting everyone to their path.

"Turn off the sirens!" Dan demanded.

Fitz silenced the car and turned off the flashing lights. "Are you okay?" He braced for the incoming rage.

"What the hell do you think?"

Fitz didn't seem offended. He just nodded as the car flew farther and farther out of town. "This is unbelievable. I thought he killed the kid when he killed her."

"He wanted a son. He always had. I bet he never knew about

Vythica." His voice held no tone. The fury had drowned every other emotion. "Hadrian needed more money than he was able to access when I killed Wretchkinsides. He used what he'd taken to get the photographs of Rainer and Emily on their honeymoon hoping to get several million from the press. He put the hit out on Vitrio and then came after me."

Fitz parked the car a block from the house. The same place they'd left the car all those years before. Dan pulled a pistol from the glove box as Fitz popped the snap on his holster. They casted and chambered the weapons then moved past an outbuilding on the property of the abandoned, derelict home.

Vile revulsion washed over Dan's body. He'd been here too many times before. They moved like the well-synchronized machine they'd always been. Fitz and Dan kept their backs pressed firmly to the warm steel of the shed. Their pistols were drawn by their faces.

Dan ducked and took in the house. He kept most of his body behind his makeshift shield. He could see two men through the shattered windows of the house set off by the overhead sun slowly making its way across the sky.

Malden was pacing and shouting angrily. He didn't have his father's patient, ominous calm. He wasn't the spider waiting endlessly to web the fly. He was nothing more than a bastard child trying to prove his worth with no real ability to do anything at all.

Both men were in the back of the house maybe twenty yards from where Fitz and Dan were hiding.

They needed to maneuver around the shed and move to the front of the house to take them without being seen.

Dan motioned to the ground. Fitz nodded as they lowered themselves into a low crawl and stayed hidden in the high grass.

Dan halted Fitz just before they fell from the shadow of the shed. He held up one finger and motioned to the side of the house. Fitz shook his head. If he took out one through the window, Malden would know they'd been found.

Sweat dewed on Dan's forehead as he edged through the undergrowth of the unkempt shack. He could feel it pooling on his back as the midday sun beat down relentlessly.

He tried to shut down the thoughts swirling violently in his mind. He needed to concentrate, but everything that had happened to him since the last time he'd been to this house, all of the horrific loss, all of the tremendous gain, tallied in his mind. He dragged himself along the ground.

"Please be careful," Fionna's voice echoed against his skull. He was in the worst possible position he could be in should he be seen. He kept his eyes trained on the windows on the side of the ramshackle house and forced his shield out over himself while praying that Malden wouldn't see the brilliant green glow.

"I want my Daddy." Aida's terrified peal fractured his heart, and fury and hatred bled from the recently mended seams. They made it to the front porch, and he allowed himself to breathe.

Relief flooded through him as he panted silently. He pulled himself into a seated position and leaned against the lattice work that had once constructed the wide front porch, gone decades ago. The entire building was tilting off of its foundation from bombing during the war, and Dan tried to shut down the memory that forced its way through all of the barriers he'd erected in his mind when he'd arrived on the property.

The last time he'd been on that porch, he'd taken out two of Wretchkinsides's men through the front window. That's how the glass had been shattered. He remembered the sound of the glass exploding in the night.

He'd ducked and barely gotten out of the way in time after shooting the powerful electrical cast. Glass rent the night sky and return fire rained down all around him.

He'd been certain for a moment he was done for. At that time in his life, he'd welcomed the end, but the pulsing, relentless, fury had saved him again. Determination had bound him back together. He wasn't dying by Cascavel's gun. The viper would go down first. Dan would make certain of that.

He'd leapt through the window he'd shattered, slicing his legs. The feeling of the jagged shards piercing his skin had only driven him harder.

Fitz had come through the front door. The house was crawling with Wretchkinsides's men. They'd fought. They'd taken out man after man, but Cascavel had escaped. He'd slipped through his fingers once more, and Dan had lived to fight another day.

Memories of all of the days between that night and the present moment ran through Dan's mind like a flip book. His heart thundered in his chest.

The funeral, the sleepless nights, the endless days, the liquor, the drugs, the grueling work, the relentless fight for every inch he gained.

Cascavel, the Russian board, Pendergrath's sneering scowl, the after party, the house in Alexandria, Sydney, his angel appearing to carry him on, the hospital, the baby, the loss, Kauai island, the leis washing out to sea, the wedding, what their love had created on their wedding night, the little girl who held his broken heart in her tiny hands. It spiked his blood as it pooled heatedly in his veins.

Fitz elbowed him and ripped him forcefully from his abstraction. He held up two fingers and gestured to the window above Dan just slightly to his left.

Dan pointed to Fitz and then moved his finger in a low semi-circle showing Fitz that he should move on the ground to the front porch and take out the man in the window.

He then pointed to himself and to a window on the side of the house indicating he was entering that way nearest Malden.

Fitz nodded and began edging toward the front of the house. Dan slid on his ass, ready to leap in a single sinewy move through the window that no longer contained any glass at all.

"Please be careful." He heard Fionna's voice reverberate through him again. Clenching his jaw, he strengthened his shield. He'd never set it that night. Either too arrogant or too desperate, he wasn't certain the reason, but he never had.

He listened between his heartbeats as they thundered in his ears. The men were still talking. Neither seemed aware that anyone else knew where they were. Malden had no idea Fitzroy had tracked his phone, but he was about to find out.

Fitz slid his body into position at the front of the house. They shared a nod, and in the length of one heartbeat, Dan sprang through the window, and Fitz clobbered the accomplice. He knocked him out cold on the thin floorboards.

Malden took aim and fired. The bullet ricocheted off of Dan's shield and onto the sparse wood floor, missing several of its slats. Fury propelled his every move. Dan tackled Malden, driving all of the air from his lungs as he fought for control of the gun.

When their skin connected, he felt it. Something sickening twisted inside of him. That piece of malignant energy in his soul recognized its kin. It infuriated him.

"Did you think you would win, you motherfucking asshole?" Dan chanted as he jerked the gun out of Malden's hands and tossed it to Fitzroy.

Fitz had it unloaded in a split second as he threw Dan cuffs. Dan shoved Malden into a three-legged, wooden chair and bound him in cuffs. With a long piece of elastic cording that he casted and stretched, he made certain he couldn't move.

"You are one fucking stupid son of a bitch." Dan snaked toward Malden. Swinging his leg to the side, he knocked the chair to the ground, listening as Malden's head hit the wood.

"Did you not think?" Dan drawled as Fitz placed his boot on Malden's rib cage. "Were you really stupid enough to believe that I wouldn't turn over every single stone, that I wouldn't hunt you down to the ends of the earth like a bloodhound in hot pursuit, that I wouldn't end the bastard that dared lay a filthy hand on my little girl?"

It was in Malden's answering scowl that Dan saw it. His face was that of his mother, but he had his eyes—his cold, malevolent eyes.

Dan shoved Fitz away and quickly righted Malden's chair. "That reminds me." He swung his fist across Malden's cheek. He reveled in the retribution and release as his knuckles shattered his jaw and teeth.

Abject hatred pulsed through him as he recalled Fionna's cheek.

"Daddy not teach you not to hit girls, you punk-ass prick? Nobody hits my wife!"

Fitzroy's eyes goggled in shock. He clearly hadn't noticed Fionna's cheek. "I can't believe you hit Fionna and you're still breathing, quite honestly, Hadrian."

Dan took a step closer and leaned until his face was inches from Malden's as Fitz kept his pistol locked on his heart.

"When I ask you a question, you better give me an answer. You understand what I'm saying to you, motherfucker?" Dan backed away slightly. "Come on, Dietrech!" He dealt the blow as Malden's eyes goggled. "Tell me, did you really believe you'd make off with one of my girls, and that we would let you continue to pollute this earth by drawing breath?"

Terror played in Malden's eyes. He couldn't hide it.

"Gonna avenge him? Gonna try and rebuild what we systematically took apart piece by piece until it all shattered down around you in crumpled useless remains? Do you want to try to avenge the father who never wanted you? He obviously knew about you. She named you after his father. His grandson. A child of one of many unnamed mistresses. Bet that made Grandpa furious when he found out. Heir to the Wretchkinsides throne."

Malden spat out teeth and blood. "You gonna kill me too? That's right, isn't it? Vindico never has to play by the rules. Everybody feels sorry for him and he gets away with cold-blooded murder," Malden hissed like the snake he was.

Dan chuckled ominously then moved back to Malden's face. "Did you put your disgusting hand on my baby girl?"

"You know I did!" Malden defied.

"Then you already know the answer to that, don't you?"

Malden trembled, but Fitzroy's pistol never wavered.

"Just one thing first." Dan toppled the chair back on its side. As Malden's hands hit the ground he brought his boot down on top of them, crushing every bone in the hand that had left the bruises on Aida's arm.

Malden screamed in searing pain as Dan and Fitz glared hatefully. "Yeah, I remember your mom now." Fitz nodded after Malden had piped down. "Vivianna Malden. I can't believe I never caught the name. You know he killed her. She showed up wanting us to protect you, but you were never in danger, were you, Hadrian? He already knew about you. She'd been working her way through the organization, and Daddy found out. He hated that. It was her he

404

wanted, not you." Fitz began to piece together the remaining pieces of the puzzle.

"Yes!" Dan staggered as his other Predilection began to seep through his awareness. "Vythica is only your half sister, isn't she? Vivianna told Nic she was his as well, but he knew better." Dan pulled Vythica's face back into his mind's eye. He'd recognized the vicious scowl, but he'd credited it to the wrong miscreant. "My God, she's Cascavel's!"

That was why Wretchkinsides had allowed Cascavel to take on the Elite forces alone when he'd taken Samantha. That was what Wretchkinsides wanted. He never cared if Cascavel killed Dan or if it went the other way. He'd waited decades to get his revenge. He'd waited until he had Adderand trained as Cascavel's replacement.

"Too bad you'll never get to meet Marlisa," Fitzroy sneered.

"Yeah, you could've spent Christmases together. Talked about the good old days with dear old Dad."

Fitz tried not to smirk. "So, what shall we do with you, Hadrian Jr.? We're the only ones who know you're here. We already took out your security detail." He gestured his head to the man handcuffed and unconscious on the floor.

"Seeing as how you provided your little gang with the address to my house, I'm tempted to load enough lead in you to add several pounds to your pathetic ass. But, since it's his little girl who's bloodied and bruised and his wife who's lying in a hospital bed right about now, I'm gonna let Dan decide how many pieces we're going to tear you into and how many different countries we're going to bury you in.

"Of course, if he should, in some preposterous twist of fate, decide to let you live, you'd stand charges of attempted kidnapping, a half dozen privacy laws in regard to the Lawsons, along with treason, assault, and planning the siege on my house. That worked well for you, didn't it?" Fitz mocked.

Realizations continued their assault on his mind. Dan grabbed the back of Malden's hair and jerked his head backward. "It was you! It was you that night! You got Cascavel out. Saved Daddy's prizefighter trying to prove your worth." His voice was laced with menace and rage pierced his soul.

"Ah." Fitz nodded. The final piece of the puzzle slipped into place. "And helping a wanted man escape." He added to the arrest charges.

Dan released Malden's hair and raised his pistol.

Malden shrank before him, grimacing and hiding his face like the coward he'd been raised to be.

Dan shook his head. "Oh, come on. Grow a pair. At least Daddy looked me in the eye when I killed him."

"He hated you!" spat from Malden spitefully as he turned his terror-filled face back to Dan..

"Oh yeah? Well, believe me, the feeling was mutual."

"He didn't hate anyone as much as he hated you. You had him at every turn. That's why he was always gone because you never let him be!" He regurgitated the shit his father must've convinced him of.

"Is that what he told you, little boy?" Dan huffed. "And yet knowing that, you still somehow thought I wouldn't find you after you hurt my girls?" Dan laughed derisively.

"I would've done more than hurt her if you hadn't taught that whore you married to throw a shield. I heard you knocked her up again. What happened? You take care of that little problem as well?"

Rage fueled the swing of his fist. He shattered Malden's eye socket and nose and watched as blood poured from his left eye. "Keep talking like that and see what I break next."

Fitz shook his head in utter disbelief. "What? You figure your minutes are numbered so you're just gonna implode in a sea of your own shit, you stupid fool?"

"Look at me, Hadrian." Dan centered his pistol over Malden's heart. "Do not ever, ever go anywhere near my wife or my daughter ever again. And if you decide you'd like to play another round of this sick game, remember this warning—I don't do chances. If you come near my girls, or my wife, or my godsons ever again, the next several days of your sad pathetic life will be extremely painful for you, and then I'll bury you right beside Daddy. Trust me!"

He slowly cocked the gun and watched Malden attempt to curl

himself into the fetal position. With one quick move, Dan released the elastic cording and hoisted Malden upright.

He wouldn't do what Nic would have done. He would never give in to the darkness. In that moment, he killed the energy he'd felt inside of himself since he'd taken on Wretchkinsides.

"Hadrian Dietrech Wretchkinsides, you are under arrest for the attempted kidnapping of my baby girl among many, many other things, and I feel certain that Crown Governor Haydenshire will be amenable to having you extradited, so let me say how much I hope you enjoy a life sentence in Coriolis Prison."

Within moments, Fitz had French Iodex officers surrounding the house as the men inside were loaded into shield-casted police wagons.

CHAPTER 42
A BETTER MAN

Dan sprinted inside the American Hospital in Paris. "Fionna Vindico's room, please."

"Yes, sir." The woman checked her computer. "She's in a secured room, sir. I can't give you that information. You'll have to have an Iodex officer admit you."

Fitzroy joined Dan at the window. "Will I do?"

"Oh, yes sir, Captain Fitzroy."

Dan raced to the elevator and casted it. He exited a minute later.

Maddie met them in the hallway. "She's all right. They've sedated her to keep her from having another panic attack. She was so worried about you. I couldn't get Aida to come out here with me. She's sitting beside her in the bed." Maddie's chin trembled, and Fitz wrapped her up in his arms.

Dan swallowed down the gut-wrenching pain and slipped into Fionna's room.

"Daddy!" Aida pled in relief as she held her hands out to Dan. She'd been sitting right beside Fionna, patting her hand as tears poured from her eyes. Her head was bandaged in a cool-casted wrap.

"Baby." He lifted Aida into his arms and cradled her tightly. "Are you okay?"

"They gave me medicine and put this thing on my head. They

made Mommy go to sleep, but she said not to 'cause you weren't here yet."

"I'm here now. I've got you." Dan tried to sound soothing as he gazed at Fionna lying in the bed. He seated himself in the chair and cradled Aida in his lap.

"Did you catch the bad guy?" She hid her face in his neck.

"Yeah, baby. I did."

"Did you take him to jail?"

"Mr. Fitzroy did."

"Will he get out of jail?" She shuddered in horror.

"No, baby. He won't ever get out of jail."

Medio Capusan came into the room to check Fionna. "Mr. Vindico, I didn't realize you'd returned. We'll turn off the drip and let Mrs. Vindico awaken on her own."

"The baby?" Dan choked.

"She's just fine. It was your wife I was worried about. The baby is healthy although keeping things a little lower key would be best for the rest of her pregnancy."

Dan assumed that lying on the beach in Kauai would probably be the best remedy.

Medio Capusan removed the IV and then left the room.

"Does your head hurt, baby, or your shoulder?" Dan forced the question from his mouth though he felt the bitter acid burn his lips.

"The medio lady person put an ice pack on my head and that hurt worse, but then it felt better. They gave me medicine for my tummy and put this on." She pointed to the bandage wrapped around her head. My shoulder hurts if I touch it." She lightly pressed her own shoulder. "But it's not bruised anymore."

A timid knock sounded on the door. Alex rushed inside with Maddie right behind him.

"Are you okay, Aida?"

She nodded but then tucked back into Dan.

"I'm sorry you got hurt." Alex was on the verge of tears. Dan grinned at his godson and scrubbed his hair.

"I want Mommy to wake up." Aida's chin trembled. It had simply been too much. She could no longer feign bravery for Alex or anyone else.

"She will in just a few minutes, sweetheart."

"Let's go, Alex. We'll check on everyone in a while." Maddie guided Alex back out of the room.

"Aida!" Fionna gasped when she finally woke up.

"Shh, baby." Dan reached for Fionna's hand while keeping Aida tucked on his shoulder with his other arm. "I've got her."

"You're here." She began to cry.

Aida reached for Fionna hesitantly.

"Here." Dan turned Aida, cradled her like a baby, and laid her beside Fionna. "Now, I can see all of my beautiful baby girls."

"Are you okay?" Fionna studied Dan closely.

"I'm fine. Fitz took Malden to jail, and there's a whole lot more to that story we'll discuss later."

"He's in jail?" A smile fought its way through her tears.

"How's the radar feeling?" He leaned and brushed his lips across hers. He couldn't help himself. Her color had returned and her perfect rosebud lips beckoned him.

"I'm perfect. I feel back to normal."

Medio Capusan returned a few minutes later. She was rolling a screen into the room followed by a Gifted sonogram technician. "Medio Haydenshire thought this might be a good idea."

A few minutes later, the technician was summoning and sending sound waves through Fionna's womb. Tears rolled down her cheeks as she squeezed Dan's hand.

He pointed to the screen. "Look, that's your little sister." He showed Aida the fuzzy blob on the screen. She looked deeply concerned.

The medio chuckled and pointed to the screen. "See, there's her head, and that's the umbilical cord, and those are the beginnings of her little arms and legs."

"She looks funny," Aida whispered.

"She'll look much more like you did when you were a baby once she gets here. She still has so much growing to do."

"I don't remember what I looked like when I was a baby."

Dan and Fionna laughed.

"Well, she will be beautiful just like you are now. And I believe you have some very special visitors."

She smiled as Fitz knocked on the door. "May I?"

Dan edged the blanket back over Fionna's abdomen, and he nodded. Crown Governor Haydenshire, Garrett, Rainer, Logan, Adeline, and Emily followed Fitz and Maddie inside the room.

Fionna was thrilled as Garrett rushed to her. She clung to him for several long minutes.

"Well, son, I'd say maybe, just maybe, it's really over this time." Governor Haydenshire offered Dan his hand.

"You're here!" Fionna and Emily embraced next.

Adeline hugged Fionna and then immediately began studying the ultrasound and Fionna's file.

"Garrett!" Aida squealed. Garrett lifted her and threw her in the air.

"Son, she has a concussion. Please don't throw her," Governor Haydenshire commanded saving Dan the trouble.

"Oh, right. Sorry." Garrett held her gently instead. "Are you okay, Miss Aida Mae?"

"Yes, Daddy made the man stop hurting me." She touched the bandage on her head.

Garrett's eyes closed. Dan knew he was letting the fury work through him as he nodded his understanding and squeezed her tighter. "Dan and I will always keep you safe," Garrett vowed.

"I know because I'm your girl." She squeezed him with more force. "And Mr. Fitzroy took him to jail."

"That's right, sweetheart. I did," Fitz assured her.

"I knew Daddy would make him stop hurting me and Mommy because we're his girls too," Aida concluded as she reached for Fionna's hand.

There wasn't a dry eye in the room as Aida leaned and crawled back into Dan's lap. He hugged her tightly.

"Daniel, if you've ever thought, even for a moment, that you hadn't done a whole lot right in this life, I'm pretty sure you stand corrected," the governor vowed.

Dan nodded his acceptance as he forcefully fought the tidal wave of emotion threatening to engulf him.

Governor Haydenshire smiled. "I've spoken with the French Prime Minister, and in just a minute, you'll be heading back to the Parliament to give one recorded testimony on your discoveries today, and then one on the attack the other night. After that you'll be allowed to leave with your girls and head home with all of us."

"Thank you, sir." Dan was certain he hadn't heard sweeter words all day.

CHAPTER 43
WILDFLOWER

"I just packed everything Aida owns," Dan called as he raced into the bedroom to begin getting ready for the reception. "May I join you in there, Mrs. Vindico?" He stripped and knocked on the shower door.

Fionna was beaming as she opened it. "I'm pretty sure your mom wouldn't approve of us showering together before our wedding reception."

Relief flooded through Dan every time he saw her beautiful smile restored to its previous peace now that the danger was really truly behind them.

"Well, baby doll,"—Dan stepped into the shower behind her—"I've never been all that good at doing things my mother approved of, and I put a ring on it and then I put my baby in it, so I'd say you're mine and to hell with what my mother thinks." She spun in his arms, and he devoured her mouth. Her energy, strong and calm, was the antidote to his every terror.

"You know, your littlest baby girl is getting harder and harder to hide. I'm pretty sure everyone that might not have believed the papers will see the proof tonight." Fionna placed her hands on her burgeoning bump.

"Good." Dan gave her a cocky grin.

"What's Aida doing?" Fionna sighed contentedly and laid her head on Dan's shoulder as he began running his lathered hands up and down her curves.

"Aida and Phoebe are catching up on the past week's Supernovas, and she seems almost as happy to be home as I am."

Fionna nodded against him, but her energy shifted and she tensed.

"What, baby?" Dan kept her cradled to his chest.

"It just sometimes pops back in my head, and I have to work my way through it again."

"I'm right here, and if you need a break tonight or you need to come home, you say the word. I'll make it happen, okay?" The terrifying reality of all that had happened still had to be dealt with even if it was behind them.

After their shower, Dan tied his bow tie and then moved on to his cufflinks. Fionna had already gotten Aida in her dress and fixed her hair in a sweet braid that circled her head and hid the swollen knot.

Fionna emerged from the bathroom, and Dan's mouth hung open. "Wow!" He shook his head, unable to believe anything that beautiful could possibly belong to him. "You look gorgeous."

She beamed as he took her in, dressed in a creamy-white sleeveless floor-length gown.

"Dan." She blushed violently.

"What, baby doll?" He couldn't take his eyes off her. She'd pulled her hair up into a sexy twist with several tendrils cascading down the side of her face. Her lips were displayed in a perfect pout, and her cleavage was on jaw-dropping display.

"I can't breathe."

Dan's eyes dropped to her bump. It was apparent in the tight dress. He couldn't help but chuckle. "Maybe you should wear something else?"

"No, I'll just try not to eat much or to sit down."

"Fi?"

"I'll be fine, and this dress is fabulous. Tomorrow and for the rest of spring and summer, I'll wear my big, huge sundresses with plenty of room for Halia. I'm just asking her for this one night."

Dan checked his watch. "All right, fine, but let's go get our little girl and head to the Fairmont. I don't plan on pissing off Marion until the end of the night."

"Dan," Fionna warned, but she couldn't quite hide her delighted grin.

∼

The valet attendant opened Aida's door. Dan and Fionna watched her sprint into her Aunt Kara's arms.

"Are you okay?" Kara embraced her readily.

"I'm okay," Aida assured her.

"Fionna." Kara threw her arms around her. "You look amazing!"

"Thank you." The dress seemed to give way slightly the longer she wore it, and she was moving with more ease as Dan escorted her into the vast banquet room.

"Dan." Governor Vindico was shaking his head as he moved toward them on the verge of tears. "Son, I just...I'm so glad you're all okay."

"Yeah, me too, Dad." Dan allowed his father a lengthy hug.

"Everything looks beautiful, Governor Vindico." Fionna smiled.

"I think the decorations have been upstaged by the bride, but that's the way it's supposed to work, isn't it?" The governor kissed Fionna's cheek.

"Thank you."

"And how's my girl?" He lifted Aida into his arms.

"I'm okay," Aida supplied as she glanced around the large room with dozens of tables covered in white linen cloths with navy blue brocade runners. There were tremendous floral centerpieces that covered the width of the tables. White stargazer lilies covered nearly every available surface. Dan shook his head. His mother had managed to pick Fionna's least favorite flower.

The room was decidedly cold. *Russian Winter,* Dan recalled.

"Olivia," Aida nearly shrieked as Tim and Meredith appeared.

Governor Vindico released her and watched as his granddaughters hugged each other fiercely.

"Mommy said you got booboos on your head and on your shoulder," Olivia worried.

Aida nodded as Dan and Fionna made their way over. "My head hurts a little still, and it was scary. I don't think I want to go back to Paris, France, only I'll miss my friend Alex."

"I think Alex and Alfred will come here and visit us," Dan assured her.

Aida looked thrilled with this information.

"Daniel, Fionna, now I'd wanted you to make an entrance after everyone has arrived. I've located a little staging room you can wait in. It's the first door on the left once you're in the hallway," was Mrs. Vindico's greeting.

"Hi, Mom. How are you? We're fine after our harrowing trip to Paris where your pregnant daughter-in-law was hospitalized twice, and your granddaughter was given a concussion. Thanks for asking," Dan huffed indignantly.

Ignoring him as usual, she barked more orders at the caterers. Turning back to Dan and Fionna, she drew a deep breath and touched the sides of her mouth making certain her lipstick hadn't smeared.

"Daniel, go now. First door on the left. I'll send someone when it's time for you to appear."

"Because abracadabra doesn't work anymore?"

"Dan." Fionna tried not to laugh.

"Mom, let's let Aida and Olivia play. They aren't going to see each other all summer. We'll watch Aida while you hide Dan and Fionna away." Meredith rolled her eyes.

"Fine."

Dan shook his head and allowed Fionna to lead him to the appointed room. She broke out in hysterical giggles as she opened the door to what was nothing more than a janitor's supply closet.

A long string of expletives spat from Dan. "She is un-fucking-believable!"

Fionna led him inside the closet and wound her arms around his neck with a mischievous grin. "Ever play seven minutes in heaven, Mr. Vindico?" she drawled flirtatiously.

Dan gave her a smirk and nodded his head. "Never with anyone as gorgeous as you."

"Wow, use that line much?" She remembered her part perfectly. He couldn't help but grin as he recalled her asking him in that pool in Sydney, Australia, if he'd ever skinny-dipped.

"I'm sorry, baby. I know this looks nothing like a reception you would have planned." He touched their foreheads tenderly together as he gazed into the most beautiful eyes he'd ever seen.

"I already had a reception I planned, so let your mom have hers."

Dan's hands slid down the dress and settled on her hips. He wanted desperately to get the reception over with, to take his wife home, to give her a bath, and to get a jump on their Hawaiian vacation. Dan gave Fionna a naughty smirk.

He set his hands on the shelving behind her and feigned impression. "These are pretty sturdy. This might work," he teased. "Turn around and hold on for me, baby doll."

Fionna giggled. "Wouldn't your mom love that when she comes to make us appear?" She did look rather intrigued with the idea.

"Wait 'til you see my magic wand," Dan continued just to hear her laugh.

As she continued to crack up, Dan was in awe yet again. They'd been stuck in a closet containing wet mops, brooms, and industrial strength cleaners, but she was laughing and laying her head on his chest. That was all that mattered. He was overcome with how much he loved her and how much he loved the life she'd given him.

Inhaling deeply, he let the heady vanilla coconut scent of her wash through his lungs and into his shield. "I love you so much."

"I love you too." A seductive heat tracked up her neck and settled in her cheeks, only adding to the need that had quickly settled in his groin.

"Since I already let you knock me up,"—she giggled again as Dan grinned broadly—"does that mean I might get a kiss before our reception?"

"Baby doll, you can have anything you want before, during, and after our reception. Just say the word and I'll go get us a room in this swanky hotel. We can recreate our wedding night."

"I'll just take the kiss for now, but when we get home..." Her invitation made his tux pants suddenly feel three sizes too small. "I think we should probably use up the rest of our oil of 'Ōhi'a lehua tonight. Tutu might not like it if we don't ask for more as soon as we arrive tomorrow."

Dan gave her the shuddering growl she was after. "You wanna be rubbed down inside and out, baby? I will definitely take care of that. And I believe I promised you a session with me and a certain vibrator."

"Kiss me." Her command caressed his lips with her heat. A hungry groan tore from his lungs. He caged her between the shelves and his body. He kept his hands on either side of her head and pressed his strain into her abdomen as he devoured her mouth.

"Yum." She turned her head, hungry for more, and traced her hand up his zipper line.

Dan wrapped his arms around her. "That's it. Think about how good that's gonna feel deep inside of you," he demanded before consuming her mouth again.

Fionna moaned in his mouth as she groped him. He slipped his hands to her breasts, squeezing and plying them through the dress he wished he could tear off of her.

Suddenly, the door swung open, and light flooded the darkened closet.

"Daniel!" Mrs. Vindico shrieked in horror. Dan jerked his hands away and wiped the lipstick from his mouth. "Just what do you think you're doing?"

Fionna's expression was caught somewhere between fear she'd upset Mrs. Vindico and hilarity that they were being asked that question.

"Well, Mom, I was just making out with my wife, you know, the mother of *my* children." Dan knew he was driving his mother crazy but found himself woefully unable to stop.

"I think you both need to keep your hands to yourselves," Mrs. Vindico commanded. That did it. Fionna cracked up. Tears leaked down her face from trying so hard not to laugh.

"I...I suggest you both go get straightened up. It's almost time for your appearance." Mrs. Vindico puffed before spinning in her indignation and returning to the banquet room.

"Come on, baby doll." Dan found the restrooms and freshened up.

"What are we supposed to do when we go in there?" Fionna clung to Dan's arm.

"I could grab your ass or unzip your dress. I could squeeze your tits. You could stick your hand down my pants." Dan offered her several scenarios.

"Would you behave?" Fionna demanded though she couldn't quite stop grinning.

"Marion sent me up here and told me to say something humorous," Governor Vindico projected his voice. Dan and Fionna could hear him from their location just outside of the room.

"Oh god, my Dad's doing stand-up." Dan panicked which only made Fionna laugh harder. "But I'm not certain I'm the guy for humor," Governor Vindico admitted humbly to polite chuckles from the guests. "So, how about if I say how much it means to Marion and me that all of you are here to celebrate with Dan and Fionna. And let me also say that Daniel's made a few decisions in his life that left me scratching my head. But when it came down to the important things, to the things that make life worth living, I don't think he could have chosen anyone more perfect for him than his lovely bride, Fionna, and his beautiful little girl sitting right over there with her other grandparents, my sweet little Aida. So, without further ado, let's welcome Daniel and Fionna in."

Tears pricked Fionna's eyes from the governor's sentiment as Dan guided her into the room to applause and beaming grins from their friends and family.

They were halted under a floral archway for photos. Trying not to grimace, Dan wrapped his arm around Fionna. Then with a smirk as he caught Governor Haydenshire's eye, he placed one hand tenderly on Fionna's stomach.

All of the Haydenshires laughed, but Mrs. Vindico looked mutinous. Once they'd been allowed to sit, the food was served. Aida and Olivia had to be reminded to eat several times as they seemed to much prefer whispering and giggling with one another.

Dan was rather impressed with the braised pork loin and scalloped potatoes.

"This is really good." Fionna seemed astonished as well.

Dan laughed. "Thankfully she let the caterers choose the food."

Things went smoothly, and Mrs. Vindico seemed thrilled with the evening as Mr. Styler wheeled in the cakes.

Dan had to laugh. "My mother did not order that for me."

"Do you think she'll be mad?" Fionna had her father create Dan a cake that was an enlarged Colt Special to go beside the traditional four-tiered wedding cake.

There was also a cake that was a copy of the Vindico crest that Dan thought was way over the top. They were shoved to the cake table by Mrs. Vindico.

Dan shot his bride a mischievous smirk and took the piece of cake he was to feed her.

"Dan!" Fionna warned though she was beaming. With that, he quickly smeared just a little of the icing on her lips. Before she could bat his hand away, he put a smudge on her neck and then two on the very tops of her swollen cleavage.

Fionna shrieked as he proceeded to lick it off before he plunged the cake in her mouth. The crowd went wild, applauding and whistling raucously.

As the cakes were sliced and served, Garrett and Chloe appeared, still laughing over the cake incident.

Dan shook Garrett's hand. "Thanks for coming yesterday and tonight."

"Just remember I loved her long before you did." Garrett hugged Fionna and brushed a kiss on her cheek. He grimaced and slid behind Dan a second later. "I'm trying to stay out of your Mom's path. I'm kind of crashing this shindig."

"What?" Dan gasped.

"Wait, you mean you didn't get invited?" Fionna quizzed in disbelief. Fury tensed in her normally calm energy streams.

"He's my date, so it's fine. I keep telling him that," Chloe scoffed.

"Mother!" Dan demanded hotly as he saw her trying to hide behind Zach.

"Yes, Daniel, did you need something?"

"Did you really fail to invite Garrett, one of my best friends, the best man in our wedding, the guy who has always taken care of me and my wife and my little girl when I couldn't?" Dan wanted Garrett to know just what he would always mean to him and Fionna.

"Don't be ridiculous. I invited all of the Haydenshires. They are the ruling family." She gestured around the room to the many varied Haydenshire children. "His invitation must've been lost in the mail. Now, it's time for the first dance."

Dan rolled his eyes as he led Fionna to the center of the assembled tables where a small dance area backed up to a subdued DJ.

A song Dan was certain he'd never heard before warbled from the enhanced speakers. He and Fionna attempted to sway for only a few seconds before it was too awkward to go on.

"It's the "Dance of the Snowflakes" from *The Nutcracker*." Fionna giggled.

With a deep sigh, he kept her hand in his and moved to the DJ. "Throw out the list my mother ordered you to play and just take requests. I'll see that you get paid."

"You got it!" The DJ looked thrilled with the new arrangement.

Dan winked at Fionna, after he made the first request. Then he tucked her back into the safety of his embrace.

"Now, let's dance, Mrs. Vindico."

"Surfer Girl," by the Beach Boys began to drawl from the speakers. They swayed rhythmically, stopping every few minutes to kiss with a great deal of fiery passion.

Mr. Styler danced with Fionna to "Over the Rainbow" as Dan danced with Aida, bringing on swoons from the guests.

After a few more songs, Chloe and the Angels decided it was time to give Fionna a proper send-off. Chloe instructed the DJ on which songs to play and then she jerked Fionna out onto the dance floor with all of her former teammates.

"Come on, Mama. Show everybody how you got him," she chanted which thoroughly embarrassed Fionna.

The Angels' favorite rap song blared from the speakers, and the girls all began to shake everything God had so graciously given them.

Fionna was caught in the converging tides of the life she'd lived previously and the one she'd begun with Dan. Desperate to rescue her, he wasn't certain how to help.

Garrett stepped in immediately. He shoved Dan onto the dance floor as he moved to Chloe. Dan laughed as he headed to Fionna who was half-heartedly performing the moves. He raised his left eyebrow and beckoned her with his index finger.

With a delighted smirk, she slid right in front of him, then turned to shake her sexy ass. Dan ground his pelvis against her, and she let loose and shook it for him. He gave her lust-filled, hungry looks as she spun and shimmied her chest in his face.

He let his hands move over her waist and hips as he thrust against her.

She spun again. Dan gave everyone an eyebrow waggle as he let his hands caress what she was shaking for him.

Rainer was pushed on the floor after the first verse so Emily could dance for him.

Right up to that point, Governor Haydenshire had been chuckling and shaking his head, however he began to scowl as Rainer's hands rested on Emily's backside as she strutted her stuff.

The song ended with the ladies surrounding Fionna and hugging her fiercely. Everyone save Mrs. Vindico was laughing. The horrified scowl on his mother's face made the entire thing worth it in Dan's book.

After a few minutes, Fionna emerged, laughing through her tears as she tried to move toward Dan.

"Hey, let my baby mama through," Dan commanded loudly. He beamed as the entire room whistled and applauded his confirmation of Fionna's pregnancy.

"Maaammmaaaa!" drawled from several of the Angels as they crowded around her again.

Mrs. Vindico was fit to be tied by the time the Angels wore out and exited the dance floor for more punch.

"This is not the kind of reception I envisioned, Daniel," she spat as she cornered him.

"Everyone's having fun, Mom, and quite honestly, after the last few months, Fi deserves to have fun with her friends and her husband if I may."

Fionna appeared beside him, flushed and smiling as he wrapped his arm around her.

"You both need to speak with your guests," Mrs. Vindico commanded.

Fionna gave Dan a sly grin as his mother turned and stalked off in a fitful huff. "I take it she didn't care for our dancing."

"You could say that. I, however, will be downloading that song so that you can dance for me, say, naked in our bedroom."

The flush in her cheeks deepened in intensity. She tucked her head on his shoulder and hid her face toward his neck. "Those were some pretty hot moves you had there yourself."

He cradled her to him and gave her a moment to allow her former life and their new one to unite in him.

"I love you so much, my sweet Maylea," he whispered in her ear. He knew each and every part of her, and he adored every delicate petal that made up his beautiful wildflower.

"Dan, it's so good to see you."

Fionna turned and smiled, but Dan's lungs refused him another breath.

"Isabelle," he forced. "It's nice to see you too. This is my wife, Fionna."

"It's so nice to meet you." Fionna offered Amelia's little sister her hand and her kind smile.

"You too." Isabelle nodded. "Uh, this is my husband, Brian, and our kids, Xavier and...Amelia." She introduced the toddlers her husband was holding. There was certainly no need to explain the namesake.

"Nice to meet you." Dan offered Brian his hand.

"You as well," Brian offered uncomfortably.

"I heard Dan say you were expecting?" Isabelle studied Fionna.

"Yes, at the end of November." Fionna rubbed her abdomen.

"Congratulations," Isabelle smiled. "I'm really happy for you. Really."

"Thanks." Dan couldn't bear to look Isabelle in the eyes. They were identical copies of her older sister's. The Richmonds joined Isabelle and Brian.

Dan shook Gerald's hand and offered Faith a hug. "Thank you for coming."

Fionna nodded her agreement.

"We wouldn't have missed it. Congratulations to both of you," Faith offered.

"Marion said you'll be spending the summer in Kauai, and that you'd taken a job at Venton," Gerald recounted.

Dan felt Fionna slip her hand in his and begin to supply him with her calming life force.

"Yes, sir. Fi grew up in Koloa. Her family owns a farm there. We'll be helping out and recuperating a little before school starts in the fall."

"Yes, we heard you two both have had quite the time of it lately." Gerald sounded truly sorry for all that Dan and Fionna had been through. "It sounds like you might've finally accomplished everything you set out to do so many years ago though." His voice fractured slightly, but he recovered well.

"Yes, sir. I certainly hope so."

Gerald slapped Dan's shoulder consolingly. "You have a beautiful family, Daniel. Faith and I are very proud for you."

"Thank you, sir."

"We better get the little ones home." Isabelle offered everyone an out.

"Thank you again for coming. It really means so much to us." Fionna grasped Faith's hands and then gave her a hesitant hug.

They made their way around to most of the guests and eventually sought respite at the Haydenshires' table.

"See, not so bad." Governor Haydenshire gestured around to the festivities. Mrs. Haydenshire wrapped Fionna up in a tight embrace.

The ladies sat down at the table where the Haydenshires had been sipping coffee with Governor Willow and his wife.

"Sir, thank you again. I really appreciate you getting the French Prime Minister to let me come home," Dan urged.

"I do what I can, and it was very clear that you and all three of your girls needed to come home."

Dan seated himself in the chair the governor directed him to.

Aida crawled up in his lap. "Hi, Governor Haydenshire!" she offered with a sweet smile.

"Hey there, Miss Aida. Are you feeling better, sweet girl?"

"Yes, sir. Mommy put ice packs on my head three times today, and Daddy did that thing the medios told him to so my head will be all better soon, but I don't like the ice very much."

"Are you still casting her, Daniel?" Governor Haydenshire looked concerned.

"Yeah, they healed the actual concussion in the hospital, but she was pretty upset when they got her there. She blocked them out for a while. They didn't want to force all of the swelling down immediately since she's so little, and it was a head injury. Adeline's going to check it before we leave tonight." Revulsion pumped through Dan as he explained everything he'd been instructed at the hospital the morning before.

"It's all over. Go to Kauai. It certainly seemed to bring about healing the last time you were there." He gestured his head to Fionna who was intently listening to Mrs. Haydenshire's advice.

"That's certainly my plan."

Most of the guests left around ten. Chloe rushed to Fionna. "Let's go out! You look hot, and Anglington's is doing half price drinks."

Fionna rolled her eyes, shook her head, and chuckled. "Chloe, I'm pregnant and therefore I can't drink. My little girl has to be taken home and given a bath. I have to hold an ice pack on her sweet little head while my amazing husband casts her so that we can all move to Kauai for the entire summer tomorrow. Then she has to be put to bed. Then Dan and I have to finish packing, and then I'm going to collapse in my husband's arms when I finally go to bed."

"And all of those are perfect examples of why I am never getting married or having kids," Chloe scoffed.

"Ah, music to my ears." Garrett sauntered up in time to hear the end of their conversation.

Chloe beamed and then immediately wound her body around his.

"Oh yeah," Dan quipped. "Change the station, man, because you have no idea what you're missing out on."

CHAPTER 44

HOME

It was nearing two in the morning when Dan finally convinced his wife to stop packing. He guided her to bed, stripped her down, and cradled her tenderly on his chest.

"Thank you for being so amazing. Thank you for always taking care of me and for figuring everything out. I love you so much." She nuzzled her face against his chest.

"I love you too. You're just incredible. I honestly don't know how I got so lucky."

She feathered a kiss on his neck and then one on his jawline. "Well, you're not getting lucky tonight because I'm so freaking tired."

Dan laughed. "That's all right, baby doll. We have all summer. I'm already working out positions for us to use when my baby girl is taking up all of your belly."

"Are you?" She giggled.

"Definitely. I consider it part of my job as a good dad."

"You are an amazing dad." Her tone lost all sense of teasing.

She yawned. Her energy was weak and draining.

"Go to sleep, sweetheart. You're exhausted."

She nodded, and as he pushed soothing rhythms through his shield, she relaxed. A minute later, she was in a deep sleep.

Dan tried to force the harrowing images from his mind. It was over. He didn't want to keep replaying it. But Wretchkinsides's son, Fionna's cheek, Aida's shoulder and head—it all haunted him. He didn't want to close his eyes. If he just stared at Fionna and felt her rhythms as she slept, she would keep the nightmares at bay.

He slipped his hand down her side and touched her growing bump. Closing his eyes, he concentrated and locked on to Halia. He pushed his calming rhythms through Fionna's womb.

She reacted. Her energy seemed to pulse in a happy cadence.

"Hey, baby girl," Dan spoke in a choked whisper. "I'm so sorry, sweetheart, for all I've already put you through, but I promise you I will always keep you safe. It's over. It's really, really over."

"Okay, sewing machine?" Frantic tension furrowed Fionna's brow as she stared at her list.

"Got it," Dan assured her.

"Fabric?"

"Was it with the machine?" She nodded. "Then it's in there."

"Aida's new books and the pregnancy books Kara gave me?"

"Baby, it's all in the car."

She glanced around their home nervously.

Garrett shook his head at her. He was coming to the airport with them to drive the Mercedes back to Dan and Fionna's after they left. "I'm sure Danny Boy will buy it for you if you forgot to pack it, baby."

Dan nodded his agreement.

"We forwarded the mail?"

"I took care of it." Dan offered her his hand as Garrett drove.

She laced her fingers through his and drew soothing energy from him.

"Still amazing every single time." He brought her hand to his mouth and brushed a kiss across her knuckles.

"Aida." Fionna grinned as she turned to glance back at their baby girl who was reading in her pink flower seat.

"Yes?"

"You know how my name is Fionna?"

"Yes, but I get to call you Mommy, and Halia will get to call you Mommy when she learns to talk, but no one else."

Dan and Garrett both chuckled.

"Okay." Fionna wasn't going to point out that they might decide to extend their family beyond their two baby girls. "Well, in Kauai, where I grew up, everyone calls me Maylea, because that's what my Mommy called me when I was a little girl."

"Before she went away?" Aida asked solemnly.

Fionna swallowed back emotion as Dan continued to supply her with calm. She managed a nod.

"Is my name different in Hawaii too?"

Fionna and Dan shared a grin. "No, baby, unless you'd like a Hawaiian nickname."

"Like what?"

"How about Hanai?"

"What does that mean?" Dan asked quietly.

"My precious chosen child."

"I like that name, but I think I like to be Aida too, maybe just a little bit more."

"Okay, you be Aida and I'll be Maylea, except for you and Halia."

"Deal."

As they were boarding the plane, Fionna's cell phone chirped. They seated Aida beside the window. Dan helped her buckle in as Fionna read the text. Her brow knitted.

"What?" Dan pulled his iPad from his bag and handed it to Aida along with his headphones. Even on a fully staffed Senate jet, it was going to be a long flight.

"Malani says she and Kai have a surprise for us that they're bringing to the airport."

Dan shrugged. He couldn't fathom what Malani might have in store for them.

"Daddy, the plane is going down like this!" Aida woke Dan up several hours later with her arm tilted downward. She sounded concerned to the point of panic as she stared out at the surrounding ocean beneath them.

Dan rubbed his eyes and yawned deeply. "We're landing in a few minutes, baby. It's okay. The plane is supposed to do that."

"And Mommy's friend will be at the airport when we get there?" She was a little nervous about their extended trip.

"That's right, and you'll really like Malani," Dan whispered. Fionna was still asleep on his shoulder. "Do you know why?"

"Why?"

"Because she reminds me a lot of Mommy."

The plane dropped again, and Dan kissed the top of Fionna's head as one of the coolant officers projected his voice throughout the plane. "Senate flight 39884 will be landing at Lihue Airport in approximately eight minutes. If you could, please prepare your children and belongings for arrival."

"How do you prepare me?" Aida stared up at him wide-eyed.

Dan winked at her. "I say, 'Aida, baby, we're gonna land in a few minutes. Give Daddy back his iPad and put Phoebe and your coloring book in your backpack.'"

"Are you going to prepare Mommy too?"

Dan nodded and kissed Fionna again. "Wake up, baby doll. We're almost there." He rubbed his hand along her thigh.

She lifted her head, took in the brilliant blue waters, and beamed.

"You're home," Dan whispered as the plane touched down and bounced slightly on the runway.

"Only because you're here with me."

His guilt over all he'd put his girls through begin to ebb slightly.

He lifted Aida onto his shoulders as they moved out into the Lihue airport.

"Maylea!" rang from Malani as soon as they made their way to baggage claim. Fionna giggled delightedly. Dan's mouth dropped open, and Fionna gasped as a very pregnant Malani rushed toward them. Kai was grinning ear to ear as he followed behind her.

"What? How?" Fionna stammered.

"Well, I think you know how," Malani teased.

"Yeah, but..." She pointed to Kai confusedly.

"Yeah, I'm pretty sure it's mine," he goaded as Fionna hugged Malani fiercely.

"I just couldn't tell you when you were here last, not after everything that had happened. I would've been the worst best friend ever, so I just kind of wore really big sundresses and shirts. It wasn't that noticeable then." She was clearly worried Fionna would be mad that she hadn't shared the news. "That's why I couldn't wait for you to get here, so I could finally tell you."

Something is different about Malani. And something far away feels dark. Dan recalled a conversation he and Fionna had when they'd been in Kauai after the miscarriage. Another haunting chill set in his bones. He laced his fingers through Fionna's and inhaled the healing Kauaian air. He tried to wash away the events of the last few months.

"When are you due?"

"Sometime in August. I keep praying you'll still be here when she comes."

"How did I not feel this?"

"You did, baby doll. Remember? You just weren't quite yourself last time we were here. You weren't sure what you were feeling. A lot had happened," Dan eased.

"But now we can be pregnant together with girls. And they can be best friends!"

"Yes! And this is Aida, my precious little hanai." She beamed up at Aida who was in Dan's arms, biting her lip nervously.

Dan set her on the ground.

"Hi, Aida!"

"Hi," Aida supplied shyly while gripping Dan's hand.

Malani placed a small pink and yellow lei she'd made around Aida's neck. Delighted, Aida dropped Dan's hand so she could hold the lei out and study it.

"I'm your Auntie Malani, and you have to love me."

"Okay." She gave Fionna a bewildered glance.

"Come on, baby girl." Dan took her hand once again and guided her out of the airport. "She comes on a little strong, but she really does love you."

A half hour later, they all spilled out of Malani's Jeep once they arrived on the farm.

"Tu, they're here," Fionna's grandfather, who was carrying a large wicker basket full of papaya, called into the house.

Tutu appeared at once with a broad knowing grin.

Papa rushed to hug Fionna tightly. "You look so much better, Maylea. You had me worried last time, sweet girl."

"I'm good, Papa. Dan always takes care of me." Fionna reached back to take Dan's hand.

"Well, let me see you," Tutu commanded as she pulled Fionna in for an all-encompassing embrace. She took her hands and smoothed the loose dress Fionna was wearing flat against her. Smiling, she took in the tiny bump growing each and every day.

"Very nice work, Daniel." She laughed as she hugged Dan fiercely.

"I do what I can."

"And this must be my very special little Aida." Tutu leaned down to study Aida and grinned at her adoringly.

Aida tucked back into Dan.

"Did you know that I knew you were coming to be in our ohana before they knew?"

"Ohana means family," Fionna whispered to Aida.

"You did?"

"Yes, the island rhythms told me the night your mommy and daddy married that there would be two granddaughters coming to my island very soon."

"Me and Halia?"

Tutu gasped as she stood to gaze at Fionna.

Fionna's grin fractured her tears. "Halia Elisabeth Amelia Vindico." She ran her hands over the tiny swell again.

Tutu hugged her again. This one lasted much longer than the one before. Both of them cried and laughed simultaneously.

As the sun sank softly into the Pacific and the majestic mountains gave off their burnt-orange glow, Dan and Fionna guided Aida into the room in the guest cottage where they would be spending the summer.

"Tomorrow, you can ride with me on the tractor, my sweet girl." Papa was overjoyed to have Aida on the farm and in the family.

"I don't know what that is."

"Well, by the end of the summer, we'll have you surfing and tractor riding," Papa assured her.

"I saw the ocean in Paris, France, but I wasn't allowed to go outside Alex's house. I don't know how to swim in it."

"Your Mommy is an excellent teacher, and we're going to teach you to do all kinds of fun things while you're here," Tutu explained.

"Okay." Aida looked excited to get started.

"We should explain to her at some point that all of France is not called Paris," Dan whispered to Fionna.

"I know." Fionna giggled. "But it's so cute when she calls it that."

"I brought in some of your old toys, Maylea." Papa pointed to an old wooden chest that had been added to the room since Garrett slept there the night before Dan and Fionna's wedding.

Tutu had made Aida's double bed up with her prescribed white bamboo sheets, one down comforter, and two homespun quilts.

Dan smiled as Fionna moved to the bed and blinked back tears. "You found my old quilt." She ran her hands over it tenderly.

"I've had it all this time. I was waiting on you to need it again," Papa soothed. "We cleaned it up on your wedding night. We knew what was coming." He gazed at Fionna like he couldn't possibly love anything more.

Fionna nodded as tears leaked down her face.

"In a few months, we'll put your old crib in here as well." Tutu wiped away Fionna's sudden tears.

"Aida, this is the quilt that I slept under every night when I was a little girl."

"You don't have to share it with me. It's very special."

Malani and Tutu both clutched their chests over Aida's vow.

"No, baby, there isn't anyone else in the world I want to share it with but you." Fionna cried harder.

Confusion cast Aida's sweet face, but she nodded. "I promise to take very good care of it."

Fionna regained her composure after a fierce hug with her little girl.

"Do you know what else you get to do when you come to Tutu and Papa's farm for the summers, my sweet little Aida?" Tutu's eyes sparkled as she cradled Aida's face in her right hand.

Aida shook her head.

"You get to come up to my house and have a tea party with me and Papa every night after dinner just like your mommy used to."

"I get to have a tea party every night?" Aida's gasp delighted everyone in the room. "Wow!"

Tutu kissed Aida's forehead. "And that way Mommy can take her bath and get ready for bed."

Fionna's mouth dropped open as she scowled in horror.

Dan furrowed his brow until she explained. "My parents were taking baths together and having sex while I had tea parties with Tutu." She sounded completely horrified.

Dan cracked up as he wrapped his arms around her.

He fell onto the sofa beside Fionna after Aida was sound asleep in her new room. His mind reeled backward for a moment to the last time he sat on that very couch. The phone call to his parents to inform them that he was marrying Fionna in an hour's time had taken place on that couch. He thought of all that had happened from that moment to the present.

Fionna was sipping her evening tea supplied lovingly to her by her grandmother. Maylea's coffee was stacked on the counter by the coffee maker. The cabinets and refrigerator were stocked full of the ingredients to make her favorite meals, along with everything for her tea, Dan's favorite beer, and Dr Peppers.

Their bedroom contained oils for their baths, candles arranged on the dresser and bedside tables, and a beautiful bouquet of Hawaiian wildflowers freshly picked from the farm. There were numerous jars of oil of ʻŌhiʻa lehua to be used with regularity throughout the spring and summer.

There were also the oils and ointments that Dan had already been rubbing Fionna down with each night on both nightstands.

He let the feeling of truly being cared for and of being surrounded by people who loved his girls almost as much as he did soothe his weary soul. He'd gotten her here. She was safe and content, and they had almost four months to actually heal from all they'd suffered.

Her rhythms were already stronger, and they'd only been there a few hours. He reveled in everything he drew from her.

"It feels different," Fionna whispered in the soft night air.

"What feels different, baby?" Dan kissed the side of her head and enveloped her in his body.

"Than the last time we were here. It feels like it's all really over. Last time, it still didn't feel over because it wasn't, I don't guess." She fumbled confusedly in her explanation, but he knew what she was referring to.

"I'm so sorry for all I put you through."

"Stop. You promised." She'd begged him to stop apologizing on the plane home from Paris.

"This time it just feels like we're really safe, and we can really heal. Aida can heal, and little Halia can grow and grow." She ran her hand over her bump contentedly. "She knows she's here." Fionna gazed up at Dan, wondering if he believed her. "She's a child of the land."

A broad smile spread across his face. "Can I feel her?"

"Yeah, let's go take our bath."

As it was the middle of the night in DC, Dan assumed Aida would sleep at least until the sunrise, so he brushed a kiss across her cheek and pulled her door closed.

He joined Fionna on the screened-in porch as she ran the water. Dan lit the candles with his hand and supplied Fionna with the oils before he stripped her down.

After helping her into the tub, he joined her and immediately felt the soothing island rhythms begin to course through him once again.

He closed his eyes as Fionna relaxed languidly against his chest. He wrapped his arms around her and placed his hands on her baby bump. He felt the tiny rhythms almost instantly.

"Does she feel different to you?"

"Yeah, she really does." His little Halia's rhythms were stronger and clearer than he'd ever felt them before. She did know where she was, and she could feel that Fionna was really truly relaxed and content.

They spun and tilted again when she felt Dan's energy moving through her.

Fionna was ecstatic. Tears of joy rolled down her cheeks as he held her tightly and pushed his loving rhythms to both his wife and his baby girl.

CHAPTER 45

SANCTUARY

BEGINNING OF AUGUST

Dan held Fionna's hand as he drove Papa's old truck out to the airport.

"We should have borrowed Malani's Jeep," Fionna fussed again.

"Baby, the truck is fine. There's plenty of room for both of my parents, and their luggage will go in the back." He hated that the only time in the last three months she'd been stressed out was due to his parents' arrival on the island.

It was nearing four o'clock, and Dan also regretted the fact that he wasn't helping Papa take in the avocado and ginger crops they'd been working on steadily for the past few days.

Dan found working the farm and the vast gardens to be extremely cathartic. No one was more surprised by his love of the work than he was, but he deeply enjoyed watching what he'd helped plant in the spring come to fruition. He loved watching Aida water the gardens and tend the flowers.

The physical labor gave him time to heal, to work through all that had come to pass, all that he'd been through, and all that he felt he'd put Fionna and his girls through. The physical release was extremely healing, more than anything Dan had ever experienced save for Fionna.

He enjoyed it all almost as much as he loved watching her bloom and ripen full of his baby, the seed he'd planted on their wedding night. Halia was no longer just a tiny bump.

Though she never believed him when he told her, Dan was certain he'd never seen anything more beautiful.

As he pulled into a parking space, he tried not to chuckle over thoughts of his mother climbing up in Papa's ancient Ford truck and being taken to the farm and then making the hour-long trip to the other side of the island since she'd insisted that she and the governor were staying at the Club Wyndham in Princeville.

He opened Fionna's door and helped her out.

"I'm sorry. My center of balance is just a little off." She clung to his hand as she scooted out of the truck.

"Sweetheart, it's my fault you need help, and I love helping you."

They walked hand in hand into the Lihue airport.

"Tutu's packing a picnic for everyone to eat out on Shipwreck." She sighed as she eased into a seat near the area where the Gifted Senate flights would disembark.

"That'll be fun, and Aida can swim a little before bed." Dan knew she was concerned his parents wouldn't like the beachside picnic. "They're coming to Kauai for vacation, and Shipwreck is beautiful even if it's not the North shore. Aida loves it." He was unable to believe that anyone, even his own mother, wouldn't like the Kauaian shorelines.

Dan rubbed his hands over her shoulders and wondered what his father would think of the calluses that had developed from his summer working as a farmhand.

Fionna had informed him the night before as he'd given her a bath and then rocked her body with his own in their bed that she loved the way his rough, callused hands moved over her silky skin. According to her, most of his calluses had always been on the inside surrounding his heart and his spirit. She thought they were working their way out, so they could be healed.

Fionna had let the island consume her as she healed from the harrowing months that had preceded their trip. She never wore makeup. Her cheeks were pink from the sun. Her skin was slightly darker. She'd spent most of the summer with her beautiful body wrapped loosely in sundresses and a flower tucked behind her left ear.

He was astounded by her natural beauty, and by how the island moved her and Halia. When they were alone in the cottage or even in the yard surrounding their summer home, she was most often topless. She let the sunlight and the sea breezes touch her skin and soothe her spirit.

They would lie in their bed each night with Dan's hands on her bare stomach. He would talk, and Halia would respond. He watched in awe as he felt his little girl move inside of Fionna.

A broad grin spread across her face. "She has the hiccups again." Fionna rubbed her hands over her bump. She seemed to think her caress would ease Halia's hiccups.

Dan seated himself beside her and placed one hand over hers. He felt her stomach jostle rhythmically. Every time he felt Halia move, he was overjoyed. It took his breath away.

"There's the plane," she sighed.

Dan grimaced. "I know sharing this with them isn't something you really bargained for. I'm sorry."

She shook her head though she offered no verbal argument. He knew she was giving away a piece of her soul, and she was sharing it with a woman who'd never been loving or accepting of her.

He helped her stand as he tucked her back to his chest. His hands wrapped around his wife and his baby girl.

She leaned her head to the side and let him kiss her cheek. "I love you, Maylea."

Her energy changed quickly to elation from his vow and his affectionate embrace. A replete grin spread across her face.

"Of course." Dan sighed as his parents made their way off the plane.

Fionna tried hard not to giggle at the aloha shirt his father was sporting, which was created of the very same fabric as his mother's long snap-front shirtdress. His father had also donned a khaki Aussie hat. The band around the crown matched the shirt and dress. They were a walking portrait of cliched tourists.

Mrs. Vindico was carrying the same large straw bag she'd carried on every trip Dan recalled from his childhood. He knew the gaudy bag contained a large bottle of water, every edition of *Women of the Realm* she'd been able to locate in the house, and her vacation planner —a thick day planner she used to plan out each and every moment of their day while on vacation.

Dan had never understood the point of planning out your vacation beyond purchasing plane tickets and making reservations. He chalked it up to his mother's inability to relax in any situation and offered his parents a smile as they neared.

The memory of him and all three of his sisters scheming together one summer, when they'd been forced to endure a car trip with their parents to the Florida panhandle, had him trying not to laugh.

He and Lindley had lifted the vacation planner from their mother's straw bag discreetly. Kara and Meredith had been in charge of hiding it in different places in the car throughout the day.

Mrs. Vindico had spent the entire day frantically searching for the book. It had culminated with her shrieking angrily at the governor that they could be missing something on their drive and that she was certain that they were supposed to see a button museum that *Women of the Realm* suggested and that it had a special display that contained a car covered in buttons, but that their tickets had been in the planner. She'd continued in her rant to conclude that it was also the planner she'd ordered from *Women of the Realm*.

Dan and his sisters had nearly choked from trying to contain their hysterical laughter as they'd ridden along.

When they'd arrived at the hotel that evening, the governor had offered his children a crisp hundred-dollar bill to be divided among them if the planner would magically reappear.

"Aloha!" Fionna gave them her sweet grin as she moved toward Governor and Mrs. Vindico to welcome them to her island.

"Looks like you might've put on a little weight there, sweetheart," Governor Vindico teased as he hugged Fionna tightly.

Certain he would not have said something like that, Dan grimaced as he hugged his mother.

"Just a little." Fionna ran her hands over her bump again and smiled sweetly.

"Son." Governor Vindico offered Dan his hand.

"Hey, Dad. Did you have a good flight?" He shook his father's hand and then pulled him in for a hug.

"I really think you should phone Stephen, Arthur. That landing was very rough. Perhaps that pilot team should go for a little more training," Mrs. Vindico huffed.

"Marion, they landed two hundred and fifty thousand pounds of steel on a twenty-five mile island in the middle of the Pacific. I think the fact that we're here in one piece is remarkable," the governor quipped.

"We brought the truck. We thought we'd show you the farm first. Fi's Grandmother fixed a picnic to take out to the shore tonight for dinner," Dan explained hesitantly as they made their way toward the parking lot after retrieving his parents' luggage.

"I was thinking we should just rent a car, that way we won't be in your hair so much," Governor Vindico offered kindly.

Fionna looked thrilled with the idea. Dan chuckled discreetly. "Whatever you want." He gestured toward the car rental area of the airport. "You'll have to take the shuttle to get a rental. There's the truck over there." He pointed out Papa's F-100, circa 1976 to his parents.

He watched his mother's eyes goggle in horror. "Daniel, you're not letting Fionna and the baby ride in *that*."

Fionna bit her lips together to keep from laughing.

"Mom, that truck is solid steel. It's probably the safest car on the road, and Fi likes the truck." He winked at his wife as he recalled the evening they'd spent in the truck a few weeks ago. They'd watched the sun set over the shoreline. She'd been wearing a bikini with a loose sarong.

Aida had been invited to a birthday party of one of the little girls in her hula class, and Papa had walked her there since he was friends with the little girl's father.

Tutu had insisted that Dan and Fionna go out and have some fun. Parked in a discreet cove overlooking the water and the brilliant orange sun that displayed the full spectrum of colors as it sank into the ocean, it had taken Dan a few short minutes to have Fionna out of her bikini and on him.

"The truck is my favorite. It has plenty of room." Fionna smirked. Dan couldn't contain his laughter.

"We'll be getting a car," Mrs. Vindico insisted.

"Great." Dan waited with Fionna while his father secured an Enclave for the week.

He helped Fionna back into the truck and waited so his father could follow him back to the farm.

"Tutu really wants them to stay in one of the guesthouses," Fionna reminded him.

"I know." He wondered if he should broach the topic with his parents. Truthfully, he didn't want them to stay on the farm. He knew he was only experiencing a modicum of what Fionna was going through trying to share the very essence of her soul when she didn't want to, but the farm had quickly become his sanctuary as well. They'd worked, cooked, and eaten nearly every meal together as a family.

They'd been embraced by not only Fionna's relatives but by the community around them. Aida had blossomed before their very eyes. She adored Tutu and Papa and did indeed have tea parties with them most every night.

At least once a week, she would spend the night with her great-grandparents who spoiled her rotten. On those special evenings, Dan and Fionna would engage in long, intimate lovemaking sessions that often lasted hours. They began with a bath, moved from tender kisses to voracious bites, and then to the all-encompassing love that passed between them as Dan made them one. He permeated her body and her soul as she filled his. They talked, and most importantly they healed and formed an unbreakable bond that ran invincibly through their family.

Dan didn't want to share the farm and what it had quickly come to mean to him. He didn't want to share Fionna or Aida, even with his own parents.

Fionna would awaken every morning and make coffee, and then she and Malani typically attended a maternity yoga class in town together.

After that, she returned to the farm and helped Tutu turn the plants and flowers that Dan and Papa had harvested that morning into her oils, treatments, scrubs, and ointments.

There was always time to walk the shorelines or teach Aida to swim in the ocean in the afternoons, and twice a week they would walk hand in hand to take Aida into Koloa town for a hula lesson at Miss Leialanie's Hula Halau which she loved. They would head over to the coffee shop for coffee or out to the shave ice cart while Aida danced. Then they would make a trip to the library near Poipu for Aida to acquire more books before they headed back to the farm.

Tutu's shop was open on Fridays. The locals would stop in for her salts, scrubs, oils, teas, and ointments. They came in a steady stream, and often Dan and Fionna ran the store so Tutu and Papa could have a day off as well.

According to Tutu, the broad grin that spread across Dan's face whenever Fionna directed someone to the oil of 'Ōhi'a lehua lubricant had quadrupled their sales from the last several summers.

Aida's adorable insistence that the kukui coconut oil was how Fionna had gotten so beautiful meant that nearly every customer left with a bottle of that as well. Tutu and Papa had enjoyed a very lucrative summer.

The parking brake gave its rapid rhythmic clicks as Dan parked the truck by the farmhouse.

Papa and Aida were seated on the front steps. He was helping her finish the leis she'd been working on for Dan's parents.

Aida beamed and held out the identical leis she'd worked so hard on. Dan's heart swelled. She'd grown at least an inch over the summer. Her eyes no longer held any traces of the dark shadows that her years of not sleeping properly had given her. She'd gained weight. Tutu's remedies had cured her dry, itchy skin. Her hair was healthy and full, and her smile lit Dan's soul.

Papa touched her back, urging her on.

"Aloha!" Aida giggled as she moved to Dan and Fionna who joined her as she made her way toward her grandparents.

"Well, hey there, sweet girl. My gosh, I hardly recognized you. You've grown so much," Governor Vindico gushed. He leaned down to allow Aida to place the lei around his neck. She repeated the action for Dan's mother who was studying the farm with a bewildered expression.

"Aida made them all by herself," Dan bragged.

"Papa helped me with the ends." Her confession made Papa chuckle.

"Papa, these are Dan's parents, Governor and Mrs. Vindico." Fionna made introductions.

"Governor." Papa extended his hand.

"Please just call me Arthur." Governor Vindico shook Papa's hand heartily.

Tutu made her way out of the kitchen. "Maylea, before I forget, I took those nighties off of the line. They were dry, and it looked like rain. I laid them on your bed."

"Thank you." Fionna grinned.

Dan found the balance of life on the Kauaian farmstead to be intoxicating. The fact that her grandmother had taken in the hand-washed lingerie that Fionna had hung on the line to dry was the perfect example of the balance he knew they would never achieve in DC.

She was well aware that Dan and Fionna had a very physical, intimate relationship, but she also knew that it was an important part of their marriage. It was something that should be cultivated and explored, not something that should be hidden away and shamed. She often encouraged them to take a little time for the two of them and to leave Aida in her care. Dan and Fionna always agreed.

"I've gotten our picnic ready. After you show our guests around, we'll head out." Tutu chuckled at the expression on Mrs. Vindico's face.

"Mrs. Iona." Governor Vindico offered Tutu his hand and a kind smile.

Tutu laughed. "Just call me Tutu, Governor. Everyone does."

Dan had to grin. He'd never heard anyone refer to Fionna's grandmother by her surname or even her first name of Tua.

"Did Dan and Maylea tell you that Papa and I would love for you to stay with us on the farm? We have several guest cottages to spare.

But if Kai doesn't relax and leave my poor Malani alone, she's gonna ship him over here."

Dan and Fionna laughed. Malani was nearing her due date, and Kai followed her around like she was a ticking time bomb. He wanted to help her sit, stand, eat, and apparently even knocked on the door to check on her during her frequent trips to the restroom.

Fionna had pointed out that Kai only did these things because he adored his wife and his baby, but Malani was extremely uncomfortable and not in the best of moods.

Dan hoped he wouldn't be quite so panicked or overbearing come November, but he did completely understand Kai's desperation to care for Malani.

"Aunt Malani's going to have a baby soon, and I get to hold her," Aida announced.

"Malani's been my best friend since I was born," Fionna supplied.

The Vindicos nodded their understanding.

Mrs. Vindico bristled. "Well, we've made the kids reservations at the Wyndham with us. It can't be far from here, just on the North end of the island."

Tutu tried to hide her laughter as she nodded her understanding.

"Mom, I have told you repeatedly that we have a cottage here. This is where we live, during the summers anyway. We are not staying in Princeville. That would be like you staying at the Holiday Inn in Arlington." He tried to make his mother see his point of view. "However, if you'd like to accept Tutu and Papa's hospitality, I can assure you that there isn't a nicer place to stay in all of Hawaii."

Tutu beamed as Papa slapped Dan on the back. "See, Tu. Maylea knew what she was doing when she found aloha." He winked at Fionna who glowed with his assessment of Dan.

"Well, why don't we see this operation?" Governor Vindico took Aida's hand.

"We'll let Dan and Maylea show you around. I have need of Papa's assistance before our picnic," Tutu explained.

Fionna shook her head at her grandmother who laughed.

Dan knew immediately what Tutu needed assistance with.

"This is our house," Aida announced as they walked through the brilliant green pastures and sauntered up to the cottage they'd been living in for the past few months.

Dan braced. He knew that nothing on the farm would suit his mother, and it meant so much to him and Fionna. His jaw clenched as he pulled open the screen door and allow his parents into their refuge. Fionna laced her fingers through his.

Mrs. Vindico took in the mismatched living room furniture, the small kitchen with the painted table and chairs that Tutu hand selected to suit different statures and offer them comfort. To the cursory eye, it appeared that a matching table and chair set couldn't have been afforded.

Fionna pulled a cutting board out of the refrigerator. She'd chopped fresh mangos, avocado, and papayas that Dan had pulled from the crop he'd harvested that morning, to make a beautiful display

"I cut these up a little while ago if you're hungry after your flight. Dan picked them just this morning."

"Dan picked them?" Governor Vindico chuckled. He helped himself to some of the mango slices. "This is outstanding, Marion. Try some. Apparently, our son picked them. You know, the one who used to stomp around the house slamming doors and huffing if I asked him to mow our quarter-acre lawn when he was a teenager."

Fionna laughed as Dan rolled his eyes. He lifted Aida into his arms and handed her a piece of the papaya which she loved.

Fionna beamed at her. "Go put your swimsuit on. After we show Grandma and Grampa the rest of the farm, we'll go to Shipwreck Beach and swim."

Aida wiggled down out of Dan's arms and raced to her bedroom.

"Is that a bathtub on the porch?" Mrs. Vindico stomped into Dan and Fionna's room without invitation.

"Uh..." Dan followed his mother as he recalled that a few of Fionna's nighties had been laid on their bed.

"You bathe out of doors?" His mother sounded appalled as she stepped down onto the screened-in porch.

"Well, there's a shower in Aida's bathroom, and you can lower the screens," Fionna defended her Grandmother's belief system.

"We're the only people on the farm, Mother, and trust me, baths are incredibly good for you."

Fionna kissed Dan's cheek. "There are bathtubs like this in all of Tutu and Papa's guest cottages. If you decide to stay here, you could try them out," she explained with a mischievous gleam in her eye.

"Seems relaxing to me." Governor Vindico came to Fionna's defense as he began to take in the lush paradise surrounding them. "Nice big tub," he commented with a wry chuckle.

"Is that a bed?" Mrs. Vindico continued her inquisition.

"Yes, ma'am." Fionna ran her hands lovingly over the swinging platform topped with a mattress on the far end of the porch.

"And you sleep out here as well?"

"Dan and I usually nap out here in the afternoons. Aida's slept out here a few nights. It's very peaceful." His mother's disdain was chafing at the raw.

Dan narrowed his eyes. "The farm is very private surrounded by trees and vegetation, not to mention the numerous fields between here and the road, which only people who live up here even use. Don't knock it until you've tried it."

The governor looked impressed with Dan's reasoning. "He's right, Marion. We could stay here with the kids for a few nights and then go to the resort."

Dan and Fionna shared a hesitant glance. Aida returned wearing one of her many swimsuits and her sandals. "I'm ready. And I remembered to take off my panties and to go to the bathroom," she informed everyone of the things she'd forgotten on occasion.

"Aida, darling, we don't say that word," Mrs. Vindico corrected.

Aida frowned, not certain which word she'd said that was wrong.

"My God, Mother, stop it!" Dan demanded.

Fionna drew a deep steadying breath. "It's an article of clothing, Mrs. Vindico, and she's allowed to say the word. There's no shame in it," Fionna insisted tersely before she turned her attention back to Aida.

"Good job. Why don't we show Grampa and Grandma your garden and then we can let them see another one of the guesthouses before we go back to get Tutu and Papa. Aunt Malani and Uncle Kai are going to pick us up in a little while."

Aida was excited to show the Vindicos the small patch of lush land that Papa had designated as Aida's garden. He'd let her plant anything she'd wanted, and he'd taught her how to care for each and every flower she'd chosen.

"Do you want to see my garden? Papa and I planted purple flowers!"

"Sure, sweetheart, lead the way." Governor Vindico grinned.

She rushed out the front door with Fionna following after her.

Dan hung back momentarily. He wanted to hear what his mother was really thinking.

"Arthur, we are not staying here. We are a governing family, not commonplace hippies."

Fury tensed in Dan's shield as he watched out the front windows. Fionna took Aida's hand and beamed at their little girl as they meandered toward her garden.

"We do not bathe out of doors, and look at our son's room." She returned to the bedroom. Dan edged closer to the front door to stay out of sight. "Candles, oils, whatever this is!" She lifted a jar of the oil of ʻŌhiʻa lehua .

Dan saw her eyes goggle as she shuddered and then set it back down on the bedside table after reading the label.

"Marion, may I remind you that we decided to come to Kauai so that you and Dan could try to forge a stronger relationship. I can assure you that attacking Fionna and her family will cause him to sever any ties he has to you at all. I'll also remind you that of the two men who went after her, one is in prison and the other is dead. I don't think it would tax him in the least to cut you out of his life completely. Now, I personally have never seen Dan look so happy or at peace, and Fionna is the reason he's no longer slowly killing himself on a daily basis."

An audible humph was the response to the governor's warnings. Dan headed out the front door to join his wife. He reached for her. He desperately needed to feel her and be soothed by her.

She smiled up at him and clasped his arm with both of her hands. Her calming energies entered him, and he drew from her deeply.

"It's not for everyone," she whispered though Dan noted the pain in her voice.

The Vindicos joined them a moment later. Aida had picked up her watering can and begun watering her flowers.

"I love you, Daddy." She'd felt his fury as well.

"I love you too, baby." Dan helped her with the large can.

"Tell us what you've been doing this summer, Aida." The governor kissed the top of her head.

She smiled, set down her can, and caressed the flower that had drooped under the weight of the water. "So many things. I love it here. I get to work on the farm and ride on the tractor with Daddy and Papa. I get to make lots of stuff with Mommy and Tutu that I get to squish with my hands. I get to take hula lessons on Tuesdays and Thursdays with my friends Harper and Sarah, and then we go to the library. On Fridays, I help Mommy and Daddy run the store. Uncle Kai surfed with me four times, and I can swim almost as good as Harper. I can paddleboard with Daddy and sometimes by myself but it's hard not to tip over sometimes if you try to stand up. I get to go to Tutu's and have a tea party every night while Daddy gives Mommy her bath. Sometimes, I get to spend the night, and Papa makes me pani popo for breakfast. I get to play in the waterfall, and go to the beach lots of times, and Mommy and I have been sewing baby Halia's blanket. Mommy even puts flowers that float in my bath sometimes."

Dan grimaced. It was painfully obvious that Mrs. Vindico had heard nothing after, *Daddy gives Mommy her bath*. The governor laughed heartily, but Dan's mother was not impressed.

"The other guesthouses are this way." Fionna coaxed the group along.

Dan kept his arm wrapped around her. She laid her head on his shoulder as they walked. She seemed to resign herself to the fact that Dan's parents were not going to understand the things that had become such an integral part of their life.

They looked around the guest cottage where Dan and Fionna had stayed on Dan's first trip to the island.

"There's a shower in the bathroom there." Dan pointed to the only bathroom in the small cottage. "If you decide to stay here, you don't have to use the outdoor bath." He narrowed his eyes at his mother, daring her to comment.

The governor looked deeply disappointed.

"So, your grandparents' store is here on the farm?" he quizzed Fionna, still trying to smooth over Dan's irritation.

"Yes, sir. It's just down along the road at the entrance to the farm."

"We'll have to stop in on Friday and see what that's all about."

Fionna smiled. "I'm sure Tutu will open it for you if you want to see it today or if there's anything you were interested in using."

Dan caught the dejection as it began to permeate her energy. "Fi created most everything that's in the store now with her own hands from the things we've been growing all summer." Dan was furious with his mother's snobbery.

Fionna's cell phone chirped from the pocket of her sundress. She smiled as she read the text. "Aunt Malani wants to know if you'd like to invite Sarah on our picnic? She says she'll pick her up for you," Fionna offered Aida.

"Yes, please!"

After everyone, save Dan's parents, had changed into swimsuits, Governor and Mrs. Vindico climbed back into their rented Buick while Dan and Fionna joined Aida and Sarah in Kai and Malani's Jeep.

They followed Tutu and Papa in the truck to Shipwreck Beach. Dan and Kai carried the numerous baskets and casted coolers through the large parking area to the waterfront. The girls raced ahead of them.

Everyone spread out on the numerous quilts Tutu provided while the girls jumped in the water. Fionna and Malani sank down in chairs while everyone else sat around them on the quilts.

Mrs. Vindico still hadn't been able to rejoin her lower jaw with her upper, a problem she often had, after Fionna had climbed out of the Jeep. It had taken Dan a moment to understand that Fionna and Malani both wearing bikinis and showing off their pregnant bellies infuriated his mother.

Fionna's hand flew to her stomach a moment later. "Wow!" She smiled as Halia made her presence known. Dan beamed as he saw Fionna's stomach bulge in one small spot.

He placed his hand where Halia had just kicked. "Hey there, baby girl," he drawled in his deep, rumbling intonation near her belly. Halia moved again, and Dan laughed. He brushed a tender kiss where she'd just kicked.

Fionna and Dan shared a tender intimate gaze for a full second before they realized Mrs. Vindico was horrified.

Tutu shook her head as she began handing out food. "Not everyone wants to be helped, Maylea." She handed Fionna a platter of sandwiches.

"Why do you call Fionna Maylea?" Mrs. Vindico demanded suddenly.

Tutu shot her a look that said for her to tread carefully. "Because that is my granddaughter's name. It means a great deal to her and to our family. If you are quiet and allow yourself to really listen, you will often hear your son refer to her as Maylea when he wants her to know just how much he loves and adores her, that he understands who she is.

"Those who've been granted access to my sweet Maylea's tender spirit, to her soul, call her as such. Those that only want to access her in pieces call her Fionna." She left no room for argument.

"Well," Mrs. Vindico smarted. "*Fionna*, I really don't feel it's appropriate for you to be so uncovered on a public beach. You are our daughter-in-law." The bitter disappointment in her tone had Dan's eyes flashing in fury.

Before he could begin shouting, Tutu stepped in with quiet wisdom. "Maylea is aware of who she is, Mrs. Vindico. She is pregnant with your granddaughter whether she's covered head to toe or in her natural state. It is very apparent to everyone that she and your son have created something beautiful out of their love. Why should she hide that?"

"Good question." Dan raised his eyebrows to his mother awaiting her response.

Governor Vindico stepped in to try and smooth over the heated standoff occurring between Dan and his mother. "You know, Tutu, I think Marion and I will take you up on the offer of staying on the farm for a few days. We'd like to spend more time with Dan and Fionna and little Aida." He glanced out to the gentle waters that Sarah and Aida were playing in.

"We'd be happy to have you. Can I offer you a few oils for your baths or things that might help you both relax?" Tutu offered kindly, though everyone listening was well aware she wasn't going to be pushed around or allow her granddaughter to be judged and bullied.

Mrs. Vindico stared at her husband in horror as she tried to formulate words but came up with nothing more than huffs and puffs.

"Daddy, come lift me up like this," Aida called from the waters. She held her arms up over her head.

Dan grinned and pulled off his shirt.

"Son, did you join a gym out here as well?" Governor Vindico gasped.

"No." Dan shook his head.

Papa chuckled. "He works like a horse. I thought I was going to have to hire two hands this summer, but he gets more done in a day than three men. I have to remind him to relax and nap with my Maylea. To take her for walks on the shores, and to conserve his energy for the girls." Papa gave Dan a pride-filled smile.

"I like the farm work. It's nice to be working for life instead of for death." Dan quipped before he ran out to Aida and threw her up in the air over the warm ocean waters. He let her squeals of delight heal his fury.

Fionna met him with a towel as he returned to the quilts later. He finished his dinner and called the girls in to eat.

"Goodness, Halia." Fionna sweetly returned her hand to her stomach.

"Can I feel her, please?" Aida begged. Fionna took Aida's hand and held it over the places where Halia was kicking.

"Do you feel her?"

Aida's eyes lit and she nodded excitedly.

"Are you going to bring your baby sister back next summer, Aida? Can we play with her?" Sarah sounded thrilled by the idea.

"Yes, and as soon as I teach her to walk, she can go to hula with us."

Everyone save Mrs. Vindico laughed. The girls ate, and Dan kept his hands on Fionna's stomach. He knew why Halia was agitated. She could feel Fionna's irritation. He tried to soothe his wife and his baby girl with his rhythms as he caressed the places she was kicking her adamant disapproval.

As the sun sank into the Pacific, everyone headed back to the cars.

"Okay, if it gets too bad, I will gladly trade Kai for you so just call me," Malani instructed Fionna in a conspiratorial whisper.

Fionna giggled. "Yeah, but I might miss Dan despite his *mother*." She thought he couldn't hear her.

"You can hide out at our house. It's only a week."

The ladies were still giggling. They kept their arms linked. Malani shot Mrs. Vindico a look that said she could go straight to hell. In a show of solidarity, she informed Kai that she was riding in the middle with Maylea.

Dan's jaw clenched until his molars ached. He slid into the passenger seat beside Kai who offered him a sympathetic smile. "They've been like this for as long as I can remember." He gestured his head to Malani and Fi. "You come for one, you're getting both," he whispered.

Dan nodded, but he wasn't letting his mother do this. She was not going to drive a wedge between him and his wife. He'd send her packing much farther away than Princeville. She wasn't going to push Fionna into the arms of her best friend because she was so hurt over the way she was being treated.

Dan preferred not to discuss his mother in front of Malani and Kai, but Fionna and Malani were whispering heatedly behind him and the word bitch was spoken more than once.

A few minutes later, they guided Aida into the cottage as Kai drove away. Dan's parents had pulled in behind them.

"Baby, can you get her ready for bed? I'm gonna get my parents settled, and we're going to have a long chat."

"Sure. Do you want me to take her to Tutu's, so I can come with you?"

"No, you just relax here. I'll be back soon to give you your bath."

He kissed her forehead and let the words he needed to say to his parents begin to take shape in his mind.

"Okay." Fionna gave him his smile. She knew he was going to take care of her. She trusted him above all others. She believed the vows he'd made even if no one else did.

She could see the change in him because she *was* the change in him. She wasn't going to go running to Malani. She was going to stay by him, and he should have known that.

"I'll be right back."

"I know." She followed Aida into the cottage.

CHAPTER 46
FIRE AND WATER

Determination set his jaw as he marched to the Enclave parked at their home. "Here, let me drive." He ordered his father out of the seat. "It gets a little narrow toward the back fields." He made no effort to soften his growl.

"Sure, son."

Uncomfortable silence drowned the car, as Dan drove the dark lane to the smaller cottages.

"I cannot believe we are staying here when Bev and Jim went to all of that trouble to work up our itinerary," Mrs. Vindico sniped.

"We're here to see Dan and the girls not to go on guided tours of the island. Fionna grew up here. Jim and Bev spent one week here. I'm certain she can play tour guide if you'd like for her to."

"And why does her grandmother insist on calling her that ridiculous name?" Mrs. Vindico huffed to Dan. She crossed her arms over her chest defiantly.

"Mother!" Dan spat, but he wanted to remain in control. He wanted to have a real conversation with his parents, sitting at the table, looking them in the eye.

He drew a deep breath and began again. "Truthfully, Mother, Maylea is a whole lot more Fionna than Fionna. It's just like Tutu told you, she *is* Maylea. Fionna is the name she was given at birth. Maylea is who she is."

"And you call her this as well?" Mrs. Vindico sneered.

"Yes, I do. Quite often, actually."

"Well, I've never heard you refer to her as such."

"Well, you also never listen." He slammed the Buick into park and helped his father unload the luggage.

He flipped the switch to turn the overhead lights on in the cottage instead of casting them. Dan set his parents' suitcases in the bedroom before returning for another load. Papa halted him out by the car on his return trip after his parents had moved into the house.

They shared a knowing gaze. Papa gave Dan his soothing chuckle. He held up one of the wooden crates that contained several of Tutu's oils and creams.

"You know they're not going to use those," Dan lamented.

"I wasn't so sure you would use them when you first brought my Maylea back to me. Of course someone handing you oils and telling you to strip my beautiful granddaughter down and give her baths makes a man of your caliber listen more intently, I suppose," he teased.

Dan found it odd that he was able to chuckle with such ease. "I certainly wasn't going to argue with her."

Papa grinned. "If we have the cure, but we don't share it with the ailing, then why are we here?" The wisdom of the man permeated his tone.

"Here, I'll give it to them."

Papa relieved himself of his burden. "Do you remember what I told you just before you married Maylea?"

Dan thought back. There had been so many things.

"You have fire in your soul, Daniel."

"Yes, sir." He recalled that conversation well. "And Maylea is the water that can soothe the burn."

"That's right." Papa seemed impressed that he'd remembered, but Dan would never forget.

"Your mother's spirit is choked with worry and doubt. She is weary and desperate for approval, but she listens to no voice other than her own. She searches for a rule book that doesn't exist to save her ego. She may not listen tonight, but that doesn't mean that you should stop talking."

"I won't let her do this. Maylea's been through hell at my hands. I won't let anything hurt her again."

"Maylea is strong, son. She is much stronger than even you. Her mighty strength is in her quiet grace, in her dignity, and in her soothing spirit. She can help quell your mother's fire as well, but she needs your shield around her. You must work together if this is going to work at all."

"I know, but she's been strong long enough. I'll always be her Shield, sir, but tonight fire is going to meet fire."

Papa nodded. "And that just might be the beginning, but at some point the fire must cool and the island must form. I wish you luck. It will be a mighty task." He handed Dan a large picnic basket that was near his feet. "Tell your parents if they need anything to let us know."

Dan added the basket of provisions to the crate of oils and tinctures. He marched toward his parents' heated whispers from inside the front room.

"Don't kid yourself!" the governor demanded. "Daniel will pack our bags for us and make certain that we end up a lot farther away than the Wyndham, and you'll never see him, or Fionna, or our granddaughters ever again.

"She is everything to him, Marion. His whole world. Not me, and not you. Fionna, and Aida and the little one. That is all that matters to him, and I want a relationship with my son and with his family. So, please stop trying to change him and change the woman who saved him when none of us were able to."

Dan watched his father begin to pace.

"Let me go ahead and lay out the cold, hard facts for you, *dear*. Right now, they're coming home in a few weeks' time, and Dan's going back to work. Late one night a few months after that she's going to wake him up terrified and overjoyed because she's in labor. I would like to think we would make the call list somewhere above Stephen and Lillian, but trust me, right now we'll be lucky if we get a call a week after they've brought little Heleena home from Georgetown."

With a sigh, Dan stepped into the cottage. He set down the picnic basket and the wooden crate on the single countertop.

"It's Halia, Dad. Halia Elisabeth Amelia Vindico. That's what Fi wants to name her."

The governor was visibly moved, but Dan's mother was still scowling.

"Don't you need to get back to May-lea?" she spat viciously.

"Marion!" Governor Vindico roared.

"Do not call her that!" Dan kept his voice calm but menacing. "You don't even know Fionna, so you're sure as hell not going to call her Maylea. That's not a right. That's a privilege you haven't earned. Actually, it's a gift," he amended, "but not one you've been given or deserve." He gestured to the table. "Sit down."

His mother jerked one of the chairs back and threw herself into it fitfully. The governor and Dan eased chairs back and joined her.

"Why are you here, Mom?" He was mildly impressed at his ability to rein in his temper, but he was certain it was Fionna and the healing island that had his rhythms calmer than he was accustomed when he was so hurt and so furious. "Really, why did you come here?" He genuinely wanted to hear her answer. "Did you come so you can tell your friends that you vacationed in Hawaii? Did you come to follow Jim and Bev's vacation itinerary? Because you didn't come to see me, and you sure as hell didn't come to see my girls, so why are you here?"

"I did want to see you and Fionna, but you have to admit this is not exactly a Hawaiian vacation."

He let her words sink in. "No," he agreed. "This is a farm—my wife's family farm in the middle of paradise. The place where the phenomenal woman who agreed to marry me and bear my children, despite all of the hell she's gone through at my hands, has been able to heal and relax and become whole again."

"This is not how you were raised. I don't understand this. I don't approve of this."

Impressed, Dan drew a deep breath. "Okay, but that doesn't make it wrong. It's not DC. I understand that. In fact, that's why we're here.

460

DC never offered me anything worth having other than my wife, but Kauai has offered me nothing but a life worth living. You don't have to understand it or approve of it, but I will not allow you to make Fionna uncomfortable or allow you to make her feel like she's not good enough for you."

"You cannot allow her to walk around on a public beach with barely anything covered. Your father is a Realm governor. We are a ruling family."

With a quick spiteful thought that she should have seen Fionna on Secret Beach a few weeks before wearing nothing at all, Dan tried to think of a way to make her understand even a small part of his life.

"I'm well aware of what my father does for a living. What I can't understand is how that changes the fact that Fionna is pregnant with our baby. If the press wants to take pictures of us out on the beach with my hands on my wife's stomach, then let them. I did that. It's mine. The Realm knows she's pregnant. What on earth is wrong with that?"

"The way you've been living this summer is inappropriate. This is not the way our family conducts itself. This place is like some kind of hippie intimate relations camp," she shrieked and shuddered in horror.

Laughter spilled from his mouth over his mother's verbiage.

"Marion, for heaven's sake." The governor rolled his eyes.

Dan shook his head. "No, Mom, the way I've been living isn't the way you'd like me to live, but it is the way I've wanted to live, and the way Fionna wanted to spend the summer. Aida has grown and healed, and obviously Halia is coming along just the way she's supposed to. So, why can't you ever just see the good?"

Governor Vindico stepped in with a sigh. "In your mother's defense, not that she has much of one, it is different. You were the man who drowned himself in his work so he never had to deal with anything at all. You would work until I found you the next morning asleep at your desk in the Iodex office.

"As happy as I am that you've changed and you're really living now, it wasn't that long ago that this wasn't you." He gestured both of his hands to Dan. "And now you're helping to run a farm, taking naps with your pregnant wife each day on a screened-in porch, and running a store that sells home remedies and bath oils. You run your hands and your mouth all over your extremely pregnant wife's stomach in front of anyone and don't give a damn. Remember that you and Fionna have been living this every day for three months. We've not even received so much as a phone call until we asked you to pick us up at the airport. So, we can obviously see the change, but we weren't a part of it."

Dan nodded. "I know, and I really do understand that. But you don't seem to understand that the guy who slept in his office more days than not, *that* wasn't me." His voice rose in accordance with his fervor. "That was some shadow of the hell I was living, some kind of demon's existence. This is me, and Fionna is the one who chiseled me out of the shell I existed in." His voice finally came to a shout, desperate for his parents to hear him.

"Okay, fine," his mother's sudden fury shocked him. "But this isn't me! And I have a very difficult time believing that I raised a son who is perfectly willing to allow his wife to run around barely dressed, letting everyone and their brother see her in the state she's in. Or that gives her baths outside on a screened-in porch. Or that lets his daughter announce that she remembered to remove her undergarments, and uses the things in that store to do things without your clothes on outside of the house!

"I'm sorry, but you've never been any more accepting of me and the things I believe in than I have of you. And I will not sit here and pretend that I believe the way you and Fionna have chosen to conduct your life is appropriate." She blinked back tears.

Dan shuddered in an effort not to scream. "You don't have to agree, and you don't have to approve. The only thing you have to do is keep your mouth shut!" he snarled but then drew a deep breath. "Be polite to my wife, her family, and her friends. I may not agree or accept the way you choose to conduct your life, but I don't call you out in front of your friends. I do try to keep the majority of my opinions to myself although I will admit that I haven't always done so well with that either."

His mother glared at him. "Do you ever think that I might be right?

Did you ever for a moment stop and think that it might not be good for your seven-year-old to know that you and Fionna are bathing outdoors every night? Or to see her mother walking around barely covered? I'm certain that if she'll wear that to the beach, she probably wears less around the house." She baptized herself in her sanctimonious indignation like a pig in muddy waters.

"Do you want Aida to turn out like Lindley?" She finally punctured the actual horror, the actual fear, that had driven her to such extremes.

Dan and his father shared a solemn glance.

"Mom, I want you to listen to me, and please know that I am not saying any of this to hurt you. I knew something was wrong with Lindley when she was much younger than Aida. We all did.

"And did you ever stop and think that maybe part of the reason I jumped into bed with Amelia when I was barely seventeen years old, after years of pressuring her before that, or that the fact that Lindley does the things she does might have something to do with the fact that you don't even want to acknowledge that sex exists?

"You spent most of our lives trying to convince us that it was bad, and it isn't bad. It's life. In fact, it's the way life begins, but you were so adamant that we shouldn't know anything about it you made it that much more tantalizing. It is a beautiful, magical experience when it's with the right person at the right time.

"I'm sure that Fi and I will make our fair share of mistakes as parents, but I am beyond certain that I don't want my daughters to grow up ashamed of their bodies or ashamed of desire. Do I want them to act on it when they're seventeen? Hell, no. But the only way I know to prevent that is to make them understand that they're worth waiting for. They are the most beautiful and the most brilliant girls in the world, and any guy who doesn't make them feel that way isn't worth having in the first place." He tried to explain the things he hoped to instill in Aida and Halia.

"So, yes, I do give my wife baths almost every night, and yes, I keep my hands on her, and I talk to Halia, and I kiss her stomach, because she's mine, both of them are mine. I want them to know that and to be proud of that. And yes, Fionna has certainly laid out, walked around, and slept topless while she's been here. And Aida's played in the sprinklers on the farm wearing nothing at all, but that's okay. Because they *are* the most beautiful, brilliant girls in the world. Not because Fi has an incredible body but because they have beautiful hearts and souls and spirits. It doesn't matter what they look like on the outside. All women are beautiful and should be proud of who they are because there is no shame in sexuality and there is no shame in being a woman." He shook his head and wondered what his mother was actually hearing.

"If Aida knows I give Fi baths, so be it, because she also knows that I adore her mother, that I love her more than life itself, and that I would do anything in the world for my wife and for my daughters. And as much as I'll hate every single minute I'll have to endure of giving them away, if my girls find a guy lucky enough to be with them, who adores them as much as I adore my wife, then I can't deny them that. I want that for them.

"My marriage isn't going to be divided into what we let the Realm see and the way we are when we think no one's looking. We're going to be us. Dan and Maylea and Aida and Halia, and you can take it, Mom, or you can leave it. The choice is entirely up to you, but Dad's right. If you can't find it in yourself somewhere to stop attacking my wife and the way we choose to do things, then you probably won't be seeing much of my family over the next few years."

Silence filled the humid night air, and a timid knock sounded on the door.

A breathy chuckle escaped Dan. "The quelling tide," he whispered as the governor stood to let Fionna inside.

"Hey, baby." Dan pulled Fionna to him. He just needed to feel her, to breathe her in. To let her douse the flames that had begun to consume him.

"Hey." Fionna smiled timidly. She glanced down uncomfortably for a moment. He saw it then. She'd been crying.

She was wearing a sleeveless sundress that she often donned after going to the water. It was a brilliant teal blue, and the elastic top clung to her heaving cleavage that wasn't bound in a bra. The long dress flowed out over her bump, and he knew that was all she was wearing.

She was natural just like he preferred. But he also knew that his parents were probably also as aware of that fact. She'd seemed to realize this as well. That's why she was even more uncomfortable.

"Uh, Papa's with Aida. I didn't leave her there or anything. She's asleep. The water wears her out. I just wanted to make sure Tutu got the cottage ready for you. I brought you some fruit salad for your breakfast." She held up a glass bowl from their own cottage that contained a mix of tropical delicacies. "Papa said he packed you some coffee." She gestured to the picnic basket. "But you're welcome to come down to our home for breakfast if you'd like."

"Thank you, Fionna. That was very kind of you." The governor glared pointedly at his wife. His brow furrowed a moment later. "Uh, did you want us to call you Maylea, sweetheart?"

"No, sir," she answered just a little too quickly. She tried to hide the willful shudder her body gave. Dan held her tightly against him. She wasn't giving any more of herself away, and he wanted her to know she didn't have to. His parents certainly hadn't earned the privilege.

He turned his gaze back to his mother as he held his wife fiercely to his chest. If she wanted to know where his loyalties lie, all she had to do was open her eyes. The ball was in her court, and everyone waited with bated breath to see her next move.

"Thank you, Fionna." Mrs. Vindico stood from the table. With an audible breath, she seemed to forcibly unhinge her jaw as she moved to the counter. "I'm not certain what all of this does." She opened the picnic basket and touched the brown bottles in the small wooden crate as if they were a den of cobras that would strike at the slightest movement.

With a timid chuckle, Fionna paced toward Mrs. Vindico. Dan followed in her wake. He kept her balancing forces shielded in his own, using his fire to protect her and give her light.

Fionna helped Mrs. Vindico unpack the foods from the picnic basket.

"Tutu knows guests sometimes like to have a meal alone or even just to have coffee and breakfast on their own, so she usually makes certain you know it's okay with her if you and the governor eat up here." She placed coffee cake and a container of malasadas from the local Hawaiian bakery in the small breadbox.

She glanced at Dan who nodded his encouragement. "These are oils for your bath." She pulled four small brown dropper bottles from the crate. "Lavender will help your rhythms relax, and this detoxes your body. Rose oil helps with balance. Ylang ylang, uh..." Her voice had lowered to a whisper, and she refused to meet anyone's eye as she forced herself to go on. "Helps you relax and increases..." She shook her head before the words sexual desire made their way out.

Dan filled them in for her.

Fionna nodded and continued. "These are just some scrubs and lotions. This helps clear up dark spots from aging." She pulled the large tube from the crate.

"Really?" Mrs. Vindico was suddenly intrigued.

Fionna's head shot up. "Yes, ma'am. It really works. We grow the aloe vera plants here, and Tutu has a honey supplier on the Big Island. She doesn't have any age spots, and she's been in the sun her whole life. The face oil she packed will help thinning skin as well."

Fionna's voice lowered again. "Kukui oil and coconut oil are excellent for everyone's skin. I've used them my whole life, and it's how Dan and I cleared up Aida's eczema." She willed Dan's parents to believe her as she set the oil on the counter.

"Dan rubs them on my belly every night, and I don't have any stretch marks so far," she began but halted abruptly as she recalled his mother's scowl on the beach.

"There are a few teas in here. Tutu believes that health comes from within and then can be cultivated from the outside. You are what you eat kind of thing."

"Uh." Her voice faltered as she removed the screw-top jar from the crate.

Dan stepped in. She didn't have to do this alone. "Tutu believes that just about anything can be cured if you eat lots of island food, take long walks in the waters of Kauai, take long baths with her prescriptions, take afternoon naps, and have long lovemaking sessions," he stated firmly and watched his mother fight her abashed scowl.

If he wanted his parents to accept his sex life, he supposed he had to admit to himself that it was probably part of their marriage as well, although he wasn't certain of that.

"This is for that last part." He held up the jar of ‘Ōhi‘a lehua lubricant.

"And she just sells this in her store?" Mrs. Vindico was trying, but she couldn't bite back the harsh words.

"Yes, ma'am." Fionna shuddered from the emotions assaulting her by way of Dan's mother, but she went on. "We have quite a few customers in your age bracket that find it helpful."

"It's part of life, Mom," Dan quipped. "That's what we do here on the farm. We cultivate life."

Fionna turned, and Dan wrapped her back up in his arms. She'd been strong long enough. He let her hide in him, and felt Halia move against his waist.

A sudden smile lit her beautiful face as Dan's hand moved instinctively to her stomach. "Did you feel that?"

"Yeah, baby." He stroked his hand over her stomach, pressing lightly until Halia responded again.

The governor had edged to the counter and was studying a few of the things Tutu had provided. "I wonder if she has anything for my shoulder. It's been hell on the golf course."

Fionna pulled away from Dan. "Oh, yes, sir. Helichrysum and lavender oils will help with inflammation, and Tutu has oils you can put in a compress to relieve sore muscles."

Dan drew a deep breath and tucked Fionna back into his chest. "We're gonna go. Think about what I said, and use whatever you want. They all really do work." He guided Fionna out of the cottage.

"This is so not how I saw this working when we left for the airport this afternoon," Fionna confessed on their walk. "I didn't even feel this."

Dan nodded. "Well, I think everyone's pretty shocked they're here, even them."

"I heard what you said there at the end," she whispered as they meandered to their home. "I don't want you to cut off your family for me."

"Hopefully I won't have to, but I won't let her hurt you. She needed to be given some boundaries. What she said to you on the beach was way out of line. I won't have it. That will not happen on my watch. I will always, always be your Shield."

"You're just amazing," Fionna choked as tears rolled down her cheeks.

Dan halted their progress and wrapped her up in his arms. He let her cry. "Shh, baby. It's all over. We'll see what happens tomorrow, but she has her ultimatum, and I'm not backing down."

"I know." Fionna shuddered as she tried to quell her tears, but the water flowed from her because the water *was* her. It always would. It was who she is.

Several minutes later, they entered the cottage. Papa had fallen asleep in one of the chairs.

Fionna grinned as she kissed his cheek. "We're back. Thank you."

Papa stood and gazed at Fionna adoringly. "Are you okay, Maylea?"

She nodded and leaned back against Dan as he nestled her in his arms.

"Can't fight the tides, Daniel. No matter how big the fire," Papa stated wisely.

"I know, sir. The water is always the stronger force."

"*Pa'ipunahele*," Papa whispered as he kissed Fionna's cheek and waved goodbye.

Chuckling, Dan kissed the top of Fionna's head. "Hey, you're my favorite love too."

"You're getting so good I hardly ever have to translate for you anymore." She gifted him with one of his smiles.

"*Ko aloha, makamae e ipo*," he murmured in her ear and felt her energy soothe as she let her eyes close to hear his vows. "*Nau ko'u aloha.*" He whispered kisses on her cheek as he told her how much he loved her. "*Na'u 'oe.*" He breathed his claim of ownership and felt her heart pick up pace as she began to pant. "*Nou no ka 'i'ini*," His voice turned to gravel as she spun and laved his mouth with a kiss.

"And what do you desire to do with me?" she urged in a heated pant.

"Come here, Maylea. I'll show you." His voice was low and breathy.

He burned for her. He needed to bury himself deeply in the cool, soothing waters of the incoming tide.

Dan awoke to someone knocking on their front door. He sighed. He didn't want to move. Fionna was curled against him. Her breasts and belly were on full display against his skin.

Halia was awake as well, but Fionna was sound asleep. He smiled as he felt his little girl glide through her mother's womb. Dan eased from the bed, still astonished after three months' time how comfortable they were.

He pulled on a pair of shorts and closed the bedroom door after covering Fionna tenderly.

He headed to the door. He had no idea what might be coming.

"Hey, Dad." He rubbed his eyes and yawned deeply.

"I thought farmhands got up with the sun?"

"Yeah, well, not here. Here we sleep." Dan allowed his father into the cottage.

"I can't blame you. That bed is astounding. I've never slept better. I plan to order one when we get back."

Dan paced to the kitchen to start the coffee. "Good luck with that. Papa makes the beds from Hawaiian hardwoods, and the mattresses are made of Hawaiian cotton and bamboo, so you'd have to have it shipped over. It'd probably cost you as much as your house."

"Really?" The governor sounded both impressed and disappointed. "Is there anything he can't make?"

"He's one of the strongest Occamy Predilects I've ever met."

"Your Mother's still asleep. I can't think of the last time she slept so late."

Dan nodded but gave nothing away as he waited on the coffee to perk and then poured his father a cup.

"I just thought I'd see if I could help out with the farmwork. I'd like to spend the day with you."

Dan offered his father a smile. "Sure, if you want, but you're on vacation."

"I was kind of hoping if I helped out maybe we could work some and then see a little of the island with you and the girls this afternoon."

Dan smiled. He was genuinely touched. "That'd be great. It means a lot to me, and sure, we can do that."

Governor Vindico drew a long restorative sip of the Kona coffee that was Fionna's favorite.

"Have a seat." Dan gestured to the table. The governor took the seat that suited his stature. He was several inches shorter than his son and not nearly as muscular.

"Tutu doesn't believe furniture should match. She believes it should be comfortable for the people sitting in it." He gestured his hand with his own coffee mug to the table where they were seated.

"Smart woman."

Dan was exceedingly thankful that his father happened to have chosen the chair that placed his back to their bedroom. Fionna opened the door dressed in a loose pair of polka-dot pajama shorts. They were slung low under her bump, but that was all she was wearing.

Dan's eyes goggled as she grimaced and closed the door back quickly. He was fairly certain his father hadn't seen anything. Dan tried to smooth over his momentary panic.

She made another appearance a moment later. This time she'd added one of Dan's T-shirts over the shorts. It was pulled tight against her bump.

"Hey, baby doll." Dan kissed her head as he stood to make her coffee.

"Good morning, Governor," Fionna managed after her first few sips of coffee.

"Good morning, sweetheart. Did you sleep well?"

"Yes, sir. Halia woke me up. I guess I should get used to that though."

"Oh, you definitely should. I don't think Dan slept through the night until he was fourteen."

Fionna giggled and shook her head at her husband.

. . .

Papa and Dan showed the governor how to harvest the aloe and ginger that was ready to be cut.

Mrs. Vindico encouraged Fionna to go on to her yoga class with Malani, while she and Tutu looked after Aida.

That afternoon, Dan and Fionna took the Vindicos to Poipu and then Dan paid for the table to enjoy The Beach House restaurant, one of Kauai's more prestigious locales.

The next day they made their way to Kappa and spent the day shopping and enjoying the beach. They stopped in for coffee and cupcakes at Dan and Fionna's favorite shop.

"That's where Mommy and Daddy got their swirly tattoos," Aida announced to her grandparents when they passed the tattoo parlor after having Fionna's favorite fish burritos.

"What does that one mean, son?" the governor quizzed. Dan was impressed with the lack of judgment in his tone. His father had not been pleased with Dan's tattoos when he'd gotten them years before.

"It's the symbol of hapai. It means pregnancy, or more appropriately in this case, to carry forever."

His father gave him an understanding and heartfelt nod as he slapped his shoulder.

Fionna's cell phone chirped, and she pulled it from her purse. "Oh my gosh!"

"What?" Dan asked.

"Malani's water just broke! I have to go. I'm the person who's supposed to tell her she wants to be casted!"

"We can take Aida back to the farm," Mrs. Vindico offered very kindly.

"I want to see Aunt Malani's baby," Aida begged.

"Baby girl, it won't be here for a long while. You go with Gramps and Grandma, and Daddy and I will take you to see her tomorrow, okay?" Fionna begged.

Disappointment shadowed Aida's face, but she nodded her agreement.

"Thank you!" Fionna embraced Mrs. Vindico which seemed to shock her.

She and Dan flew to the truck, and Dan did his best to get to

Wilcox Memorial Hospital in a hurry. Fionna had been given a checkup there just a few weeks before.

He sat in the waiting room with Malani's father, Tutu, Papa, Kai's parents, and his brother. He called his parents to check on Aida several times. They'd helped her water her garden, and then she'd fallen asleep with the governor as he'd read to her.

At four thirty, Dan smiled. His head lifted from his drowsy state. He heard the customary shrieking wail of a newborn as she drew her first breath.

Fionna appeared after several long minutes. She pulled off her mask and beamed at him. "She's so beautiful!"

"What's her name?" Dan tried to envision the people who would be waiting on him to appear with the news of Halia's birth.

"Leilanie Maylea."

Dan nodded his understanding and guided her to him as she began to cry.

EPILOGUE

LAST WEEK OF AUGUST

As he stepped out of the shower, Dan tried not to feel the harrowing sense of loss that twisted and tossed in the pit of his stomach.

He toweled off and glanced at the packed suitcases on the bedroom floor. They were leaving in the morning, headed back to Arlington, back to a life Dan hadn't missed at all.

He reminded himself that he'd signed a contract to teach. If Fionna and the girls wanted to move to the farm after that, they could. He ran his brush through his wet hair.

Fionna had been in tears off and on all day long. She'd spent the morning with Malani holding little Lanie with both women sobbing that they wouldn't be back together until the next summer.

Aida had wandered around dejectedly to all of her favorite places on the farm, verbally telling each of them goodbye while effectively breaking Dan's heart.

There were meetings he had to attend before school started the next week. They were posing for pictures for the first of many articles and brochures for the Auxiliary International Adoption program.

They had to get Aida set to start second grade. She was to meet her teacher Thursday night.

He reviewed all of the reasons they had to leave, but none of them seemed viable at the moment.

He'd helped Papa plant what would become the winter harvest. He tried desperately to keep the feeling of the volcanic soil, the feeling of growing life, cemented in his mind and in his soul. He would need that to get through the next nine months until they returned.

He noted the crates and crates of oils, lotions, ointments, and teas for Fionna, Aida, and for little Halia stacked beside the luggage as he moved into the bedroom.

He pulled on the khaki shorts he'd laid out after packing everything else but what he planned to fly home in. He saw it as he located his T-shirt. There was a note on his pillow.

While praying that Aida hadn't written him to declare that she refused to go back to Arlington and was moving in with Tutu and Papa, Dan lifted the paper.

Ko'u Aloha. Dan began translating. *My love,* he smiled as he went on.

E Kipa Mai. Come to me. His heart begin to pick up rhythm. *Nou No Ka 'Tini,* I desire you. His face pulled into a hungry grin. "*Wailele,*" was the next word. The waterfall. Dan recalled the word as he stood and located his shoes quickly.

He folded the note carefully and slipped it in his wallet before he rushed out of the cottage.

Aida was spending the night at Harper's house. They were having a going away party with the other little girls from her hula class. Dan broke out into a quick run toward the north end of the farm.

He slipped out of his shoes as he came into the vegetation that surrounded the waterfall.

Her clothes lay on the stone bench beside the falls. His heart beat disjointedly as he saw her partially obscured form behind the rapidly falling water.

She was bare in the water, letting her hands feel the warmth of the spring as she pulled them rhythmically through the water.

Overwhelmed by her beauty, Dan undressed and stepped into the water hidden by the surrounding plants and bushes.

He half walked and half swam under the falls.

"Hey, baby doll."

She gave him his smile. She moved to him and laid her head against his chest. Their naked bodies melded in the water.

"You know, I used to date this really phenomenal woman who had a waterfall fantasy."

She grinned as his cock swelled against her. "And what did you do with her, Mr. Vindico?"

"Well," Dan let his hand slip down her slick body. He placed one to her extremely pregnant swell and the other on her lush backside. "First, I married her, and then I promptly knocked her up."

He reveled in her delighted giggle. "So, what you're saying is this is your fault." She wrapped her hands lovingly over her belly.

"All mine," he growled as he let his hands move over her breasts, gently squeezing and kneading them. He slipped her puckered nipples between his fingers as her breaths came quicker. The water carried her energy to him in craving hungry pulses. It understood her. It was her.

"What does my sweet Maylea want?"

"I need you." Her voice was low and raspy in her need.

"I've got everything you need, baby doll. I just need the fantasy so I can make certain it comes true."

A shuddering moan escaped her as she writhed in his hands. "Turn me around. Make me take you against the rock wall. Tell me how bad you want me, and what you're going to do. Make me take it hard."

A low thundering growl echoed around them from deep within Dan's chest. She was exquisite. "Every time I see you, Maylea, I want you. Every time I think of you and of how good you feel when I pull you over me, when I fill you up, I know nothing will ever feel as good as that, baby doll. God, you make me hurt. I ache to pump you full of me, to hear you make those sweet sounds you make only for me, to feel you clench tight around me. It's incredible." A breathy moan permeated the air around them. "That's it, baby. I want to hear you."

She went wild as he leaned and devoured her mouth. He sucked her tongue and dragged his teeth over her bottom lip. Nipping the swollen skin, owning her.

"I want to take you rough, baby. I'm gonna pound those sweet lips until you're screaming for me, and then I'm gonna slow it down and make it last. I'm gonna make you beg me for more, because the only thing you want is for me to set you free. But I'm not going to let you have it until you just can't stand it anymore." He could feel her heart race as she wrapped her hands around his throbbing strain, letting the water lubricate him as she began to torture him with her hands.

"Give it to me, please." She began her begging.

"Be a good girl and spread your legs for me," Dan commanded. No longer able to access her from the front while she stood, he traced his hands down the center of her backside.

She was frantic, and the fear of leaving the island still pulsed under the drowning emotions of her desire.

"Let's see if I can't take the edge off a little, sweetheart."

She tensed and pitched against him. He let his fingers trace tiny figure eights over her clit as he moved his mouth to her right breast.

"Mine." He let his tongue sweep over her nipple in languid vacillations and then flicked it against them with more force, as her moans spilled in heady need from her lips.

"All mine," he growled as he moved up her breast, sucking and marking the thin skin at the top of their swell. As he sucked her, he dipped fingers deep inside of her, letting the warm water move to her most sensitive spots as he caressed her deeply.

"Yes, more, please!" She arched her back, pushing him deeper. Her energy spun in tight rapid twists, frantic to be loosed.

"You need to come for me, baby. I can feel how badly you need to let go."

She shuddered and pulsed around him as her breath caught and her temperature spiked hard.

"That's my good girl." He pulled her breast deep in his mouth, suckling the fevered mound as he let his fingers work her over.

She grasped his hair and held his head to her breast. Her nails dug into his scalp as she spiraled out of control.

He pulled his head away as she convulsed and clung to him fiercely. He held her in the safety of his embrace, letting the waves wash over her as she writhed and begged for more.

"I'm not finished, baby doll. Not even close. I'm gonna take good care of my Maylea." She fought to catch her eluding breath.

Dan forced himself to slow. He took her hand and wrapped it around his strain. "Feel me. Feel how hard you make me, before I make you take it all. I'm gonna fill that tight little pussy so full you can't feel anything but me deep inside of you."

She grasped and groped him. Her fingertips explored the thickened veins and spun over his head. It drove him wild.

He turned her around and flipped her wet hair to one side as he kissed the back of her neck. Working his lips down her wet skin, he let his teeth drag over the spot where her neck and shoulder met and listened to her furtive moans.

He traced slow tedious patterns down her back and massaged her breasts from behind her as he pressed his strain to her sexy ass.

She leaned. She wanted more. They needed to be one. She was desperate for him to permeate her, to fill her with his length and with his energy. She needed to feel his love and to know that he would always be hers for eternity.

"Are you ready, sweetheart? You ready for me to make you mine?"

"Now," she begged.

"Take it, baby doll." Dan grasped her hips and slipped deeply inside of the slick heavenly paradise that was all his. He filled her to overflowing then reset slowly. He let her envelop him inch by inch. He pulled away and pushed in again, slowly and rhythmically. "Such a good girl," he urged.

He listened to her frantic pleas to be taken harder and faster, and he answered her cries. He fulfilled every desire as he transitioned and began to pump her full and pound into her.

She clawed the rock wall as the first release broke over her in a riptide of drowning need.

Dan pulled her body back to his and wrapped one hand over her breasts and the other around her swell. He kept himself inside her, letting the orgasm pulse around him.

"I'm not finished with you. You ready for more, baby? Be a good girl and take a little more for me." He groaned from the ecstasy of her rippled tugs all around him.

"Oh, God, yes. Give it to me. I want all of you."

"Oh, baby doll, don't you worry. You're gonna take it all," he growled as he began to pound into her once again. He moved his hands to her hip bones, burying himself inside of her perfection.

"God, you are so fucking beautiful!" He watched his strain be consumed by her body through the clear, rippling water. The sight was too much. She pulsed fiercely, and it was more than he could withstand.

She was too perfect and felt far too good. She was his, all his, full of him, full of his baby, and as she broke again, he followed her, straining tightly against her walls. Their releases combined inside of her as their gasping groans echoed off the rock walls and were drowned by the falling water.

Dan panted for breath as he withdrew. He turned her back around and held her tightly to his chest. "I love you so much, Maylea."

They stayed in that position, clinging tightly to the only thing that would ever matter, the only thing that made life worth living.

"I'm not finished, sweetheart," he warned.

"Oh god yes," she pled. "More."

When they finally emerged from under the falls, Dan helped her out of the pool. "I'm glad you remembered towels. I was done for after your note. I hardly remembered to get dressed." He dried her off and then helped her pull her sundress over her head.

He managed to redress while keeping in constant contact with her.

"Wanna go get some fish tacos and then go watch the sunset on Salt Pond?" He repeated her invitation from the first night he'd ever been to the farm.

"That's perfect," she agreed but was still scared to leave their sanctuary and to leave the serenity of all they'd forged on the farm.

They sat out on a quilt eating fish tacos and watching the sun begin its descent into the ocean.

"This is where we decided to get married and to make Halia." She whispered, but he needed no reminder.

"I know, baby. I'll never forget."

"I've been so scared all day."

"I knew that too." He cupped his hand and then let his shield surround her.

"But then I realized," she whispered as he began dragging his fingers gently through her hair. "It doesn't matter where we live or even where we are. What we have, the things that bind us together as a family, they don't just exist here. If I'm beside you, that's all that matters."

"I will always be right beside you, Maylea, no matter where we are. Right beside you is the only place I ever want to be. I love you."

Fionna leaned up and kissed Dan's jaw as her energy began to settle and calm from his shield.

"Me too."

The End

ABOUT THE AUTHOR

J.E. Neal (aka Jillian) vastly prefers coffee to tea, guac to salsa, the beach over anywhere else, and the world inside her head over the one outside her front door. She also loves not having to choose.

Driven by the question 'what if,' J.E. Neal's world began to manifest. What if there were people with powers the rest of us couldn't see? What if the energy of our world could be summoned and used at their will? Characters with these amazing abilities took shape in her mind. She created—and continues to create—an endless number of stories full of delicious escape from our reality where emotions are visible, desire is palpable, and danger is universal.

Learn more about J.E. Neal at JillianNeal.com

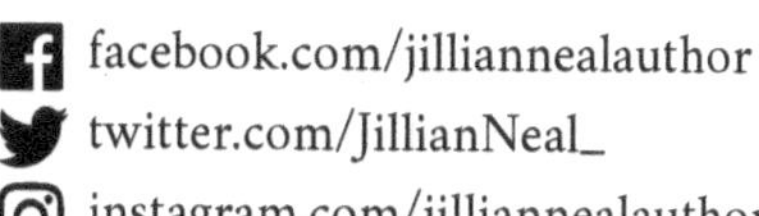

facebook.com/jilliannealauthor

twitter.com/JillianNeal_

instagram.com/jilliannealauthor

ALSO BY J.E. NEAL

ENERGY OF MAGIC

Shield and Shattered Cages (Book 1)

Shield and Faltered Steps (Book 2)

Shield and Splintered Oaths (Book 3)

Shield and Humbled Crown (Book 4)

Shield and Vile Serpents (Book 5)

Shield and Coveted Splendor (Book 6)

Shield and Guarded Shadow (Book 7)

Shield and Worthy Sinner (Book 8)

Shield and Sacrificial Heirs (Book 9)

www.ingramcontent.com/pod-product-compliance
Lightning Source LLC
Chambersburg PA
CBHW060723190726
48285CB00001B/42